SNOW

Speed Demons MC: Book 3.5

Jules Ford

ISBN: 9798394934346

Copyright 2023 by Jules Ford.

All rights reserved.

This is a work of fiction. Names, characters, business, places, and incidents are either the product of the author's imagination or used in a fictitious manner. Any resemblance to actual living persons, living, or dead, or actual events is purely coincidental.

ALL RIGHTS RESERVED

This book contains material protected under International and Federal Copyright Laws and Treaties. Any unauthorized reprint or use of this material is prohibited. No part of this book may be reproduced or transmitted in any form, or by any means, electronic or mechanical, including photocopying, recording, or by any informal storage and retrieval system without express written permission from the author/ publisher.

Cover by JoeLee Creative

Formatting by Md Foysal Ahmed

www.facebook.com/foysal.rumman1
www.fiverr.com/foysalrumman

Editing and proofreading by Ellie Race

With thanks.

Dedication

For our Veterans and their families.
Thank you for your service.

I would like to send Katie a very special thank you!
Your help with this book has been essential.
I appreciate you and all the time you dedicated.

Snow's Playlist is Available on Spotify

https://open.spotify.com/playlist/3KQ49S91ECxBiqiZnMaJ3z

Locked on Her: Book One of the Three Kings MC by Amy Davies, mentioned in this book, is available to read on Amazon

Other Books by Jules

Speed Demons MC
Bowie
Cash
Atlas
Snow
Breaker ~ Coming Soon

Soulless Assassins MC
Tyrant's Redemption (Co-author Raven Dark)

Glossary

A-Team/A-Teaming ~ Four soldiers make up a team—a noncommissioned officer and three junior enlisted soldiers. Teams with special functions may also include officers or warrant officers.

CHU Containerized Housing Units

CM Court Martial

Dear John Relationship break-up letter

DFAC Dining Facility or Mess

EOD Explosive Ordnance Disposal

Evac Evacuation

Fugazi Fucked up/ (alt FUBAR) (slang)

Hurry-up-and-wait Ordered to hurry to a place to complete a task, only for nothing to happen.

IED Improvised Explosive Device

ISAF International Security Assistance Force

Joe Soldier (slang)

LT Lieutenant

M224 Light-Weight Company Mortar System

M4 Carbine/Compact Military Assault Rifle

MG Major General

MK-23 Special Operations 'Offensive' Handgun

Moon dust Powder-like, light sand found in Afghanistan (slang)

NATO North Atlantic Treaty Organization

Nut to butt Soldiers packed together in an enclosed space

NJP Non-Judicial Punishment

Para Paratrooper

Pop Smoke To leave/ Resign from military duty

PPE Personal Protective Equipment

Ruck Rucksack

SPC Specialist (Military Rank)

SSG Staff Sergeant

TERP Interpreter

T-Man Taliban

VBIED Vehicle Borne Improvised Explosive Device

Note to Readers

The book was originally going to be part of Breaker Speed Demons MC Book Four.

Only when I began researching Kit's time in Afghanistan did I understand that had to change. I felt uncomfortable minimizing the character's time in the military and what he and others endured.

So, here we are, an extra book in the series that was never planned but I feel is essential to Kit and Kennedy's story.

This book details ISAF and U.S. troops' endeavors in Afghanistan, particularly between 2010-2014.

Along with such endeavors came casualties and the deaths of civilian men, women, children, and soldiers. This book details such deaths graphically.

This book also contains graphic scenes of murder and other violence.

Drug use is also prevalent in this book, along with other addictions, including violent and sexual. All of which may be uncomfortable to read.

If violence–sometimes of a sexual nature, death—including child death, prolific drug use, the development and effects of severe PTSD, and associated depression and suicidal thoughts are upsetting, **please do not continue**.

Additional Note

This book also contains Game of Thrones spoilers, though if you haven't watched it by now, I'd say it's time.

XOXO

Table of Contents

Chapter One 1

Chapter Two 13

Chapter Three 29

Chapter Four 41

Chapter Five 66

Chapter Six 70

Chapter Seven 74

Chapter Eight 85

Chapter Nine 90

Chapter Ten 103

Chapter Eleven 110

Chapter Twelve 125

Chapter Thirteen 129

Chapter Fourteen 148

Chapter Fifteen 164

Chapter Sixteen 184

Chapter Seventeen 192

Chapter Eighteen 204

Chapter Nineteen	223
Chapter Twenty	230
Chapter Twenty-One	235
Chapter Twenty-Two	254
Chapter Twenty-Three	264
Chapter Twenty-Four	280
Chapter Twenty-Five	291
Chapter Twenty-Six	299
Chapter Twenty-Seven	307
Chapter Twenty-Eight	321
Chapter Twenty-Nine	333
Chapter Thirty	349
Epilogue	363

Chapter One

Snow ~ Ten years ago

"Fire in the hole. Fire in the hole. Fire in the hole."

A thunderous explosion rocked through the air. The truck my ass crouched behind swayed with the force of the blast but stayed intact. Burning heat from the fireball hit my face even though the vehicle shielded me. I let out a low whistle. "Jesus, fuck, that was a hot one."

"Bet I got the trajectory right," Ben said beside me. "You can't get closest every fuckin' time."

I chewed my gum and stood straight. "Benny, when you gonna get with the program? I always get closest." I gave him a hard clap on the shoulder, nodding toward the bomb. "That fucker blew up and out. I guarantee it."

He folded his arms across his chest, shaking his head. "Nah. It went left for sure."

"Squad!" I heard Lieutenant call. "Get your asses over here. Let's see who hit the jackpot."

"Guess we'll find out now," Ben said with a laugh as he started to make his way toward the hood of the truck. "But I'm telling you, it blew left."

I fell into step beside him. "What are we betting this time? I feel bad taking your money from you; it's embarrassing."

"Smartass fuck." Ben turned to me with a cocked eyebrow. "If I win, I get first dibs in Vegas. If you win, you get the cream of the crop."

I bit back a laugh 'cause there was no way that my best bud, Sol 'Benny' Benedetti, was gonna get closest. I had a knack of seein' which way a blast would blow. It was what made me one of the best. I knew where and how to set off an explosive for maximum impact. I knew which direction it would blow, how high it would blast, and how much damage it would do. It wasn't somethin' you could train into me. I just seemed to know.

I'd been in the 756th EOD Company for two years, and there was nowhere else I'd dream of being. It was where I was needed, where I was most useful.

Growing up in an MC with two older brothers who both suited the lifestyle way better than me didn't bode well for my ego. Surprisingly, Explosive Ordnance Disposal seemed to be where I felt most at home, which was weird as fuck considering there was a massive chance of me being blown up in the blink of an eye.

Life on the edge, baby. There was no feeling like it. The danger. The rush. Cheating death. It all gave me a hard-on so big that you could almost see it from space.

Our lieutenant inspected the explosion as the other men in my platoon and I approached the blast site. He looked up at us before writing something down on his pad. "This is getting tedious as hell. Same shit, different day. Up and out. Snow wins."

Mutterings sounded up from the other men.

Benny blew out a hard breath. "You've done it again?"

I looked around at the pissed-off faces and smirked as my unit groaned and cursed. "Looks like I get first dibs. Were goin' to Vegas, baby."

"Fuck!" Ben said under his breath. "I was sure that one was gonna blow left. The gusts are strong as hell."

My smirk turned even more smug. "Watch and learn, Benny boy."

"You've got talent, Snow," Lieutenant stated. "Shame you screw around so much. You could go far. Even I thought it would blow some to the left the way the wind is. What made you think it would go high?"

"It's not gusting much, sir," I replied. "Plus, the device was buried deep. Had a gut feeling, so I gambled on up and out."

Lieutenant shook his head while he wrote on his clipboard. "Good call. You got a talent for this. Heard you achieved the best time in snuffing out that IED last week, too."

"Yes, sir," I confirmed.

"And you're a natural with the robotic arm. All round EOD superstar by all accounts." His eyes met mine and narrowed slightly. "Can't wait to see how you fuck it up."

"Ain't gonna do that, sir," I clipped out. "This is my calling."

"Yeah, yeah. Heard that shit before, Snow. You'll fuck it up." He glanced at Benny. "You boys all still going to Vegas?"

"Yes, sir," Ben replied. "Thought we'd let off some steam before we deploy."

Hollister began writing on his clipboard. "Don't wanna hear any horror stories about my soldiers. Any shit from you men, and I'll come down on you hard. Have a good time. God knows that it'll be your last bit of fun for a while. No fighting, and I don't want any women turning up at this base looking for you two. Had enough of that shit with Higgs. Any lovesick damsels come calling, and I'll court-martial your asses so fast your heads will spin. Make sure you leave there with a clean break."

My eyebrows scrunched together. "Got no intentions of getting hitched while we're there. Not my style, sir."

Lieutenant glanced up from his clipboard. "Just make sure you don't do anything stupid. Look at Higgs and learn a lesson."

"Yes, sir," we said in unison before walking away and heading for the truck.

"Fuck," Benny murmured. "Don't think he likes us."

"No shit. Especially after the prank with the condoms. I swear there's still a lingering smell of burning rubber in the barracks."

Ben grinned. "Funny as fuck, though."

I returned his smile. "Still wanna bust a gut at the sight of the LT's face when he stormed in and saw those burned-out condoms hanging from the windows."

"Me too. But our little stunt didn't go over well. Now Hollister's got it in for us. If we get in any more trouble, he's gonna come down on us like a rainstorm in March."

I grabbed the driver's door handle, hauled it open, and jumped inside. "Ain't about us staying outta trouble, Benny boy. The trick is, don't get caught."

"He said we're looking at a CM next time we fuck up." He slipped into the passenger seat and reached for his seat belt. "We gotta be careful, Snow. He's gonna throw the book at us if we bring any more shit to his door. I can't afford to lose my place here. It's okay for you; there's something for you to go home to, but for me, there's nothing except night security shifts at the local mall."

I checked my mirrors. "Relax, Ben. We'll go to Vegas. Take in a show. Have a few beers and lose some money. What can go wrong?"

Benny looked at me and heaved out a breath. "Fuck me."

Glancing at him, I laughed. Poor fucker was beside himself.

Benny was my opposite. He worried about the little shit while I was a 'no fucks given' kinda man. Being so different made our friendship solid. Together, we were the whole package. We'd come to the EOD team together and developed a bond that I sometimes felt was more robust than the one I had with my blood brothers back in Wyoming.

I would've laid my life down for Benny and all my military brothers, and they would for me. All soldiers said the same thing, but the EOD was something special. Maybe it was because we knew that our lives and deaths depended on a kill switch that could detonate at any given second. Every day we went to work could've been our last day on Earth.

That was the reason I made the most out of life. I lived for the day, laughed, smiled, and had fun. Unfortunately, having too much fun was also why Lieutenant Hollister watched us like a hawk.

"Snow," Benny said as he put his seat belt on. "Have you heard the one about the U.S. Army lieutenants and the prep talk?"

"No."

"Well." He chuckled. "A huge battle was about to start, so the captain gathered his soldiers and three lieutenants for a final prep talk. The first lieutenant stepped forward and shouted, 'My name's Will because when I go into battle, my will hardens, and I want to put the enemy down!' They all give him a whoop. The second lieutenant steps forward and shouts even louder, 'My name's Heart because when I go into battle, my heart hardens, and I want to put the enemy down! The soldiers go crazy cheering. The third lieutenant steps forward but stays silent. The captain gets pissed, goes up to him, and says, 'What about you?' The lieutenant leans in and whispers, 'My name's Dick.'"

I chuckled, shaking my head. "Ben. They're getting worse."

He shrugged. "Made ya laugh though, fucker."

A loud bang sounded from the back of the truck. "Yo, assholes. Don't hog the transport. We all need to get back."

Benny rolled his eyes. "Can we pretend we didn't hear him?"

I shook my head. "He'll only tattle on us if we go without him. Fucking prick."

The back doors opened. "Can't believe you selfish dicks are hogging an entire truck to yourselves. We all need to get back to base."

"Just like those two," another voice rumbled, "not thinking about anyone but their punk ass selves."

I craned my neck to address the two assholes who were buckling up. "You snooze, you lose, fucknuts. You'll get stranded if you stay behind to lick Lieutenant's ass clean."

Benny let out a snort.

I glanced at him, rolling my eyes as I put my foot on the gas and headed the truck toward the base.

The team got on great, mostly. Unfortunately, two assholes ruined the mood. Kyle Simmons and his sidekick, Lee Baker.

I met Simmons the day I joined the EOD and disliked him immediately. He was talking shit about Benny to his little minion, and we nearly came to blows.

Since then, our relationship had gotten decidedly fucking worse. Simmons was a smug asshole who sucked our superior's asses so hard that I was surprised that his big mouth wasn't swollen from the workout.

Fuck Simmons and fuck Baker.

Asswipes.

"Can't help it if he likes us more than you, Snow," Simmons muttered. "Maybe if you stopped fucking around, he might like you, too."

I looked at him in the rearview and rolled my eyes. "You're such a chick, Simmons. Believe me, I've met the worst bitches you could imagine, and you still take the fucking cake. It's embarrassing. Bet your parents are proud."

His eyes narrowed. "Don't talk about my fucking parents, Jon Snow. Especially when yours are dirty biker trash."

I ignored the pang that gripped my chest and, instead, barked a laugh. Couldn't let the snaky prick know he'd gotten to me, especially when I had game, too, and I wouldn't give him the satisfaction of knowing he'd scored a point.

"You think that bothers me, Simmons? Jesus, like I haven't heard it all my life." I glanced over my shoulder, throwing him a cocky grin. "I may come from a long line of dirty bikers, but we're rich as fuck. Not like your family of broke asses."

Word was, Simmons didn't want to enlist, but his parents were so poor that he needed to get out. Apparently, he had good grades and wanted to go to college, but his family needed green, so here he was.

In a way, I respected that. Maybe we could've even been friends in an alternate reality. But he took his troubles out on good people by fucking them over. Therefore, in this reality, I fucking detested him, seeing as the thing I hated most was a rat.

You could take the man outta the MC, but you'd never take the MC outta the man. I'd been raised to despise snitches, and Simmons was the worst of 'em 'cause he did it for sport.

"Heard you and your motley crew are going to Vegas this weekend, Snow," Simmons murmured. "Just be careful. Lieutenant wouldn't be happy if you did your usual trick and fucked up again. He's already watching you after the burning condom incident. Would hate you to get a CM for behaving like the lunatic you are. Especially when you're going for that SPC promotion."

We approached the security gate, where I saw a woman arguing with the guard. My gut dropped when I saw who it was.

"Is that Higgs's woman?" Baker gave a high-pitched whistle. "Hollister won't like that. He already told Higgs if she turns up here again, he'll be in deep shit."

"Fuck," Ben kept his tone low so the assholes in the back couldn't hear. "Hate to say it, but he's right."

I showed the guard my ID, and he opened the barrier for us with a wave. "Don't worry your bitch ass about Higgs, Simmons. You worry about yourself getting laid on your trip home from that high school sweetheart of yours." My voice took on a mocking tone, trying to take his attention away from Higgs's ex-fuck buddy, who by then was pleading with the guard. "Wait. That's right, she dumped you, didn't she? Heard she got engaged to someone else. Sorry 'bout that."

Simmon's face twisted. "Fucking prick."

I parked the truck, switched the engine off, and we all got out, slamming the doors behind us.

"Like I said, Jon Snow. Be very fucking careful," Simmons warned. "Word has a habit of getting out, and don't think I won't tell the boss about it. He's already gonna hear about Higgs's woman at the gate again." He turned his back on me and began walking toward the mess hall with his crony.

"Yo, assholes," I shouted at their backs.

They came to a stop and turned toward us.

"Carry on being a dick. I'll visit your hometown and fuck your girl myself. I'll video that shit and show the boys." I smirked.

"Jesus, Kit," Benny muttered. "You're asking for trouble."

"Better me than Higgs," I murmured while watching Simmon's face turn bright purple. "Bet she'd fuck anyone if she fucked you, Kyle," I called out. "Maybe we should visit all the ghettos in Alaska, Benny. We'd come across Simmon's hovel sooner or later."

Simmons snarled. "I'll kill you, fucker." He squared his shoulders, getting ready to charge.

Baker, the minion, grabbed his arm, pulling him back. "Chill, Kyle." His eyes flashed at me. "Not here. We'll teach Snow a lesson without being pulled before Hollister." His mouth twisted into a sneer. "He'll keep."

"Yeah," Simmons smirked. "Let's go see Hollister now. I'm sure he's gonna love to hear all about Higgs giving our unit a bad rep yet again."

They turned, sauntering toward the building where Hollister's office was. As they got to the door, Simmons looked back at me and smirked.

"He's a fucking dick," I bit out. "Wouldn't trust him as far as I can throw him."

Benny after them, deep in thought. "We gotta have each other's sixes in Afghanistan, Snow. Kyle's a dick, but I wouldn't mind him taking my back if I was under fire. Gotta admit he's dedicated." A grin spread across his face. "Shame he's such a rat bastard."

We made for the building where we were housed, ascending the steps. "Yeah. He's a good soldier. Gotta give him his due. But why does he have to fuck us over? We're all brothers. I know he wants to make his way, but he don't gotta step on us to get there."

"I concur," Benny agreed. "But if you want that SPC role, you've gotta find some common ground with Simmons. I reckon you're in for a good chance of getting it if you use your big head."

I shrugged as we entered the living quarters and turned down the maze of corridors. "Chances are Hollister won't give it to me. He's still up my ass about the last prank. *If,* by some miracle, I get lucky, I'll tolerate Simmons, but I can't be buds with a man who fucks people over to get on in life. How are we meant to trust our brothers in battle if we can't trust them out of it?

If he was part of an MC, they'd have shot him in the head by now. Bikers are smart-asses, but there's no question about their loyalty."

We walked down the long corridor to our dorm room. "Yeah, I get it," Ben replied. "Especially after he stirred shit with Higgs. Can't believe that girl turned up again today. That's been every day for the last two weeks. Hollister's gonna freak."

I nodded as I thought about my pal's predicament.

Higgs was a solid friend and colleague. He'd met a girl during leave in Atlantic City and fucked her solidly for a week. Before he left, he gave her his info, thinking he'd never see her again. She showed up at the gates two weeks ago, begging to see him.

He went down there, was a gentleman, and told her he was going on deployment, wouldn't be able to carry things on. Unlucky for him, she wouldn't take no for an answer and kept turning up, screaming, and getting aggressive with the guards. We reckoned it was Simmons who reported it to Hollister. However, it wouldn't have mattered, seeing as our MG passed through the gates a week ago, saw her screaming and shouting, stopped, and got her story. Turned out that some asshole Jarhead had ghosted the MG's niece the year before, which by all accounts meant that Higgs was fucked. He'd been accused of bringing the military into disrepute.

Simmons had been stirring shit and taunting Higgs ever since. The day before, Higgs lost his cool and went for him. We pulled our boy back and calmed him down, but a passing officer saw it all.

It was a shitshow to end all shitshows.

"Wonder if Higgs is out of his meeting yet?" Benny mused.

I nodded toward our dorm room door, which had been left ajar. "Looks like it. C'mon. Let's see what's going on."

We entered the room to see Higgs lying on his bed, throwing a baseball at the wall and catching it. Poor fucker looked like someone had pissed in his beer.

My heart went out to him. Higgs was well thought of by all until this incident. The dude had a college degree and could've enlisted in officer training. Instead, he wanted to work his way up through the lower ranks. He said he'd better understand his men if he'd been in their position.

That hadn't gone unnoticed by Hollister, who I'd heard had done the same thing.

"Are you okay?" I asked Higgs. "What did Hall say?"

He didn't even look at me. "I got an NJP. Two weeks' pay docked and confined to barracks until we deploy."

"Fuck!" Benny spat. "You can't come to Vegas?"

"That's the least of my worries," Higgs retorted. "Hollister nixed me from the SPC promotion. He said I was a shoo-in but couldn't be seen as a good role model because of my conduct."

My gut sank.

Higgs had been working toward the promotion to Specialist for an entire year. In his spare time, he trained and studied, almost sweating blood for it. All that sacrifice for nothing because of a wild week and a woman.

I'd been studying for the same promotion. I'd taken my final test alongside Higgs and Simmons. I'd been looking forward to working alongside him.

Jeez!

"I'm sorry, man," Benny murmured. "We know how much you wanted it."

Higgs threw the ball again. "Got a note on my file, too. Not permitted to apply for any promotions for two years." He sat up and scrubbed a hand down his face. "It's gonna put me back so far that I may never catch up."

I took in his face, devoid of color. His eyes were red-rimmed with purple smudges underneath. He looked like shit, though that was expected, seeing as his career had just been wiped out.

Jesus, if that happened to me, I'd be forced to pop smoke and go back to the MC. The thought made me shudder. Once you got a note on your file, it took time for your career to recover.

My jaw clenched as I thought back to Simmons's smug face. The asshole enjoyed screwing people over, but now he was on my shit list. I'd make it my mission to get some payback for Higgs.

I'd teach that fucker a lesson if it killed me.

Chapter Two

Snow

My mouth twisted into a wry smile as I glanced back at Harry Reid Airport. We had four days of R&R ahead of us and were chomping at the proverbial bit to get started. The heat of Las Vegas hit my face, making my footsteps falter. I closed my eyes and looked up, basking in it briefly.

We needed this trip badly. We'd been stuck on base for months getting ready for deployment. We were shipping out the following week; I was determined to make the most of my time on U.S. soil. Our LV party trip was gonna be memorable. I could feel it in my blood.

A dull stab went through my chest when I thought of home.

Maybe I should've gone to Hambleton this weekend–most of the team were returning to their hometowns. Still, I didn't feel any pull toward Wyoming. I loved my folks and siblings, but the military was my life, as was my team, and I wanted to have a good time with them.

However, I couldn't help feeling a little guilty, especially as I knew my mom and Iris would've loved a quick visit.

"Vegas, baby," AJ whooped. "I can almost smell all the green I'm gonna win later."

AJ's excitement made me smile. "I'm with you there, brother."

Benny hoisted his backpack securely over his shoulder. "I don't intend to get any shuteye tonight. It's rude not to go crazy on our first night here, and at least we'll still have three days to recover."

"That's what I'm talking about." Puck clapped Ben on the back. "I like your way of thinking."

I took my shades from my backpack and slid them on before nodding toward the long line of taxis waiting outside the airport. "Let's get to the hotel, dump our bags, and hit the bars. Time to get the weekend started."

"Good idea," Benny said. "But first, we need to talk." He looked at all of us in turn. "Okay, after what happened with Higgs, we talked about giving fake names to any women we meet, right?"

We all nodded.

"Last thing we need is to slip up and call each other by the wrong name. We've been told during training that if you lie to the enemy under interrogation, keep it as close to the truth as possible. That way, you'll remember details better. So, I was thinking. Why don't we give out the names of people we know? That way, we won't forget them."

My face twisted, confused. "Who do you wanna be? The Easter bunny?"

Benny rolled his eyes. "Who do we know that narks on everyone?" His eyes bugged out. "Think about it, assholes. Who would we love to get their comeuppance?"

His meaning dawned on me, and a laugh rose through my throat. "Genius! You gotta let me be Simmons."

"I'll be Baker," Benny confirmed.

AJ thumbed his chest. "I'm gonna be Hollister."

Puck laughed. "That leaves me with Espinoza."

Snow

Benny looked between us all with a playful smirk. "Let the games begin."

I drained my beer, placed the bottle on the table, and looked around the club.

The guy at the hotel recommended this place. He told us that even Vegas residents came to this particular strip club. He'd done good.

Red velvet couches and chairs were situated around black lacquer tables. The walls were decorated in a grey wallpaper with swirl patterns. The lights were low, casting a subtle red hue around the vast room.

The massive stage in front of us had a black lacquer floor and curtains drawn tightly closed. I'd been in some shitty strip clubs before, but this one was classy. But then we were in Vegas, the capital of sin, and like everyone said, sex sells.

This place must have turned over a fortune. I just hoped the dancers lived up to the same hype. If I wanted to watch a bunch of skanks dance, I'd have gone to the Speed Demons clubhouse bar and watched the whores grind on each other.

I'd always been a take-it-or-leave-it kind of dude when it came to women and sex.

It wasn't something I actively went out looking for. I lost my virginity at fifteen to a club hang around. Though, I could've lost it much sooner if I'd wanted to.

I'd grown up around sex, so it wasn't something I revered. It stood to reason that when a man witnessed sexual acts every day of his life, he got jaded. I did it when I needed to take the edge off, but more recently, I'd gone without it for years. My right hand gave me what I needed, and there was no awkwardness afterward. That was exactly how I liked things. Simple and easy.

I watched Benny weaving toward me from the bar, beers in hand. He set them down on the table, pulled the chair out next to me, and sank his ass down.

"Even the bartenders in this place are fucking gorgeous." He craned his neck and nodded toward the bar. "That little redhead's cute as fuck. Funny, too."

I followed the direction of his gaze to see a tiny little thing behind the bar popping tops of bottles of beer. She glanced up and caught Benny's gaze, blushing prettily, before turning away to place the bottles on the bar top.

"She's hot, Ben," I agreed, picking up my beer and swigging it. "I forgot women could blush like that. She seems sweet."

"Yup," he murmured thoughtfully, turning back to face the stage. "She's from Connecticut, too. Not far from where I grew up."

I shook my head. "Didn't take you long to get her life story."

Benny took a long pull from his bottle. "Never does." His tone was nonchalant, but I could tell by the way he kept glancing furtively over his shoulder that he was into the girl.

"Go talk to her, Ben," I told him, pointing the neck of my beer bottle toward the bar. "You obviously like what you see. Have a good time; you won't be able to soon."

He shrugged. "Nah. We're flying out to hell next week. It's not fair to start something new. And come on, man. She works in a strip club. She's probably got dudes hitting on her all the time."

"Jesus, Benny. It's not like she's a stripper. She doesn't whip her tits out. The woman deals in cocktails, not cocks." I chuckled at my own joke. "I could understand your hesitation if she let it all hang out for a living, but that's not the case here."

"What's wrong with stripping?" he asked, eyebrows furrowing. "Never took you for a snob."

"I grew up in a biker club, ain't no snob, but believe me, I've met a lot of skanks and strippers, and unlike Red over there, they're not the kinda girls you get to know. They're good for something, but it ain't meeting your ma."

Ben shook his head slowly. "Never took you for a judgmental cunt, Snow. That's more Simmons's speed."

"Ain't judging." I retorted. "Live and let live, Ben. I'm just saying you get serious with some girls and others you don't. Strippers strip 'cause they don't make good wives."

"Jesus." He pursed his lips. "You're an asshole."

"Just telling it like it is, Ben. Ya gotta—" I was cut off by the crackle of the sound system.

A loud voice boomed, *Ladies and gentlemen. Welcome to Crimson Velvet. Voted Vegas's best exotic dance club for two years running. Now, without further ado, let's welcome our first goddess dancing for you tonight. Put your hands together for... Raven!*

A speck of light shone on the stage, and excited whispers turned into a loud roar. The crowds of people standing at the bar moved toward the tables and chairs, their full attention glued to the black curtains that started to swish open. The atmosphere was so juiced that I could almost see the air crackle with electricity.

The pinprick of light grew until the form of a woman appeared, and the opening bars of Beyonce's 'Partition' started to pump through the room.

Her back faced the baying crowd, dark brown skin glistening under the stage lights. She was dressed like a Victoria's Secret model in a white lacy bra, panties, and enormous white wings that spanned a few feet to each side. She was curvy, ass big, high, and round.

Fucking beautiful.

Sitting back, I watched Raven's ass pump in time to the beat of the music. A huge smile took over my face. "I think we're in for a treat tonight, Benny."

My bud cleared his throat, eyes still glued to the woman as she swung around to reveal her beautiful face and bright red lips. Her waist-length plaited hair swung out like a fuckin' halo around her.

One side of Ben's mouth hitched up. "Snowy. I think you're right." He leaned back, eyes never leaving the dancer, who was on her knees, crawling across the stage floor toward us. "Jesus, fuck," he muttered, beer bottle suspended mid-air, halfway to his mouth.

I laughed. "Jesus, fuck, indeed, Ben." I cast an appreciative eye over Raven's ass. "Enjoy the show, brother.

An hour later, our eyes were still glued to the stage. Between intervals, girl after girl gave us a show unlike anything we'd seen.

All the strip clubs I'd been to before had been seedy as fuck. This place was something different. The décor clean, the bartenders pretty, and the dancers—well, they were strippers but with a difference.

Every girl had talent. Their routines were classy, and I got lost in every grind of their hips and seductive smiles. They were more like professional dancers than strippers.

After every routine, the stage fell into darkness. The male—and female—patrons surged toward the bar, grabbing fresh drinks before the next girl appeared under the spotlights. The buzzing atmosphere never wavered. Each dancer received encouraging shouts from the crowd as they entertained, then sashayed from the stage, blowing kisses to us.

The owner of the place must've been sitting on a goldmine. He obviously knew his clientele and business well. He'd created something special. I made a mental note to tell Pop about it one day. There was obviously some scratch to be made with a club like this.

At some point, AJ and Puck walked in and sat with us, but I hardly noticed because my attention was caught on a beautiful red-haired woman flying through the air to

Snow

No Doubt's 'Hella Good.' She leaped, somersaulted, and tumbled like an Olympic gymnast until her clothes came off.

Puck surged to his feet, cheering as she finished her dance. The crowd had gone wild for her, and underwear-clad women strategically weaved through the tables, holding buckets for us to throw our cash into.

Throughout the night, I'd been relieved of a few hundred bucks. Not that I noticed or even cared. Those girls were worth every penny, and I didn't have much else to spend my scratch on. They were fucking welcome to it.

Time went by fast, and a lot of beer was drunk. Eventually, I glanced at my watch, eyes widening, when I noticed it was already past midnight.

My stare returned to the stage, where a brunette woman dressed in bondage gear cracked a whip through the air. She wore a Maleficent headdress and writhed around to The Red Hot Chilli Peppers 'Give it Away Now.'

I bobbed my head along to the banging of the drums vibrating through the sound system. AJ had jumped to his feet, shouting encouragement along with every other man in the room.

I'd never seen anything like it.

Every woman was beautiful, sexy, and classy. Some were exotic looking, others like sexy little girls next door. I was so engrossed in their dancing talent that they didn't register sexually. I'd been raised around tits and ass, so it wasn't anything I hadn't seen a thousand times.

But there was no getting away from the fact I was entertained. So, when one of the waitresses rattled a bucket beside me, I gladly threw another fifty inside. I grinned at the thought of the dancers getting their cut. Those girls must've been loaded, but funnily, I didn't begrudge it one bit. We'd had a great first night in Vegas, so they'd earned it.

The closing bars of the song died before a huge cheer went up around the room. People stomped their feet, shouting their appreciation to the woman, who gave a broad smile, blowing kisses to the crowd. Their shouts increased as she exited the stage.

The speakers gave another crackle, and silence fell over the club as the compere's voice came through.

Ladies and gentlemen. It's the moment you've all been waiting for. Please put your hands together for the last act of the night. She's known as the sexiest woman in Vegas. I give you the one and only... Kitten!

For a split second, you could hear a pin drop before a howling roar went up. It seemed to lift the roof off the joint. A loud chant cut through the air, every man in the room yelling, "Kitten. Kitten. Kitten." The opening chords of 'Welcome to the Jungle' pounded through the room so loudly that the drum and bass seemed to thump through my chest.

I sat up, back slowly straightening.

Something made me look, take notice, a feeling. My breath caught inside my throat when the silhouette of a woman suspended mid-air appeared through the backlit closed curtains.

The placement of the beam shining from behind her meant all I could see was a shadowy figure thrusting and gyrating horizontally, seemingly levitating. It was eerie and other-worldly. Fuck, it was the most compelling thing I'd ever seen in my goddamned life.

As Axl screamed, 'Welcome to the jungle,' the girl flipped herself vertically.

She threw her head back while simultaneously punching her arms outward to make the shape of a cross. Every stage light beamed onto her as the curtain swept back, revealing her for the first time.

My body jerked as something punched me in the chest.

Snow

Heart hammered and pulse thrumming, I leaned forward, resting my arms on my knees, hands dangling down.

I couldn't look away.

She was incredible. Long blonde hair flowed down to her tiny waist. The swell of her hips accentuated her long, shapely legs. Her perfect tits were encased in red lace, matching the panties that whispered across her pussy.

Palms suddenly clammy, I rubbed them absentmindedly against my jeans. I thought about glancing at my boys, just to see if they were as mesmerized as I was, but for the life of me, I couldn't look away from that goddamned stage.

Still suspended by invisible wires, her hips rolled in time to the pumping bassline. She bounced her head up and down like a crazy woman, making her light blonde hair fly everywhere.

The crowd's roar was so loud I could hear it as distinctly as the music.

It reminded me of being at a gig where the fans were so rabid they drowned out the band. I rubbed at the goosebumps trailing down my arms, still unable to wrench my stare away from the sex kitten.

"Jesus, fuck!" AJ muttered from beside me. "She's fucking gorgeous."

My gut twisted.

An urge to pull his eyes out of their sockets hit me. I wanted to stop him from looking at her. My fingers twitched with the compulsion to knock him the fuck out.

The chorus hit, and she twisted just before her feet hit the floor. As if in a trance, I zeroed in on her face.

Her head still banged in time to the music, hips writhing as she contorted her body into positions and shapes that would be physically impossible for the average person. But then she wasn't anything like average whatsoever.

Long blonde hair flew over her features, making it impossible to see her appearance. I needed to see her face. Was she as beautiful as she was sexy? If she was, I was fucked.

"Come on, baby girl," I whispered, leaning forward. "Show me what you got."

She couldn't have heard me over the music or the screaming crowd. But maybe we were somehow connected in another way because she supermodel stomped her ass toward the edge of the stage and looked directly at me.

Big cornflower blue eyes caught mine.

My breath hitched as I watched a small smile curve her beautiful, full mouth. Her gaze pulled me in like a fucking tractor beam.

My mind went blank for a few seconds before a fire flickered to life inside my gut. I had to force my ass to stay in that fucking chair to stop myself from leaping up on the stage and tossing her over my shoulder.

I watched her high, firm, little ass thrust in time to the music. My mind conjured up images of crawling on top of her, digging my fingers into her ass, and doing some thrusting of my own.

She must've seen the blatant desire on my face because she looked me up and down, licked her lips, and shot me a sexy little wink.

I stopped fucking breathing.

The heavens opened and shone a white light down on her.

My cock pulsed, hard as rebar, as a realization hit me.

I'd sailed through life, never being affected by much. Not family, friends, or women. This girl had made me sit up and take notice. Something told me I'd never forget that one fleeting moment in time.

She'd flipped a switch inside me and brought me to life.

Kitten twirled and thrust, all the while shooting me seductive glances.

It was almost inhuman how her body contorted. She dropped to her knees, head circling so vigorously that her silky hair flew out in all directions. Jumping to her feet, still crouched, she slowly rose to a stand, ass first, glutes undulating as she shook her perfect booty in my face.

My mouth watered at the sight of her toned muscles rippling under her golden skin. Cock aching against my zipper, I watched her twist around until her back was to the audience and grind her ass. All that covered her crack was a tiny thong, which didn't leave much to the imagination.

She looked like an angel and a sinner. Her light blonde hair gave her an air of innocence, and then she'd whip around, flashing me a devilish smirk. It was confusing and compelling at the same time.

The final bars of the rock song blasted through the speakers. A thread of panic twisted inside. I didn't want it to end. I could've happily sat there watching her for the rest of my life and died a happy man.

She spun around to face the audience again, let out a piercing yell, and as the last riff echoed from the guitar, she ripped her bra open from the front, revealing firm, high tits. The lights cut out, and darkness suddenly bathed the stage.

I closed my eyes, cock leaking inside my shorts as another roar rose through the vast room. Feet stomped, glasses crashed, and yells of 'Kitten' pounded the air.

I sat back in the chair, mouth still hanging open.

Jeez, is it hot in here?

"Close your trap, Snow." Benny laughed from beside me. "Trying to catch flies?"

I gulped.

"She was fucking hot," Puck muttered. He glanced at me mischievously. "Wonder if she gives lap dances."

Fire swept through me. "Don't even think about it. Keep your goddamned hands off her."

Benny's face froze comically.

Puck side-eyed AJ, smirking.

I knew he'd be an asshole. I loved my team, but we all went hard on each other. It didn't usually bother me. It was all part of being in the military, but I didn't like the idea of them being pricks where the sexy little kitten was involved.

A bucket rattled next to us. I went into my wallet, plucked two Benjamins out, and tossed 'em inside.

My brain still whirred with Axl's shrieks and Kitten's moves.

It was like someone had come along and tasered my ass because I couldn't think straight. My hands were clammy, and my shirt felt like it was strangling my goddamned neck.

Benny watched me, shaking his head slightly. "You high-rolling tonight?"

I ignored him while I took a pull of my beer.

AJ waggled his eyebrows. "More for me." He turned to the waitress. "Can I book a lap dance with the Kitten?"

My jaw clenched so hard I was surprised I didn't crack a tooth.

"AJ," Ben warned. "Don't be a dick. He'll bury you."

The waitress looked between us, lips twitching. "Sorry. Kitten doesn't do private dances. Raven or Ruby will be happy to oblige, though." She glanced at her watch. "The girls will be ready in about fifteen minutes."

My shoulders relaxed.

Puck leaned forward in his chair. "Ruby. Is she the redhead?"

I smiled at the thread of excitement in his voice. Puck had always been partial to women with red hair. It was an in-joke. He liked finding out if the carpet matched the drapes.

Snow

"Yeah," the waitress replied. "Want me to book you in?"

He nodded enthusiastically.

"Room three. Pay security on the door," she instructed. "Though I must warn you, boys, you can't touch. This is a clean place, not a brothel. Management looks after us."

Puck nodded, rubbing his hands together with a grin. "Well, boys, that's my night planned. I'll see ya back at the hotel." He got to his feet and made his way in the direction the waitress was pointing.

"Well, it didn't take him long to abandon us," I muttered. "First sniff of pussy, and he runs like his ass is on fire."

Benny laughed. "He always was easily led."

"Yeah," I agreed. "By the short fucking hairs. You'd think he'd never seen a woman before."

"Where we're going, it'll be a while before he sees one like Ruby again." AJ's tone was thoughtful. "Leave him to his fun."

Ben shook his beer bottle. "I'm empty. You boys ready for a fresh one?"

I nodded.

"Not for me," AJ told him, getting to his feet. "Puck's got the right idea. I'm wondering if that tasty little brunette who was on second from last gives lap dances. Gonna go and get my fill before we ship out." He gave us a loose salute and disappeared in the same direction as Puck.

Benny watched him go and stood up. "AJ," he called.

Our friend stopped and turned, cocking his head questioningly.

"Remember our pact. Don't get chatty; above all else, don't forget your name."

AJ jerked a nod and turned before disappearing down a corridor.

Benny turned to me. "You gonna spend money to get a hard-on? Nobody would blame ya, Snowy."

I recalled the curve of Kitten's ass as she shook it in my face earlier. I doubted I could even get a half-chub unless she was the one coaxing it outta me.

I shrugged. "Nah."

A smile took over my buddy's face. "I know who you're thinking about. The minute she came on stage, you looked shell-shocked." He let out a low whistle. "Did you see her on those wires? Girl's gotta have a strong core to do that shit."

"Did you see the way she moved? Thought my cock was gonna bust open; she was so goddamned incredible."

"She was. But you've known a lotta beautiful women. Never saw you react that way before."

"Can't say I remember reacting like that either." I scraped a hand down my face, suddenly feeling exhausted. The adrenaline coursing through my veins when Kitten was on stage faded fast. "Maybe I should just get some shuteye back at the hotel."

Benny looked at me thoughtfully. "Stay for now. I'll get us another beer."

One shoulder lifted in a shrug. "Guess I can sleep when I'm dead."

Benny clapped me on the back. "Trust me, Snowy. I'll show you a good time."

My eyes followed him as he turned and strolled toward the bar. "Yeah," I breathed, watching him call Red to serve. "Your good times usually end in disaster."

I loved my military brothers; I'd die for them, but they were pains in my ass. It was weird how I'd trust them to have my back and save my life but wouldn't trust them with everyday things like talking about a woman I was into. That was the military for you. Practical jokes and evil banter reigned. Soldiers dealt with things civilians couldn't imagine, so it was easy to understand why we needed to let off steam in our downtime. We made the most of life because we knew it was fragile. Laughing helped us cope with the darkness.

Especially in the world we were living in.

The good ol' U.S. of A had always taken pride in their military forces. Still, after nine-eleven and the worldwide backlash, our soldiers felt the pressure.

I'd missed the Iraq war but enlisted just before the government sent troops into Afghanistan. The EOD boys wanted nothing more than to help fight the good fight.

Our Vegas trip was designed to help us forget, even briefly. We needed to live like average men without a care in the world. We needed a weekend to reflect on while spitting hot sand from our throats.

My head swiveled toward the bar where Benny was chatting up the little redheaded bartender. Their heads were together, thick as thieves, and she laughed at something he'd said.

He was a smooth bastard. His Italian good looks meant he wasn't short of a conquest or two. The ladies loved him, and he loved them right back, at least for a night.

I'd been raised around casual sex and one-night stands, which never appealed to me. I was looking for something more, some kind of connection.

I immediately thought about the sexy little kitten who had blown me away. I'd felt a connection there. When her eyes met mine, something passed between us. A sense of déjà vu, like I'd met her before but couldn't remember the details.

My pulse quickened when I recalled how she twisted her body, threw her hair, and shot me little looks while she danced like her life depended on it.

Kitten performed just for me. I could feel it. Now, she seemed like a missed opportunity, someone significant who I was missing out on. The girl gave me big-assed FOMO.

I tried to think of a way to talk to her. If I asked the waitresses, management would think I was some weirdo trying to find her and take her back to my lair. She probably had creepers trying to get to her all the time. I'd been watching the room, but she hadn't appeared. Some of the other girls had swept out and were working their magic, but not Kitten.

A big old ball of emotion rolled through me.

I'd have liked to have gotten to know her, but how could I? If I lived here, I'd have had time to work something out, but we were only in Vegas for a few days.

Fuck my life.

Benny approached the table. "Get your shit. We're going." He picked up his cell from the table and slipped it into his pocket. "Come on, Snow. Move your ass. pronto." He glanced at the bar, sending Red a wink. "We ain't got all night."

My brow furrowed. "Ain't got all night for what?"

He popped a piece of gum in his mouth and smirked as he began to chew. "You'll see, Snowy."

Confused, I stood and patted my pockets, ensuring I had my cell and wallet. "What the fuck's the hurry?"

Benny barked out a laugh, clapping me on the shoulder. "Gotta little surprise for ya, bro. You can thank me later."

"The last time you had a little surprise for me, I almost ended up with a court fucking martial," I grumbled as we weaved through the tables toward the main entrance.

"I promise you're gonna like this one," Benny said under his breath as we exited the club. He pulled out his cell. "Need to call a cab if we're gonna catch you a kitten."

I froze. "Huh?"

Benny dipped his chin, rubbing his hands together. "We gotta double date."

Chapter Three

Kitten

I couldn't stop my face twisting as Chloe told me about the stupid fix-up she'd arranged without me knowing jack about it. Honestly, I could've killed her. I'd just gotten out of a crazy situation with a guy who I thought was okay but turned out to be a fanboy.

Things got so crazy that Marco's guys had to pay him a visit. It was the only way he'd leave me the hell alone.

A girl—a stripper at that—had to be careful if she didn't want to end up as just another statistic. Shit went on in this town, shit that even I couldn't believe sometimes, and I'd lived here since the day I was born.

Did I like violence? Hell no. But if it was a choice between an asshole stalker and me, I'd volunteer him as tribute all day long. Only it seemed now Chloe had put me straight back to square one.

"What if they turn out to be nut jobs?" I demanded. "This shit never ends well, Chlo. There's a real good reason Marco doesn't like us meeting clients away from the club."

"I promise it will be fine," my friend murmured, signaling to the waitress for a refill. "It's a couple of those soldiers Rave and Natalie were swooning over. They're gorgeous, Kitty. Just relax and enjoy yourself. You're always so uptight."

I leaned back in the chair while the waitress filled our cups with java.

As soon as Raven returned to the dressing room after her dance, she chatted excitedly about the tall, good-looking guys sitting by the stage.

"Soldiers for sure," she'd said, then told us about her daddy. Turned out he'd been a career officer. Her family moved home every few years whenever he got stationed somewhere new. She'd grown up around military personnel and reckoned they had a particular way of moving, which she could spot from a mile away.

Throughout the night, as the girls went out to do their thing and then came back to the dressing room talking excitedly about how hot the guys were, I grew more curious.

I was on last. I'd taken the coveted final spot for the previous few weeks. The crowd was friendly and warmed up for me. I couldn't wait to perform the new routine, which had taken me weeks to put together.

Something inside me sparked when I looked down and caught golden eyes.

His stare flicked over my body, leaving a burning trail on my skin.

It felt so intense that I couldn't stop my gaze from wandering toward him every few seconds. Before I knew it, I was dancing for him alone. My steps—usually well-rehearsed—became tailored by his reaction. By the end of my number, I felt his appraisal somewhere deep inside my cooch. He affected me.

Still, I was a single young woman living in Sin City. Statistically, I was prone to get kidnapped, raped, or trafficked, so I had to keep my head. Marco told us we weren't to date clients. He'd looked after me like a big brother, and I trusted his judgment.

My boss wouldn't be happy about this.

"You don't know who these men are, Chlo," I insisted. "I have to steer clear of trouble, or Marco will be pissed, especially after he had to deal with the last weirdo."

"I'm a good judge of character," she insisted. "These guys are cool and totally fucking hot. The one I was talking to is from Connecticut, just like me."

"Oh, well, that's fine then." I deadpanned. "Ted Bundy was good-looking and charismatic too, then lo-and-behold, it's all strangulation and crowbars."

Chloe rolled her eyes. "Go home then, Kitty. I'll be fine."

I sighed, eyes softening as I regarded my pretty friend. "You're my girl. I'm not going to leave you alone with them, am I?"

As I said that, I heard the bell tinkle above the doorway.

"They're here," Chlo said under her breath. "Jesus, help me. They're hot."

Slowly, my gaze lifted to meet golden eyes.

It was him.

My tummy pitched like I was on a rollercoaster ride when I saw the man who'd been on my mind for the last hour. He seemed bigger, over six feet. Muscled and toned. His beautiful, tanned face made my breath catch in my throat.

Tall, dark, and handsome may have been my catnip, but add in charismatic and beautiful, and it was 'hello downfall.'

My heart thudded once, then raced as he stalked toward our table, his eyes holding mine while he approached.

Something sparked inside my belly and began to warm me as I observed him saunter over and pull the chair out next to me. It scraped as he maneuvered it across the tiled floor. The scent of his cologne hit me, and my tummy swirled as I breathed it in. Fresh, with a hit of sandalwood.

My mind blanked, and my tongue tied up in knots.

Usually, I was never shy or stuck for words, but this man robbed me of all reason. My mind seemed to revert to a fifteen-year-old girl who'd just been asked out by the football team captain.

I looked ahead, avoiding his eyes, trying to scramble my brain back into a working organ again, but I could feel his gaze heat my skin, just like it did on stage.

"Good evening, ladies," the guy seated beside Chloe greeted.

"Hey!" she replied. "Glad you could make it. Kitty's been freaking out."

I felt *him* shift beside me. "Why?" he rumbled.

Jesus, even his voice sounded beautiful. It was molten lava. Gravelly, dangerous, and burning hot. It seemed to flow straight toward my panties because my vagina immediately heated.

"She's freaking out because we don't know you," Chlo continued. "Clients tend to give her trouble. They get attached and make her nervous."

I shifted in my seat, suddenly uncomfortable.

"You're okay," the guy sitting with Chloe assured me. "Snowy gets it. He's you with a cock. Women flock to him."

The man, Snowy, cursed at his friend.

Chloe burst into giggles.

My brain latched on to the information and thankfully began to settle. I turned to my right to see golden eyes already on my face.

God, he was gorgeous.

"Snowy?" I asked softly.

He dipped his chin, his eyes holding mine hostage. "Snow's the handle my team gave me."

I felt my mouth hitch up at one side. "Why Snow?"

His stare darted to his friend. I noticed his neck redden slightly as he looked to the other man for help. "Umm—"

"—He looks like the Jon Snow character from that Game of Thrones show," the other guy interrupted quickly. "He got his name the day we joined the same unit."

I turned back to examine his face. I hadn't watched Game of Thrones, but it was everywhere. Yeah, I could see the likeness.

Something pinged suspiciously as a look passed between them. They seemed to be having a whole other conversation telepathically. That was rude. "Is everything okay?"

"Yeah," Chole's guy assured me. "Let me introduce myself. I'm Lee." He nodded toward his friend. "This is Kyle."

Kyle's stare veered down at his hands. His face flushed almost nervously as he slid his eyes back to mine. It seemed like he wanted to say something, but he rolled his lips together, staying quiet.

"Are you military?" I asked.

"Yeah," Lee confirmed. "We're bomb squad." He turned his body to face Chloe and whispered something in her ear.

She giggled girlishly.

A sick feeling washed through me. "Isn't that really dangerous?"

"You look different," he rasped, completely ignoring my question. "You're younger than I thought back at the club."

Chloe and Lee were already engrossed in their conversation, so I turned toward Kyle and shrugged. "No makeup. The first thing I do when I come off stage is take it off. I hate the feel of it." I started to babble. "But I find if I wear it when I dance, I'm more confident."

"You look more beautiful without it," he rumbled quietly. "You looked incredible on stage, but it was a mask. Now I can see this version, I realize I prefer it. The woman at the club was beautiful, but the real you's better."

Emotion sprung up my throat at his words.

Kitten was a character, the persona I adopted to get me through my dances with confidence and flair. I wasn't ashamed of stripping; it came naturally to me, but being someone fake to the clientele meant I could keep something real back just for me.

People saw me on stage and immediately thought they knew me.

I gave them the character they wanted, but she wasn't anything like me. Kitten was sexy, confident, and a man-eater. Kennedy had more of a quiet confidence and a ton of ambition, which burned inside.

I'd been judged on my looks all my life.

People thought I was a pretty airhead when, in reality, I'd graduated high school a year early and finished college in two. I was nineteen with two college degrees and graduated at the top of my classes.

I did that. Nobody helped me. No parent motivated me. I motivated myself.

There was only one family member to whom I was remotely close to. My uncle Hustle.

He was part of Vegas's most prominent MC. He loved me and wanted to take me in when my mom took off, but I wanted to look after myself. My best friend Sophie's mom became my legal guardian until I turned eighteen. She tried to help me financially, as did Hustle, but I didn't want handouts, and I didn't want charity.

I wanted to work for everything I had because, that way, nobody could wrench it away from me.

I'd always been independent. Maybe because my mom flitted from man to man while depending financially on them all. She was beautiful. All the women in her bloodline were the same way. Blonde, blue-eyed, good genes.

Snow

Mom's looks were her meal ticket. Her lifestyle depended on how rich her latest beau was. She relied on everyone but herself, which made my childhood precarious.

I swore I'd never be that person. I paid my own way and didn't need anyone to buy me. I was happiest doing everything solo, which was great but also made me a loner. Mom had never really been present anyway, so I was used to it.

However, looking at Kyle in that diner, I felt like I wanted to be around him. He unnerved me and put me at ease at the same time. He was almost familiar like I knew him from somewhere.

My fingers tremored slightly as I lifted my mug. "Have we met before?" I asked, taking a sip.

He smiled widely to reveal perfect, white teeth. "Yeah. I reckon we have. I feel it, too."

"When?"

He studied my face. "I'll tell you later when we're alone."

"You wanna get me alone?" I teased softly. "I don't know you enough to go somewhere with you alone."

"Not yet," he confirmed. "But you will." His eyes kept sweeping over my face. It was a little distracting.

"Why are you looking at me like that?"

"Committing you to memory, Kitten. We're shipping out next week. I wanna be able to remember your beautiful face." He smiled broadly.

I usually would've rolled my eyes at his cheesy lines, but from him, the words made my tummy fizz and pop. "You hardly know me. For all you know, I could be Aileen Wuornos wrapped up in a prettier package."

Kyle laughed. "I highly doubt that, Kitten. Tell me everything. What about your family? Are they in Vegas, too?"

I looked at him thoughtfully. We were playing a dangerous game here, but weirdly, I trusted him. My instincts had never let me down before, and they were telling me he was special.

"My dad took off just after I was born, then my mom took off when I was sixteen. My best friend's family officially fostered me until I was eighteen, and she went off to study medicine. I stayed because I got accepted to Harvard to study for my MBA in business. I'm dancing so I can save every penny before I go."

"Jesus," he breathed. "You're fucking fascinating." His hand slipped over mine, resting on the table. Warmth enveloped my fingers, and I shivered.

Nobody had ever called me that before.

"What makes you tick?" he asked. "What lights a fire in your belly, Kitten? What is it inside that makes you get up every day and put one foot in front of the other?"

I froze.

Jesus. Who is this guy?

My eyes slid over his face, taking in his honest and open expression.

One of a kind, my inner voice whispered.

I was the most practical girl you could meet, but I also believed in fate and the premise that everything happens for a reason. For me, people seemed to leave my life when the time was right, always making way for new people to come in.

It had been proven to me time and time again. My parents left to let Lois and Sophie in. Then, I met Marco the day I got my Harvard acceptance letter. I was so in my head about how I'd afford it that I wasn't watching where I was going. I bumped into him and was his new dancer within ten minutes.

People came in and out of my life as and when needed.

Maybe he had, too.

My only constants were Sophie and Lois. They were my soulmates, the ones who'd been by my side for centuries. The ones who my soul recognized and kept

Snow

close. No man had ever been close to me. I'd never been in love and never wanted to settle down.

But this man felt different.

He felt right.

"Success makes me tick," I finally replied. "Making something of myself. Taking something for me, then giving it back when I've made it. It's all yin and yang. Life balances out. You roll with the good times and learn from the bad."

"My mother would fucking love you," he murmured.

That made me laugh and feel warm at the same time. "The only mother who's ever loved me is my foster one."

He shrugged. "Some people are insecure. A lot of mothers I know have a special bond with their boys. In my experience, we're just scared to lose the people we connect with the most."

My brow furrowed. "Is it like that with your family?"

"In a sense. I'm from a military background. Dad, Grandpa, and Great-Grandpa all fought in one of the big wars. It was either enlisting or joining the family business. Ma knows I've always wanted to serve my country, so here I am."

"That's nice," I murmured. "Having purpose."

He splayed his fingers through mine. "You've got a purpose. Harvard. Taking the business world by storm. You'll make it, Kitten. I see great things for you. I can feel it in my bones."

A lump formed in my throat. "You think?"

He threw me his sexy grin, and my heart fluttered. "I know it as well as I know the back of my hand. You're gonna change lives. I've known you for a few hours, and you've already changed mine."

Wow.

He must have heard my sharp intake of breath because his fingers squeezed mine, and in that moment, I knew I'd met him for a reason.

He felt like mine.

Over the next few hours, we continued to go deep. Deeper than I'd been with anyone ever before. I didn't notice people enter the diner or leave. Even Chloe and Lee seemed to fade away, though they sat at the same table.

He was all I saw, all I felt. My skin thrummed every time his fingers skated over mine, and my heart thudded a little faster. My reaction to him was physical, emotional, and spiritual. We loved the same music the same food. We had the same moral compass and the same outlook on life.

We laughed together, and he gently wiped away a stray tear that spilled over with his thumb when I got overly emotional.

He never once made me feel stupid or acted like I had nothing to offer. He asked me everything, and I answered because I wanted him to know everything, too. Men before called me a hippie chick and said I needed to come back down to earth, but Kyle seemed to respond most to the spiritual side of me.

He accepted the essence of me. That made me feel like I was floating. My skin buzzed, my heart raced, and my stomach flipped.

And I loved it.

We were startled out of our bubble when Lee announced it was getting late or early, depending on how you looked at it.

"You've let me talk about myself all night," I murmured, mouth hitching into a smile.

The soft look he gave me made my heart soar. "You're really interesting. I've never known a woman like you before."

"Bet you've known lots of women," I joked.

He busted out a laugh.

It immediately struck me how vibrant he looked. So joyful and alive. "I've known women," he admitted. "But not as many as you might think."

"It's because you're so handsome." I shrugged. "People think if you're good-looking, you must be getting it all the time."

"You think I'm handsome?" he asked gently.

"That's what you took from what I just said?" I teased, smiling, then shrugged. "I get the same thing. People think because I'm pretty and a stripper, I've known many men, but it's not the case."

"Yeah," he agreed. "After talking to you tonight, I don't think you have."

"Only one, in fact." I smiled as I thought back. "My high school boyfriend. He took me to prom and then to a fancy hotel. He'd saved so hard to pay for everything. I didn't have the heart to say no."

Kyle's eyebrows drew together. "You shouldn't ever feel pressured, Kitten. Never do anything you don't wanna."

The warmth swirling through me told me I liked that he cared. I liked that he wanted the best for me. I wished someone had done that for me when I lost my virginity. I mean, it was okay but forgettable.

I looked down to see his pinky finger loop around mine, and my heart swelled. "I like talking to you," he muttered. "I don't want this night to end."

The longing in his voice made my stomach clench. "It has to end sooner or later. Everything does."

"A cynic." He smiled.

"A realist," I corrected. "If a spiritual one."

A slow grin spread across his face, his eyes darting between mine. "Let's do something good for our souls, then. I wanna watch the sunrise with you, Kitten."

Lee must've caught that because he interrupted. "Good idea."

Chloe snuggled into his side. "Why don't we take them to Lone Mountain, Kitty? It's not far, so we'll catch it in time."

"Are the trails open?" I asked.

"Who cares? We don't have to go through the main entrance. I always go running up there, so I know all the routes. It'll only take us an hour to get to the top, and there's no actual climbing, just a hike."

"What do you think, Kitten?" Snow murmured beside me. "Wanna come to watch the sunrise with me? It's up to you, baby. No pressure. But it seems we got two choices here. We can part ways and leave tonight as a beautiful memory. Or..." he paused.

I turned to see his golden eyes on my face and a small smile playing around his mouth.

My heart beat a little faster for the hundredth time that night. "Or what?"

"Or, we can go and watch the sunrise and just be." He ducked his head, suddenly bashful.

Cold slithered through me at the idea of this beautiful soldier being just a memory. It didn't make sense. I wanted to spend time with him, make the most of him while I could, and then say goodbye when I had to. I knew he'd leave, and I'd have to accept he could only ever be a memory, eventually.

Everything happens for a reason.

I slipped my hand back into his and squeezed, smiling as he gently squeezed back. "The way I see it, life is for living." I went to stand. "Let's go."

Chapter Four

Snow

Hand in hand, we exited the diner laughing.

"Follow me," Chloe suggested, pulling Benny toward a silver Ford Focus. "We'll see you there."

I sent Ben a chin lift before looking at Kitten's fingers, which still held tight onto mine.

She'd surprised me. When I saw her on stage, I thought she was in her early twenties, maybe a little older than me. It was only when I walked into the diner and saw her fresh face and her hair in a ponytail that I realized she was younger.

I didn't like that she was stripping at her age, not one bit. But I understood.

Life hadn't been kind to her. It had forced her to be independent. She wanted to make it alone despite her neglectful mother and absent father. Kitten had a fire in her belly that wouldn't quit; I admired her a lot. I'd been raised by strong women, and I knew one day my wife would be the same way.

My mind had whirred with fantasies about us all night. But I had to keep my shit contained, for now, at least. There was something there, something beautiful, but we were both too young for any big commitment. Kitten was working toward something, and I didn't wanna fuck that up. She deserved to achieve her goals, and as much as I wanted to wrap her in my arms and never let her go, I knew I needed to let her. I was about to deploy to one of the most dangerous places on Earth. We couldn't start something serious, not yet, anyway.

Still holding my hand, Kitten led me toward a black Audi A7 parked no more than twenty feet away.

My eyes bugged out. "Is that your ride?"

She threw a smile over her shoulder. "Yeah. Isn't she cool? She's a supercharged V6 with fuel injection."

"Nice," I murmured, running a hand over the hood. "You know about cars?"

"Yeah." A faraway look fell over her face. "My uncle used to take me to work at his friend's auto shop. He taught me everything about them."

"Bet she cost a fortune," I mused, eyes sweeping over the shiny, black vehicle.

Kitten laughed. "The insurance alone would make you shit yourself, but I can afford it." She went to walk to the driver's side but paused, turning toward me. "Here," she said, throwing me the keys. "You wanna drive?"

I reached up and caught them midair. "You sure?"

"I'm sure." She cocked her head, narrowing her eyes, a small smile hovering over her mouth as she looked inside my soul. "Please. Just be gentle with her. That's all I ask."

I immediately got her double meaning.

Still smiling, I shook my head, staring deep into her cornflower-blue eyes. "I'll treat her like a queen." Grabbing the door, I pulled it open and helped Kitten inside, watching as she slipped her seatbelt on. Then, I pushed the door closed, jogged around the other side, and jumped in the driver's seat.

The smell of new leather assaulted my senses, making me smile. "I usually ride a motorcycle," I explained. "But I gotta say, I'm looking forward to this."

Snow

I looked right just as she looked left. Our eyes met, and my heart gave a hard jolt. "You ready, Kitten? You've still got time to back out."

She smiled at my double meaning that time and nodded slowly. "I'm ready."

I started the car, revving the engine a couple of times. Pressing down on the gas, I exited the parking space and turned the vehicle toward the main road to catch up with Chloe, who was already speeding away.

"Then hold on tight, baby," I said, slipping my hand onto her knee. 'Cause you're in for a helluva ride."

I didn't let go of her hand while we climbed Lone Mountain.

Clingy wasn't a word I'd ever associated with myself, but when it came to her, I just didn't want to break our connection.

So, for a mile, I held onto her while we hiked.

When the terrain got a little rougher, I grabbed her waist to steady her or pulled her up a steep incline, but I never released her hand once.

I'd always laughed it off when my Dad said Stone men fell hard, fast, and forever.

The thing was, I didn't remotely fit into the Stone Man mold, so I'd never believed it would be the same way for me. My pop and brothers all lived for the club, just like my grandpa Bandit did. I knew there was more to life than the Speed Demons MC, so I enlisted the day after I graduated from Hambleton High.

I'd always felt less important than my brothers, especially Xander, the golden boy, the next prez. Bowie was his best bud. I was just the annoying little shit who used to bug them to spend time with me.

Even then, it was clear I didn't fit in.

But maybe I was more Stone than I realized, though, because the minute I saw Kitten, I'd tumbled into a world where I never wanted to let her go. A world where it was just her and me, and nobody else existed.

So, I decided I wouldn't let her go. At least, not until I had to.

"There's a little seating area," Kitten said, pointing to a wooden bench. "We can get a good view of the sunrise from there."

We weren't at the top of the mountain, maybe thirty feet below, but we were close enough, and the ridge we were on gave us a great view of Vegas. It felt like we were standing on top of the world.

The blackness of night had been waning for the last half hour. It was nearly time for the sun to come up, and I wanted nothing more than for her to be in my arms when it did. I gently dragged her toward the bench and made sure she was seated comfortably before I plonked my ass down by her side. "Are you cold?" I asked.

"No. Are you?"

I shook my head, realizing I hadn't felt cold since the second I'd seen Kitten levitating on stage. She brought me all the warmth and fire I needed.

"You said we've met before," she reminded me gently. "You said you'd tell me where from when we were alone." She swept her arm out. "We're alone now."

My chest panged. Why had I said that? Earlier, it'd just slipped out, but now I worried she'd suspect I was one of those nutjobs who got too attached. "You're gonna think I'm crazy," I muttered.

"Try me." She rubbed her thumb over mine, waiting.

Do or die.

"My mom's into all that past life stuff. She's gotta theory that we go through life meeting up with the people we loved before." I pulled her into my side, resting my face on her head. "She says we get a feeling of recognition when we meet some people. Maybe that's what happened with us."

"So you're saying we knew each other in a past life?" Kitten let out a soft chuckle. "I don't think it's crazy at all. It's beautiful. I love the idea that we never really leave the people who mean something."

She pulled her cell out of her jeans pocket and tapped before finally resting it against her thigh. Soft music began to play. Synths mixed with a piano played a tune that was as uplifting as it was pretty before the lyrics kicked in.

My eyes rested on the rays of light that pierced the purple sky. The sight was so pure, so magical. Light shimmered around us as the first beams of pink sun pierced the sky.

The beauty and honesty around us made the prospect of playing games seem wrong. Kitten had reached inside me and flicked a switch that had lain dormant until now. I wanted her to know how she made me feel.

A ball of emotion bounced through my chest. Maybe I was wrong to lay my cards out, but it felt right.

I closed my eyes and just spoke from my heart. "Baby. I think you've been mine a thousand times over. In every life we've ever lived."

A shiver ran through her. I saw tiny goosebumps trail down her arms. My free hand reached out, took hers, and I threaded our fingers together. "Maybe it's fate, Kitten."

My words died as a ray of light pierced the horizon, and she sucked in a sharp breath.

Vegas was suddenly bathed in oranges and reds as the sun burst over the horizon.

My heart swelled at its beauty. I took a mental snapshot of the colors racing across the city and lighting up the world, but also of Kitten being in my arms and how it made me feel at peace.

Being deployed never scared me. If anything, I looked forward to the experience. Seeing new places and experiencing new cultures was part of the reason I enlisted. Liberating Afghanistan and its people was a cause that I believed in and wanted to be a part of. Being on the right side of history was essential to me.

But that was before I'd met this woman. As ridiculous as it sounded, a part of me didn't want to leave her. I'd never feared death before, but my gut dragged when I thought there was a chance I might never return for her.

"I can't believe Chlo and Lee went off to her place," Kitten murmured, burrowing her head deeper into my throat. "They missed pure beauty."

I nuzzled my cheek against the top of her head, noticing how soft and silky her hair felt against my skin. When we arrived at the mountain, the other couple told us they'd changed their minds and were heading out. Benny had charmed the panties off his girl.

I'd thought about doing the same. Hell, I was tempted, especially when I considered how goddamned hard Kitten made me, but I decided not to. I didn't wanna be a stranger who passed in the night. Not to her. I wanted us to be something more.

The sun bathed us in its warmth and light. I leaned back and closed my eyes, breathing it all in. The scent of peaches from Kitten's shampoo hit my senses, and I breathed deeply, letting it settle inside my soul.

So, this was what living felt like?

It was everything.

My face turned upward to allow the already rising heat to warm my face. I basked in the feeling of the sun on my skin and my kitten in my arms until she suddenly shifted.

I opened my eyes to see her stand and smile dazedly as she looked over Vegas. "I've never seen anything more beautiful," she said, laughing. Her head turned, and she looked at me over her shoulder, her grin brighter than any morning sun.

Snow

I took a mental snapshot and tucked it away.

My eyes never left hers. I needed to convey what I felt at that moment, so I grinned back at her and murmured, "Neither have I, baby. Takes my goddamned breath away."

She knew I wasn't talking about the view.

The song, still playing through her cell, built to a crescendo. Kitten's ass began to sway, and she sang along to the words. Turning suddenly, she leaned down and grabbed hold of my hand. "Come on. Dance with me."

I laughed. I wasn't no dancer, but I wasn't stupid either. We'd never be in this moment again. Never feel the way we did right then. Why waste it?

I stood and drew her into my arms.

Her hands slid up and around my neck. "I'm so happy," she breathed.

A chuckle escaped me as we began to sway together in time to the music. "Can't say I've ever danced on a mountaintop with a beautiful girl snuggled up to me. Can't say I hate it."

"Stop being a grouch," she chastised playfully. "Where's your sense of romance?"

Jesus. This girl.

"Never done romance in my life, Kitten. You're just gonna have to teach me."

She rested her cheek against my chest, letting out a contented sigh. "Don't worry, Snow. You seem to be doing okay. You've won *me* over."

A bubble of laughter rose through me.

If Atlas could see me now, I'd never live it down.

Our SAA was a good brother but still a typical asshole biker through and through. I doubted he'd ever dance on a mountaintop with the girl he was falling for. Jeez, the thought alone made me wanna bust a gut.

I cursed as a loud rumble came from my stomach. "Shit."

Kitten burst into laughter and looked up at me. "Hungry?"

I gave a sharp nod. "Starving," I admitted.

She blushed prettily. "You wanna grab breakfast and eat at my apartment?" Her eyes shone excitedly. "We can watch Game of Thrones. I always wanted to start it. What better time than with Jon Snow himself?"

My heart jolted. Here we were, already.

Decision time.

Should I say thanks but no thanks, kiss her goodbye, and leave? Or should I go and eat at her place and start something up?

We were at a crossroads. One path led to nothing but a memory, a moment in time when I met a beautiful woman in Vegas and watched the sunrise with her.

The other fork led to something a whole fucking lot more complicated.

I wasn't in the right place for serious, and I certainly couldn't offer Kitten any kind of commitment. I was too young and way too dedicated to serving my country. But, still, I didn't have to think about my answer. There was no question, not really.

"Yeah, Kitten." I gazed into her eyes and softly brushed her hair away from her face. "I'd love that."

We stopped at a small strip mall near Kitten's apartment.

It was around six thirty by the time we got from the mountain into Kitten's car. The drive back to Vegas didn't take us long. Time was made quicker by singing along to the radio and laughing hard.

She told me all about the bakery nestled in the small row of stores. Apparently, they made the best pastries she'd ever eaten. They also served coffee, so we could get everything we needed in one stop.

The smell of fresh baking hit me as we walked inside, and my guts rumbled again.

Kitten looked at me, her face lighting up with laughter. "Martha," she called out. "Got any croissants ready yet? Got me a hungry man here."

A pretty woman stood at a big coffee machine. She looked up and smiled. "Morning, Kitty." Her eyes slid to me and widened. "Well, this is a turn of events. Nice to actually see you with someone."

My eyes went to Kitten as a pink flush stained her cheeks. "Jeez, thanks, Martha. You make me sound like a lonely old cat lady."

I laughed gently at that.

Obviously, Kitten didn't bring guys around much, if at all. This was her everyday life, the real her. Martha's teasing indicated that Kitty was telling the truth when she said she didn't bother with men romantically. Not that I ever thought she was yanking my chain. Still, I liked that I was one of the few men–people even–she let into her sacred space.

I liked it a hell of a lot.

"Here," Martha said. She cut a pastry in half, putting each piece onto a napkin before handing it to us. "New recipe. Tell me what you think."

"Thanks." Kitty took one half, took a bite, and rolled her eyes.

I took the other. "Much obliged, ma'am," I said with a respectful nod."

Martha smiled. "A gentleman. We don't get many of you in Vegas, eh, Kitty?"

Kitten sent me one of her sexy, teasing looks. "I know, Martha. Snow here's one of a kind." She finished her pastry and ordered four coffees.

I munched happily on my pastry while Martha made them up and chatted to Kitten about her mom.

"She got her disability benefits, Kitty. Thank you so much for your help with all that paperwork. She'd never have been able to do it herself."

"Oh, it was nothing," Kitten assured her, waving a dismissive hand. "It was one day out of my life. Honestly, I loved talking to her. She told me about your dad when he served in Vietnam. It was fascinating."

"She said she loved talking to you, too. You have a way with folk, Kitty. People can sense your warmth."

I got a little gut punch from those words.

Martha was right. Kitten did have a warmth about her and a sweetness that lit her up. Everyone could see it. Me, Chloe. Even Marco, I reckoned. It was no doubt why he hired her, at first sight, to dance for him.

If you could bottle Kitten's spirit—her aura—and sell it, you'd become a wealthy man.

Watching Kitten interact bewitched me. She was tactile and attentive. She spoke to Martha like she was the most important person in the world. The respect Martha had for my girl was written all over her face.

"These are all on the house," Martha said quietly. "A small thank you for helping Mom."

Kitten shook her head. "I couldn't. Some of these are for Ed and Paulie."

Martha looked between us, placing two pastry boxes on the counter. Already got theirs ready, honey. I put Paulie's cream and sugar in too. You're all set."

Kitten squeezed the woman's hand, conveying her thanks before turning to me. "I have to drop these off at Ed's, then run to Mr. Kowalski's for milk."

I took the coffees and boxes from her. "Come on, Kitten. Let's get your shit done. I wanna get back and eat more than ever after trying those pastry things."

Martha blushed.

We said our goodbyes and walked outside, turning right.

Snow

Kitten took two coffees from the holder I was carrying and one of the boxes. "Follow me," she ordered gently. "Ed's shy around new people. Let me go first."

She turned toward a narrow alley between a small grocery store and a laundromat.

A knot formed in my stomach.

What the hell is she doing? "Kitten," I snapped. "Get back from ther—"

"—Ed? Are you home? Breakfast time," she called out as I went to pull her away.

After a few seconds, some dude lumbered from the alleyway. He was dressed in dirty clothes, and his hair was unkempt—obviously a homeless guy. "Morning, darlin'," he greeted with a deep, scratchy voice. "You look pretty today."

My shoulders slumped, the knot unraveling as I watched Kitten hand the guy a coffee cup.

"Where's Paulie?" she asked, handing the guy the coffees and box.

Ed looked uncomfortable as he shifted from foot to foot. "Still sick, darlin'. He's asleep."

Kittten's face fell, which made my gut drop, too. "Wait here," she said, hurrying toward her car.

Ed went into the alley. I heard muttering before he returned, still holding one of the coffee cups.

"Hey, man," I greeted, nodding toward the alley. "Everythin' okay?"

He shook his head. "My bud's sick. He developed a fever last week. It moved to his chest. Think he's got an infection."

My heart went out to him. He looked fucking devastated, chewing on the inside of his cheek, eyes filled with worry.

"Can't you get into a shelter?" I asked.

He shook his head. "I wouldn't take up the space. We can take care of ourselves out here. Others need it more than us."

"Except you're getting sick," I pointed out.

Ed's stare slid downward, and he nodded.

I reached into my pocket and took out my wallet.

"No, man," he insisted. "Not taking your money. Ain't a charity case."

"Ain't charity," I replied, tucking several Benjamins into his pocket. "Take your bud. Go to a motel and hole up for a few days. Keep him warm and chill out for a while."

He nodded, eyes misting over. "I won't spend it on booze."

I shrugged. "If a bottle of cheap whisky brings you and your bud a moment of joy, go for it."

He laughed.

My neck craned as footsteps sounded behind me.

Kitten hurried back, clutching something in her hand. "Here," she said, handing a bottle to Ed. "It's antibiotics. They're generic, but they should help Paulie out."

"Kitty. Are you sure?"

She nodded. "Marco got them for me. There are two weeks there. There's more if you need them. Just let me know."

He visibly relaxed.

Kitty touched my arm. "I'm just going to Mr. Kowalski's store to get milk."

"Thanks for everything, Kitty," Ed muttered. "Paulie and me are going to a motel. We'll be back, but don't worry if we're not around for a few days."

She stepped forward and wrapped her arms around him, hugging him tight. "See you soon, honey. Take care of each other."

My heart filled with emotion.

This fucking girl.

Kitty turned toward a small store. "Need anything?" she asked me.

I shook my head, unable to speak because she choked me up. My gaze followed as she walked into the store.

Snow

Sweet and so fucking kind and generous; she took my goddamned breath away. How the fuck was I supposed to walk away from her? How the hell could I give her up?

"She's special," Ed murmured. "She cares, you know?"

I nodded, eyes still on the door she'd just disappeared through.

"She brings us coffee and pastries most mornings," Ed continued. "She works until late but still finds the time to come here for us." He snorted. "We'd probably starve without that girl."

Still in a trance, I nodded again.

"Hey," he said.

My head swiveled to face him.

"You like her?"

I thought about his question for a minute. It didn't seem enough, somehow. "Yeah," I admitted. "Dunno if I should, though. I'm deploying to Afghanistan next week. Typical that I'd meet the right woman at the completely wrong fucking time."

His face paled.

My eyebrows knotted together. "You okay, man?"

He nodded. "I was a soldier. Got sent home from Iraq five years ago with a knee injury."

I looked around and took in the conditions he'd been dealing with, my heart plummeting because a war vet was living in a fucking alleyway. "What went wrong?" I asked.

"Came home a different man. My wife left me for someone else. She couldn't handle my PTSD. Took my kids with her. Haven't seen them for three years now. The fact is, they're scared of me. Scared of my fucked-up head. Scared of my nightmares. Scared that I ran for cover every time I heard an exhaust backfire. Couldn't hold a job, so I couldn't pay my way. Took me six months to lose everything."

My stomach sank as I went back for my wallet, emptied it, and handed it all to him.

"No," he insisted. "Can't accept it."

"Take the fucking money," I ordered. "I got plenty."

He stared at me. Must've seen I was serious because he finally took the cash.

"If you ever need a change of scene, get your asses to a small town called Hambleton, Wyoming, a little way north of the Colorado border. Ask around for the Speed Demons compound. Tell 'em Snow sent you."

I turned on my heel, heading straight for the convenience store, my guts jerking as I went. I didn't look back. Maybe I wanted my eyes on Kitten because Ed had unsettled me.

It was easier to see him as a bum. A guy down on his luck, another homeless person who society forgot. But he wasn't, was he?

A phrase my mom always said sprang to mind.

There for the grace of God, go I.

Could that be me one day? Unable to function within society's parameters because a war fucked with my head.

I fucking hoped not.

Clearing the dark thoughts from my mind, I went in search of Kitten. A bell tinkled above the door as I walked in, looked up, and stopped dead.

My Kitten was being held by an old man, giggling hysterically as he waltzed her up and down an aisle. The look of joy on his face made me smile. It was contagious.

"You're such a charmer, Mr. Kowalski," she teased. "I bet you had the ladies falling at your feet when you were younger."

"You wouldn't have stood a chance," the guy said in a thick accent. "If I met a girl like you when I was a young man, we'd have grown old together."

Kitten threw her head back and laughed before she saw me out of the corner of her eye, stared, and gave me one of her smiles. "Well, this is embarrassing," she said, not looking at all bothered.

That was when I saw it, saw her.

My girl was determined to inhale life and experience everything the world had to offer. She lived for the moment, which was beautiful and courageous because she reveled in every so-called embarrassing thing she did.

She'd told me back at the diner that life was for living, and by God, did she live it.

I felt it down to my soul.

Cold fingers crept up my spine—some kind of premonition, maybe.

What if I broke her? What if she broke me? What if I'd found my one, the woman my dad always said would bring me to my knees, and the worst happened? What if I took hold of her, made her mine, then she lost me? Would her beautiful spirit stay intact?

A dark lump formed in the pit of my stomach.

And standing in a convenience store in Vegas, watching a beautiful girl make an old man happy, I got scared.

"Oh my God," Kitty shrieked, throwing me a wide-eyed glance. "He just pushed Bran out the window."

"I'm more concerned with him fucking his sister," I muttered, shock still reverberating at the final scene of the episode of Game of Thrones we'd just watched. "It's all backstabbing and killing. Never seen so many goddamned tits in one place." I smiled at Kitten. "No offense intended."

"None taken." She turned her face up to look at me, waggling her eyebrows. "Wanna watch the next one?"

I grinned. "Fuck, yeah."

She dropped my hand and got up from the couch. "I'll get the popcorn. We may be here a while."

The cold air made me shiver slightly the second she stood.

My kitten was like a little furnace, and I liked having her heat warm me up. I watched her ass swing as she walked through the door to her tiny kitchen. Her apartment was small but okay for what she needed. She'd already told me she was saving for Harvard, so I wasn't shocked it was so tiny.

The urge to help her out was strong, but how the fuck could I do that without offending her? Jeez, I was turning into a sap. I'd only known the woman for twelve hours and already wanted to throw my cash at her.

A quiet chuckle escaped me when I thought about what the guys in the MC would say if I told 'em I wanted to send my money to a stripper I met in Vegas. Fuck me, Atlas would hunt me down just to slap me upside the head.

That cold chill went down my spine again.

Fuck. I couldn't make Kitten mine.

My brain was already spinning scenarios like we had a future. I was here for a couple more days. My boys had already been blowing my cell up, asking where the fuck I was. And all I could think about was playing happy families with a woman I hardly knew. And a stripper to boot.

Fuck. I needed to get the hell out of here before I did something stupid. What was I thinking, starting something like this when I may not even be coming back to U.S. soil?

Cupboards banged from the kitchen. "Kyle," she called. "Want anything?"

I winced. *Fucking Kyle.*

I knew it was a mistake when Benny opened his mouth and gave the girls the fake names.

Snow

Okay, so we made a pact, but that was before I met Kitten. She tried to tell me her real name on the way back from Lone Mountain, but I'd stopped her. I told her I didn't need to know and explained that she was my kitten, which was good enough for me. I spun it into the notion that she didn't know me and should keep her cards close until she trusted me, but I was lying.

If I didn't know her real name, I'd feel less guilty that she didn't know mine. I didn't want to make her mad and screw up our limited time together. What was the point when I was leaving soon?

Also, I'd known her for half a day. She was golden, and I knew she was stable, but I'd been working toward the SPC role and didn't wanna fuck it up over a woman like Higgs had.

Every time she called me Kyle, though, I wanted to puke. Of all the fucking names I could've given her, I regretted more than anything that it was the asshole I hated. Didn't think that one through at all.

I heaved out a breath. *Fuck it.* It wouldn't matter after today.

My cell buzzed again from the table, reminding me why I was here in Vegas. All of a sudden, my collar felt tight. I was too hot. Fuck, I needed some air. I needed to get outta there.

My eyes slid to the door.

It would be so easy to walk out. No goodbyes, no emotions, just freedom. Kitten would be okay. She'd understand, wouldn't she?

My brain tried to talk me into jetting, into taking the easy way out, but I couldn't. It would be one regret too far. There'd be no coming back from that bullshit. The thought of her hating me made me ache.

I stood slowly, going to the kitchen where Kitty was cleaning up. Leaning against the doorjamb, I watched as she sang under her breath while loading the dishwasher. My heart squeezed at the view of her ass in her denim cut-off shorts, and another mental snapshot got filed away in the recesses of my mind. My heart bounced because I'd need those snapshots of her pretty soon to get me through the night.

Stop it, Kit. You're already too attached. You gotta end it.

I thrust my fingers through my hair, a vein throbbing in my temple.

She must've sensed me there because she turned and gave me a smile that lit me up from the inside. My heart seemed to drop into my gut because I knew it would hurt to leave her.

It was gonna hurt both of us.

I held my hand out. "Come here."

She straightened, looked down at my fingers, and slipped her hand into mine. "Is everything okay? You seem sad."

I slid my arm across her shoulders and led her back into the living room. "We need to talk."

"Uh oh." She sat down on the couch, pulling her legs up under her. "The 'we need to talk' speech never ends well, Kyle."

I settled down next to her, twisting my body until we faced each other, and took her hand. "That's the first thing we need to discuss. Nobody calls me Kyle, ever. Everyone calls me Snow. You call me Snow."

She shrugged nonchalantly. "I prefer Snow anyway, especially after watching that." She nodded toward the TV. "Jon Snow's hot. Best roleplay ever." She started giggling.

I let out an exasperated sigh. "Can we be serious for a minute, baby?"

Her cheeks flushed, and she ducked her head.

My brain scrambled for the words that I didn't wanna say. Every instinct screamed at me to keep my mouth shut, but my head ruled my heart.

I didn't have a choice.

"The boys and I came here to let off steam before we shipped out on deployment. You know that, right?"

"Yeah," she said, smiling softly.

My chest ached with the words I was about to say. "I never expected to meet you. I don't have women I see all the time or date. It never appealed to me, and I never met anyone I wanted to take that step with. I see myself being in the military for a long time, Kitten. Years. I love what I do and what I get out of it, ya know?"

She bit the inside of her cheek and nodded.

"You've got plans too, Kitten," I continued. "You're dancing your ass off to give yourself a better life. Would you wanna waste it on me?"

Her eyes welled up, but she smiled. "It wouldn't be wasting it, Snow, but I know what you're asking, and my answer's no. I have plans. I wanna go to Harvard. I've got goals I want to achieve. I can't do that pining after you. I've got dreams, too."

Hot emotion rose through my throat.

I think a tiny part of me would've liked to hear her say she wanted to give it all up for me, but I'd never admit that to anyone, and regardless, I'd never let her do it.

"Is this your way of saying you don't want to pursue this?" she asked softly. "Be honest with me, please."

"No… Well… Maybe." I reached up and tucked a loose lock of hair behind her ear. "I'm deploying for three months, Kitten. Anything can happen when I'm over there…" my voice trailed off, throat burning.

Her forehead creased, and she bowed her head.

"I'm sorry, baby," I murmured. "I wish things were different. I wish we had more time."

She kept her head bowed and nodded.

I reached out before my brain engaged. I wanted to look at Kitten's face one last time, but my hand dropped before it reached its target.

If I touched her, it would be harder to leave.

Getting to my feet, I patted my pockets to ensure my wallet was secure and picked up my cell off the coffee table. I needed to go, immediately, before I did something stupid like begging her to never let me leave.

As I approached the door, Kitten's voice whispered from behind me. "I'll never forget you, Snow. You're one of a kind. Take care of yourself, honey."

I stopped in my tracks, wondering if I'd ever be able to get the piece of me back that I'd just left bleeding out on the couch. Did I even want to? Perhaps it was always meant to be hers.

Another crossroads, two more forks in the road. One leading back to her and the other one leading away. I hoped to God I was doing the right thing because it didn't feel like it.

Leaving felt all wrong, but I didn't have a choice. I couldn't keep myself alive if my head was full of her. She'd already consumed me in the space of twelve hours. If I stayed with her two more days, I'd be completely fucked. We both would.

I pulled my shoulders back, still facing the door. "You take care too, Kitten." I swallowed past the lump in my throat before walking through her little cloakroom and out the front door. I closed it behind me and took note of the apartment number. My chest clenched when I saw it was twenty-one, the same as my age. Too fucking young to find something so meaningful. Too fucking young to have to worry about a girl back home.

I was doing us both a favor, Kitten especially. Her life was all about college and business and hustling to get where she wanted to be.

Mine was about heavier stuff, which would drag me down like a ton of weight. The last thing I wanted was to drag Kitten down with me. She'd been through enough abandonment.

Snow

If I wanted to survive, I needed to keep my head straight and keep her in a box tucked away in the recesses of my mind.

My life depended on it.

Two A.M. and Harry Reid was packed.

Vegas never slept. It was as bustling in the middle of the night as in the middle of the day.

The boys had all gone to Crimson Velvet as a last shout before our flight back to Nashville. We were to report for duty at midday and fly to Kabul the day after. The boys asked me to go and told me I'd regret it if I didn't see her one last time, but I said no 'cause I was a stubborn prick.

After I left her crying in her apartment, I returned to the hotel, sat at the bar, and drank until I could fall asleep. The next day, I woke up and did it again. I'd been in the same bar for days, fighting with myself.

She was all I could think about.

I could still feel her, smell her scent. Her laugh tinkled in my ears, and her voice kept whispering through my mind.

I'll never forget you, Snow. Take care of yourself.

The alcohol had numbed me for the past two days. It had helped me stick to my guns by muting my feelings, but now I was sober; there was no escaping them anymore.

My chest was weighed down, and it ached like fuck because I'd made a colossal mistake. Screwed up with the one girl who had ever made me feel something.

I closed my eyes, remembering the chest punch I got the first time I saw her. How everything inside came to life when she smiled at me.

I thought about dancing on a mountaintop with a kind, beautiful girl who cared about everyone around her. Sitting on a plastic seat in a busy airport, waiting for my flight to be called, it hit me that I'd royally fucked up.

Since the second I left her, acid had burned through my gut and up my throat. I recognized it as the bitter taste of regret.

How could I have left her like that? How could I have taken off and left so much unsaid? I bent over in my chair, head in hands, rubbing at my temples, trying to think of a way to contact her. Getting to her club and back would take me at least an hour. I quickly checked my watch, my heart clenching when I saw our flight was about to be called.

Fuck.

I pulled my cell out to check Crimson Velvet's website. It was pretty basic, just a page detailing their opening and closing hours and contact information. Still, at least I could call there for her. I was just about to click on the number when I heard boots stomping.

"Snow!" I recognized the voice calling me, but I was so engrossed in getting a hold of Kitten that I ignored it, lifting my cell to my ear.

"Snow!" Benny shouted louder. "Got something here for ya."

I swung around, face set in a snarl, about to cuss him out, and froze.

Benny stood ten feet away with his arm slung around Chloe's shoulders. AJ and Puck were on his right, but it was the person on his left who caught my attention.

My cell phone fell from my hand and clattered on the floor, but I hardly noticed. All my focus was taken by the beautiful blonde woman gazing at me, nervously biting her lip. She looked different with her stage makeup of black-rimmed eyes and scarlet lips, but it was still her.

My feet moved toward her simultaneously as she started to float toward me. My fingers twitched with a

Snow

deep need to touch her, my throat thickening with all the apologies in the world.

She was in my arms within seconds, and I breathed in her peachy scent. "I'm sorry. I'm sorry. I'm sorry," I chanted into her hair.

She looked up at me with tears in her eyes. "I wanted to say goodbye properly. No hard feelings, Snow. I don't regret a thing."

My insides jerked as a loud voice announced our flight.

Fuck. Why did I waste all that time?

I cupped her cheek, eyes flicking over her face. My mind took another snapshot, filing the image away. "I don't wanna walk away from you. I'm such a fuckhead. I've sat here going crazy thinking, instead of getting spooked, I should've asked you to be my girl."

She paused for a second as her eyes searched mine, then she threw back her head and laughed exuberantly. "You are a fuckhead, but it's okay. We're okay."

A woman's voice came over the speaker system. S*outhwest Airlines flight 2762 flight to Nashville boarding now. Please make your way to gate three.*

"I'm gonna come back," I promised. "We're gonna finish Game of Thrones, and we're gonna talk about everything."

"I won't watch it without you," she promised. "I'll wait." Her arms snaked around my waist, burrowing her face into my shirt.

Her peachy scent wafted up, and I inhaled deeply, breathing her until she settled inside my heart. "Can I write to you?" I pleaded in her ear. "Gimme your address, quick."

She laughed again, nodding to Benny. "Already gave it to Lee," she explained. "Just in case."

I closed my eyes, mentally kicking myself again for my stupid lie. I told myself I'd be honest about what we did and make it right when I saw her next. "I need to explain a few things when I return, Kitten. I'm gonna tell you all about me next time, okay?"

"Okay," she breathed.

Last call for Southwestern Airline flight 2762. The gate is about to close.

"We gotta hurry, man," Benny yelled.

My hand cupped her face and angled it up. Our eyes met, hers full of sadness, mine full of regret for all the days I'd wasted getting drunk alone in a hotel bar.

In that instant, all I wanted to do, all I could do, was try and show her what she meant to me. So, I bent my neck and caught her mouth in a kiss that made my heart do a backflip.

Her lips were soft against mine as they moved. I touched my tongue to hers, and her body seemed to melt. She tasted like mine, which made me deepen the kiss, trying to get everything I could out of it. I knew it would be months before we could do this again. It would have been so easy to stay and grab Kitten, get a cab to her apartment, and just hole up, but I knew I couldn't.

Running my lips across her face, I nuzzled her cheek. "I have to go."

"I know."

My arms released her body, and again, I was left cold. I bent down, picked up my bag, and grabbed my cell phone, still on the ground from when I'd dropped it.

"Be safe," she said gently. Still smiling. Still brave.

I nodded, slipped my cell back into my pocket, and turned on my heel without a backward glance. Looking at Kitten would've made me second-guess everything.

I showed my ticket as I went through the gate, smiling robotically as the boys gave me back claps. Their appreciative words about our Vegas weekend didn't even register. How could they when I was so consumed with her?

For the entire walk to the plane, I could still feel the softness of Kitten's lips. The pang of missing her made me realize she'd already burrowed so far under my skin that a part of me was already hers.

We walked up the plane's steps, found our seats, and got settled for the flight back to Nashville. I was there in body, but my spirit remained in the airport where I'd left Kitten. Maybe it was better off there. My girl could keep it safe for me.

The plane's engines began to roar, and within seconds, we were careening down the runway, about to take off. My eyes slid to the window toward the airport where I'd left my girl, and I wondered for a split second if I'd ever see her again.

If only I knew then what I know now.

Chapter Five

Snow

Our pre-deployment briefing threw up some unbelievable shit. I couldn't believe people in this century still lived that way.

Pictures showed people living in huts and caves. We were told that farmers worked their crops carrying M4s like it was normal. But what disturbed me most was the premise that bombs were sewn into children's clothes before they were sent out to murder.

We were told our troops were there for peacekeeping and to train the Afghan Army in weaponry and bomb disposal, which would help in their fight against the Taliban.

The U.S. Marine unit on our Airbus told us so much more.

Their entire unit was pissed. Two weeks after they returned to US soil from their last tour, they were shipped back to Afghanistan. They were on their way to their third deployment in five years. This one, lucky for them, was just a three-week mission.

Hearing that made me think.

Our deployment was designed to be for three or four months, but it was expected our time there could be extended. How would Kitten feel about that? Was it remotely fair to ask a girl like her to wait?

Even sitting in the plane, feeling the force of the engines whir through my guts, my head was still in Harry Reid with Kitten in my arms. I burned to touch her skin and hear her sweet laugh. But the address she gave Benny didn't include her number or even her email address.

It looked like we were doing this the old-fashioned way. Pen to fucking paper.

"Place is a fucking trip," Fritz, one of the Marines, said, leaning back in his seat. "It's hotter than Satan's asshole in Summer, then Winter hits, and you can't even feel your nuts."

"Remember that British Paratrooper who got a frostbitten ball?" his team member sitting beside him said, nudging him. "He just shrugged and said, 's'alright, mate. I got another one.'"

A couple of them barked out laughs.

I looked at Ben as if to say, 'What the fuck?' These guys were lunatics, but then you had to have a certain level of crazy bastard to be a jarhead.

"He was a wily fucker," a guy with Pandy written across his lapel muttered. "Remember that farmer he had the run-in with?"

Benny sat up a bit straighter. "Farmer?"

I heaved out a hard breath. This was some goddamned bullshit.

One side of Fritz's mouth hitched. "Last tour, we'd been briefed that a terrorist cell was holed up in a cave system in the East. We were sent in with coalition forces to capture and kill."

"Our mission was strictly recon along with some British Paras and a few Seven Guns," Pandy explained. "It was all going like clockwork. A few miles from our target, we crossed a field and found a farmer hiding in the long grass with two fucking goats."

Fritz snorted. "Poor fucker almost pissed himself. He made a run for it. Fuck knows how he thought he could outrun us, but he fled like the devil himself was after him."

"Did you catch him?" Benny asked.

"Yeah, we caught him." Pandy laughed. "We chased him through that field like something out of a fucking Laurel and Hardy sketch. Every time we got close, the skinny fuck darted in the opposite direction. In the end, one of our boys who played college football tackled him like a pro."

Fritz hooted out a laugh. "Can you imagine the scene? A Haji farmer in robes lying in a field with eight M4s trained on him. Luckily, we had a TERP with us who spoke Dari. Asked him why he was running."

Something panged inside my gut.

Shit like that was why we called them Gung-Ho's. They were all about the action. They didn't seem to give much of a shit about the Local Nationals being terrorized by men sent there to protect them.

Pandy shook his head, grinning. "The enemy had been there two days before and took the fucker's fattest goat. Get this. When we made him tell us whose side he fought on, he told the TERP that he was on the T-Man's side yesterday, but he was gonna switch that day 'cause we were there."

A few of my boys chuckled, Benny included, though he looked sheepish when I sent him a hard stare.

My eyes rested on the Marine. He was full of bullshit and bravado. The thing was, I'd heard stories like that a lot, especially after the war in Iraq.

Nine-eleven had created a culture of U.S. men who wanted retribution for our country, me included. I'd dreamed about being a soldier for as long as I could remember. But sitting in front of the TV as a kid, watching those iconic buildings burn, my dream became a calling.

The conflict made the lines muddy, but I was determined to go in there and do my job. I didn't need to make friends or enemies with the Local Nationals. I just needed to keep them and the Allied Forces safe from IEDs.

Would I fight, even kill, if I had to? Yep. But I could still have a conscience while I did it.

Puck regarded Fritz for a minute, eyes never leaving his face. "How many men have you put down?"

He shrugged. "Ain't giving you my number. That's personal. But I will say I did two tours of Iraq and some Afghanistan deployments. Been involved in covert ops, rescues, and explosions. Hell, I've been in free-for-all barrel-to-barrel gunfights. I'll just say this, Crab. I'd need three hands to count them all."

Benny nodded thoughtfully. "What scares me the most is killing an innocent. Not sure how I'd live with that on my conscience."

Fritz closed his eyes slowly as if he was reliving a memory. "You're gonna be caught up in a situation where someone will be in the wrong place, doing the wrong thing, and you have to make an instant decision. Not only for you but also your boys." His eyes lost all humor as they rested on mine. "But think about this. Is it better to be judged by twelve men or be carried by six?"

A heaviness settled in my gut as the Jarhead stared at me with eyes devoid of all emotion before saying three words that would one day come back to haunt me.

"Choose your path."

Chapter Six

Snow

We were stationed at Camp Eggers.
It was a melting pot of command and security forces, which were all part of ISAF. Men and women from NATO countries were based there, as evidenced by the different accents and languages floating through the air.

It was hot and so humid that my formerly pristine combats dripped with sweat. I pulled at the neck of my shirt, trying to get some breeze onto my skin, but the clammy air of it just made it worse.

The place was massive, like a really eclectic, gated community. As we got further in, I noticed containerized housing units everywhere. I recognized them as climate-controlled metal box units that housed the soldiers, known as CHUs.

"You will get a map of the base. Use it," Hollister commanded. He began to call names out, giving us keys. "These are your assigned CHUs. Go in, see what you need, then get down and get it from storage.

"Where's storage, Lieutenant?" Cheng asked.

Hollister raised an eyebrow. "Check the fucking map, asswipe. I ain't your papa. Not here to hold your hand."

He turned his stare on us one by one. "Briefing a 0600 hours. It'll be a few days before we go out on our first sweep. When we do, we'll hit the ground running. Do not be late. Tonight's yours. Go eat. The mess hall's open twenty-four-seven." He smiled evilly. "And I believe we've made it for karaoke night."

Groans went up.

Hollister's smile dropped. "Whatcha waiting for? Time to move in." A smirk took over his face. "Welcome to Hell, boys."

Our CHU was a box containing just a bunk bed. Thank fuck I wasn't claustrophobic because that ten by eight room housing two people would've ended me instead of the Taliban.

The one saving grace was I'd been assigned to share with Benny. Maybe Hollister wasn't all bad, as we got housed with our closest brothers. I was also used to sharing a bathroom, so it could've been worse. Soldiers were dirty-mouthed and would break your balls, but we were trained to be clean.

We were going to pick up some drawers for our shit and look for a TV, seeing as the base got the Armed Forces Network streamed in. We would call in, get what we needed, drop everything off, call into the mess, and turn it in.

Everyone we passed seemed to know where they were going and what they were doing. I wasn't nervous but felt like a fish out of water. It would take time to get my bearings, but until it came easier, I'd just have to deal.

I missed U.S. soil, but my dad or brothers didn't take up my headspace. Instead, I recalled blonde hair and soft skin, just a whisper against my cheek. I think being so far away was what made me yearn for her. I could hardly get a weekend pass and visit. Still, that was the life of a soldier. Time would tell if Kitten could handle it.

Something told me she would, though. I'd seen her inner strength the second she appeared on stage.

We'd picked up some plastic drawers. A big, muscled German soldier dropped off a tiny 32-inch TV just as we reached the storage unit. He told us his team was going home the next day, so we snapped it up. Within thirty minutes, we'd hauled everything back, set everything up, then come to the dining facility or DFAC.

It was coming up to 23:00 local time. Eight hours ahead of the US. We'd been traveling since 0300 hours. We had to report for duty in six hours, but I'd be golden as long as I got five hours in.

"What do you think, Ben?" I asked over the rim of the coffee mug I held to my mouth. "This place is weird. Can't say I feel completely at ease yet."

Ben sat back in his chair, chewing the sandwich he'd just bitten into. "It's gonna take time, Snow. We're small fish in a big pond, but we'll work it out once we get into our roles here. Our soldiers have been doing this since Iraq. We're in good hands."

"I know, Ben," I agreed. "It's just so different. I feel like a hamster in a wheel. We can't leave the base and go for a beer. We're insulated inside a pressure cooker, and the heat's killing me."

"Just give it time, Snow. We've only just arrived. I know it's unsettling, but we have to get used to our new normal."

I nodded my agreement as I took in Benny's worried expression. Jeez, I had to snap out of it. It wasn't fair to bring him down. "I'll be fine. Ignore me. I'm just being a whiny cunt 'cause I fucked up with my girl. I'll be cool after a good night's sleep."

"Snow. Did I ever tell you the one about the soldier and the rattlesnake?"

I rolled my eyes. "No."

"Well," he began. "While conducting drills up a mountain, a soldier gets bitten on his cock by a rattlesnake. He yells out to his partner, 'Fuck! A snake just bit me on my dick! Quickly, run down for help!' His partner runs down the hill, finds his Lieutenant, and explains the sitch. The Lieutenant says to the soldier, 'Okay, look. We fucked up and forgot the medical supplies. You're gonna have to run back up the mountain, locate the wound, and suck the venom out. It's the only way we can save our brother. Go on. Move it.' The soldier who got bit is on the floor, groaning in pain. He sees his partner strolling up without a care in the world and says, 'Thank fuck you're back. What did the Lieutenant say?' The other soldier replies, 'Sorry bro, LT said you're gonna die!'"

I began to chuckle. Fucking Benny and his lame-ass jokes. He always knew how to get me out of a bad mood. The worse the joke was, the more I busted a gut.

But underneath my amusement, my insides still churned.

Afghanistan was one of the most dangerous places for an American soldier. Half the population was out to kill us on sight. And the other half was no doubt scared shitless of us. We'd have to watch each other's backs if we wanted to get home without injury.

My mind returned to the Marines we talked to on the air carrier.

They talked about their time here and in Iraq like they ruled the roost. I got it. War in Iraq dictated the shit that happened over there, but we weren't in a war now. We were a peaceful task force sent in to help the Afghan people take back control and help build infrastructure. The only thing we were here to fight was oppression.

We'd be fine. EOD would do our duty and go home in one piece.

But even as I tried to convince myself, that kernel of doubt spread through my bones.

I had a bad feeling about this.

Chapter Seven

Snow ~ Day Five at Camp Eggers

The last few days had consisted of briefings, training, and getting the lay of the land.
We reported for duty at 0600 hours and worked solidly until about 1800 hours. Some of the men were given night duties. God only knew what that consisted of, but I saw the guys looking weary the next day. They must've been put through their paces.

I was beginning to acclimatize at last.

The heat still made me fucking nauseous sometimes, but the thought of cooling down in my CHU after my shift kept me going. The base was huge. They had coffee shops, DFACs, and even an area where the local women set up a bazaar twice a week.

Most of the battalions stayed inside the wire. Life outside the base was precarious at best. We could do what we wanted, but they worked us so hard that the thought of walking around Kabul didn't inspire me with enthusiasm. Plus, the risk of being targeted by a suicide bomber was always on my mind.

We'd been led into a briefing room at 0630 with some soldiers from the 2nd Infantry Division. We'd gotten to know a few of them as their CHUs were close to ours. Three of 'em, Yates, Renz, and Brown, were much like me, Benny, and the boys, so we naturally gravitated toward them.

We were packed in the room like sardines when Lieutenant Hollister and the 2nd Infantry's Staff Sergeant Marks joined us. They went to a small, elevated stage, stepped up, and turned to address us.

"Good morning," SSG Marks yelled. "Now we've got you nut to butt; let's talk about the day ahead."

The quiet chatter in the room quickly died down as one of the guys called out, "What's on the agenda for today, SSG?"

Marks cocked his head. "Some fucking bullshit, Ballas. But we're our country's finest. We will prevail."

Chuckles rose through the room.

"Same thing every day," Brown muttered beside me. "Someone asks what we're doing. Sarge always replies with 'some fucking bullshit, but we will prevail.' It's like our mantra now."

I chuckled under my breath and turned back to the officers.

Hollister stepped forward, surveying the room. "EOD has been tasked with clearing an area a mile from the airfield. Intelligence has told us there have been wires spotted. Tactically, the area's important, so we need a clear route for our guys. We're going out in three teams. Two in the Buffalos and one observation team who'll carry out imaging. Our objective is to clear the route over the next forty-eight hours."

"Our unit is there to protect the EOD boys," Marks confirmed. "We're gonna set up teams and surround them from every direction. We're also gonna assign two men for each Buffalo. They'll be carrying out close protection. If the T-Man comes'a calling, we'll give 'em a U.S. Army welcome."

The officers continued to review the details, but I couldn't, my mind wandering. This was our first mission outside the wire. It had come just in time; I felt antsy about being cooped up in the base. At last, I could do what I did best. My mind could go into the zone I loved and finally accomplish something over here.

Pulling my back straight, I tuned back into the briefing, carefully listening to Marks and Hollister review the details of the mission and our roles.

"Are we clear on our objectives?" Hollister demanded.

A 'Yes sir' chorus rose, and we all filed out of the briefing room.

"Snow!" Hollister yelled. "Get your ass back here."

My heart seemed to stop. Whipping around, I caught Benny with his eyes bugging out. "What the fuck does he want?" I cursed under my breath.

He grimaced. "We haven't done anything to screw up while here. It's either an old prank or something's happened back at home." He nodded toward the room solemnly. "Go on. I'll wait outside."

I shot Benny a last look before turning on my heel and returning to the room.

"Shut the door, Private Stone," my lieutenant ordered.

Private Stone? That sounded serious. My gut jerked, but I did as I was told and made my way over to him. Something Cash used to say came to mind. My ass was nipping. My insides almost quivered when I saw he had eyes on me the entire time.

The fucker could make the President himself nervous with the killer stare he was sending my way. It was enough to make a grown man wither away and die. I was also used to it, seeing as I was a man who bent the rules. Hopefully, my fuckery wouldn't come back and bite me in the ass.

Hollister leaned back against the table and folded his beefy arms across his chest. "Had word from Fort Campbell an hour ago, Snow."

My heart dropped. "Is it my family, sir?"

"Nope," he said. Popping the 'p.' "It was Command. Remember the tests you took for promotion to Specialist? Seems you passed with flying colors. You're not just a pretty face with a shitty attitude. You've got some brains, after all." He smirked.

A slow grin took over my face. About a week before we went to Vegas, I'd taken the aptitude test. I'd been so busy finding my feet that I hadn't stressed about it. I thought it would take longer than a few weeks to get the results in.

"You scored top of your class, Snow," he continued. "Two marks higher than Simmons. You did well. See what you can do when you stop fucking around? Your instincts are as good as any I've seen. Over here, that could be the difference between life and death for you and your brothers in arms."

For the first time ever, my LT gave me a friendly clap on the back and fuck me if a lump didn't appear in my throat.

Hollister had never spoken to me like I meant something. Nobody had. All my life, I'd been the youngest Stone. The annoyance. It was part of the reason I enlisted. I wanted to step away from Xander and Gage's shadow. Wanted to be my own man and not get bogged down under the bullshit of the MC.

Never in my life had I felt pride in myself or my accomplishments, but right then, my chest was warm and buoyant. I felt like I was king of the fucking world. If Hollister had put an M4 in my hands and sent me out to fight, I think I could've taken on the T-Man single-handedly.

"I've recruited two new specialists into the unit. You and Simmons. From now on, you two cut the bullshit. You'll have more responsibility than your peers and be involved in decision-making when we're out on missions. I need you two to get along."

Snow

My face must have fallen because Hollister cocked an eyebrow. "Don't look at me like that, princess. Your name ain't Dawson, and this ain't no creek. Work your grievances out. Do you copy?"

My lips twitched. LT was a witty cunt when he wanted to be. "Yes, sir."

Hollister nodded toward the door. "Now, fuck off, SPC Stone. See you at the Humvees."

Grinning, I saluted, turned, and marched toward the door, all the while thinking how fucking sexy SPC sounded to my ears.

It was still sinking in.

The fact was, I wasn't expecting to get anywhere when I took the tests. Hollister wasn't my number one fan, and he had a say in the decision-making. I was shocked he gave it to me.

My curiosity about why he chose me far outweighed my common sense because as I approached the door, I stopped and looked back over my shoulder. "Can I ask you something, Lieutenant? Off the record?"

He nodded once.

"Why me? I know you don't hold me in high regard. Aren't there other men who deserve it more than I do?"

He studied me for a minute with his all-knowing stare. "Why don't you think you deserve it?"

My eyebrows drew together. "You've always said I'm a fuckup."

"Never asked you why *I* don't think you deserve it. Asked you why *you* don't think you do." He left the words hanging briefly as he thought about his following ones. "Is Simmons a better soldier than you?" He shrugged. "Yeah, in some ways, he is. He's a stickler for the rules, and if idiots like you think you can break them whenever you want, we'd have out-and-out anarchy. But, the thing is, Stone, there ain't no rules in war. War *is* anarchy. We need men who can think outside the box, improvise, and go with their gut. That's your strength, SPC Stone. That's why I chose you."

Again, a lump of emotion appeared in my throat.

Before then, I didn't much care what Hollister thought of me. I'd believed my lieutenant had written me off as a prankster and not to be taken seriously.

But I decided then I'd work hard to fulfill the potential he saw in me. He was the first to dig deeper to see what I had to offer. I was gonna make him proud.

"Thank you, sir," I rasped, throat heated. "I won't let you down."

He nodded slowly, face thoughtful as his stare burned my skin. "You know what, Snow? I don't think you will."

"Fucking moon dust gets everywhere," Brown complained, clearing his throat loudly. "Once it's down your gullet, it's all you can taste for a week."

"Joys of working in a place which resembles the Bible." Yates laughed. "I'll be glad to get home to the green fields of Minnesota."

We were in an area just outside Hamid Karzai Airfield, awaiting instructions from the ground team, mapping out the site with our imaging equipment. In twelve hours, we'd safely disposed of four IEDs.

The heat inside the Buffalo was stifling, but at least Benny and I were safe inside. Well, safer than the ground crew, anyway. There was chatter that insurgents had been spotted in the area, so we were taking a break while some of Marks's team carried out recon.

Benny twisted his body around to face Yates. "Minnesota? I got a cousin there. He loves it, says it's beautiful country."

Yates smiled fondly, eyes glazing over as he thought about my words. "I never understood how beautiful it was

Snow

until I came here. Always thought living in Minnesota was akin to waiting to die. But now I know differently. I'll be home with my woman and kid in six more weeks." He rummaged inside his uniform and pulled out a photograph. "This is my Laura." He proudly pointed out a pretty brunette holding a toddler on her hip. "That's Joshua there. He's five now."

Carefully, I looked at the image of Yates's perfect family. My heart sank. God, he must've missed them so fucking much. "How does she feel about you being here?" I asked. "Must be hard on you all."

He looked thoughtful for a minute. "It is hard. Sometimes, it's torture, but what can you do? We've all got choices, and this was ours. I didn't wanna work in my dad's hardware store, and Minnesota's hardly crawling with opportunities, at least not where I'm from. My choices were the U.S. Army or shopkeeper." He held his arms out theatrically. "And here I am, boys."

Our chuckles filled the air.

"All we've talked about all day is our women and kids," Brown stated. "What about you two?"

"Young, free, and single." Benny grinned. "Just before we came out here, we enjoyed a Vegas weekend. It was a good time."

Brown shrugged. "Never been, but I've heard some stories. Did you drink, fight, and fuck all weekend? Guess there's not much else to do there."

An image of my girl floated through my mind, and I smiled to myself.

Yates caught my expression and let out a soft laugh. "Guess I got my answer right there."

"I met someone," I admitted. "Kitten's fucking beautiful. Smart too. Can you believe she's saving up for Harvard? She's ambitious but also kind. Never thought I'd ever meet a girl like her."

Brown let out a low whistle. "She sounds like a girl a man could fall for. Gotta picture?"

I shook my head, not for the first time, kicking myself because I hadn't thought of getting one. We didn't have time, especially after my head fuck. I made a mental note to get one the next time I saw her. I'd seen some of her with her friends in frames all over her apartment. I'd take one of them if I had to.

"We didn't get a chance," I mused as if to myself. "One minute, we were together. The next I was here."

Benny rolled his eyes. "Didn't help that you holed up in the hotel bar for two days feeling sorry for yourself."

Yates looked confused. "You did what? What the fuck happened?"

The question was easy to answer. All I'd been thinking about for the last week was my tweak and why I got spooked. "The second I saw her, I knew she'd be important to me if I let her. At first, I made a judgment and thought she was someone she wasn't, so I didn't really think about having anything beyond a weekend. Then I learned about her life and saw all her beauty inside and out. I knew it could go somewhere."

"So, why did you choose the hotel bar instead of locking her down?" Brown asked me.

"Because I was coming here. Even after twelve hours of knowing Kitten, I felt strong enough that I didn't want her to experience more loss."

"Ahh," Yates said knowingly. "Those noble intentions are a fucker, aren't they? Had a few of them myself back in the day."

I smiled self-deprecatingly. "Yeah. Until I got to the airport to catch the flight home and freaked the fuck out. I went frantic when I sobered up. Knew I'd screwed everything up. Lost my shit for a few minutes there."

"And that was where Uncle Benny came to the rescue," my friend interjected. "Me and the boys knew what a fuckhead he was being. Snowy here has good intentions, but they often bite him in the ass. We picked her up and brought her to the airport to say goodbye. I knew he'd be regretting his shitty choices."

We all chuckled.

"Me and Lau have had the conversation," Yates murmured. "You know, what happens if I don't get home. I held off on marrying her when I first enlisted because I felt the same way as you did. Eventually, I realized we already loved each other, so what was the difference? Married or not, she'd still have to mourn. At least with my ring on her finger, she'd get benefits if the worst happened."

Brown nodded, deep in thought. "I just think we should hold on to every little piece of beauty we can. My wife says we should make the most of every moment, so why not do it together?"

A small weight lifted off me. "That's a fucking nice way of looking at it."

"It's like my lady always says, Snow." A teasing look fell over his face. "Wifey knows best—"

—Chaos three, Chaos three. This is Chaos Six. The radio crackled.

Brown spoke into the receiver, "Chaos three, copy."

T-Man was sighted two kilometers east. Joe set to engage. Hang tight, Chaos Three. We'll keep you updated. Chaos six out.

A muscle ticked my jaw. We'd been talking about this all day. We were out in the open, without cover, and working on an area that was tactically important to both sides. It wasn't a shock that the recon team had spotted the Taliban a few kilometers east of our position.

Sounded like Marks's men were about to engage.

My breath began to quicken. We were stuck in this Buffalo with just our rifles. It was an armored vehicle, but we'd be sitting ducks if the T-man got through.

A few seconds of silence reigned before Yates muttered, "Sounds like trouble's on its way." He went for his M4 carbine and started to check the ammo.

"What you got, boys?" Brown asked, doing the same.

I leaned over to our sealed container of weapons we stored inside the Buffalo before we went outside the wire.

The vehicle was armored up to the eyeballs but had no built-in attack weaponry like you'd find on a tank. We always kept a stock of weapons on board during these missions in case of attack.

Hands shaking, I pulled out three M4 carbines, a couple of pistols, and a shit ton of ammunition which should've been able to keep us going for a while.

"Got every faith in Sarge," Brown explained. "He won't let them through, but we need to be ready in case they go black on ammo." He caught the unease on my face and laughed. "They won't, trust me. But what we gotta do apart from getting ready?"

I nodded and began to check the weaponry, getting everything loaded and laying out the ammo for easy access.

My gut leaped as a pop-pop-popping sounded in the distance.

Brown and Yates glanced at each other before scrambling to the window. "That was quick. Our boys have engaged. The T-Man must've been a bit close for comfort." He pointed outside. "Look."

Heart pounding, I hauled myself over to the window where, in the distance, little lights flashed in the twilight. The sound of gunfire carried over the air, making my blood pound through my veins.

"Over there. See?" Brown stated. "Watch. Marks will have them surrounded soon.

Sure enough, the flickers of light began to slowly reposition.

"Jesus," Benny said from over my shoulder. "Makes you wanna get out there and join in. It's a fucking rush."

He was right. My pulse raced as I looked down at my hands, shaking with the adrenaline coursing through me. It was much like when I saw Kitten on stage. My body slowly came alive.

Inside, my brain kept chanting, *get out there, join in*, to the point where I had to consciously stop myself from opening the doors and jumping down. It was a high-to-end all-highs. It would be easy to get hooked.

Snow

A colossal bang echoed in the distance before a plume of smoke filled the air. My eyes were glued to the scene as the popping stopped for a few seconds, then started up again.

"What the fuck was that?" Benny demanded, awestruck.

"Staff Sarge's M224." Brown chuckled. "It's his favorite toy. His trick is to herd the T-Man together, surround them, and then blow 'em sky high. It's his signature calling card."

Yates and Brown laughed.

The noise of gunfire died down. I watched and waited, holding my breath while listening for the radio.

After a few minutes, it crackled.

Chaos Three. Chaos Three. This is Chaos Six.

Brown spoke into the handset, "Chaos Three, copy."

T-Man is eliminated. As you were, Chaos Three. Chaos Six, out.

Brown and Yates looked at each other smugly. "Looks like we're back to work, boys." Brown's mouth hitched up. "Enemy is down."

Nodding, I ran my clammy hands down my pants before moving back to the controls, thinking of how anticlimactic the whole thing had been. I'd been expecting to get caught up in the thick of it. Instead, I'd sat back and waited while other people had all the fun.

My relief at the moment was palpable, as was my disappointment.

Little did I know, I'd gotten off lucky.

Being in the thick of it wasn't always what it was cracked up to be.

Chapter Eight

Kitten

My mind was on him every moment of every day. Even at work, he was there in the background, even when surrounded by people.

I danced for him on stage, imagining my beautiful soldier watching me from his table. Then, later, I went to bed and cried for him. Not because I needed him with me—though that would've been ace—It was because of what I imagined he was enduring.

CNN became my best friend.

I'd sit for hours reading the books I'd bought in preparation for Harvard. But one ear was always on the news, which by then I had playing twenty-four seven. Slowly, it became my new obsession. Listening, watching, trying to see one man in a crowd of many, all wearing the same uniform.

But it was futile.

In those first weeks, I'd comfort myself with memories of how he looked at me like he could see inside my soul. I'd play music and daydream about the next time Snow came to see me. His smile was etched on my brain. Sometimes, I'd imagine I heard his deep, throaty laugh in a crowd full of strangers.

My music tastes turned from rock and house music to the country twang of Carrie Underwood singing how she'd see her man, her soldier again. It said everything I felt and made me a little less lonely.

I waited.

And I waited.

The weeks turned into months, and the spark of hope he'd ignited began to wither and die. The logical side of my brain told me Snow would be okay. He was trained to look after himself. Still, after hearing all the horror stories coming out of Afghanistan, my less logical side began to torture me.

Every day melded into the next. Every Sunday, I'd ask myself if it would be the week I got a letter, but I never did. People used to tell me absence made the heart grow fonder, but I began to hate him for leaving me in limbo, traumatizing me with worry.

I almost gave up, almost stopped looking out for the small envelope that meant so much, until six weeks and four days after he left.

I'd been up early, disturbed by a dark dream that had disappeared from my mind the instant I woke. I was about to put my sneakers on and run to Mr. Kowalski's for groceries when the mailman knocked.

I opened the door to see he had a parcel under one arm with a letter on top held together by a rubber band. "Morning," he chirped.

I smiled and began to chit-chat until he handed me the package. My heart leaped into my throat when my eyes caught the brown paper-wrapped parcel, and I suddenly focused on the envelope stamped with the two words I'd been yearning to see.

'U.S. Army.'

My hands turned sweaty as I muttered a goodbye and swung the door closed.

I stared at those two words for what felt like hours, mouth gaping.

Snow

It was funny because I'd been praying for weeks to hear from him, and the minute my prayers were answered, my stupid knees turned to jelly.

Like on autopilot, my feet carried me to my couch, and I sat, almost dazed, looking at those two words. My stomach churned; my throat tightened. Why didn't I want to open it after waiting so long?

What would I do if he was writing to tell me it was over?

I bit my lip, eyes flicking over the faint streak of dirt and the slightly crumpled edges of the paper.

Logical and less logical began to argue with each other again.

What if he doesn't want you? He left you before.
He regretted it, didn't he?
What if he's done with you?
So what. You'll deal.

With trembling fingers, I pulled that envelope from its rubber band and tore into it like a woman possessed. My eyes flickered over it, trying to get the gist of the words so I could prepare myself for the worst. My heart galloped to the point where I started to feel faint.

Calm down.
Just read.

Closing my eyes, I evened out my breathing and began,

Kitten.

Hope this letter finds you well.
Sorry I didn't write sooner. We've been up to our ball sacks in training and getting settled in. I remember arriving and thinking I gotta write soon. Next thing, I turned around, and 4 goddamned weeks had passed.

Well, we're here in sunny Afghanistan. It's okay, I guess. Could be worse.

I'm struggling with the heat, which my unit thinks is great cos it gives them a reason to crucify my ass. Goddamned soldiers. LOL.

This heat wipes me out. All I do, when I come off duty, is sleep. The other night I dreamed of Vegas and Lone Mountain. We watched the sunrise, and it felt like I had everything I needed in my arms, but when I looked down, you were gone. Hope it's not a sign, baby, cos I can't wait to be with you again.

Those nights in Vegas when I wasn't with you, I was in the hotel bar thinking about life and where our choices could take us. Being here has made me realize we can't plan shit, especially in hellholes like this. All we can do is our best and hope it's enough.

Sometimes I wonder if it's all worth the battles, struggles, and violence. But then I look down at the faces of the Afghan girls who're finally allowed to get an education, and I know I'm here for a reason.

The kids here are spectacular, Kitten. They've got nothing, but their smiles are so big. We passed through the bazaar the other day, and some boys dragged us into a soccer game. We had a great time, and it made them so happy that it made me happy, too. I couldn't wipe the smile off my face for the rest of the day.

Did you know the enemy uses kids here, Kitten? They strap bombs onto their little bodies and send them out to die and murder other innocents as they blow themselves up. It's a shitshow. I hope my being here helps them. Hope me being here is doing some good.

Fuck, Kitten. I miss you. Every time I close my eyes, you're all I can see. I can't believe I wasted two days I could've spent with you. I'm such a fucking idiot.

I'm coming back for you. After this deployment, I get a few days off, and I'm flying in as soon as possible. I'll let you know when the minute they tell us. Can't wait to hold you and kiss you. I don't intend on leaving your bed all the time I'm there, so be prepared. We'll watch Game of Thrones. Don't watch it without me. Can't wait to see what happened to Bran after he got thrown out of that fucking window.

I think about you all the time. Please don't give up. It's not easy, but hopefully, it will be worth it one day.

Tell Chloe my boy says hi. He knows they agreed not to keep in touch, but tell her he's okay.

Hope everything's cool at the club and your studies are going well. I was telling some guys from another unit how smart you are and how goddamned pretty. Every time I look at you, it's like I can't breathe. I wish I had a picture of you to show them. Can you sort that out?

Anyway. Gotta get some shuteye. I'm on night duty for the first time next week, so hopefully, I'll get a minute to write you again.

Take care, baby.

Your idiot.
Snow.

Chapter Nine

Snow

Five of us got picked for night duty. Me, Benny, Higgs, Cheng, and, believe it or not, Kyle 'fucknut' Simmons. Since we'd been out here, I'd mostly avoided him. Hollister tended to post us on separate teams since we both got bumped up to Special Private. The lieutenant wanted to spread out our expertise.

Finally, it felt like I'd started to get into my groove.

The heat was still a fucker, but it wasn't making me nauseous anymore. My gut churn wasn't something I wanted to live with again. It was hard enough being out here. It was nothing like home and a complete culture shock, so constant sickness wasn't something I wanted to deal with on top of that.

The last week had been difficult because there'd been a spree of suicide bombers attacking close to the base. The booms of their explosives would jar me awake at night, wondering what the fuck was happening. The noise led to disturbed sleep, which, over time, led to exhaustion.

It was much the same for Benny, too. The easy smile that used to be continuously plastered to his face had faded somewhat. It was a challenging environment, but the silver lining was we had each other. Brown, Yates, and their crew had become good buds too. There was nothing like the threat of being blown up or shot to help build close relationships.

Our sergeant had sent us on a short break, so we'd come to the DFAC to grab a coffee. It was about 0200 hours, and we were due to come off duty at 0600. We sat down, discussing how Brown's team had been sent to Helmand Province. ISAF had gained control over the area, previously a Taliban stronghold at the center of their opium production and distribution.

ISAF had a strong presence there, but the region was problematic, to say the least. Tactically, the province was essential to the T-Man, so there was a constant power struggle.

"Bet Marks is letting M224s off left and right." Cheng laughed. He was part of the ground crew carrying out imaging when the Insurgents got too close. He witnessed what happened the day we were stuck in the Buffalos.

"He'll be happy as a pig in shit," Higgs agreed. "You should've seen him in action. Sarge knows what he's doing. He was the first one running into the thick of it. I could see why his unit thinks so highly of him. Hope we can get some action before we leave. It looked like a good time."

I regarded Simmons, who leaned back in his chair, holding his mug to his mouth, and remembered Hollister's comments about cutting the bullshit. I guessed it was as good a time as any.

"What do you think, Simmons?" I asked. "Wanna see some action this tour?"

His eyes lifted from his cup, visibly startled because I addressed him. "Yeah. I guess so. It might—" He was interrupted by a loud boom in the distance.

The DFAC almost rattled with its force. I sat up straight as my stomach tied itself into knots. "That sounded close."

Snow

Benny stood, taking a last gulp of coffee. "Come on. We better get back to Espinoza."

Chairs scraped against the floor tiles as we jumped up and made our way through the door and down the corridor that led to the room where we'd set up a training facility.

As we approached, Sergeant Espinoza stalked out of the door. He spotted us and crossed his arms across his barrel chest. "We've had an IED attack 'bout a hundred feet from the gates. Suspected car bomb. We're up."

My gut jolted. "Any casualties, Sarge?"

He nodded once.

The look on his face should've clued me in on the gravity of the situation. Still, my mind immediately went over the drills we'd completed for similar problems. We got into our tactical gear and checked our equipment while Espinoza relayed our objectives. Our orders were to sweep the area and ensure there were no further VBIEDs present. As well as securing the site.

Just before we left, Espinoza stopped us, his eyes sliding from one face to the next. "Remember, boys. Initial success or total failure."

"Yes, sir!" we chorused while together, saluting the motto of the EOD.

Within minutes, we were in the Humvees and speeding through the gates. We'd been joined by a team of Marines–thankfully, not the assholes on our flight over. The vehicle smelled of smoke, metal, and apprehension, the only sound being our hard breaths sawing in and out.

I looked over, seeing Benny's lips move as he gave himself a pep talk. Fucker was probably saying his Hail Marys and holding his grandmother's rosary beads, which he always kept in his pocket. Couldn't blame him. His faith comforted him. Right then, it would've been nice to believe a higher power was watching out for us.

Our eyes met.

This is it. We're on, his stare relayed.
We'll be good. I've got your six, mine replied.
He gave me a slight nod.

I closed my eyes, trying to breathe through the pulsing in my veins as adrenaline began to spike. We'd mastered breathing techniques and calming exercises throughout our EOD training and beyond. All my hard work and training had all been for this one moment in time. This was the reason I'd enlisted in the first place.

To serve my country.

My body jolted as the Humvee slowed and came to a stop.

"Ready, boys?" Espinoza demanded.

"Yes, sir," rose through the Humvee.

"I want Simmons and Cheng on imaging," he ordered. "Higgs, you're relaying. Snow, Benedetti. You're with me."

Another chorus of "Yes, sir," and we were out of the Humvee, unloading the equipment.

Espinoza strode over to talk to one of the soldiers in charge, allowing me to look around for the first time.

We were parked at the mouth of a dark walkway. The smell of burning was acrid from the small billows of smoke floating from the alley. The place was a hive of activity. Soldiers were physically forcing a crowd of Afghan civilians back as they crammed together, trying to see what was happening.

My first thought was they were crazy to wanna hang around an area where bombs could detonate any second, but then I heard wailing, and my heart jolted.

Looking for the source of the screams, I saw a group of women wearing robes holding a younger female back from the walkway where the IED had detonated. The woman cried as she screamed a name. "Azyan! Azyan!"

My heart clenched.

If anyone had been down the walkway when the device detonated, they wouldn't have stood a chance.

The alley was a narrow, tight, enclosed space. If they weren't eviscerated in the blast itself, the force of the explosion and flying debris would've gotten them.

Espinoza clapped the officer on the back and made his way back to us. "Snow. Benedetti. Full tac gear, night vision, and head cam. Hollister's requested to tap into the feed from the base. Smile. You're gonna be on camera. There's no way we're getting a robot down there, so we're gonna it the old-fashioned way. Bomb suits, handheld imaging, and our wits."

"Was someone down there, sir?" I asked, gesturing toward the alley.

"We've had a report that two teens went down there a few minutes before detonation. We're gonna do some recon. See what we can find."

A sick feeling swooped through my gut because I already knew what we would find, and it wouldn't be pleasant.

My heart started to race again.

We were walking into the unknown, and God only knew what we'd find there. Our checks hadn't detected any further charges or switches, but the space was so compact we couldn't be sure.

I began breathing exercises again while we fitted our protective masks, ensuring our cameras and comms worked.

Finally, we got into our bomb suits. That was my time. That was when I got my head in the zone.

The other guys helped strap us in, ensuring the built-in Kevlar shield was situated correctly, and the Velcro around the wrist cuffs was pulled securely. Next was the electronic panel strapped to our arms, which controlled our body temperature and our headgear lights. Finally, our protective collars went up, and we were ready.

Ben and I glanced at each other through the glass panel in the headgear, then nodded our assurances before moving toward the alley.

"I'll take the lead," Espinoza declared quietly through the comms, unlocking his M4 and hoisting it up into position. "Snow at my back. Benedetti, take our six."

"Yes. sir," we both murmured.

My hand lifted to switch on the comms system. It crackled slightly before a voice said, *"Good evening, princesses. Beautiful night for it, doncha think?"*

Hollister.

It was weird. I didn't relish the idea of the LT having eyes on our mission. He'd chew my ass out if I did the slightest thing wrong. On the other hand, his being there seemed to calm my racing heart. The panic in my throat seemed to dissipate at his no-nonsense tone.

"Evening, sir," I muttered.

"Snow. Remember your training. Your strength is dealing with the unexpected. Trust your instincts and do everything Sergeant says. He did two tours in Iraq, and he's still alive."

"Yes, sir," I breathed.

"Benedetti. You're our eyes and ears. You're my attention to detail. Keep your position. Look and listen for anything that shouldn't be there."

"Copy, sir," Benny replied.

Espinoza looked down the alleyway, then glanced over his shoulder at me, nodding once.

And off we went.

The alley was dark, but some smoke had cleared, so at least we had limited vision. The fumes from the burned-out vehicle were so strong it would've been impossible to walk toward it without wearing PPE. I could feel we were getting closer because the heat was ramping up with every step we took.

All I could hear were the sounds of the blast's aftermath and my own heaving breaths. It was hard to breathe through PPE anyway. The adrenaline pumping through me made it even more tricky.

"Show me those walls, Snow," Hollister ordered.

Obeying, I slowly swiveled my head left, then right, allowing Hollister to see through the camera fitted to my helmet. The centuries-old, thick mud walls had turned from sand color to black.

"The walls are intact, Snow. What does that tell you?"

The answer had already come to me. The Taliban meant to cause maximum damage. Either their explosive devices were big, or they set up a collection of smaller ones. "Looks like a small device. We need to look for more," I relayed to Hollister.

The comms link crackled. *"That's what I'm talking about, soldier. Proceed with caution."*

I nodded. "Yes, sir."

The further we got into the alley, the more rubble we had to contend with. I was surprised the walls were still mainly intact, but they were built thick and designed to last. Still, you could never entirely predict what a bomb blast would do in an uncontrolled environment.

The smoke was getting thicker. That told me we were getting closer to the blast site. We must have been in the alley for maybe thirty minutes, but it felt like hours. Apprehension was a fucker for making time slow down.

The sounds in the alley slowly began to silence. All I could hear was the blood rushing in my ears and the thud of my heartbeat. I was in the zone, finally.

For one second, all I could see was smoke. The next, we were upon mangled, burned-out metal. Jesus, it was a mess. I'd seen this shit in a controlled environment. I'd even bet on which way they blew, but that burning vehicle was way more sinister than anything I'd experienced.

"Benedetti. You're up," Espinoza ordered.

"Yes, sir," Benny muttered as he moved beside me and began mapping out areas for imaging. There wasn't much equipment, just a sizeable hand-held X-Ray machine that could detect switches and timer signals. It had been designed for small areas like this. It was portable and light. Easy to lift and get into tight spaces.

We helped him maneuver around what was left of the vehicle. Pulling back hot metal to enable him to get into tight spaces. We were careful, imaging every section as we approached, which held us up somewhat. Still, within an hour, we'd determined there were no further threats.

My relief was palpable. The second Espinoza gave us the all-clear, our shoulders slumped, and we heaved a collective breath.

We'd gotten through it, but not without my blood pressure rising.

Hollister had been giving instructions over comms while we worked. The system crackled slightly before he said, *"Good job. Now we gotta clear the area. The FBI man's coming down to carry out an investigation on this one. Any sign of life?"*

"No, sir," I replied.

"You heard the lieutenant," Espinoza called out. "Let's drive on so we can get back behind the wire. My bunk's calling me. We need to clear a walkway for the other units. Benedetti. Start clearing that pile of debris." He gestured further up the alley. "Snow. Go move the other pile that we imaged. Try and shove it against the wall. Let's make it easy for our boys, yeah?"

"Yes, sir," me and Benny chorused.

He nodded. "Have each other's sixes," Sarge ordered before walking back to where we came. I heard him on the radio, summoning Simmons and Yates to help.

Benny looked at me bug-eyed. "That was a rush."

I couldn't help laughing at him. Trust the crazy fucker to get my head back on track.

"It was," I agreed. "Didn't like not seeing where we were going, though."

Benny shrugged. "Never thought I'd be grateful they trained us to operate in dark, enclosed areas. It killed me back in the day, but now I'm glad for it. Espinoza knows his shit, too We were always gonna be okay."

I gestured further up the alley. "Better get to work."

Benny nodded, swiveling toward the pile of metal that was once a vehicle.

Turning, I began to make my way further up the alley. I still had a tremor in my hands from the adrenaline rush. I hoped my nerves would improve the more missions we did. An EOD expert with the shakes was a liability.

What I'd discovered walking up the alley was that no amount of training prepared you for the real thing. We'd been all over the world dealing with everything from defusing old WW2 bombs and disposing of others, but it was all well controlled.

Operating in a war zone was different.

We didn't get hours to stand in a field imaging and discussing the best way to move forward, as we had on missions before. Here we were, in and out. Command carried out instant assessments and gave us our orders accordingly. It was our job to follow them, no questions asked. Our lives depended on what came down from the top.

But Benny was right. It was a rush.

I was still distracted as I approached the massive pile of debris I'd been ordered to clear. The adrenaline that minutes ago had pumped through my bloodstream slowly faded, leaving exhaustion in its wake. The danger was over, and I was morphing into autopilot.

Maybe it was why I didn't see her at first.

Looking back, I think my exhaustion had clouded my vision and made me less aware of my environment. It wasn't until I was in front of the pile of metal that I trod on something soft.

Weird.

I glanced down, expecting to see some cloth or foam from the seats of the exploded vehicle. Instead, I spied a small hand.

My gut took a nosedive.

The adrenaline, which had burned itself out a few minutes before, sparked to life again. Using strength I didn't know I had, I started to haul the pieces of crumpled metal away. Despite my efforts, I couldn't shift the big sheet covering her little body.

"Ben!" I yelled. "Need ya! Now!"

Within seconds, footsteps echoed as Benny and Espinoza ran toward my position.

"There's a kid under there," I yelled. "Help me get her out."

I assumed she was a little girl from the smear of red nail polish slashed across one of her fingers.

"Wait!" Espinoza ordered. "If imaging didn't pick her up, we might have missed an IED. Get back!"

"I'll get the camera," Benny muttered, disappearing back down the alley.

By then, I was frantic. My vision blurred, and I realized some tears had welled up. I began to pace. "Let me help her, sir," I pleaded.

"You've been given an order, Snow," Espinoza grated. "We wait for Benedetti. We'll get her out as soon as we know it's clear."

My comms crackled. *"Report. Now!"* Hollister demanded.

Espinoza began to relay the information back to the lieutenant. It was weird because I knew what he was saying, but later, if someone had asked me what words he spoke, I couldn't have told them.

All my attention was on the little hand as I rasped, "Please let her be okay. God. Let her be okay." I didn't notice the time pass. All that registered was Benny finally declaring the area safe after what felt like hours of waiting.

Snow

By then, the other guys had joined us. Between them, they got to work, shoving the heavy metal away.

I stayed with her, crouched down, holding the little hand, and talking gently because I knew she'd be scared. At one point, I had to let her go to allow the boys to get into position. That was when I discovered what I thought was nail polish was actually her blood.

All hope she was alive faded away.

Finally, the boys managed to haul the massive sheet of metal away.

My eyes slid up her body, and my entire body froze at what I saw.

She was lying among the metal and the rubble, strangely at peace. But the sight of half her body missing made sickness roil through my gut.

That innocent little girl had been severed apart at the waist.

My throat thickened with tears. Or was it puke? Maybe it was both. All my strength left me, and I fell back onto my ass, holding my head in my hands.

"Fuck!" Benny muttered.

"Jesus," Simmons exclaimed gently. "Poor kid."

It was like watching the aftermath of an accident. You knew looking was wrong, but you couldn't help yourself. I was no exception because my eyes traveled back to her.

It was crazy how her bottom half looked so gruesome, but her top half didn't. My eyes rested on the kid's face, and another wave of sickness hit me.

She looked uncannily like Freya.

Her empty, staring eyes were a golden brown, her little pink lips full. Thick dark hair with some natural curl splayed out around her amongst the rubble.

I couldn't help thinking she looked like an angel.

Sensing movement, my eyes lifted to Espinoza. He mimicked the sign of the Holy Cross over his chest and looked up to the heavens, lips moving in prayer.

The comms crackled, and Hollister let out a curse.

That was when I realized my head cam was still running, and the lieutenant could see the horror splayed out before me.

"Snow. Get your ass up. Now, he ordered. *We can't help her, but we can respect her. I'll hold the other teams off for five minutes at most. Look around, gather up any pieces, and zip her up. If the FBI gets in now, they'll just bulldoze over her. We can arrange to return her to her parents for a proper burial."*

Fuck, he was right. "Yes, sir," I croaked.

"Whatever you're feeling, shut it down. Now. Get up and find the rest of her. That's an order, Snow."

I scrambled to my feet, nodding. "Yes, sir. I'm okay, sir."

Espinoza clapped me on the back. "C'mon, SPC Stone. We'll find her. We'll do right by her."

I nodded, unable to speak because my throat was so thick with emotion. "We will, sir," I finally rasped.

So we searched. Whenever somebody found a little piece of her, they'd hand her to me so I could dust her off and place her inside a body bag.

Never before had I felt such reverence and determination to do what was right. I treated every piece of her I touched with respect and honor because a thought occurred to me. In another world and time, that girl could've been Freya. The only difference between her and my sister was geography.

As I gathered up the little girl's remains, hatred for the enemy began to claw at my throat because how could they do this? How could they hurt the very people they professed to love and protect?

Something inside me twisted as I heard Hollister's order in the back of my brain. *Shut it down, Snow. Shut it down.*

So I did. I shut down everything I felt and buried it deep.

Snow

I couldn't help that girl anymore, but I could avenge her and every other kid the enemy manipulated. I could get revenge for every child they strapped a bomb on and sent out to murder others.

I could pay the T-Man back tenfold.

That was the moment a monster stirred inside, changing me forever.

Chapter Ten

Kitten

I was on my way to the dressing room when a deep voice permeated the distant thumping of the bass. "You ready, Kitten? You're on in ten."

I gave Marco a nod as I breezed past him into the packed dressing room.

He was a tall, dark-haired, wiry guy. Good looking if you were into the whole hot nerd look. He wore small, round glasses; I'd never seen him in jeans. It was all designer suits.

"On it, boss. I'd never be late for you." I threw him a smile, cracking the door open and hurrying inside. "Jesus. He's on my ass constantly," I complained, approaching an empty chair and slumping down onto a seat.

"He's probably worried you'll run off with your soldier boy," Raven said knowingly. "You know what men get like when they sense you're pulling away." She gave a theatrical shudder. "Clingy."

The other girls laughed with calls of 'Amen' and 'Preach, sister.'

Smiling through the tightness in my throat, I shrugged nonchalantly. "That's a long way off yet. Harvard's still my dream."

"That's what they all say." Raven smiled, eyes still on the mirror as she swiped red lipstick across her beautiful, puffy lips. "Make sure you do it, Kitty. Don't waste it."

My belly almost heaved at her words, similar to the ones in Snow's letter that had arrived that morning.

The exact words that made me well up and smile simultaneously.

The exact words that had sparked a flicker of discomfort in my belly but also inspired me.

Compared to his last letter, he seemed low.

That wasn't a problem for me. Snow was allowed to feel anything he wanted in that place. The drudgery of it would get into anyone's head. The news channels reported stories about the soldiers who had left the recent war in Iraq and their state of mind. The term PTSD was discussed much more. No doubt Snow would need time to adjust, too. I got that.

I simply just plain old worried about him.

I simply just plain old missed him.

And I simply, just plain old, couldn't wait for him to return to me.

I had everything planned.

First. A hero's welcome at the airport because he was a hero, just like every other man and woman who donned that uniform and put themselves in danger for us every day. They deserved nothing less than everything.

Second. I'd take Snow straight to my apartment, where we were going to crack open the industrial-sized box of condoms that I'd already stashed inside my nightstand. Planning had gone even further in that respect. I'd been asking the girls for tips. Now, I had some stuff in my repertoire that I was pretty sure would take his mind off Afghanistan for a while.

Third. Talking, getting more connected, Game of Thrones, and more sex. In fact, way more sex. I was gonna sex him up and down, and in and out until Snow

Snow

was so sexed out that when he left me, he'd have a dopey smile on his face and a bunch of spank bank items that he could call upon day or night.

Perfect!

We just had to get through.

He just needed to keep his wits about him and get back to me in one piece.

I'd do the rest.

I smiled, my heart suddenly feeling a little lighter.

"We're heading out, Kitten," Mae called out. "Wanna meet us at the casino after your dance?"

Her voice startled me a little. I'd been so deep in my head that I hadn't realized the girls had collected their stuff and were already heading out. Being the headline dancer was great, but it also meant that I was often stuck here later than the other girls.

I twisted my body to face them. "Not tonight. I'm bushed. I bought a new book about the relevance of economics within business management. My night is planned."

Raven looked at me approvingly. "Make sure that you remember us when you're a top CEO. We can't strip forever."

The girls laughed.

"I won't forget my roots," I assured her. "The world will always need ex-strippers to discuss their portfolios with."

Raven laughed. "See you next weekend, Kitty."

We all said our goodbyes, and they headed out, slamming the dressing room door behind them.

My smile still played around my lips as I watched them leave.

The girls had been great with me. They were amazing, always cheering me up when I struggled to breathe through missing him.

You'd think putting a bunch of strippers together would be the recipe for a catty, hair-pulling, eyes-scratching disaster, but not here.

Just like me, some were paying their way through school. Others were moms and wives and wanted to earn for their families. Some just loved dancing, which was their way of living out their passion. It helped that the Crimson Velvet was different from other clubs. Marcus wanted a show. We were more like a burlesque troupe than your run-of-the-mill strippers.

My mom taught me jack about women supporting women. Frankly, she was only out for herself. My best friend Sophie and her mom made up for that, though. Then the Crimson Velvet women got thrown into the mix, and it couldn't have made me any prouder to be a part of their sisterhood.

In the last few months, they'd sympathized with me all that time I didn't hear from him. Shared in my joy when I finally did and generally propped me up when I needed support.

My mind went to the letter in my purse, and I couldn't help smiling to myself.

It was already getting dog-eared from being read so much. An urge swept over me, and I leaned down, grabbed my purse, and pulled out the paper with the U.S. Army stamped over it.

I smiled at the fizzing sensation popping through my belly.

Just one more read before I go on.

Kitten.

Can you believe I've been here nearly three months already?

Some days, it seems like a year. Others, only yesterday. I've acclimatized now. LOL. It's fucking typical that I get used to the heat at the ass-end of my deployment.

I don't know what you see on the news channels back home, but things here are sketchy. A few weeks ago, there was a bombing on a courthouse, and since then, it's been attack, attack, attack. At the moment, it's like the Wild fucking West, but with IEDs instead of pistols.

It's the kids I feel sorry for. Imagine growing up in a place like this? We're not only fighting a physical enemy but also an ideology. Some men are so fucking scared that the girls will be Westernized that they give them to the enemy to use as weapons. They'd rather their girls get blown up than be educated. Can you believe that?

Shit—look at me whining. Sorry, Kitten, it just gets to me sometimes. We're all safe, even though I've seen much more action since I last wrote. We work outside the base a lot more, especially with all the IEDs and explosions constantly detonating. However, there's not much we can do for the victims after the fact except pick up the bodies.

I worry about coming home sometimes. I've made so many friends here from all over the world. Even got a mate who's a Brit. He's bloody mint. (See what I did there. LOL)

I worry about leaving them because I know we're coming back. My Commander already said we'll get at least three deployments here. Some EOD units are on their fifth, so we've been lucky. I worry that I'll return and all my friends I've made will be shipped out or dead, and I'll have to start all over again.

You know what I'm looking forward to more than anything in the world? Seeing you.

Even thinking about it brings a smile to my face, Kitten. Talking, watching TV—just being. It's gonna be amazing.

Sometimes I forget your face. I know what you look like, but I can't summon up the details. That scares me because, without the thought of you, I'd struggle to get through in this place. We spent a night outdoors last week. We all took a shift of guard duty, and in that hour, my head was full of nothing but you. Thinking about Vegas, us, and Lone Mountain is the only thing that makes me feel like my old self again these days.

I can't wait to hold you, Kitten.

I better shut it down. Can't get emotional. I'll save that for when I see you.

I hope your studies are ok. Work hard, baby, please. Western girls are so lucky compared to the oppressed ones all over the world. Don't waste it. Do it for the young women who can't. Some girls here would love to go into business, but they're not allowed. Instead, they marry and have kids. Sometimes to a good guy, often not.

I'm so proud of you for making shit happen! If I ever have a daughter, I want her to be like you. Strong and beautiful down to her bones. Kind and sweet, with a little bit of edge to keep her guy on his toes. Maybe one day we'll make that happen. LOL. Ignore me. I'm talking like a stage one clinger. Still, when you've nothing but time on your hands, your thoughts go to the meaning of life and what you want out of it, especially when you're surrounded by so much brutality.

I'll write again as soon as I know when our deployment's up. I'll book a flight and tell you the date and times. All the details. I don't even know if you'll want me by then. You may have met someone else, but in my heart, I know it hasn't happened because what we had felt like beautiful.

Tell you what, meet me at the airport when I fly in, and we'll take it from there. Let's not waste even a second of it. I did enough of that on my last visit. I'm still sorry about that. Wasting that time is one of my biggest regrets because those precious moments in time are all we've really got.

Snow

Anyway, Kitten. We're heading down to the DFAC. After we eat, I'll take this letter to the postal facility, then I'm crashing for the night. Gotta get my strength up for when I see you again cos the next time we meet, I'm not gonna let you go.

So long, for now, baby. Be safe.

Your idiot.
Snow.

Chapter Eleven

Snow

Benny sat bolt upright on his bunk and punched his arm in the air. "Booorn in the USA! I was—"

I jumped up from my bottom bunk. "Booorn in the USA! I was—"

"Booorn in the USA, I was."

"Booorn in the USA-A-A."

Benny jumped to the floor as the drums kicked in, and we started yelling along to Springsteen's words.

It had become our nightly ritual, at least inside the wire. We went through extreme highs and dark lows, so I reckoned it was healthy as fuck to let off some steam.

The ground bounced as we started jumping up and down, punching the air and shouting along to the lyrics. We only needed a mosh-pit and could've been at any thrash metal concert.

Our door flew open to reveal Higgs and Simmons at the threshold, grinning at us.

Suddenly, Higgs's arm flew up into the air, and he made a fist. He looked like a fucking rock god as he yelled the words to the song. He leaped into our CHU, pushing an imaginary microphone under my chin so I could join the show.

Whoops and hollers rang out as the song looped back to the chorus. We all jumped around the enclosed space like crazy men again, shouting along to the words. I was no dancer. I'd definitely leave that shit to my Kitten, but it turned out that I played a mean fucking air guitar.

Music had become one of the most important things to me while I'd been at Camp Eggers.

I'd always loved it, even felt it deep inside. Music affected my mood and personality. It had become a significant factor in my everyday life. The Brit boys listened to a guy called Raleigh Ritchie. His music spoke to me. I'd lay in my bunk and listen to a song called 'I Can Change' for hours.

The words resonated so deeply with me that my eyes misted and my throat clenched. Hollister's voice would often float through my mind, yelling: *Shut it down, Snow. Shut it down.*

So I'd shut it down.

It was easier that way. Melancholy was rife. I'd seen soldiers walking around with their hands behind their backs and their heads bowed, and it would bring me down. It was terrible for morale.

The worst times were when we lost someone. The air of silent anger in the camp would become almost tangible. Officers would stomp into the DFAC, and I'd know by the force of the savagery pounding from them that they'd just lost a team member.

Every time it happened, the churning in my stomach would start. The only thing that would make it stop was the vow I'd make to avenge that soldier, the same way I vowed to avenge the little girl who we pulled out of the rubble.

Savagery was way more appropriate than melancholy in the environment we were stuck in. Hence and the team jumping around the CHU like fucking lunatics who'd been released from the asylum.

After a minute or two, the song began to fade out.

Snow

I sat, flopping back on my bed, exhausted. One minute, I was exuberant; the next, bone tired. I chalked it up to the heat, even though I should've been used to it by then.

Higgs took the one chair we had space for while I shifted up my bed to make room for Benny and Simmons.

"I needed that," Ben announced. "Been antsy for days."

"Air guitar always puts me right," Simmons agreed. "When we're outside the wire, I'm constantly on high alert. I find it hard as hell to let that go when we're back on base."

My lips twitched as I thought—not for the first time—how unexpected the change in Simmons had been.

Baker had transferred to another unit about a month back. Seemed he wasn't cut out for EOD. Soon after, Simmons seemed to have undergone a personality replacement because he chilled the fuck out. The man was a prick at Fort Campbell but had morphed into a decent brother since we'd been in Kabul. He looked out for us the same as we did him, thankfully losing that chip on his shoulder in the process.

Hollister called me into his office about a week ago, and we chatted about it. Lieutenant reckoned that seeing that girl blown in half changed him made him see the bigger picture. He said that he'd seen it time and again in Iraq. Men went out as loners and misfits and returned home as part of a family.

I kinda liked that, seeing as I'd felt like a misfit all my life.

"Anyone heard when we're leaving this shithole yet?" Higgs asked. "Our time's almost up. It started at three months, then four. We're about two weeks away from that, right?"

Benny cracked out his cell and checked his calendar. "Nearer three, but who's counting?"

Simmons closed his eyes and smiled. "Can't wait to fuck my girl. I'll have her walking like John Wayne when I finish with her. My nuts are the size of fucking watermelons. It's starting to hurt."

Higgs laughed. "Shouldn't be with how many times you whack off in a week. It's like living with a twelve-year-old boy."

My eyebrows slashed together. "Wait, Simmons. Thought she dumped your sneaky ass?"

He grinned. "We got back together on our last weekend before deployment. You know, when you dirty fucks went to Vegas."

Benny ducked his head to cover his smirk. "Ahh yeah. Good ol' Vegas."

I wondered if I should tell him I faked his name when I met Kitten. We were close enough now. He could take it. It seemed like nothing after being in this place for weeks on end, just schoolboy shit.

My mouth curved into a grin. "Guess what, Simmons."

He looked at me, cocking his eyebrow at my playful tone. "What now?"

"You did go to Vegas that weekend."

He reared back, face twisting. "Huh?"

Benny began to crack up. "We gave fake names to the girls we met. I was Baker. Snow was you."

Higgs busted a gut.

"You fucking asshole." Simmons punched Benny's arm. "What if she turns up at the base for me? Or worse, tracks me down and speaks to my girl?"

"Well, that was kind of the point." I nodded to Higgs. "After you gave this one so much shit, we decided you needed some payback."

We all began to roar with laughter. I had to bend double to stop from pissing myself. After a few seconds, even Simmon's mouth hitched up. "Pricks." He cursed under his breath. "You better make it right."

I nodded as Kitten's beautiful face flashed through my mind. "I didn't think it through. The funny thing was, she was calling me Kyle, and it got me so pissed that I had to tell her to call me Snow."

"Should've seen his face." Benny put on a sultry voice and pouted while he flicked imaginary long hair. "Why do they call you Snow?" he said breathily before laughing. "Snowy here shit himself."

"I'm sure he did," Simmons deadpanned. "Especially since we call you Snow because you've got the same name as that actor who plays him. How the fuck did you dig yourself out of that hole if you'd already told her your name was Kyle Simmons instead of Kit Stone?"

My friend stood up, put his hands on his hips, and snapped his back straight, striking the classic Superman pose. "Benny to the rescue!" He laughed and relaxed his shoulders. "Told her that we think Snowy here looks like his namesake."

Simmons's eyes bugged out. "I can't see it. You look like an ugly fuckhead to me."

Laughter filled the room again.

I thought back to that night the same way I had a thousand times while I'd been in Afghanistan. It turned out to be a pivotal moment for me. I should've shut Benny down when he opened his mouth 'cause I had to explain the truth when I saw Kitten again.

"I'm gonna tell her everything when we get back." My heart swelled as the feel of her soft skin burned through my memory. "I just hope she doesn't cut my balls off. My Kitten's got claws. But I can't have her crying 'Kyle' out when I'm inside her. Being reminded of you when we fuck is a surefire way to lose my hard-on."

Simmons grinned. "You could throw an IED at me when I'm fucking Lisa; I'd still stay hard. I'm so fucking horny that she could call me Kyle, Snow, or Martha goddamned Stewart. Couldn't give a fuck."

We all laughed again.

"I'll tell her everything," I reiterated. "She's a cool chick. She'll give me some shit, but I think she'll understand where my head was at." My voice took on an earnest tone. "Never met a chick like her. She's funny, sweet, doesn't take herself too seriously—"

"—And a stripper," Higgs interrupted.

Kyle smirked. "Don't worry, Snow. At least your mom's used to being around girls like her. Though she's probably a nun compared to the skanks you usually take home, right?"

"Could be worse," Benny added. "She could've already fucked all your brothers. Your pop will think it's Christmas when you rock up with a stripper instead of a club girl. At least he hasn't been inside this one."

The boys cracked up, letting out hoots and hollers.

"Smartass fucks," I muttered, but I didn't care. They didn't mean anything by it. They were just being assholes. I would've been saying the same shit to them if the boot was on the other foot. Giving each other shit was what we did best.

Just then, someone banged on the door. "SPC Stone," a voice called from the hall.

My heart leaped. Nobody went knocking on doors around here. They just strolled in. What the fuck was going on?

Higgs stood from his chair and swung the door open to reveal Espinoza standing just outside. He folded his arms across his chest. "Ahh. An orgy. Should've known. Get your asses to briefing room four, ladies. We're going on a little vacation. Lieutenant Hollister thinks you need a break from the base. Want you all in full tac gear. You've got five minutes."

He walked away, banging on doors as he summoned the rest of the unit.

"Fuck. What now?" Benny muttered.

Snow

"God knows." I rubbed my chin, mind ticking over all the scenarios Hollister could want us for but coming up blank. "But it doesn't look good."

Surobi was a district about fifty miles east of Kabul.

It was home to hundreds of little villages, probably due to the Kabul River that ran through the district. It was greener than I imagined, again, no doubt because of the river.

In our briefing back at Eggers, Hollister told us that the people who resided there weren't fond of U.S. soldiers or peacekeeping forces. He explained that in 1998 U.S. Missiles leveled the Khalid Bin Whalid terrorist training camp in retaliation for the U.S. Embassy bombings that occurred earlier that same year.

The place was a hotbed of insurgents with a score to settle, and the area was rumored to house more than one man who'd been placed on Interpol's most-wanted list.

U.S. Marines had discovered a stash of IEDs that had been buried in the floor of a house in one of the villages. We'd been sent in to neutralize them.

The area bustled with activity. We stopped our vehicle next to some Humvees parked in front of a building. The village was everything you'd expect. Dusty, sand-colored, and traditional.

My eyes narrowed on a group of Marines. Their weapons were drawn as they yelled at a group of civilians to stay back from the hut.

The air felt full of underlying aggression that sank into my skin, immediately putting me on edge. I caught the eye of a bearded man in robes. He stood at the edge of the crowd. His eyes hardened as they caught mine, hatred flickering across his features as he sneered at me.

I sneered back at the ungrateful fucker. We were here to stop the village from being leveled. All he wanted was to throw attitude. It wouldn't be a shocker if he was one of the T-Man who put the explosives there. Fucking scum.

The gut churn began. It seemed to affect me a lot more these days. I'd started to suspect it was more than the heat getting to me, but I didn't care to think about it too much. I'd just have to deal with whatever it was, so what was the point?

We exited the Buffalo and waited for the others to pull up behind us in another Buffalo and two Humvees. We didn't have to carry light because we could drive directly to the target. We also had the robot on board. That made me feel better by miles. It was comforting to know we had all we needed, especially as we often had to cart handheld stuff through small spaces.

I fucking loved that Buffalo. Fuck, it made me feel safer.

Vehicle doors slammed as our unit jumped out of the transports, gathering around Hollister, who gave orders to Espinoza. The sergeant moved toward the door of the house—which was actually more like a hut—that the Marines appeared to be protecting.

"Okay, boys," Hollister began. "First, imaging. The men who found the IEDs have already mapped out the floor areas that they think are safe, but they ain't EOD, so I want it double-checked before I send Rosita in."

Calls of 'yes, sir' went up, and we got to work.

The imaging equipment and the robot were unloaded first, and we began to set up. The robot could easily fit through the door of the hut, meaning we wouldn't even have to enter unless there was an urgent need.

Our robot—otherwise known as Rosita—was our eyes and often our hands. If any devices were deemed a risk, we could guide Rosita using a control pad to place them in a chamber and blow them up remotely. A few would be kept to take back to base for investigation, but the rest would go *boom*.

Within an hour, we'd determined they were duds. The devices were half-made and didn't contain all the necessary components to explode. There were different types of IEDs, but they needed a power supply–or charge–to get heat into it, or else they couldn't detonate. The charges on the IEDs in the ground had yet to be fitted.

"Cheng and CJ. Suit up," Hollister ordered. "I want those devices in containers within the hour. It's karaoke night tonight, and I feel some Sinatra coming on."

Good-natured complaints and whines went up. Everyone wanted in on dealing with the IEDs.

"Now, now, girls. No need to cry," Espinoza said with a chuckle. "Everyone needs a turn at the good stuff. Snow, Benedetti, Simmons, and Higgs have been hogging all the action. Remember. Sharing's caring."

He stopped talking as one of the Marine sergeants approached. "Everything okay?" he inquired.

The Marine scraped his hand down his face, looking stressed. "Things are getting rowdy over there." He nodded toward the crowd, who were by then baying for blood. "I've got another unit en route. ETA seven minutes. Can you spare any of your guys to help us hold the line until then?"

My eyes flashed to the crowd. While we'd been working, things had gotten much more aggressive. Their shouts had turned to screams and curses, and they were actively trying to break the line to get to the team.

A cold shiver went down my spine at the thought of the Marines losing control of the villagers.

Hollister stepped forward, looking around at the boys who were waiting expectantly. His eyes darted to mine, then to a couple of the other guys. "Snow. Puck. Simmons. You're with me. The rest of you are back up. If any of these people get through, shoot them on sight."

He headed into our Humvee and grabbed a sealed weapons container before passing M4s out to us.

"Listen to your guts," Lieutenant ordered. "This ain't our day job, but we're still soldiers. You're all proficient, and I'd trust you at my six. Now get into position."

My gut leaped buoyantly as I did my weapons check and loaded up. I was comfortable with a gun in my hand. I was born for this shit.

I'd been shooting since I was five years old. My Grandpa Bandit used to take us to the woods at the back of the clubhouse for target practice. That made me the best shot in the unit, so I wasn't shocked that Hollister had picked me.

Our LT gathered us around him for a quick chat. "Don't mind saying, boys, that I've been a little tweaked since I stepped outta that Humvee," he said quietly.

I froze, remembering my gut churn from earlier.

Everything seemed to slot into place as it dawned that it seemed to come on every time I was in an uncomfortable situation. The last time being when we found that little girl. Soldiers talked about a feeling, instinctual. It could be mental or physical, like a warning. Was that my tweak sign? Jesus. It all suddenly started to make sense. It made me grateful in a way because instincts that strong were gonna come in fucking useful.

"Look out for anyone acting out of the ordinary," Hollister continued. "Humans have a pack mentality. Anyone not with the pack will be up to no good. Do not think. Shoot. Nine came out from the wire, and I want nine going back behind it. Do you copy?"

"Copy, sir," we chorused.

He nodded once. "Get into position."

We made our way over to the line of soldiers. Some stood back with their weapons pointed at the crowd as they screamed and yelled obscenities in their own language.

One of the Marines glanced at me as I got into position beside him. "TERP says that building is where the village prays. Your being in there desecrates it. That's why they're losing their shit."

I shook my head. "Crazy how they don't give a fuck about the IEDs desecrating their place of prayer, though."

"It's a war we're fighting," the Marine said outta the side of his mouth, eyes still glued to the crowd. "Maybe they believe anything that can kill us is sacred to them."

I hoisted my M4 and pointed it toward the crowd, muttering, "This is some fucked-up shit."

The Marine just smirked.

Locked and loaded, I took in the crowd of faces twisted with evil intentions, shoving at the line like crazy people.

Men, women, and children pushed against the Marines surrounding the hut, screaming in their faces. Our boys kept their cool. They were an immovable force even though they were getting jostled badly, even struck at in some cases.

A tendril of fire flickered through me. I felt my body harden, my lungs burning in response to the scene before me. *These people would stone you in the street even though you want to help them*, a small voice said in my mind. *These people blow up little girls just to prove a point.*

My jaw clenched. I was breathing shakily by then. Of course, it was the adrenaline, but also something else.

Something dark, almost primitive.

These people were almost animalistic in their aggression. Why were we here when they didn't want to be helped? We could be somewhere else, assisting in building a school for the part of the population who showed us a modicum of gratitude instead of dealing with this bullshit.

I don't know what made me glance left. Looking back later, I think I saw the flash of black in the distance that stood out among the lighter robes. I recognized the man who had sneered at me earlier. He'd changed his clothes. Now, he was dressed differently.

Initially, I thought he was moving to join in with the crowd, but there was something off about his movements. They were stiff and puppet-like.

My gut began to churn, and I knew.

Immediately, the Lieutenant's words flashed through my mind. *Anyone not with the pack will be up to no good.*

The man's movements quickened, and he began to sprint toward us.

My gut churn intensified to the point I thought I was gonna puke.

The sounds quietened. Every holler, every scream faded to silence until all I could hear was a ringing in my ears and my breath sawing in and out of my lungs.

The world around me shrank inward to a small point of tunnel vision. Until it was just him and me.

I knew he felt my stare. His head swiveled, and he glared at me. My heart's racing slowed as I watched his panicked face morph into a mask of determination.

That was when I knew.

Without a thought, I took my shot.

Lieutenant Hollister's elbows rested on the arms of his chair, fingers steepled against his chin as he thoughtfully regarded me in silence.

I shifted in my seat. Fuck, my LT made me nervous.

Turned out that if I hadn't shot that insurgent, the Marine next to me would have. He seemed to feel my reaction and quickly put two and two together. He was just about to fire, but I beat him to it.

After the shots splintered the air, all hell broke loose.

Snow

The crowd dispersed as panicked men, women, and children ran for shelter, screaming.

Within seconds, the other Marine unit rolled into the village and quickly restored order. Lieutenant and Espinoza bundled me straight into the Buffalo, got Benny to stay with me, and ordered me to remain there while they reported to Command.

You know what was funny?

I sat there, hands shaking like a big ol' leaf, thinking I'd just stepped into a big pile of shit. Benny kept trying to speak to me, make sure I was okay, but I was too far inside my head.

The incident wasn't about some heartbroken, crazy girl turning up at the barracks and giving me shit. The incident could've been deemed a war crime for all I knew.

While I sat in that Buffalo chewing my nails off and fretting that they were gonna CM me, I didn't give the man I'd shot a second thought. Everything had happened so fast. All I had was my instincts to work with.

All worry eased when Espinoza climbed inside the Buffalo wearing a shit-eating grin. He informed me that the man I'd eliminated was wearing enough explosives around his chest to wipe out that entire village and everyone in it, including us.

Turned out I'd saved everyone from a suicide bomb attack.

Since then, I'd lost count of the back slaps, the congratulations, and, in some cases, the genuine respect thrown my way.

Back at Eggers, people stared at us as we marched straight into briefing room four. They grinned, calling out congratulations. Didn't know most of them, but obviously, word traveled fast.

All in all, I felt like a fucking superstar.

The lieutenant debriefed us. Conveyed his thoughts about the incident and dismissed everyone–apart from me.

We'd been sitting silently for at least two minutes while he eye-balled the shit out of me.

"You know, Snow. My first kill was a lot like yours," Hollister declared out of nowhere, making me almost jump out of my skin. "We were sweeping a village situated between Baghdad and Karbala. Intelligence had a tip-off about a stash of IEDs hidden underground. Very much like today." His eyes glazed over as he thought back. "Two Insurgents appeared from nowhere and just started firing. God knows how I didn't get hit. Next thing I knew, I was standing over two dead men, trying not to puke." He slowly leaned forward, elbows on the desk. "How do you feel? And I don't want a generic 'fine.' Think, Snow. How do you feel," he tapped his temple twice, "in there?"

My eyebrows drew together as I thought about Hollister's question.

The fact was, I didn't feel anything. I was almost numb. There were thoughts and feelings inside, but nothing freaked me out. It felt much like another day at the office.

"At first, I freaked out," I replied. "I was stressing that you were gonna CM me. When Sarge gave me the details, and I settled, I wondered why I didn't feel more. The fact is, I'm sorry that life got lost. Nobody wants it to come to that. But for me, there was no choice."

Hollister nodded. "Sounds like it hasn't hit you, Snow. If and when it does, you knock on that door, and I'll get your head straight. I've been where you are. I can relate."

My chest warmed. "Thank you, sir."

"When we return to Kentucky, I want you to see the army psychologist. Just talk over what happened and see if he can give you any tools you can use if it starts fucking with your head. Copy?"

I almost groaned out loud. Didn't need no psych asking me about my feelings. I couldn't think of anything worse.

But Hollister needed to think I was playing along, so I kept my mouth shut and nodded.

It didn't matter, anyway, 'cause I didn't care one way or another that I'd killed that man. If it was him with the M4, he wouldn't have hesitated to blow my head off.

I was golden.

Chapter Twelve

Kitten ~ Two weeks later.

When I saw the U.S. Army postmark, I was shocked.
It was two months between letters last time. This one arrived about four weeks after the previous one. I didn't even hear the mailman come. I'd been cleaning the apartment with the music turned up loud and missed it completely.

I'd done that a lot lately, clean.

I also shopped and worked extra shifts—even doing Marco's admin occasionally, just to keep going—I hung out with Raven and the girls. We drank coffee, chatted, and laughed.

I jogged.

Went to the gym.

I went to Martha's, checked in with Ed, and flirted shamelessly with Mr. Zowalski.

One night after work, I went to the strip with the girls and saw a billboard light the night sky in bronze hues that reminded me of his eyes. It was an image of a beautiful male model. He had perfect muscles, golden skin, and cropped hair. The model reminded me so much of Snow that when my head was too crammed full of dark thoughts, I'd go and stare at it for hours.

I knew it wasn't my handsome soldier, but it still made me feel closer to him.

I did everything possible to stay busy and make time go faster so he'd return to me sooner. Over and over, I asked myself what it was about Snow that made me feel everything after one weekend of knowing him when I didn't feel much for my high school boyfriend, even after three years.

I put it down to chemistry. Me, plus him, equaled beautiful.

Every time my thoughts turned to Snow, my belly fluttered. And because I thought of him a whole damned lot, I constantly had butterflies, feelings, and emotions coursing through my bloodstream, making me feel alive, if a little on edge.

I was happy and sad and lonely and content. One minute, I had faith. The next, I was sick to my stomach at the thought of him being hurt.

So, when I saw the letter lying on my floor, boasting that distinctive postmark, my emotions got the better of me, and I almost threw up. It was unexpected, to say the least.

One minute, I stood, staring at the envelope resting on my floor. The next, I sat on my couch with my legs under me, carefully tearing it open.

I took a deep breath to calm my fluttering pulse, and I read,

Kitten.

I MISS YOU!
The mere thought of you grounds me, while the memory of you keeps me sane.

Things have gotten worse over here. Every mission is more dangerous. Not helped by the ideology that we're fighting against.

Looking back at when we first arrived here, we seemed to coast through, but now shit's gotten real. I'm on guard constantly. My days consist of looking for and disposing of IEDs while continually looking over my shoulder. I'm even on guard when I sleep.

How is that a way to live?

I dream of lying next to you, holding you, and sleeping without the sound of gunfire waking me. That's what I crave more than anything, a connection to something good, clean, and beautiful.

Anyway, there's a point to this letter.

I've good news, Kitten.

Guess What?

I'M COMING HOME!!!!

Command confirmed that we have three weeks left of our deployment, then we're home free.

Did you notice the sneaky fuckers tagged a few weeks on? LOL.

Also, they've told us not to get too comfortable. We may only be back on U.S. soil briefly before they ship us out again, but I'll worry about that when it happens.

I've got a debrief when we get back. Then I gotta get a quick visit out of the way, but I've booked my flight to LV.

I've enclosed all the details. It's during the week, so you won't be at the club. It couldn't have worked out better, baby. I haven't stopped smiling since they told us.

We're nearly there. We've almost done it. Just hold on a bit longer, Kitten. Please. I promise I'll make it worth it. I'm sorry if it's been as hard on you as it has been on me. I'll make it up to you when I see you in a few weeks.

I'm counting every second until I can touch you again. I just wanna breathe you in.

Your Idiot.
Snow.

PS Don't forget my picture.

My mouth fell open disbelievingly.
Snow was coming home!
Oh my God.
He was really coming home.
My throat thickened with emotions, and my stomach began to turn over. The letter shook almost violently because of the tremor in my hands, brought on by the excitement that started to flow through my belly.

My stare zeroed in on the date of the flight and froze. It was less than two weeks away. He'd be flying in next week. It had taken the letter ten days to arrive.

Letting out a whoop, I jumped up, punched the air, and began to dance around the room, yelling, "He's coming home. He's coming home. Thank you, God! Snow's coming home."

Chapter Thirteen

Snow

Pop sent a welcome party to collect me from the airport at Rock Springs. It consisted of Cash, Atlas, Abe, and a new guy they introduced as Colt.

I was irritated after my stopover in Denver, but at least it was one day of flying instead of a two or three-day drive. I'd arranged a quick visit 'cause if I didn't, Mom would hunt me the fuck down. It had been a minute–years– since I'd been home. Atlas would bring me back Monday morning, where I'd fly back to Denver before Vegas.

The last seven days had been filled with travel and debriefings. It had been a whirlwind of activity as we faced the challenges of unpacking the physical, mental, and emotional stuff. Exhaustion was beginning to set in.

I'd already lost a day by waiting on base to see the psych. I got the all-clear, though I knew the triggers he was trained to watch for. I told him everything he wanted to hear.

I was fine, though, not really affected at all.

As soon as I'd finished, I headed out to Nashville airport. Now, I was back in Wyoming, and all I wanted to do was get to my room and sleep. The last few months were already catching up with me, as was the jetlag. I knew I couldn't outrun it forever, but the boys had other ideas.

Cash had already messaged to tell me where they'd meet me, so I headed outside the airport toward the dead-end road, where he told me they were waiting. The gleam of sunshine bouncing off metal alerted me the boys had already arrived.

I hoisted my ruck higher across my back and shoved my shades across my eyes.

Atlas saw me first, probably helped by the eyes he seemed to have hidden in the back of his head. He raised his hand in greeting and crowed, "Yo, motherfucker!"

Every head turned toward me before hoots and hollers cut the air.

"Brought Veronica for ya, little bro," Cash called out through the noise. "She needs a good riding. It's been a while. Dad reckoned you'd wanna leave some cobwebs in the wind."

A slow grin spread across my face as the lump in my gut shifted.

My bike. Thank God. Dad was right; Veronica *would* help me blow away the cobwebs. We called our bikes after pin-up girls. Lana, Marilyn, Bettie, Jayne. Some were more modern, like Megan and Scarlett. Mine was Veronica Lake, who was my top jack-off material growing up. Fucking beautiful, and thinking about it, a lot like Kitten. Seemed I had a type.

My step held a swagger as I approached the crowd of brothers still making a goddamned racket.

First, I greeted Atlas. He pulled me in for a manly hug and gave me a resounding clap on the back. "Good to see you looking well, Kit," he murmured as he curled his giant palm around my nape. "We've seen the news. Looks sketchy as fuck over there."

"Ain't so bad," I told him in a low voice. "Got good buds, which helps."

"Well, you know how I feel about brotherhood." He grinned.

Arms clamped around my waist from behind, and suddenly, I was airborne, being shaken around. "Missed you, shit face," Cash said thickly. "Got nobody to beat on when you're off playin' soldier." He dropped me back on my feet. "Though you're turnin' into one big fucker. Your ass will be fatter than Atlas's soon."

I turned and punched him on the arm playfully. "All muscle, Cashy boy. Jealousy doesn't suit you."

More laughter rose up before my eyes landed on Abe.

Jesus, I'd missed him. Sometimes, I felt closer to him than my own pop. Abe was my go-to for advice and all the serious shit. There was nobody on this Earth I trusted more. His ol' lady, Iris, was also like a second mom.

A lump formed in my throat as I watched his stare flick over me, taking stock, making sure I didn't seem any worse for wear. His eyes rested on mine and bored into my soul.

I didn't miss his slight wince.

God only knew what he saw, but he didn't like it. Nobody would've guessed because he stepped forward and pulled me into a tight embrace. "You were supposed to come home months ago, you little fuck. Iris has been going up the goddamned wall worrying about you. She made me come and meet you to make sure you didn't fuck off somewhere else again."

I plastered a cocky expression on my face. "Vegas called, Abe. If Iris don't put out for me, I gotta get my tail elsewhere."

His eyes narrowed. "Goddamned prick."

More laughter sounded.

My stare slid to a pretty fucker who sat astride a fucking sweet ride. It had been customed in a dark, racing green color that lit up as the sun hit it. I gave him a chin-lift. "Kit," I told him.

He smiled, giving me a loose salute. "Good to meet you. I'm Colt."

I wasn't into guys, but he'd probably be my type if I was. He was tall and good-looking, with dark blonde hair and piercing blue eyes. I couldn't see exactly how tall he was, but he must've been well over six feet and was built, too.

I checked out his cut. "Not prospecting?"

"Passed three months ago. Did a ten-month stint before Prez put me outta my misery."

Atlas nodded toward Colt. "He's good with a computer. Once he showed us he could handle himself, Prez patched him straight in. He's been a big help to the club. A good brother by all accounts."

Colt's back remained ramrod straight, stare never leaving mine. I'd seen that stance before, many fucking times. "You serve?" I asked.

He jerked a nod. "Enlisted and did boot camp before completing OCS at Fort Benning. Transferred into intelligence but didn't like all the red tape I had to cut through. I can do more for my country going rogue."

Impressive. "Well, I'm glad to know you, Colt."

He gave me a respectful nod. "Ditto."

The sun's reflection hitting black metal caught my eye. I turned, all exhaustion fading away as I took in the other woman in my life.

Veronica was as beautiful as her namesake.

My Harley Dyna Glide was the first big purchase I'd ever made, and the best. I loved her, partly because I brought her with the inheritance Bandit left me. Handing the cash over for her made my eyes water at the time, but she was a good investment.

I was yet to customize her. But she was still sexy as fuck, all shiny black bodywork and silver pipes. She gave me a hard-on just sitting there looking gorgeous.

Atlas handed me my helmet. "Ready to ride, soldier?"

Snow

I jerked a chin lift and approached my bike. Throwing my leg over, I put on my helmet and started her up before nearly coming in my pants at the unmistakable pop-popping that only a Harley could emit. We got into formation. Atlas first, followed by Cash, Abe, Colt, and me. Then, with a twirl of Atlas's finger, we were off.

A smile as big as Texas spread across my face as we turned onto the main highway, making our way onto the long road back to Hambleton. My heart swelled as I thought of where we were heading.

It was weird. I'd avoided Hambleton like the plague since I'd enlisted. Still, as I headed Veronica toward the town I grew up in, with the smell of leather and exhaust fumes permeating my senses, there was only one thing on my mind.

There's no place like home.

Mom, Pop, and Iris were waiting outside the clubhouse. I'd hardly had a chance to kick on the stand before the women flew at me.

"I'm so happy you're home, Kit," Mom murmured into my shoulder, arms snaking tight around my neck. "I've been so worried about you."

I swallowed hard at the pure relief in her tone, suddenly feeling like the biggest asshole in the world. I should've come home sooner. I hadn't been fair to her and hadn't been a good son lately.

Mom pulled back and beamed a smile before it turned into a scowl. Reaching out and cuffing me hard around the ear. "You little shit," she snapped. "I've been going mad with worry about you. I thought you'd at least come home before you deployed, but your mother's not good enough. You'd rather live it up in Vegas." Her hand reached out again, clipping the back of my head. "One phone call a week isn't enough, especially when you're in a war zone."

I rubbed at the spot she caught me. "Jesus, Ma," I grumbled. "No need to smack the shit outta me."

"I'll kick your scrawny little ass if you do that to me again. I brought you into this world. Don't think I can't take you out of it, too."

I winced 'cause I knew she meant every word.

"Let him get off his bike before you beat his ass, Dell." A hand came out, grabbed my chin, and pulled me around. "How can you get more handsome every time I see you?" Iris croaked. "I've missed you all the world, my beautiful boy."

My throat heated as her eyes flickered over my face, taking stock of what she saw. Her mouth hitched into a bright smile. "You're older, Kit. Jesus. You went away a boy, but you're a man now."

My eyes misted up, and I croaked, "I guess that's what the military does, Ris."

She nodded earnestly. "Are you okay, son?"

I gave her a nod and a smile, trying to tamp down the sudden rush of emotions flooding my bloodstream. Love, fear, guilt, and hundreds more that I couldn't explain all came back, and it was overwhelming.

Big arms came at me from the side, thick fingers curling around my shoulders. The scent of motor oil and spicy cologne swirled all around me. I knew that smell. It hadn't changed for as long as I could remember.

John 'Dagger' Stone.

My pop pulled me into his immovable rock of a chest. "Good to see ya, son." His voice, still the same as I remembered, was deep, gravelly, and profound.

More emotion hit me from all sides, and I shuddered.

"Need me to get you out of here?" Dad asked in a low voice.

I nodded.

Next thing I knew, I'd been half pulled off my bike. "Taking Kit to church," Pop called. "Do not disturb."

"That fucker needs a come to Jesus moment," I heard Cash shout as I straightened and headed toward the main doors of the clubhouse.

Laugher rose through the lot.

"Abe," Dad bellowed, his arm still heavy across my shoulder.

"Right behind you," he shouted as Dad grabbed the door, ushering me inside.

"Prospect," Atlas yelled as the door closed behind us. "Get Kit's shit in his room. Now!"

The air of the clubhouse felt cool against my skin as we walked through the bar. I kept my head down, avoiding all eye contact as we swept through. Luckily, it was Friday morning. Most of the brothers would've been working or out doing jobs for the club, so at least I didn't walk into a raging party.

My knees turned to mush as we headed down the corridor toward Church. Fuck knows what was happening to me. All my emotions came from nowhere and hit me like a freight train. My skin felt itchy and hot, and stabs of nausea clenched through my gut.

"Fuck," I hissed as Dad shut the door to church with a thud.

"Sit down, Son," Dad ordered. "It'll pass soon."

I slumped in a chair, squeezing my eyes shut.

"I'll go get him a whisky," Abe muttered. "He's having a surge."

I opened one eye and squinted, watching Abe disappear from the room. "What the fuck's that?"

Dad's concerned stare swept over my face. "It's what me and my military brothers used to call that feeling you get when you're overwhelmed with all the shit you've pushed down for months. Did your Ma set you off? I told her to give you space. You've just got back from a fucking warzone."

I took a minute to do some breathing exercises. Eventually, my heart rate slowed, and I turned to Dad. "Maybe. Probably more Iris. And it wasn't strictly a warzone. Just seemed like it sometimes."

"Makes sense that the heart of the club makes yours beat faster." Dad shook his head, but I could tell he wasn't pissed with Iris. More exasperated.

I dipped my chin. "She didn't know, and she means well."

"Yup. That's why I'm not gonna say a fucking word. And really, ya little shit, you brought it on yourself. Staying away for so long has caused this. Your mom and Iris have been beside 'emselves. Your ma has hardly slept for months. She's been a fucking nightmare to live with."

Abe appeared at the door. "Here," he muttered. "Get that down, ya. It's your dad's top-shelf shit."

"Thanks." I watched as he closed the door and sat before I took a big sip of amber liquid. My shoulders slumped as the welcome burn worked its way down my throat.

I was used to alcohol. I had my first beer at fifteen. Dad believed that if we were gonna drink, he'd rather control it. He didn't want us out in the woods somewhere acting stupid.

That meant we built up tolerance slowly over time, so when we hit twenty-one, we were already used to it. It was like Pop said, kids in France drank wine at the dinner table. The legal drinking age in European countries was around eighteen. He'd rather we did it safely and under supervision, especially around an MC.

"Better?" Abe demanded in a tight voice.

"Yeah." I jerked a nod. "I'm good. It's passed."

"You got a psych on base?"

My gut clenched again. "Yeah. My lieutenant made me see him before I left Fort Campbell. He signed me off as fit duty after ten minutes in his office. He ain't concerned. I just think I got overwhelmed, like Pop said."

"A ten-minute briefing don't tell him shit," Dad snapped.

"Pop. I'm fine," I insisted. "Had a hard deployment, is all. I just need to chill, sleep, and catch up with everyone. I'm still acclimatizing, too. I've come from a different world. Everything here seems so fucking jarring since I've been back."

Abe studied me closely. "Jarring in what way?"

"I think it's the difference in noises and environment. It's like the layers of sounds that usually blend together don't at the moment. Everything's heightened. Then Iris spoke to me, and I got over-emotional."

Dad nodded. "Yeah. I get that. It's your body standing down. You've probably been on edge for the last few months. Maybe you retuned your brain to shut down so you could cope better over there, but now you're back, you're getting a delayed reaction." He leaned forward, eyes taking me in. "The boys have planned a bash for you tonight. You gonna be okay with it? If it's too much, we'll cancel and have a quiet one."

My face twisted, my annoyance no doubt written all over it. "Why have they done that? I'm not a member."

"Returning hero." Dad grinned, puffing his chest out slightly. "My son, the bomb squad tech, coming home from Afghanistan. A shindig is the least we can do. Anyway, you're gonna be a member soon, right? When you come out?"

Shit.

"Yeah. When I come out." I didn't have the heart to tell him that wouldn't be for a fucking long time.

He'd been so good with me and seemed to relate to what I was dealing with. I'd never had that from Pop before. I kinda wanted to bask in his pride while I could, seeing it was the first time it had happened to me and would probably be the last.

"A party sounds good." I flashed a grin. "My room still free? Noticed some new faces."

Dad's eyes narrowed. "Your room will always be your room, Kit. You can get that shit outta your head for a start. Your place with us is guaranteed whether you're a member or not. You're more than that, anyway. You're family."

A lump formed in my throat. "Thanks, Pop."

He stared at me for a few seconds. It reminded me of Hollister and how his eyes bored into me like he could see inside my head. It was unnerving to the point where I needed to get outta there.

"I'll go get some shuteye," I said, ignoring the weird tension in my stomach. Both Pop and Abe were eyeballing me by then, and I didn't like it one bit.

Dad got up from his chair and clapped me on the back. "Go and rest, Son. We'll talk later."

"Okay."

I went through the door, suddenly desperate to escape their all-seeing stares. I couldn't get away with shit when I was young. These two could tell I'd been up to no good with one glance.

But I wasn't a kid anymore, and I'd done nothing wrong, so why were my guts bouncing and my lungs heavy? Maybe Pop was right. It could be I was having some kind of delayed reaction.

Or maybe people just needed to back the hell off my ass and let me rest up for a while. I'd been on the move since we got on the plane back to the U.S. Travel, constant debriefs, jetlag, psych appointments, and more travel. It had all fucked with me.

I just needed a bit of rest and recuperation.

I'd be fine.

Snow

Bang, Bang, Bang.

I sat bolt upright in bed, disorientated and half asleep. "Ben," I called out. "Is that fucking Espinoza?"

Silence.

"Benny. Wake the hell up," I croaked. "I think Sarge is hammering on the door.

My eyes began to adjust to the pitch black. I saw my CHU exactly as it always looked. Our tiny TV sat precariously on top of the brightly colored plastic drawers. Our photos from home were stuck to the walls in the same place they always were.

A soft groan sounded from Benny.

"Get up, bro," I said. "An IED must've gone off outside the wire. Gotta get moving, or Hollister will be on our asses."

Another groan sounded.

Bang, bang, bang. "Snow, you there? Snow!"

The room began to spin, and a sharp pain sliced behind my eyes. "Jesus," I murmured, burying my head in my hands. "What the fuck?"

"Kit!" a deep voice sounded. "Get the fuck up. The boys are starting to arrive. Everyone's asking for you."

I raised my head and looked around the room. My entire body began to jerk involuntarily. Every nerve ending tingled, making my hands numb. That was when I realized I wasn't in my CHU. I was in my room at the clubhouse.

I swallowed down the bile that rose through my throat.

Jesus, I could've sworn—

"Kit!" I recognized the voice as Atlas's. "Wake up!"

I looked around, confused to my core. I was sure I'd heard Benny's groan, but I couldn't have done. I was alone.

"Kit!"

Fuck, Atlas was getting pissed. "Come in," I croaked, still woozy as hell.

The door cracked open, light flooding the room. "Wake up, sleeping fuckin' beauty. We got bikers, strippers, and whores congregating. You've had eight hours. Rise and goddamned shine. We've got plans for you, motherfucker."

I leaned over to my nightstand and clicked on my lamp. Immediately, my head started thumping. I rubbed my temples. "Fuck," I groaned.

Atlas must've caught on that something was wrong because he approached. "You okay?"

"Head hurts," I muttered.

"Best you start fucking drinking then. There's nothin' like a cold one to wash away the aches and pains." He clapped his hands together twice. "Chop fuckin' chop. We can't have a party without the guest of honor."

He laughed at my wince. "Jesus. It's like you turned into a senior overnight. Get your ass outta that bed."

"Okay," I acquiesced. "Gimme twenty. I need to wash up and brush my teeth."

"Twenty minutes?" he grumbled. "What are you, a goddamn chick? Need time to put your lippy on? Freshen up ya vagina? Who the fuck needs twenty minutes?"

I pressed my lips together to stop myself from launching at the fucking asshole while he continued to whine like a goddamned kid. Going on, and on, and on.

My pulse kicked up a notch while a familiar burn swept through my gut. I couldn't stop myself. "Atlas!" I snapped. "Get the fuck out of my room. I told ya. Twenty fucking minutes. Are you goddamned simple?" My hands clenched into fists, and I felt a muscle in my jaw tic.

Atlas's head reared back. He cocked his eyebrow as if he couldn't believe how I'd just talked smack to him. "Come again?" he said, tone like steel.

My eyes held his. "Get the fuck out," I ordered.

Snow

His eyes narrowed on mine, and he slowly crossed his massive arms. He looked like a mountain standing there, eyes burning through me. "Tell ya what, Kit. I'm gonna be generous tonight. I'll let that one slide on account of you just gettin' back from deployment. No doubt you're feelin' outta sorts." He took a step forward, his voice lowering threateningly. "But if you ever speak to me like that again, ya little cunt, I'll knock you from one side of this clubhouse to the other. Do you fucking get me?"

I glared, holding his stare, but that fucker didn't back down. Eye to eye, I didn't even blink, and then, in an instant, the fire in my belly waned. My shoulders slumped, and I heaved out a sigh. "Fuck, man. I'm sorry. You're right. I'm feeling outta sorts. My head's all over the place." I thrust a hand through my hair.

Atlas's face lost some of its hardness, and he nodded. "It's okay. Maybe I came on too strong. Just glad to see you back, is all."

I threw the covers back and swung my legs out of bed. "I'm getting up. Gonna jump in the shower quickly. I'll be out soon." I stood and looked at Atlas again. "I apologize."

A grin spread across his face, and he clapped my shoulder. "No harm, no foul. You've grown up. Thought you were gonna jump outta your pit and clock me for a minute. Three years ago, you would've shit your tighty whities if I gave you the death glare." He chuckled. "We'll make a biker outta you yet, Kit Stone."

Making my way to my bathroom, I almost grimaced. *Don't fucking bet on it.*

Beer bottle in hand, I leaned back on the couch and took everything in.

The party was in full swing. Bodies danced and threw themselves around to House of Pain's 'Jump Around.' The place was packed. Had to be a couple of hundred here, at least. The funny thing was, I hardly knew any of them.

I took a long pull of beer, ignoring the dark cloud swirling.

Usually, I loved this song, but the pulsing screech that ran through it hurt my head. Cash danced with some chick he'd invited, probably one of his townie regulars. Atlas sat at the bar deep in convo with Pop. Bowie, well, I hadn't seen him at all. Apparently, he was with Samantha. She wasn't much of a party girl. In a way, I always felt she looked down her nose at us, but Bowie didn't seem to notice. Either that, or he didn't care.

The image of the morning sun's reflection bouncing off soft blonde hair filtered through my mind. I swore I could almost detect the scent of peaches in the air. I checked my watch, wondering what Kitten would be doing now. She'd probably be on stage. My throat went tight at that thought. A stab of coldness made my gut sting. Weird, I wasn't a jealous guy. Kitten stripping had never bothered me before. When she danced, it was just character, a body. It was who she was inside that mattered. That side of her belonged to me.

Still, it seemed to darken my mood.

The atmosphere in the bar throbbed in time with the bass. The screeching background lyrics of the song cut through my skull. My gut constricted with the grating cold irritation that seemed to burrow deep down. Everything pissed me off.

My jaw clenched. Fuck, it was too hot in here. I needed air.

I rose from the couch, clenching my hands as I turned for the door. My knees liquified, and I almost stumbled as I went.

Snow

A touch stopped me in my tracks. Stiff, cold fingers pressed into my back almost painfully. Hands snaked around my waist from behind, leaving a trail of ice in their wake while a woman's pitchy voice whined. "Where are you going? Want some company, hero?"

My back snapped straight, and I whirled around.

The woman was tall, rail thin, with dyed black hair, and skanky. My blood boiled as I glared down where her fingers met my torso. "The fuck you say, bitch?"

She stepped forward and pressed her body into mine.

Nausea rolled through my stomach, my body recoiling like a snake. "Fuck off," I snapped, getting in her face. "The fuck you touching? Did I say you could put your cunt hands on me?"

Her eyes grew, and she began to stutter, "Umm. Err."

A fire burned my gut as I angled my face closer to hers and bellowed, "I asked you a question. Did I say you could put your hands on me?" I sneered in her face. "I ain't no biker. I don't go with whores."

Tears filled her eyes.

"Kit, brother," a low voice murmured from beside me. "That's Louanna. She's okay. She's just doing her job, man." A strong hand curled around my neck and pulled my face around. "You have to calm the fuck down, Kit. Everyone's watching."

I glanced up and froze.

In my rage, I hadn't even noticed the music being turned down. Every eye in the place was on me, including Pop and Atlas.

I sucked in a breath, then released it, trying to tamp down the tension that tightened every muscle. My jaw ached with discomfort. It was so tight.

I pulled in another deep breath through my nose that time. My nostrils must've flared because the woman's face blanched. That was when I realized she was scared half to death.

"Kit, brother. Take a step back," Cash ordered under his breath.

My stomach dropped. My shoulders relaxed as the flames roaring inside me snuffed out. "Ain't gonna hurt you," I croaked. "I'd never do that." I moved forward to grab her arm, make her see she didn't need to fear me, but she shrank back.

"Kit." Dad appeared in my line of sight as he walked up behind the girl toward me. "Let's get outside, Son. Get some air." He turned toward the bar and bellowed, "Come on, you nosy-assed pricks. Thought this was a party."

Loud shouts echoed through the room as the music turned louder once again. A new song played, but I couldn't tell what it was. I'd retreated too deep inside my own head.

"Come on," Dad said with a low growl. "You need fresh air."

I nodded as he shuffled me outside.

What the fuck had just happened?

I'd heard of zoning out before, heard soldiers talking about it all the time, but I couldn't say that was what happened. I knew where I was and what I was doing. I just felt so fucking displaced. Like I was out of tune with the world around me. That girl just touching me made me itchy and sore. All my senses heightened to the point of pain.

Jesus, I needed to chill out, or else I'd drive myself crazy.

As soon as the fresh air hit me, my chest loosened. The invisible string that pulled my spine taut unraveled, and my torso slumped.

My mind immediately went to the girl I'd treated terribly, and my pang went through me. "I need to apologize to that chick, Pop. What was her name?"

Dad grabbed me by the nape, guiding me toward a picnic bench down the side of the clubhouse. "She can

Snow

wait, Son. Louanne's been here a year now. She's seen a lot more fistfights and fuckery than the average man. Talk to her tomorrow. I'll send your ma to 'Blooms' to get you some flowers for her. She'll like that."

I sat my ass up on the bench and planted my feet on the attached wooden seat. "I just lost my head for a minute. It all got too much."

"Told ya, Kit. It's the surge," Dad pointed out, sitting beside me. "You've come back from a place where you've had to hold everything in. You've been consistently on edge for months. I guess you've hardly slept, either. Plus, you've needed to keep it together, especially in your role, or else you'll blow every fucker up, including yourself. It's your body's way of settling back down. We should'a left you in bed. I told Atlas it was too much, but you know these boys. Any excuse for a party."

"I am tired," I admitted, digging the heel of my palm into my eye. "Slept more today than I have in the last week. Even woke up exhausted and disorientated. Couldn't seem to pull myself around after that." I grimaced. "Even gave Atlas some lip."

Dad threw his head back and laughed. "About time someone did. Since the fucker made SAA, he thinks he's the big man. At's a hardass, but he cares about the club and everyone in it. Which is why I know he won't take it to heart. The man knows where you've been, Kit. We all do."

What Pop said made perfect sense.

It stood to reason that I'd have to adjust, the same way it took me a while to settle in when we first arrived at Camp Eggers. Afghanistan wasn't easy to deal with, and Dad was right when he said I lived on a knife edge all the time I was there. That was precisely how I felt then and now.

He was right. I just needed time and a fuck load of sleep.

Footsteps alerted me to someone approaching. I looked up to see Abe moving toward us. "Y'alright?" he drawled.

"He's okay," Pop replied. "Louanna pissed him off. Should'a warned her Kit doesn't go there with the whores. She got handsy, and he overreacted."

Abe gestured at me to give him room. He plonked down next to me when I shuffled my ass over. "You need sleep, Kit," he said quietly.

"That's what Pop said. I just feel fucking awful now that I scared that girl."

Abe deadpanned. "Jesus. She fucks bikers for a living. I think she's seen worse than you getting your panties in a bunch. Louanna's okay, but you know how bitchy those girls get. She'll live."

Dad laughed. "You've been away too long, boy. You forgot what those club girls can be like. If it wasn't for your ma ruling them with an iron fist, I think they'd run circles around us."

He was right. I had two days here. I'd catch up with Louanne and apologize. Right then, though, I needed to sleep.

I hauled to my feet before jumping down from the wooden seat. "Turning in," I muttered.

"I'll make sure your mom and Ris tell the others to leave you alone," Abe told me. "Sleep until you wake up by yourself. You'll feel better. I guarantee it."

I turned to face them. "Thank you."

Pop grinned at me.

Abe stared into my face again like he was looking for a sign. Eventually, he relaxed and shrugged a shoulder. "Nite, Kit."

I turned back toward the clubhouse, deep in thought.

Dad had been great with all this. Real support. He'd always run the club in some capacity. He was VP before Bandit died, then he took the reins. Sometimes, I forgot he was military, too. He'd probably experienced everything I was going through and more.

A warmth spread through me. It was nice to have something in common with Pop. Usually, he was all about Cash and Bowie. Maybe I'd catch up with him the next day and talk about soldier shit.

For now, I just needed to sleep.

Chapter Fourteen

Kitten

My hands had been shaking all day.
I'd almost crashed my car on the way to Harry Reid. I was a bag of nerves.

It was weird. I'd been looking forward to seeing him for so long. Now the day had arrived, I didn't know what to do with myself. My apartment was spotless, my closet reorganized, and my car was clean inside and out—for a change.

I'd even helped out the lawyer who worked for Uncle Hustle's MC. His paralegal was on maternity leave, so I stepped in. The Three Kings MC kept him busy, so I had regular work, which helped my Harvard fund considerably. Plus, I found the law surprisingly fascinating.

Today, I'd gotten a wax. I'd had my hair done and bought new bedsheets and enough food and drink to keep us going for a week. We wouldn't need to leave my apartment if we didn't want to.

Now I just needed Snow.

I hadn't heard from him since his last letter. There was no way to contact him, so I had to trust he'd be there and hadn't gotten cold feet. Maybe he'd been stressed too, in case I didn't show, but he needn't have worried. The thought never entered my head, not once.

I'd gotten to Harry Reid early. I was so paranoid I'd somehow miss him. I found the gate he was due to arrive at, claimed an empty chair, and sat, waiting. Looking at my watch, I saw it was 10:02 A.M. Okay, about forty minutes to wait.

My stomach was in knots, my palms a sticky mess. I worried that the sweat patches I suspected had formed under my arms would ruin all my primping and grooming work. Jesus. I needed to calm down.

I looked at my watch. 10.10. Eight minutes? Jesus, time seemed to crawl along. My stomach swirled like I was going to be sick. I rose to my feet and went to the ladies' restroom. I'd pee and splash some water on my face to try and calm the hell down.

When I finished, I went back to my seat. 10. 21. I could play Candy Crush for a while and kill some time. I pulled my cell phone out and started tapping. That lasted for about six minutes. I was so preoccupied I lost my level and had to wait for new lives.

The information board had his fight number up already and his ETA. It looked like his flight was running on time.

I checked my emails quickly and smiled to see one from Sophie. I'd told her all about Snow on our weekly two-hour phone call. She was busy at med school, and I was busy with everything else, but we always found the time to connect. She told me to be careful, but if I was sure, to go for it.

I chewed my lip nervously as a dark feeling crept through my stomach.

What if this was a massive mistake? I'd heard about things like this all the time. Whirlwind romances with people you meet on vacation. Did they ever work out? Once real life and its tedium set in, was it ever the same?

God, please stop my hands from shaking.

Snow

I checked the time. 10.38. My eyes flew up to the information board.

My heart leaped when I saw his flight landing. Oh my God. Snow was in Vegas. Well, if he was even on the flight.

I rose from the chair to get a better view of the passengers departing. It took about ten more minutes for people to start trickling through.

I held my breath, studying every person who came through departures, but there was no sign of him. I checked my watch. 10.50. He should've been through.

For the first time since he left me standing in the same goddamned airport four months ago, I began to doubt Snow. Had I been a fool? Had he played me all along?

A lump formed in my throat. Our connection had seemed so genuine, so special. Why did Snow ask me to wait if he wasn't coming back? He'd ended it and walked away. I'd just wanted to wish him luck the night I came to the airport with Lee and the guys. I wasn't angling for anything. I just wanted him to understand that even though we'd hardly spent any time together, he'd impacted my life and made it beautiful, even if it was only for a few hours.

I wanted him to know that he'd made a difference to me before he left.

My watch told me it was 11.03. Snow's fight landed nearly half an hour ago.

Tears sprang into my eyes.

He didn't come.

Fuck.

Blindly, I turned away just as my heart fractured. I almost heard the crack when it split in two. All those plans, all my preparation, all those dreams for nothing. Maybe he'd been stringing me along since that first letter. Snow probably had a girl in every city he visited. Asshole.

My feet began to drag toward the main doors. I needed to get out of this goddamned airport before I threw up. I didn't know whether to burst into tears or punch something.

That was when I heard a shout.

I froze and slowly turned. My breath hitched as I saw a flash of blue moving through the perspex tunnel leading to the arrivals lounge. I watched, still holding my breath, hoping, waiting. "Come on. Come on," I chanted, eyes glued to the tunnel. Suddenly, Snow was there. He burst into the lounge, sprinting toward me.

My shoulders slumped, and I began to laugh hysterically. My breath came out in heavy pants where I'd previously held it for so long. Jesus, this boy was gonna give me a stroke.

He saw me and immediately slowed, his feet dragging as his eyes swept over me from top to bottom. "Jesus fuck!" he yelled. "You're so fucking beautiful, Kitten." A smile conveying pure joy spread across his face, and my heart fluttered.

Tears sprang up again, but not the distraught ones from a minute before. I bounced lightly on my toes before I began walking on what seemed like air toward him. I drank him in. Snow looked the same, if slightly bulkier and more tanned.

His beauty, though. That still gave me butterflies.

My steps sped up until I was running toward him. I saw him go back on one foot to brace as I leaped, and he caught me in his arms. My legs wrapped around his hips. I buried my face in his throat, breathing him in. He smelled the same. Fresh, with a hint of sandalwood.

"I'm sorry. Fucking security thought I looked like some asshole with an alert out on him. I've argued that I'm not the man they're after for the last twenty minutes." He buried his face in my hair and breathed me in exactly the same way I'd just done to him. "Peaches," he said huskily. "You smell like peaches and sunshine."

Snow

My throat constricted.

"Pull back, Kitten. Let me see my girl."

I went to jump down, but he grabbed my thighs and held them in place. "You're not going nowhere. Pull back."

I leaned back, and we stared at each other for a minute. His features softened as he took in every inch of my face. "I'd sometimes wonder if I dreamed you up, baby. I used to think of you and wonder if my brain was playing tricks on me because nobody could be so breathtakingly pretty. I gotta say. You're even more stunning than I remember."

My heart swelled. "Welcome home, Snow." I brushed a hand across his cheek. "I've missed you."

He leaned forward and kissed the tip of my nose. "I'm desperate for you, Kitten. Let's go home." He started to move toward the exit, still carrying me. As he walked us through Harry Reid airport, people stared at our bodies fusing together. Some of them smiled at us. The more cynical ones rolled their eyes.

I didn't care.

My soldier was back.

"Up, Kitten," he ordered as he pressed the key fob. "I want you in my arms."

A bubble of laughter rose through my throat. "Can't you wait until we get to the apartment?"

"I've waited four months for you, baby girl. Ain't waitin' a second longer." He held his arms out, and I leaped up, sliding my legs around his waist. "Kiss me," he demanded.

My body sank into his, and I pressed our lips together. His tongue darted out and lapped against mine.

"Fuck," he muttered, pulling back. "Gonna fucking come."

I giggled. "We can't have that, honey. I've got the biggest box of condoms you've ever seen. I want to make a dent in them."

He walked through the underground car park toward the elevators, which took us straight to the apartments. "Don't worry." He nuzzled my cheek. "It's been a long time. Plenty stored up."

I cocked my head questioningly. "How long?"

"'Bout a year," he told me with all the nonchalance in the world.

Wow. "Really?"

He threw me a wicked grin as he reached out with one hand and punched the button for the elevator. "What do you think I am? A fuckboy?"

"No." My eyes searched his as he carried me into the elevator. "I didn't think it would've been so long for you, though." The doors closed behind us with a *whoosh*, and I pressed the number for my floor.

"Had a medical when I got back from deployment, Kitten. A clean bill of health. Had another clean bill of health twelve months before. The only woman I've kissed in the last year has been you. You're safe with me, baby. I'd never put you at risk. You know that, right?"

Tears sprang to my eyes again while my heart pitter-pattered.

Never before had anyone made me feel more cared for than Snow. How could a man who'd spent mere hours by my side make me feel so utterly cherished?

It was a profound thing for me to feel protected. Probably because it hadn't been that way for me much throughout my life. I knew I had support from my friends, Hustle, and even Marco. My boss cared for me, but more in the way a businessman protected his commodities.

Snow

But with Snow, it was evident in how he automatically walked on the side of the street nearest the road. In how he held me a little closer if a sketchy-looking dude walked past us. It was in the way he went to the pits of hell to fight for a cause he believed in.

I think that facet of him was ingrained in his DNA, and my heart told me I liked it a whole lot.

The elevator doors opened on my floor, and we were on the move again. Snow carried me down the hall to my apartment, whipped the keys from my hand, and swung open the door.

"Lemons," he muttered as he walked us inside, slamming the door closed with his foot.

"I've been cleaning a lot lately." I stared at him. "I miss you so much. I need to find things to do to keep myself busy."

His eyebrows slashed together. "Baby. I'm sorry—"

I cupped his face, covering his mouth with the pad of my thumb. "—Shh. Don't ever be sorry, honey. It's who you are. I wouldn't change a thing."

He sucked my thumb into his mouth, and my pussy clenched. "You keep talking like that, Kitten, and I'm never gonna let you go."

I gave him a devilish smirk. "Well, Snow. You better hold on tight, then."

In an instant, my back was pressed against the wall.

He stared at me. His mouth lowered to mine, and he kissed me, his body sinking deadweight against my torso. His weight held my body up, allowing him to reach behind his head and pull off his tee. "Arms up," he demanded.

I raised them slowly, giving him a show before leaning forward and touching my mouth to his.

He ripped my top off, threw it behind him, and brought his face close to mine. "Wanna breathe you in, baby girl, right down to my soul." He leaned in and sucked my bottom lip into his mouth.

A bolt of electricity shot through my pussy, and I moaned.

His hand skated over my skin to unhook my bra before he tossed it in the same direction as our tees. Golden eyes never left mine, not for a second. They burned into me until I could see everything I felt mirrored in his gaze.

Something inside my chest fluttered.

This was deep and meaningful. Nothing like the fumbling ministrations of my first time. It was sensual and intimate. By looking into my eyes, I knew Snow wanted us to connect on a deeper level, and it made my heart sing.

Suddenly, we were on the move again, that time toward my bedroom.

"My fingers are gonna touch every inch of your skin, Kitty. Then I'm gonna touch you again but with my tongue. Gonna keep the memory of you tucked away somewhere deep, just for me. I wanna make you mine in every way, baby. Nobody's ever gonna touch you the way I will." He placed me gently on the bed and stepped back. "Now. Let me see you."

I snaked my arms above my head and arched my back, pushing my breasts toward him, smiling as he groaned. My mom gave me one good thing: great genes. I knew my body was appealing. My boobs were a naturally large C-cup. My waist cinched in, and my hips and legs were shapely. I was small but with an hourglass figure. My skin glowed with health and tanned golden. Almost a year of dancing and frequent visits to the gym had toned me up nicely.

And I worked it for all it was worth.

I wanted Snow to want me more than anything else in the world. I wanted it so that when he looked at another woman, all he'd ever see was me. I wanted to bewitch him. Put him under a spell he'd never escape from nor

Snow

ever want to. I wanted Snow to be mine physically, emotionally, and spiritually.

I wiggled my way up the bed until my back was against the headboard, allowing my panties to snag on the comforter until they were askew. Then I raised my hands above my head again and smirked.

My belly pitched as he flicked the buttons of his jeans open, pushed them down, and stepped out of them. He either tugged his shorts down with his jeans or went commando because, as he stood straight, I saw he was completely naked.

He was so gorgeous I almost wept.

Toned body and arms with extra muscle packed on. Snow's abs were prominent, but in a natural way, not like the sharp ridges of a bodybuilder. He had that beautiful V-shape across his groin, which pointed down to his long, hard cock, jutting up toward his navel. Furthermore, the boy was groomed nicely.

I licked my lips and smiled like the proverbial cat getting the proverbial cream.

"Don't you look at me like that, Kitten," he ordered softly.

My reply was to raise one brow. "Like what?" My eyes widened innocently.

"You're gonna be trouble, aren't you, Kitty cat?"

I arched my back a little more. "You wouldn't have me any other way."

He put one knee on the bed and began crawling up toward me. "I'm gonna edge the fuck outta you for that," he threatened. "Gonna bring you close, then leave you cold. Gonna keep doing it until you burn for me."

"Already burning, honey." I grabbed his hand and slid it slowly up my thigh. "See?"

His hand rested under the edge of the scrap of lace that passed for panties. "For me, this is more, baby. You know that, right?" He lowered his head and skimmed his lips across the crease of skin where his hand had just rested. "What's this?" His hands went to the little ties at the sides of my panties.

"Pull and find out," I told him.

Slowly, he did as I said, and my panties fell away.

"Jesus, fuck," he muttered. "That's gotta be one of the hottest things I've ever witnessed. I love unwrapping you, Kitten. You're the prettiest gift a man could ever get."

He moved further up the bed and tugged me into him until we lay on our sides facing each other. "Where're the rubbers?" he asked.

I leaned behind me and pulled the box out of my nightstand.

His mouth widened in a smile when he saw how many were in there. "Someone's gotten herself some high hopes. Anyone would think you only want me for my cock." He pulled a few out, tossed them on the stand beside him, and threw the box in the drawer. His eyes burned into mine. "I'll take care of you, baby. I'll make it good for you." He crawled over me, sliding his skin against me, giving me his full weight. "The first time, I'll come in about two point seven seconds. The second, I'll last longer; it depends on how worked up you get me. The third time I'll wake you in the night or early morning, and I'll fuck you all over again."

My belly contracted with need.

Snow lowered his head, his eyes fucking smoldering, then his lips caught mine.

My throat made an involuntary noise as he applied more pressure. He forced my mouth open with his and touched his tongue to mine. Strong fingers entwined with my smaller ones, and he pulled my arms up the bed until our joint hands were on either side of my head.

He released my mouth. "You're so fucking perfect, Kitten," he said throatily. "And you're so fucking mine. Knew it the instant I saw you hanging from those goddamned wires. Even then, something told me this would be us one day." He ran his lips across my cheek and down my throat, pulling gently on my skin with his mouth.

The sensations his lips evoked made my brain jumble. My thoughts wouldn't line up; every time something made sense, he'd suck on my throat, and my mind would turn back to mush. He began kissing lower, working his way down. First to the dip in the base of my throat, then lower. Releasing one of my hands, his fingers slid down to one breast. A thumb stroked over my nipple while his mouth enclosed the other.

I cried out, back arching as he pulled it between his lips. My hips thrust into his, seeking purchase, any contact to help ease the heavy ache there. He released me before kissing his way over my skin to my other breast. Again, he pulled it gently into his mouth, giving it the same attention as my other nipple.

Before I knew it, he was on the move again. Lower he went, kissing every inch of skin from the underside of my breast to my stomach. His hot tongue dipped into my navel before moving from one hip to the other, kissing the angles where my bones jutted.

My skin burned for him. Every time he kissed me somewhere new, my belly fluttered, and my pussy ached to be filled. His mouth trailed the scorch marks he'd left on my skin all those months ago when I'd danced for him. I'd heard the girls talk about how good it could be, especially with the right guy. Still, I never imagined this heat or how my body set alight for him, taking my heart along with it.

I moaned as I felt his weight leave me. Cracking an eye open, I watched him sit back on his haunches and rip a condom packet apart with his teeth and roll the thin layer of latex over his thick cock with one hand.

His gaze lifted to meet mine. "I'm gonna really eat you now," he rasped. "Open your legs."

I hesitated for a few seconds, my teeth sinking into my lip.

Snow was more up close and personal with that part of me than anyone had ever been. I'd never received oral sex or given it. On my only time before, he rolled on, pumped a few times, and rolled back off.

It was nothing like this.

"I-I've never—" I stared, suddenly shy.

He stared back. After a few seconds, a self-satisfied smile curved his lips. "Good." His hand went to my hip and stroked his thumb over it. "Won't make you do anything you're uncomfortable with, baby, but you can trust me."

I nodded because there was no question.

His hand trailed from my hip to the crease where my thigh met my pussy. I clenched, the ache suddenly flaring up again. "Open your legs, Kitten. Let me see you. I *need* to see you."

My legs fell open.

His nostrils flared as he sucked in a breath, looking down at my core. "Never had anything more beautiful that belonged to me, baby. I knew you'd be perfect. Knew you were everything I was missing."

"Where did you come from?" I croaked through the burn in my throat. "Are you even real?"

He grinned his sexy grin while his body lowered until his face hovered over my pussy. "'I'll show you how real I am." He nuzzled me there before moving inside and tasting me.

My moan was husky with pleasure.

"Pretty as fuck." Snow's words vibrated against my clit as he lapped with his tongue. One finger slipped inside; his other hand snaked higher and laced our fingers together while he licked me out.

I forced my thighs wider apart, desperate to give him all the access I could.

Everything clenched. My abs, my throat, my core. The pulse point in the base of my throat fluttered. My heart hammered, and my blood raced through my veins.

Snow aroused everything inside me that had lain stagnant since I was a girl. My soul had experienced some deep cuts, often from the ones who were supposed to love me the most, but he fixed it. My beautiful soldier made it whole again.

The soft laps of his tongue turned into hard strokes. The finger he'd used to stretch me began to curl against my front wall. He started eating me with a rhythm that was incredible and relentless at the same time. Pressure began to ebb and flow. Every time I came close, he'd stop, and it edged away again.

"I've never felt like this before," I murmured, moaning long and hard.

Snow replied by taking my clit between his lips and sucking hard. The finger inside me worked faster while his hand squeezed mine.

My hips jerked, and he hummed against my clit, causing a vibration that made me whimper.

There was no sign, no build-up, just a pleasure so intense I couldn't catch my breath. An atom bomb formed inside my belly, sucking together every cell before exploding.

I cried out, overwhelmed by the pleasure coursing through my pussy as Snow ate me through my orgasm. He didn't let up. He kept licking, sucking, and fingering me until all of the tremors and aftershocks faded, and I was left a quivering mess on the bed.

Within seconds, I felt his weight pressing on me again. He eased himself between my legs, taking my head in both hands. "Look at me, baby," he demanded.

I opened my eyes to see his face almost touching mine. His mouth and chin shone from the remnants of my orgasm. "You're fucking incredible." He lifted one of my legs around his waist and softly kissed my nose. "You're everything," he whispered before pulling his hips back and slamming inside me.

My back bowed off the bed, and I let out a shriek. He filled me to the point of pain. The intrusion was too much. I wasn't prepared.

He stilled, smoothing the hair away from my face. "I'm sorry, Kitten. Stay with me. It'll pass. I'll look after you, baby."

His hands held my head in place, his stare all-seeing. "Keep your eyes on me at all times. I wanna watch your face when I fuck you."

His lips caught mine, our tongues tangling as he slowly moved. He didn't thrust hard like I thought he would; instead, he circled his hips, gently grinding into me. His lips were musky with a hint of fruit. My scent mixed with what I recognized as the body lotion I used. I closed my eyes, trying to make sense of the myriad of sensations assaulting me.

"Open," he ordered. "Look at me, Kitten."

I obeyed.

His eyes were golden flames burning into me, setting me alight. The soreness between my legs began to fade until, after a minute, it didn't hurt anymore.

It felt good.

Snow saw my eyes widen as my pussy contracted with pleasure around his hard cock. He let out a deep, throaty groan and murmured, "This is beauty, Kitten. You and me like this; nothing's ever felt more right."

The force of his movements increased. Every time he circled his hips, his cock drove deeper into me. He seemed to catch my clit with every hard turn of his groin. The trimmed coarse hair on the root of his cock skating over my sensitive bundle of nerves made me whimper.

"You're so fucking tight, Kitty." He kissed my nose again. "Your perfect little pussy was made for me. Do you feel it? D'ya feel how well we piece together?"

Snow

We still stared into each other's eyes, his hands clasped to my hair, keeping me in place. It weaved a spell of intimacy I'd never dreamed I could have with someone. He began to grind harder, propping himself up on one arm and putting his back into it. Still, though, his eyes never left mine.

A tingle began to fizz in my stomach. He circled his hips quicker, angling himself so even more pressure was pressed against my clit. My thighs started to tremble with the sensations flowing through my blood. He fucked me harder, taking me higher and higher, and I moaned again.

"Fuck, Kitty. I'm gonna come," he murmured. His hips jerked uncontrollably as he pounded his cock inside me. "This little cunt," he groaned. "Jesus."

His words set off a triggered reaction. My pussy clenched hard, and I couldn't help wailing as another orgasm spread from my abdomen.

"Fuck. Fuck. Fuck," Snow said in tandem with his hard thrusts. His face twisted, eyes glazing over, and we watched each other orgasm.

Snow shuddered as he emptied himself inside the condom. The heat from his cum warmed me from the inside. More jerks and a deep growl. Suddenly, his arms gave way, and his body dropped deadweight onto mine.

Our chests heaved as our breaths slowly began to turn to normal.

"Jesus, fuck, Kitten," Snow murmured into my throat. "Never came so hard in my life."

He lifted up again. His strong hands stroked my hair as he pecked my lips gently over and over again.

I could feel everything between Snow and me. Acute feelings flooded my bloodstream, making my throat burn. At that moment, I was more connected to him than I'd ever been to anyone before. Euphoria rose inside me, and my eyes welled with moisture.

He kissed away a single tear that fell. "I'm sorry if I hurt you. I'll make it better next time. I promise. It's been so long that I lost control for a hot minute. I meant to go slower."

I shook my head at his misinterpretation of my raw emotions. "No, honey. You didn't hurt me. Don't you see? You healed me. You made everything better."

He smiled, and I noticed how open he was. He looked young and boyish with his sex hair and a sexy, slow grin.

"Was I okay?" I asked nervously. "It's just I'm not very experienced."

He began to laugh deep, throaty chuckles, making his chest bounce against mine. "Kitten. You could lie there like a plank with that body. I'd fucking blow just by looking at you." He shook his head, quietly amused. "You were perfect."

I let out a little mewl of contentment as he nuzzled my neck. He couldn't stop kissing me, and I couldn't say I hated the tiny shivers his sweet caresses sent trickling down my spine.

I blew out a sigh full of contentment with the world around me. If I had been given the option to never leave my bed, I would've taken it without thinking twice. "Snow. Seeing it was so good, can I ask you a question?"

He lifted up again, looking at me quizzically. "Course."

I sent him a wicked smile and waggled my eyebrows. "When can we do it again?"

Chapter Fifteen

Snow

Kitty's surprised eyes slashed to mine, her beautiful mouth slack with shock. "Huh?"

I cursed under my breath. "What the actual fucking fuck? They can't do that!" I shook my head, going over what I'd just seen again, trying to make sense of it.

She shook her head disbelievingly, wringing her hands. "How could they?" she whispered. "He was the best of them all. Good guys don't lose. They can't behead Ned fucking Stark." Her eyes went wide. "Maybe it's a trick. What if some magical spell brings him back to life? This is a world with dragons and witchcraft. Surely he can't stay dead?"

I grimaced. "Beheading seems pretty fucking final to me, kitty cat. Not much chance of coming back from that shit."

She let out a frustrated harrumph, folding her arms. "I'm not watching any more of that fucking show." She threw her arms in the air. "I can't believe they killed off Ned fucking Stark." She pursed her lips, her folded arms pushing her boobs up. "Maybe we should watch the next one," she mused. "Just in case it wasn't real. You know how these shows can make it look like something gnarly happened when, really, from a different angle, it didn't. The Walking Dead does it all the time."

My head reared back. "You watch The Walking Dead?"

She cocked her head to one side, looking at me like I belonged in the asylum. "Well, duh."

Laughter rose up, and I made a grab for her. "Who the fuck are you 'well duh'ing'?"

She scurried across the bed out of my reach, giggling.

I grabbed her around the waist and hauled her back into my lap, arms holding her close.

"The Walking Dead's pure brilliance," she informed me. "We've already got a sweepstake at the club on who makes it to the end. They don't care who they kill off. No fucks given at all."

My gaze skated down her tight little tee, white panties, and big fluffy socks. Fuck, this girl did it for me. She was innocent and sexy and gave me lip like she was born for it. Kitten was soft but with an edge so sharp she'd cut you clean in half. Life had put her through the wringer, but she was quick to laugh and quick to love, and I wanted to protect those qualities above all else.

We'd been holed up in her apartment for three days. Our time had been spent fucking, laughing, eating, talking, watching our new TV obsession, and just being.

I felt much more like my old self. I still found myself startled awake by the slightest noise, but Kitten was there to sink into every time I needed grounding. I was grateful I had her to hold on to when I felt the surge. Luckily, it had only happened once since coming here, and Kitty had been asleep. Being in Vegas with her was the best thing I could've done for my soul because my girl was there to nurture it back to health.

Afghanistan seemed like a dream sometimes.

When I lay awake, I couldn't help thinking about the girl in the rubble and the man I killed. Then, my brain would go over how I acted when I returned to Hambleton.

I could see my reactions had been over the top, but I also believed it was pure exhaustion that made me behave that way. I'd felt the concern Abe and Pop were giving off, so for the rest of my time there, I'd stayed away from them. They'd only want me to open up about my feelings, but there was nothing I wanted to say. So I slept, spent time with Mom and Ris in the kitchen, and generally chilled the fuck out.

Being with Kitty had brought me back to myself. I swore the next time I got tweaked, I'd visit my girl before going home to the club. So, by the time I saw Pop, I'd be okay, and my folks wouldn't worry.

Hollister told us during our debriefing there'd be another deployment, and probably soon. The other EOD teams were burned out—excuse the pun—we'd gotten away with it so far because we were a young, inexperienced team compared to the others. However, we couldn't say that now after all the shit we'd dealt with in Kabul.

I knew reality would hit soon, but for now, I was content, though admittedly, I was starting to get a little antsy. I wasn't a man to stay cooped up for long. It was getting to the point where I needed to let off some steam.

A muffled ringtone pealed from somewhere in the room.

Kitten leaned down the side of the bed, grabbed her purse, and pulled out her cell. After stabbing the green button, she lifted it to her ear. "Hey, Raven," she greeted. "You, okay?" After listening for a minute, her face lit up. "That's amazing, Rave. Congratulations." She paused for a few seconds, listening, and slowly turned to me. "Tonight? Really? One second. Let me check with Snow." She tapped the mute button and raised her eyes to meet mine. "Raven's got a last-minute DJ gig tonight at 'Underground.' It's a really nice, exclusive club. She's asking if we'll go and support her. She'll get us on the VIP list. Some of the other girls will be there with their guys, too. What do you think?"

I thought about it for a few seconds. I wasn't a dance club kinda guy, but I'd been feeling restless since the night before. We'd been holed up for days, and as much as I loved spending time just me and Kitty, the offer of a night out had come at precisely the right time for me to let off some steam.

"Wanna go on a date with me, Kitten?" I asked, waggling my eyebrows playfully.

She punched the air excitedly. "Yes!"

I laughed. "Tell your girl we'll be there. Can't wait to dance with you, baby."

She looked confused. "Thought you didn't dance."

"I *don't* dance," I confirmed. "Didn't say I *couldn't*. Maybe I'm not at your level, but I get by."

She beamed at me.

I beamed back as I watched her tap on her cell. "Rave," she said, putting it to her ear, her eyes shining excitedly into mine as she spoke, "we'll be there."

'Underground' was big, dark, plush, and very exclusive.

We'd walked past a line of a hundred people, at least, who were queuing to get inside. Kitten had told me if they didn't wear the right clothes or even have the right look, they'd be turned away. She didn't like it said it was snobby and arrogant to judge people on their appearance. It was the reason she didn't often go out. She hated the fakery of it.

However, the right look wasn't something Kitten would ever have to worry about, seeing as she looked fucking incredible.

Snow

I'd showered and dressed, thinking I'd get another episode of Game of Thrones in and let my girl get ready without me hovering. When she'd walked outta the bedroom, my mouth fell open.

She wore a dark pink satin dress down to her knees that gaped across her boobs and fit everywhere else like a second skin. Her messy bun had been teased into a mane of long, wild hair down to her waist. My girl didn't wear much make-up, but the small amount she'd applied enhanced every feature. My gaze traveled down to see the silver sandals with a tiny bar that secured her foot and silver straps crisscrossing her calf.

My cock thickened, and I had to suppress my groan.

Kitten bit her lip nervously and did a little twirl. "Do I look alright?"

I took a mental snapshot and looked deep into her eyes. "You're stunning," I announced, voice so husky it was almost a growl.

She smiled, eyes shining with happiness. "So are you."

I looked down at my clean, black jeans, designer sneakers, and black Tom Ford button-down that Freya had helped pick out as a Christmas gift. "I look like a fucking peasant next to you, baby."

She stepped forward, straightening my collar. "No. You look so handsome. You make me wanna cry, Snow."

I caught her cheek in my palm and rubbed my thumb along her lip, my brain taking in her expression and storing it away. "How long until the cab's due, baby? I need to fuck you before we go." As I spoke, her cell beeped with an alert.

She picked it up from the coffee table and tucked it inside a tiny silver purse with a little shrug. "Sorry, Snow. Cab's here."

I grabbed her hand and led her out of the apartment, locking up behind us and pocketing the keys as we went. She'd told me a little about the club in the cab, explaining how her boss, Marco, owned shares. Apparently, some top DJs had played at 'Underground.' Raven, an aspiring DJ, had been trying to get a gig there for a while. Eventually, Marco got her a deal where she acted as a backup. Tonight was obviously her lucky break.

The cab couldn't drive safely to the entrance because the long queue spilled into the road, so he'd parked a hundred yards away. I got out, jogged to Kitten's door, opened it, and helped her out.

Immediately, a buzz went through the crowd of people.

"Is that Kitten?"

"Oh, my God! It's her."

Shouts of "Kitten. We love you," pierced the air.

Mind reeling, I watched as she stood straight, smiled a dazzling white Hollywood smile, and waved.

My stare went to the queue of people with cell phones, recording and taking pictures of my girl. My eyebrows knitting together. "Are you fucking famous?" I asked her incredulously.

She shrugged, a fake smile still plastered across her face as we approached the entrance. "No," she denied quietly. "Well—maybe a little. I'm one of the top-billed strippers in Vegas. That makes me well known, but I wouldn't say I'm famous."

I took in the glare of lights that followed my girl from all the cell phones on us. A dark tension flooded my gut. I didn't like her being so exposed. Pulling my woman closer, I slung my arm around her shoulder, shielding her from the crowd of people who, by then, were yelling louder. Quickly, I walked her to the entrance.

Fuck me, how the hell did I end up here?

I hadn't had the first clue about Kitten's notoriety. The night I saw her dance, I got how popular she was. She was the headline act, and from the chatter I picked up, some people had come a long way to see her perform.

Snow

Honestly, though, I thought her popularity was contained to Crimson Velvet.

I had no fucking idea she was so well known.

She was so fucking down to earth, too. Never once had she been a diva or even high maintenance. She wore sweats, a sports bra, and a hoodie the night in the diner. During this visit, she'd lived in tees, panties, and fluffy socks. Kitten didn't care if her hair was mussed. She didn't wear makeup unless she worked or went out, like tonight.

Either she didn't believe the hype surrounding her, or she didn't care.

My money was on the latter, and by God, in that minute, it made me fall for her just a little bit more. She was only nineteen but still possessed enough maturity to not allow all the bullshit that came with her job to get inside her head.

Five guys guarded the door of the club like sentries. They were a mix of black, Hispanic, and white. All of them looked mean fuck and not people who I'd wanna mess with.

One stood apart from the others. The second he noticed our approach, his mean look turned into a colossal smile. "Kitten!" he announced. "Rave said you were coming. You're all set up. Get your ass straight in the VIP section. Your bill's comp'd tonight." He grinned. "Order the best. Lord can afford it."

Kitten laughed as she went to give the guy a big hug. "You know I'm underage. Everything okay, Ty? How's Soraya?"

"She's great," he replied, pulling back to grin at her. "Getting big now. Only five weeks to go before Junior arrives. She loved the outfits you sent. Call her soon. You two should meet for coffee. Woman's bored out of her skull now I've made her give up work."

"I will as soon as Snow leaves," she told him. She craned her neck and nodded for me to go over. "Snow.

This is Ty. He used to work security at Crimson before Marco brought him over here."

I stepped over to them and held my hand out. "Good to meet ya, man."

He shook my hand. "Likewise." He flashed me a stern look. "You looking after our Kitten?"

It was on the tip of my tongue to tell him she was my Kitten, but I behaved. Didn't wanna look like an asshole in front of my girl. Plus, I liked that people cared about her.

I jerked a nod.

He reached around and opened the doors to the club. "Have a good night." He smirked.

Kitten took my hand and pulled me through, calling out a 'see you later' to Ty. She glanced at me as we walked through a corridor until we reached two sets of double doors manned by another couple of big fuckers.

"Kitten," she announced.

One checked a clipboard and crossed her name off with a flourish. "Your night's compliments of the house." He reached inside his pocket and pulled out a golden chip attached to a long chain. "Show this to your waitress. She'll comp your drinks."

Kitty slid it over her head, smiling her thanks as the guy pushed a door open, muttering, "Enjoy."

As soon as we'd walked inside, a crowd of women rushed over, squealing their hellos.

I recognized some of them as dancers from Crimson Velvet. They saw me and squealed again, hugging me and pulling us over to a massive, curved couch that must have held at least twenty people. Small round tables were dotted in front, with big, plush armchairs around them. Just as well, seeing as our crowd of people was fucking huge.

The vast area was dark shades of blue and very expensive looking. Enormous couches were dotted all over the room, identical to the one we congregated around. The far end held a bar, and the other side opened up into the club, manned by another two security guys. From my vantage point, it was already packed with people dancing.

A couple of the men, obviously husbands and boyfriends, were already sitting. I introduced myself before sinking into one of the enormous armchairs, nodding in time to the deep, thudding beat reverberating through the room.

"You Kitten's guy?" one of the guys asked. "The soldier?"

I nodded. "Yeah. She's mine."

He shook his head, grinning. "Gotta say. I've never known her to date, let alone have a steady guy."

My chest puffed out slightly. Couldn't say I hated that at all. "She's a special girl," I said, eyes sliding to my woman, still talking animatedly with her girls. "Sweeter than candy and twice as addictive."

His eyes followed mine. "Yeah. My wife, Sarah, says the same."

"Sarah?" I asked.

He nodded toward one of the girls, who I recognized as the acrobatic dancer who flew around the stage to Hella Good on the night I met Kitten. "That's Sarah. Otherwise known as Heaven. She loves Kitty. They all do."

"They're a close-knit group," I agreed, my mind comparing them to the club girls. "The only other women group I know don't act like these girls."

The guy who'd already introduced himself as Leon nodded. "Yeah. The Crimson girls are mostly cool. Now and again, they have their moments, but not as often as you'd think. They're out in force to support Raven. That says it all, really. They look out for each other."

Leon was right.

Eight girls must've been there, all out to support their friend. It made me feel better about leaving Kitty when I returned to Fort Campbell. I wasn't sure when I'd get enough leave where I could come back and see her, though I was determined to do that before my next deployment.

Kitty looked at me and said something to Sarah. She came over, and I grabbed her hands, splaying our fingers together before I pulled her onto my lap.

Her arms snaked around my neck, and she snuggled in. "Sorry, honey. Didn't mean to neglect you."

"Nothing to be sorry for, baby," I said, arm tightening around her. "Not a thing." I nodded to the open area of the club. "Have you been here before?"

"Once or twice," she admitted. "But it's not really my scene. It's a bit pretentious for me. I don't like mixing with the rich and famous." She rolled her eyes, gesturing to the bar when two reality TV sisters held court with their entourage. "Honestly, I'd much rather study. I love going out dancing, but it's usually to smaller clubs to support Raven's gigs."

I took a swig of beer. "Is she good? Gotta say the club scene isn't my thing, usually."

Kitten smiled. "Raven's great. I'm in awe of the way she controls a crowd. She starts off slow and sensuous, taking her cues from them and working them up slowly. She has them in the palm of her hand until they feel whatever she wants them to feel." Kitty turned to face me and began to explain, "Raven says there's a perfect speed she works up to. When she hits it, the track starts to resonate. At that point, she and the crowd are on a journey together, and there's no better feeling."

"The way you describe it sounds sexy as fuck," I muttered, willing my half-chub to go down.

Kitten laughed. "It is sexy. She says it's just like fucking. You start slowly, then build up until your blood sings and your nerve endings tingle with sensations."

As if on cue, the music lowered, and a voice came over the speaker system that fed into the VIP room from the club, introducing Raven.

"Come on," Kitty said, scrambling to her feet and pulling me up. "She's on. I'll show you."

We all rose from our seats and made our way to the side of the room that opened up into the rest of the club. Security opened the velvet rope separating the two areas and let us through.

A deep, pulsing beat began to pound through the room.

Kitty smirked. "Here she comes," she murmured. "She's something else."

The thick bass seemed to pump through my chest as an ice machine billowed smoke over the dance floor crowd. Shouts and catcalls began to sound up.

Leon tapped my shoulder. "Men stand back and watch the show, dude," he explained. "Trust me. You can thank me later."

I stood beside him, back to the wall, and did as he said. My eyes immediately sought Kitten out. I blew a hard breath when I spotted her about ten feet away on the edge of the dance floor with her girls.

The air was thick with smoke and anticipation. The smell of clean sweat and booze hung in the ether. Calls and shouts came from the packed dance floor as the crowd begged for relief.

My heart jerked as suddenly, everything stopped dead.

I glanced up at the DJ booth, suspended ten feet from the ground, and my mouth fell open.

Raven stood with her arms outstretched wide, like a God bestowing her grace on the crowd. She wore a tiny silver sequined halter top that caught the lights flashing all over the room. Her hair was teased out, her afro appearing almost halo-like and cool as hell. Suddenly, every beam shone on her, lighting her up like an angel from above.

Hundreds of hands were reaching for the heavens as a single, hard beat began to *thump* through the room. The sea of people started to move almost as one. Excitement flickered through the air, making my senses tingle. The deep, pulsating thump resonated, and the memory of Kitten's voice floated through my mind.

She starts off slow and sensuous, taking her cues from the crowd and working them up slowly.

Kitten said Raven took them on a journey and fuck me; at that moment, with the pounding beat thrumming through me, I wanted to go on it too.

My heart began to slam as a loud roar went up.

The beams flashed around the room again, tiny pinpricks of light turning everything from light to dark and back again.

The beat pulsed harder until a chorus of synths came in, carving out a sweet melody and the echo of bongo drums that added an extra layer of bass.

Every light in the place shone on Raven again. Her magnetism must've pulled the crowd in because a sea of hands reached up toward the DJ booth in worship.

Raven raised one arm high in the air, made a fist, and pumped it in time to the beat, building higher and higher, harder and harder. Suddenly, she stilled, almost suspended, as the resonating thump hit a crescendo before she crashed her fist down hard and dropped the bassline.

The crowd went wild, and every person packed together on the dancefloor moved just as a man's soulful voice began to sing,

It's true. I never meant to make you cry. Never meant to say goodbye.

I wanna come back to you and put things together.

My chest swelled. It was so fucking euphoric that my throat filled with emotion. The crowd was captured in a trance-like state of depthless bliss, making the blood hammer through my veins.

Leon nudged me. "Look."

My eyes sliced to where Kitten danced with her girls, and my breath caught in my throat.

She was moving, but unlike anything I'd ever seen before.

Her hips swayed and thrust in time to the banging beat. Her entire body moved like molten liquid as she ground and bumped along with the song.

I knew she could dance; I'd seen her on stage, and she was magnificent. But watching her thrust and grind in the pink satin dress that clung to her body like a second skin was even more enthralling than seeing her naked.

Kitten swung around to face me head-on.

My eyes lifted from her ass and caught her shining cornflower-blue orbs.

My dick kicked—hard.

She smirked while continuing to dance. That time, I didn't doubt for one second it was all just for me. With a small smile playing around her lips, they began to move as she sang along, mouthing the words at me.

My heart stuttered as her lips curved, ass still twisting and pumping in time to the bassline, which was turning funkier and heavier the longer the song played on.

Emotions hit me from everywhere as the resonating beat continued to thud through me. In five months, I'd gone from unaffected and uncaring to an onslaught of feelings. Sadness and frustration coursed through me. That shit represented all the bullshit I'd had to go through on deployment. But through all that, Kitten was at the center of my universe, along with all the unadulterated love for her that hit me deep inside.

At that moment, I swore I'd protect her from it all.

She'd never know what I knew or what I'd seen. Never would she feel the darkness. I wanted to keep her exactly how she was right then as she danced for me. Sweet, kind, and perfect. I'd make sure she lived out every dream. I'd make sure she succeeded in everything she did. Kitten was the only speck of light in a world of darkness, and I'd keep her shining brightly if it was the last thing I did.

I'd protect her and keep her safe. I'd always put her above me, every fucking time. No question. No doubt.

I caught a flash of movement outta the corner of my eye, my hands clenching into fists as some asshole made a beeline for my girl. Couldn't blame him; she was a beacon of everything good in the world. I was shocked it had taken so long for one of the fuckers to crawl outta the woodwork, but still, he'd be disappointed.

I straightened and began to stalk forward. I was closer, so he stood no chance. The thought of him touching her skin, even breathing her air, made me wanna rip him apart by the seams.

Something profound had happened to me, standing with my back to a wall in a Vegas club, watching my Kitten dance.

I'd finally had a revelation.

She belonged to me.

She'd belonged to me mind, body, and soul ever since we'd sat on a mountain, watching the sun's rays race across the city. I'd known it then. I just didn't wanna admit it to myself.

Society's constraints made me play it down in my head. *Nobody can fall in twelve hours. It's lust, not love.* But fuck that and fuck society.

There was no rhyme or reason when it came to the way I felt about her.

And there was no hiding from it anymore.

Kitten saw me approach and snaked her arms above her head, ass still swaying with the rhythm. My girl knew what she was doing; she understood her power and embraced it. I fucking loved that. She bloomed before my eyes, and what made it even more compelling was I'd had a hand in it. I nurtured that shit, which gave me a hard-on so potent my cock ached.

I caught her around the waist just as the guy came from behind. Chest heaving with desire and anger, I bared my teeth, skewering him with a look.

His face froze, and he slunk away.

My hands slid down to Kitten's hips, still thrusting with the music, and I began to dance with her.

Her eyes locked with mine, and she smiled at me in a way that made my heart feel like it'd burst through my skin. Toned, golden arms lowered and snaked around my neck as I matched the rhythm she carved out with her incredible body.

She was so carefree, so untouched by life's bullshit, and I craved that too. She made me forget all the evil I'd encountered. She gave me something decent to hold on to in a world full of dead little girls, savagery, and suicide bombers.

Kitten was going through a sexual liberation, and I was proud to be a part of that. Still, I was going through an emotional one, and it was all because of her.

My hands slid around her ass, pulling her into me. I watched her eyes shine as she felt the thick steel of my cock dig into her flat, toned stomach.

Her eyes lifted to mine, and again, she threw me that sexy little smirk that drove me half crazy, and she said two words. "Oh my."

Our hips moved together along with the bassline of the music. That word came to me again, *connection* and every part of it rang true. We were connected with our minds, hearts, and souls, and I prayed I'd never be set free.

She leaned into me. "Snow," she whispered. "I know somewhere, honey. I want you to take me there and fuck me. Fuck me like you never wanna let me go."

My cock ached as I splayed the fingers on one hand with hers. "Come on." I turned, prowling back toward the VIP area, tugging her behind me.

Security pulled the rope back while giving Kitten an appreciative look.

My jaw clenched, and I eyeballed him as I sauntered past, slinging my arm around my girl's shoulders, showing him who she belonged to.

She pointed out a door leading to the bathrooms. I propelled us there, cock twitching at the thought of what we were about to do. The atmosphere, Kitten, the music, it'd all gotten me so fucking worked up I couldn't think straight. I needed to be inside her. Immediately.

I swung the door open and walked into a quiet corridor. A sign pointed toward the bathrooms, but Kitty gestured toward a dark hall opposite. "Down here," she said breathlessly.

The coolness of the corridor cooled my heated skin as we ventured further. We turned a corner with one solitary spotlight shining from the ceiling, dimming the area.

"Here," I demanded.

Her eyes flashed. "There's an office a bit further up."

"Here," I insisted louder that time. "I wanna fuck you right here. I wanna listen to that door open. Wanna hear people moving in and out, just a few feet away, while my cock's pounding your cunt." I pushed her back against the wall, gripped her chin with my hand, and kissed her hard.

My lips forced hers apart, and I started flicking her tongue with mine, reminiscent of how she loved me licking her clit.

She moaned in my mouth, her fingers frantically clawing at the buttons of my jeans.

I kissed her long and wet, grabbing her hands and holding them over her head against the wall. All we'd done for days was fuck until we were raw, but my cock was reminiscent of iron, like it hadn't seen action for years.

I nibbled down her jaw to her throat. "Don't touch me, Kitty," I rasped. "Just feel," I murmured the words into her skin, etching them like a tattooed kiss.

My hands reached to the hem of her dress and slid it up her legs, and she moaned. "It feels good, Snow."

I dropped to my knees, pressed her hard against the wall, and nuzzled the skin at the apex of her thighs. She smelled just like she always did: sweet musk and peaches.

My cock kicked at the realization that she didn't wear panties.

Spreading her legs apart, I dived in. I didn't work up to it; instead, I found her aching, hard little clit and sucked greedily.

She let out a keening cry and thrust her hands through my hair.

I pulled back. "Hands up on the wall," I ordered. "Do as you're told, baby girl, or I won't let you come."

She let out a little huff but grudgingly obeyed.

I went back to work, smiling into her pussy. My baby was gonna get a spanking for that. The harder I worked her, the more beautifully she responded. Her hips began to thrust toward my face, her body's way of urging me on. "That's it, Kitten. Take what you need." I growled the words onto her clit, the reverberations making her moan even louder.

Two fingers slid through her pussy, picking up moisture as they went. Pushing her legs even farther apart, I began to fuck her with them, stretching out her tight little cunt, preparing it to take my cock. She was gonna get it hard and fast, but she was still so tight. I wanted to make it good for her.

Her walls began to clench around my fingers. Contracting so tightly that she sucked them inside. I continued, timing it, licking and sucking and fucking until her orgasm hovered over us both.

Then, I stopped.

"Snow," she whined. "Please, honey."

I rose to my feet and grabbed her jaw again, jutting my face close to hers. "Love it when you beg, baby girl, but it won't do you any good. When you come, it's gonna be all over my cock."

I grabbed her hair in my fist, spun her around, and pressed her tits against the wall. "Hands flat, legs open wide, and bend over. You're gonna take it like a good girl."

She obeyed with a whimper.

I slid her dress further up to her hips and kicked her legs wider apart. Reaching into my pocket, I pulled out a wrap, opened it with my teeth, and rolled it over my cock. "Want you on the pill by my next visit," I commanded. "Wanna see you filled with my cum."

She whimpered again, whispering, "Oh my God."

I grabbed my cock by the root, found the notch of her pussy, and slammed it inside.

Kitten's groan was long and guttural.

I started to thrust slowly at first, but still forced her to take every inch.

Her cunt was so fucking tight, especially when she squeezed her inner muscles around me, tempting me to come.

I gave her ass a light swat, feeling a gush of moisture flood my dick. "Fuck, yeah. That's my dirty girl," I moaned.

The thud of the bassline reverberated through the walls, and I started to fuck my kitten in time to it, creating a rhythm that made my chest wanna explode. The music suddenly got louder as the doors to the bathroom opened.

Laughter and voices sounded as two women chatted on their way to the bathroom before the music muted again and the doors closed.

Snow

Kitten flooded my cock for a second time.

She loved that I was fucking her like this, loved that we could be caught at any minute. We were literally around the corner from the doors. All it would take was for someone to walk the wrong way, and—I moaned as my cock kicked inside my girl's pussy, my mind getting lost in the fantasy.

Already, a telltale tingle started at the base of my spine. "Come, baby," I whispered. "Need you to come for me."

"I can't, Snow–I need–I can't—" Her voice was a stutter as I cut her off with every hard thrust of my cock.

My hand snaked up her back and clasped around the front of her throat. I hauled her upright until my torso pushed flush against her spine. Keeping her throat cuffed gently with one hand, the other slid down and pressed hard on her clit.

I braced as she went off like a firework. She squealed, chanting, "Oh, God. Oh, God," as her cunt clamped down, squeezing me so tight it almost hurt.

Shoving my fingers in her mouth, I groaned as my cum rocketed into the thin rubber barrier. I saw stars as I fucked her through our orgasms like an animal, brutal and savage, not letting up until she'd drained me dry.

After a minute, my girl slumped in my arms. If I hadn't held her up, she would've gone down like a sack of bricks. I wasn't in a much better state. My knees were like jello, but I was determined to never let her fall.

I held her like that, against the wall, waiting for our heart rates to slow and our breathing to return to normal. Eventually, she craned her neck and beamed a smile I felt down to my soul.

Click. Click. I took a mental snapshot of Kitten's glowing eyes and grinned back. My heart soared a mile high, and I couldn't help myself. I had to tell her. What if I never came back from my next deployment? What if I never got to give her this again?

I leaned forward, kissed the tip of her nose, and said it from the heart. "I fucking love you, Kitten. You're my fire."

Her eyes widened slightly before welling up with tears. She beamed me another megawatt smile and said the words that made me feel like I stood ten feet tall.

"I love you too, Snow. Always and forever."

Chapter Sixteen

Kitten

Over the next few days, Snow and I became even closer. We only got out of bed to shower and cook, and the funny thing was, we did those things glued together, too. We seemed to gravitate toward each other. I'd feel a pull toward him just sitting in bed together, our backs to the headboard, watching Game of Thrones.

Thinking back, I couldn't recall a time when I'd ever felt so totally and utterly joyous. The love I held inside for him warmed me. I went to sleep with a contented smile plastered across my face and usually woke up with one, too. Though, I was usually being poked in the back by Snow's beautiful cock, so that helped my mood.

There was only one black mark on the horizon.

Time wasn't on our side.

The closer we got to the day he was due to return to base, the more desperate I became.

I tried to think practically. I had to get back to work to earn money for Harvard and catch up with my study preparation. Life still marched along, and I had to march with it if I was going to achieve everything I wanted. My future included Snow, but it was still dependent on me.

Marco had given me Friday off so that Snow and I could spend his last night together and not at the club.

Though, in hindsight, maybe it would've been better for us to go out because the mood in my apartment was so low and somber.

How could my chest ache so painfully when he hadn't left me yet? Tears sprang into my eyes at the mere thought of him not being at my side, but I hid them. I was determined not to cry in front of him. I wanted to send him off with a smile, not tears. Making him feel bad wouldn't have been fair. I went into it knowing who he was and what it entailed, so I had to suck it up.

I tried to look at it positively and think of our time apart as an opportunity to plan for our future. In a way, that thought made me more determined to succeed. I didn't know if saying goodbye would be the only constant in our lives. Still, it showed me more than ever that I needed to build something to hold on to when he wasn't around, or else I'd go insane with missing him.

On our last night together, we just lay in bed talking.

Snow made me take off my tee. We'd stripped down to our shorts and panties and were talking. Maybe symbolically, it was our way of baring our souls to each other. He'd been telling me stories about his military buddies and all the pranks they got up to. I'd just been cry-laughing all through a story about them sneaking into his lieutenant's office, hanging condoms from the window, and setting them alight.

His eyes locked with mine. "I love your laugh, Kitten," he said softly.

"Thank you," I murmured. "I love that you make me laugh."

He nodded, his beautiful, sexy grin fading. "Baby. Real life's knocking on the door. There's not long left. We need to talk about something."

My heart leaped up into my throat, and nausea clenched my stomach. I shook my head, shoulders suddenly tense. "No! I don't wanna hear it."

His eyebrows snapped together. "Kitten. What the fuck?"

I took his hand, threading my fingers through his. "Last time you said we needed to talk, you walked out that door and left me heartbroken. Is what you want to say about a life or death situation?"

He shook his head. "No."

"Do you want to end things with me?"

"Fuck. No, baby." His voice sounded thick with emotion. "I love you. I don't wanna end things. I couldn't. You're mine."

My shoulders slumped. "Thank God." I blew out a long breath as a niggle of a thought came to me, making my chest ache. "Is it another woman?"

He barked out a laugh.

My mouth twisted into a pout. "Snow!" I slapped his chest. "Don't laugh at me!"

He threw his head back and roared.

I rolled my eyes and huffed. "Asshole," I muttered.

"Kitten," he cajoled, still grinning. "It's not another woman. How could it be? There's never been another goddamned woman, and there never will be again. I'm gone for you, baby. Fucked good and hard up the asshole. How the hell do you expect me to ever be with anyone else again? How could they live up to what we've got? There hasn't been a sniff of it in the last twenty-one years, and I doubt there will be in the next. I'm yours. You're mine. The only way you'll ever see another dick in this lifetime is if I get blown sky fucking high, and believe me, I've no intention of that happening. Now. Get that goddamned thought outta your head before I bend you over this bed and fuck it outta ya."

I gave him the sexy smirk he seemed to love, trailing a finger down his chest. "Don't threaten me with a good time, Snow."

He tagged me around the waist and pulled me into him. "Ain't no threat, Kitten. This is our last night. Now.

Let's get the housekeeping outta the way. Have you got those pictures for me?"

I nodded toward a brown envelope resting on the dresser. "In there."

"Is your cell number there, too? Like I asked?"

I mock saluted. "All present and correct, sir."

"Good." He grinned. "So, there's only one thing left to do." He waggled his eyebrows suggestively.

A laugh bubbled through me. "Are you sure you can handle it again?"

His hand slipped between my legs, eyes softening to liquid gold. "Oh, I can handle it, alright. Gonna lick you, eat you, make you come, fuck you, make you come again, then fuck you some more. Gonna fuck us both to sleep. And next week, when I'm lonely in my bunk, I'm gonna fist my cock and think about you. Think about us."

A tingle swept through my pussy, and warmth flooded my heart. "I like the thought of you fucking me to sleep, Snow," I said softly, looking deep into his eyes.

"Good." His eyes stayed open as his lips caught mine, and he kissed me hard, our stares remaining on each other the entire time. And true to his word, over the next three hours, that's precisely what he did.

My eyes opened slowly, almost blinded by the low morning sunlight streaming through my window. I remembered what day it was, and my heart dropped like a ton of weight in my stomach. Heat burned the back of my throat, and I sucked in a breath, trying to cool my lungs.

A strong hand squeezed my waist from behind, and Snow's husky voice murmured, "Morning, baby."

My hand covered his, touching his fingers, committing their feeling to memory. He let me play for a

Snow

while; maybe he was doing the same thing, storing away thoughts and feelings, tucking them safely inside to call on when needed.

An ache began to weave through my chest, turning every organ to dust until all that was left was emptiness.

How am I supposed to do this? How am I supposed to let him go?

"Look at me, Kitty cat," he demanded gently. "Turn around. I wanna see my girl."

I took a couple of shuddering breaths, still determined not to let him see me so distraught. Snow hadn't done anything wrong. He didn't need this guilt trip, and leaving him with the memory of my heart bleeding out on the bedroom floor wasn't fair to him.

"Kitten," he prompted. "Do as I say."

Sighing, I slowly turned over to face him.

His hand immediately lifted to cup my jaw. "I've never seen anything more beautiful." His thumb swept across my lip. "I promise, baby. It'll be easier this time. I'll write. I can call. It's not like deployment."

I held my breath and nodded.

"Thank you," he whispered thickly. "You've given me the best week of my life. I never imagined I could feel this way; didn't fucking dare to. You're my fire, baby."

I laughed a sob. "Don't. I'm trying not to lose it, but you keep giving me all this beauty, and it's just making it harder to let you go."

He dipped his chin, his golden eyes turning thoughtful. "You never have to hold back with me, Kitty. Don't ever hide from me. If you wanna cry, then cry. If you wanna laugh, laugh away. I choose you exactly the way you are, emotions and all. I'm not going anywhere. I may not be here in the physical sense. But we'll always be together here." He touched his heart, then mine. "I'm still yours, and you're still mine. Always."

I couldn't help it. A tear fell. Snow reached out, curled his hand around my nape, and tucked my face into his throat. "It's okay, Kitty cat," he rumbled. "Let it out."

So, I did. I went limp in his arms and wept as my heart cracked.

For the first time ever, I had something beautiful to hold, but now I had to let it go. My soul hurt for him. For the places he was going and the horrors he may have to endure.

I cried for everything we were going to miss. For every first we couldn't have together. I wept for everything that would happen in our lives that the other wouldn't witness. Finally, I cried at the thought of watching my beautiful soldier walk out the door and my world turning darker because he wasn't in it.

He moved suddenly. His arms went under my legs and back, lifting me against his chest and heading to the bathroom. I heard the shower start. Then he put me on my feet and kneeled before me, gently peeling off my panties. He stood again, tugging the shower door open and gently maneuvering me inside to stand under the warm spray.

He turned me to face him, eyes full of warm concern. His strong hands pushed my hair back as he angled my chin upward so he could look into my eyes. "Cry it out." He leaned down and kissed my tear-stained face. "I love you so fucking much, baby. I'm sorry I made you upset."

A hollow feeling appeared in the pit of my stomach. "No. It wasn't you." I sniffed. "I always knew you were leaving. I'm just gonna miss you, honey."

He grabbed the shower gel, squeezed a glob in his palm, and washed me. As his hands skated over my skin, I noticed he avoided my nipples and pussy. I frowned at him.

"I fucked you all I'm gonna fuck you this visit," he informed me. "This is just about being close, baby. Relax, and let me take care of my girl."

Snow

I smiled at his sweetness. "You're the hottest, cutest, most badass soldier I've ever met," I whispered. "Though you're the only hot, cute, badass soldier I've ever met."

He laughed. "There's my kitty cat. Knew I could make her smile." He pushed my wet locks of hair behind my ears, staring into my eyes. "Love you. Always and forever."

I smiled up at him. "Love you always and forever, Snow."

Ten minutes later, he wrapped me up in a warm, fluffy towel before tying a smaller one around his waist. We kept stealing looks at each other, taking everything in while we could.

My chest still ached, but I felt better.

The shower, Snow's care, and his affection had made me stronger. I tried to look on the bright side. I could return to work, earn, study, and then be free to do and go anywhere I wanted. We just had to get through the next few years. It wasn't like I'd never see or speak to him again.

This was just how it had to be for now, at least. It wasn't like I'd ever ask Snow to give up his military career for me. It would be like asking to give a piece of himself up. It was like he said to me earlier as we lay on our sides, staring into each other's eyes. I chose him exactly the way he was, military and all.

"I don't want you to come see me off, Kitten," he said huskily.

I stared at him, unable to breathe.

"I can't face the thought of leaving you crying alone in an airport. It's not a position I ever want you to be in. And then drive home in that state? No fucking way. I wanna leave you here to cry it out safely. I'll call a cab."

As much as I hated him saying that, I loved him *for* saying that. "See?" I croaked. "You give me so much beauty. Sometimes it hurts to breathe."

He grinned and checked his watch. "Got time for one more Game of Thrones. We can finish season two." He gazed at me, his golden eyes somber. "I just want you to promise one thing while I'm away from you."

I nodded. "Anything."

Grin still in place, he tugged me into him, nuzzling our noses together. His face went to my throat, and he inhaled me deeply. "Promise me you won't watch that fucking show without me."

My hands slid up his back. I cupped his nape and gave him the sweetest kiss I could muster. I put my heart and soul into it, trying to give him a tiny piece of me to take with him. "I promise, Snow. Never."

Chapter Seventeen

Snow

The journey back to Fort Campbell was uneventful.
At least I didn't have to stop off at Denver. I flew straight into Nashville, where Benny picked me up to make the hour-ish drive back to base. He'd spent the week at his folks' in Connecticut but flew back in the day before me.

I got my weekly call to Mom out of the way, sat back in the passenger seat, and listened to Ben chatter about his week.

I nodded at his stories, making all the right noises, but I wasn't present, not mentally, anyway. My head and heart were still back at Kitten's apartment, her in my arms, watching Game of Thrones.

I'd meant every word when I told her I'd had the best week of my life.

There, with her, I fit in.

Even when we went to 'Underground,' a place that usually would feel wrong to me, it felt right. Everything felt displaced when it came to my dad and brothers, but everything clicked together with her. Maybe that was the point when you found your soulmate. Nothing made sense when you weren't with your 'one' until you were touched by their grace again.

The only other place I'd ever felt remotely like myself was in the military. Now, the two things I loved most were fighting against each other for my care and attention.

Military life was good *for* me and good *to* me.

My personality was, well, frankly, full of fuckery. I got bored quickly and had a short attention span, which usually meant I got into trouble at the drop of a hat. The military taught me how to channel that energy into my work. How to focus, and how to become more regimented. I thrived off routine. It seemed to calm me down, and that was why I'd always believed that the U.S. Army was a lifelong career for me.

Then I met Kitten and finally found *home*.

She also calmed me. I felt normality with her that I'd only ever felt with the military, but in a different way. Where my career kept me focused, her free spirit called to the unconventional rule-breaker inside me. The girl danced on mountains, befriended the homeless, and cared for people who society forgot about.

And by God, I loved her for it.

The problem was, I couldn't have both one hundred percent. If I left the EOD for Kitten, who would I be? And if I left Kitten for the EOD, who would I be?

The only thing I was sure of, down to my bones, was that I'd have to choose one day.

For now, though, I'd keep both, even if it meant breaking Kitten's heart every time I left her. I knew it was the most selfish thing I could do, but what other option did I have?

She felt everything, and I knew loving me and watching me leave cut her deep, but she was vocal that she didn't want to let me go. So I'd hold on to her for as long as I could. Maybe even forever; who knew? Sometimes, forever wasn't long in my line of work, so I had to make the most of my time here.

Snow

Benny's voice permeated my brain, probably because he mentioned my girl's name. "Did you tell Kitten everything?"

My eyebrows knitted together in question, my neck swiveling left.

"How we lied about our names?" he prompted. "Did your girl fuck you up?"

I scraped a hand down my face, my insides suddenly heavy. "No. I couldn't do it. I kept my mouth shut all week. Thought I'd tell her on our last night. I tried, swear to God, Ben, but she got upset. Told me unless it was life and death, she didn't wanna know."

Benny shook his head exasperatedly. "Jesus, Snow. That's fucked up."

My jaw clenched as a hot temper rose through my throat. Ben was who gave my girl Simmon's fucking name in the first place, the hypocritical prick.

"I'll do it in my own time," I snapped, suddenly overwhelmed with the ramifications of not telling Kitten the truth. I raised a hand to rub at the growing ache in my temple, rolling the stress from my shoulders. "You don't get it. All week, we were in this bubble. She's fucking incredible. Us together is something so fucking unique that I was scared to burst it. I *will* tell her. I'll tell her everything, but I wanna do it face-to-face. It'll have to wait for the next visit."

"Okay. Okay. I'll lay off for now." Benny threw me another quick glance. "You get your pictures?"

"Yeah." I smiled. "Three. Two of her and a cheesy one of us together from when we met. Tried to get a shot of her tits on my cell, but she wasn't having it."

He busted out laughing. "Now she's shy. Half of Vegas and beyond have seen her tits."

I shrugged. "The woman you see on stage isn't who I see. She's not that character. The girl I know is a little shy and a lot sweet. A free spirit. She's got a lot of people in her corner because she draws 'em there."

"Yeah," he agreed. "She's got a way about her. Even I saw it. You need to tell her, Snowy. How are you supposed to build a lasting relationship when you don't even know each other's names? Even I know that, and I'm as dense as they come about all that shit."

"There is that," I joked, twisting my body slightly to look at him. "So, what about you? See any girls when you were home?"

A small smile floated across his lips. "Maybe."

I busted out a laugh. "The lady killer falls, huh?"

He laughed along with me. "I wouldn't go that far. It's a girl who was younger than me at school. Too young, so I never went there. Fifteen and eighteen are much further apart in years than nineteen and twenty-two."

"True," I stated. "Also, one's statutory rape, whereas the other, not so much."

"Exactly," he said, tone thoughtful. "I used to see her in the halls and have to look away. She was too young and, like your Kitten, too sweet. Plus, I had a fucking terrible reputation. We were worlds apart. Always thought she was beautiful, though. You wanna see her, Snow. Long jet-black hair and eyes the color of a stormy summer's day. Tiny, curvy, and cute as a button."

I grinned. Benny wasn't usually what I'd call poetic. Looked like this girl brought another side of him out. "What's her name?" I asked.

"Carina."

"Pretty," I murmured. "You gonna make her yours?"

He blew out a pfft sound. "Who the hell knows, Snowy? It'd be great to have a girl like her to go home to, but you know our life. We live in dangerous times, especially EOD. All I can do is visit when I can and see if we can build something. It's hard for any woman to be with a soldier. We're never home."

"Other people make it work," I pointed out. "People take their families with 'em when they get stationed in new places. It doesn't have to be constant separation if you don't want it to be."

"Can't take 'em to Afghanistan, though. And from what Hollister said, we've got another stretch coming up."

My chest panged as I thought about that.

Deployments were meant to be a 1:2 ratio. Meaning if you were deployed for six months, you had to be back on U.S. soil for twelve months before the next one. Most branches liked to keep their troops home for at least a year between deployments. The Defense Secretary could break that, though, which was happening more frequently. I'd also heard, in some cases, the powers that be had gotten around the timings by sending teams on specialized missions to Afghanistan for a few weeks and bringing 'em back. They kept doing it until the next official deployment time came around.

I accepted it. We were in a war on terror, and I'd signed up for the good fight. The soldiers in World Wars One and Two, even Vietnam, didn't get a choice of where and how long they were posted. War was war. It stood to reason that our soldiers were needed most in the thick of the action.

Also, EOD was specialized. There weren't many of us, so those rules didn't apply.

I'd seen what the U.S. Military was dealing with in Afghanistan. At home, we'd train, blow up shit that didn't matter, trying to hone our skills. At least over there, when we honed our skills it was on the job. At least there, we made a difference.

"I don't have the answers for you, Ben," I mused. "Got the same problem. I wanna keep Kitten, but I wanna keep my career, too."

Ben glanced at me. I noticed his knuckles were white as he gripped the steering wheel. "Have you ever thought about getting out, Snow?"

The thought made my brain wanna explode. "Can't say I have other than to look at my life without the U.S. Military. My dad would love me to join the MC, but it was never my thing, ya know?" I chuckled. "The thought of prospecting alone makes me wanna hurl."

"At least you've got that." He glanced at me again. "At least you can settle down somewhere and have a family."

"You could do the same," I suggested. "My dad would pull you into the MC in a heartbeat. We gotta lotta vets and ex-military in the club. Prospects who've served get first refusal. Dad likes not only the skill set they bring to the table but also their temperaments. Fact is, ex-military can take and carry out orders."

"Dunno about an MC, Snow. I've been thinking. I'd like to open my own security firm one day." He glanced at me before slashing his eyes back to the road. "Maybe we could look at that together."

I grinned. "Benny, with your skills, you'd get into a police department bomb squad."

"Yeah." He chuckled. "And get blown up? Defeats the point of leaving."

I thought about his suggestion. Honestly, it didn't appeal, but I didn't wanna be an asshole about it. Benny didn't have much to go out to, so it was natural that he'd be thinking of his future. I didn't wanna be the one to piss in his Cheerios, though.

"Look, Ben. We've got two years before our contracts come up for renewal, so we can't pop smoke now anyway. Let's lie low, do our jobs, and get home in one piece. We'll worry about the future when we have to."

"Good plan," he said, voice still thoughtful. He nodded toward the approaching sign for Oak Grove. "Nearly there, brother. Back to the grindstone on Monday. You all refreshed and raring to go?"

Snow

I slumped back in my seat, trying to ignore the heaviness in the pit of my stomach. "Yeah, Ben." I heaved out a long breath. "Ready as I'll ever be."

I'd only had time to haul my ruck to our room before a loud rap sounded from our door.

"What the fuck?" Ben muttered, rolling off the bed he'd just flopped down on. He moved toward the door and hauled it open.

My heart thudded when I saw Espinoza on the other side. "Good afternoon, ladies," he called out good-naturedly, "hope your health and spa weeks went well. I'm aware that you're not officially back on duty until Monday. Still, your favorite lieutenant would like a nice, cozy chat.

A stabbing pain slashed behind my eyes.

"Get in your uniforms, boys," Sarge ordered. "You got twenty, which, according to my rules, means you've got ten. Meet us in his office." With that, he turned and walked away.

Benny rolled his eyes, his shoulders slumping with the heavy sigh he blew out. "Fucking knew I should've stayed away until tomorrow."

I brought a hand up to rub my aching temple. "Come on. We can grumble later. Hollister will write us up if we're late."

We went to our small closets, grabbed our uniforms, and got changed. Quickly, I splashed water on my face and brushed my teeth, trying to summon the will to care. Fucking typical that Hollister knew we were back. The prick had eyes in the back of his head as well as up his asshole.

While in the bathroom, with only a basic sink and a toilet, I heard Benny call out, "Snow. Did I ever tell you about Lieutenant and the camel?"

I chuckled, rinsing my toothbrush. "No. Haven't heard that one." I walked out to see Benny getting dressed in his uniform. "Come on then, Benedetti. Tell me."

Ben checked his collar and cuffs were straight. "A newly commissioned U.S. Army lieutenant was assigned to a base in Afghanistan. He walked around to ensure everything was regulation. It was all good, except for a camel tied to a tree just inside the wire. The lieutenant asked one of the men who'd been there a while why the fuck there was a camel tied to a tree. The soldier explained that sometimes they got lonely, seeing there were no women there, so they had the camel. The lieutenant was disgusted, but being new, he let it go. After a few weeks, he felt really lonely. So he took the camel into his CHU. The camel put up so much of a fight that finally, the LT walked out, bruised and battered. 'Jesus,' he said to the men, 'that camel sure put up a fight! How do you guys do it?' One of the men responded, 'Well, usually we just use the camel to ride to the brothel in town.'"

I thought about it for a few seconds, then the punchline hit me, and I threw my head back and roared.

He grinned wider. "Just remember that when Hollister pisses us off. We'll buy the fucker a camel."

I wiped the moisture from my eyes, smiling at my friend.

What the fuck would I ever do without him? Ten minutes before, I was reeling. Now he had me cry laughing. I could always trust him to bring me around. Sol 'Benny' Benedetti was a good man and a better friend.

I nodded to the door. "C'mon. Let's go see what he wants."

Snow

Benny moved past me, and I clapped him on the shoulder. "Thanks, brother," I murmured. "Just thanks."

He turned to me, still chucking. "Anytime, Snow."

To my surprise, Simmons was waiting when we walked into Hollister's office. My eyes slid to his as if to say. *What the hell's going on?*

He looked back at me, made a face, and gave a little shrug.

Hollister sat behind his desk, reading notes from his laptop. Take a seat, men," he ordered, eyes never wavering from the screen.

I sat in the middle of my two buds.

The door opened, and Sergeant Espinoza walked in with another man by his side.

My throat closed up when I realized it was Hollister's boss. Captain Alvares. I'd had dealings with him before, but not often this up close and personal. He commanded around eighty men in total. So, most of the everyday stuff concerning our team was left to our lieutenant and Sarge.

I'd heard he was a hard man but fair. About five-ten, stocky, muscled, olive-skinned, and black-haired. Someone told me his folks had emigrated from Portugal when he was a baby and scrimped and saved to put him through college. But then you heard a lotta shit in this place—not all of it strictly true.

We all stood and saluted as he walked around the other side of Hollister's desk and dragged a chair over, slumping back in it without a care in the world. I glanced behind to see Espinoza take a seat by the door.

"Stand down, soldiers," Alvarez ordered.

We took our seats.

Hollister typed something on his laptop before clicking on the mouse and shutting it down. Snapping the lid closed, he glanced at Alvarez and sat back in his chair. Immediately, his elbows settled on the arms of his chair, and his fingers steepled at his chin, eyes regarding us thoughtfully.

"EOD," he began. "Explosive Ordinance Disposal. Our department knows explosives inside out. We know heat supplies, switches, and what makes them tick—literally in some cases." He leaned forward, arms resting on the desk. "So, I ask you, boys. Who better than to build them?"

The back of my neck prickled.

Still lounging in his chair, Alvares looked from me to Benny to Simmons. "Lieutenant Hollister tells me that he regards you three men as the best in his team."

Dayum. I had to fight my lips from tipping up.

"He also informs me that you all worked well together during your recent deployment. Says that you overcame personal issues and got the job done. In some cases," his eyes slashed to me, "excelled." He let that hang in the air for a minute before turning to Hollister, dipping his chin, and leaning back again.

The lieutenant cocked a thick brow, still eyeballing us. "Captain Alvares has authorized me to offer you men the chance to become part of a task force that builds and distributes explosives. Before I get chatty, I must clarify that you do *not* discuss this with anyone. This shit is so low on the down that it's at Earth's core. You do not talk about it, even *think* about it, unless I give you permission. Do you understand?"

My gut gave an uncomfortable clench, but I muttered, 'Yes, sir,' along with Benny and Simmons.

"This task force is sent covertly into areas which known terrorists frequent," he continued. "We build, set, and detonate. It's high-pressured, high mortality, and so intense that even with your training, it's a mindfuck. You'll be nothing but shadows. We'll teach you everything you need to know, but I want to clarify." He leaned forward, anchoring his stare on us. "It will play on your minds. You'll share space with known terrorists. You'll have your back to a wall, sometimes working yards away from the enemy. You're sent in, do what you do, and get out. Well... Usually." He smirked.

My gut churned.

I'd heard rumors about this task force. They were assembled during the previous War in Afghanistan before being sent to Iraq. That was it. That was my knowledge of them, proving they were tight and kept their mouths shut.

This shit was significant and, like Hollister told us, undercover, covert ops. The exact type of secret that the U.S. Defense Department denied even knowing the existence of.

I didn't really know how to feel about it.

One side of me wanted to run for the hills. I'm sure Alvarez and Hollister only told us what they needed to at that stage. There was a dark side to every country's military and government agencies. Secret Service, MI5, SAS, CIA, FBI—they all had an underbelly of agents who carried out the ugly shit nobody wanted to take responsibility for. It was deep, dark, and dangerous.

The other side of me, the rebel, felt like my birthday had come early. I'd enlisted essentially to annihilate the T-Man after sitting in front of the TV as a kid and watching those towers go up in flames. Hollister had offered an opportunity to pinpoint the organization behind that attack and ensure they couldn't do it again. There was also the payback. They'd go out the same way many American citizens and Afghani kids had.

They'd burn.

I'd already killed a man. If God was gonna damn me for it, I'd already *be* damned. Would taking out a few more wicked men really hurt?

"So," Hollister said gruffly. "The choice is yours. I'll respect you if it's a no, but this conversation never happened. If it's repeated, I'll make sure you disappear for good. Think about it, though. Men who carry out these ops usually leave the military with well-forged connections. You could be recruited by top-level agencies from all over the world when you pop smoke. In effect, you'll be made men."

Benny and Simmons stiffened on either side of me, and I immediately understood why.

Both didn't have much to go out to. If Ben forged the right connections, his security business could do well. Simmons could move away, get a government job, and pull his family out of poverty.

Even I could settle in one city, maybe work for one of the agencies too. I'd still be doing work that mattered and perhaps could even be involved with the military as a consultant. The only difference was I could also have Kitten by my side. She could be a CEO anywhere, and if I knew the right people, I could help make that happen for her.

The uneasiness in my stomach turned into a ripple of excitement that weaved up my chest and made it puff out slightly. This could be the solution to everything.

A sign.

My back snapped straight in my chair. "Permission to speak, sir?"

Hollister's lips twitched, and he jerked a nod. The fucker knew precisely what was coming next.

"I've already made my decision, sir." I held his eyes as my mouth curved into a massive grin. "You can count me in."

Chapter Eighteen

Snow ~ Three Weeks Later

"Snow, Simmons," Benny said in a low tone. "Did you ever hear the one about the Air Force lieutenant?"

I compressed two wires with my fingers, shaking my head while Simmons muttered, "Can't say I have, Ben."

"Well," he went on. "A sergeant in a parachute battalion was participating in a shitload of nighttime exercises. One night, he sat next to a lieutenant fresh outta Jump School. The LT was quiet, so the sergeant decided to chat with him and get his mind off things. 'Scared Lieutenant?' he asked. The lieutenant shook his head nervously. 'No, Sergeant. Just apprehensive.' The sarge looked at him like he was crazy and asked. 'What's the fucking difference?' The lieutenant shrugged and said, 'It means I'm scared but with a college education.'"

Simmons and I chuckled. "Good one, Ben," I whispered. "Mop my brow for me. If I sweat on this motherfucker we'll get blowed up."

Benny reached up with some tissue and did as I asked.

"Thanks," I nodded. "Just one more adjustment and—" I slotted the switch carefully into place. "Done," I announced quietly. "We'll disable it again while we wait for the Marines and reconnect it when we sneak in.

Jules Ford

I looked around the back of the Humvee we sat in, heart racing out my chest.

We were on our first mission as part of Task Force Fever.

Two hours ago, we'd been spirited off a plane by a unit of Marines and brought to the mouth of the Tora Bora caves in Eastern Afghanistan. Our objective was to set an explosion big enough to cause a panic that sent members of the Taliban into a trap. Our blast site area was lesser used and lesser known, though intelligence had word that one of the T-Man leaders was hunkered down close.

The Marines were currently clearing it and taking out whoever they could as silently as possible. We'd built two explosives and were ready to go.

All I needed was to calm the fuck down.

I bent my neck, steepled my fingers to my forehead, and closed my eyes. I breathed gently through my nose and outta my mouth, fighting against the adrenaline surging through my veins.

My heart rate slowly began to settle. Consciously relaxing my muscles, I continued breathing, in and out, rinse and repeat. I imagined a mountain, a sunrise, and peace. My heart slowed and began pumping steadily again.

After a few minutes, my stare lifted to watch as Benny cracked his neck from side to side, threading his rosary beads between his fingers.

Simmons stretched out his limbs and breathed much like I'd juts done.

In our first week of recruiting into Task Force Fever, the officers looked at specific points from our past EOD training and took us through them again, but on steroids that time. The main challenge we faced wasn't building an explosive but staying calm.

Espinoza taught us how to transcend to an almost meditative state for hours. Not just breathing like before but clearing our minds to the point where we could control our bodies and their functions. Within a week, when Hollister ordered me to shut it down, that was precisely what I did; I shut down my mind, my soul, and my emotions.

I morphed into a machine, and it served me well.

A quiet scuffle sounded from outside the Humvee. Just as my hand automatically went for my weapon, a Marine appeared at the window, jerking his head at us to get out.

Ben opened the door and slid his feet onto the moon dust-covered ground. Simmons followed. I went last, taking the ruck full of explosives with me.

"My team's cleared the area," said the sergeant. "We're trying to flush out any others dotted around, but if we delay much longer, someone will notice something and raise the alarm." He nodded toward a dark mouth of caves a few hundred feet away. "Keep up."

He bent forward and began to run.

The closer we ran, the more massive the caves loomed. Taliban strongholds were stationed throughout this miles-long cave system. It was where the enemy plotted crazy shit, like how they'd build bombs and strap them onto small children. This was where they planned brutal acts and prayed for the downfall of my country and its brave men and women.

My jaw clenched as an icy, dark tendril of blackness curled inside me and gripped hold tight.

The memory of a man in black running toward a crowd of people, eyes brutal and hateful, flashed through my mind. The dark void inside swelled and grew until it filled me up. Suddenly, I couldn't wait to get in there and blow everything sky fucking high.

The Marine slowed as we reached the entrance. Four of his team stood with M4s pointing downward, where a group of men in robes lay tied up on the ground with black sacks covering their heads. One made a noise, trying to get up. I couldn't see, but it sounded like he was gagged. One of the soldiers stepped forward and cracked his head with the butt of his weapon.

I smiled and ran faster as the robed man hit the dust again with a thud.

The inside of the cave was pitch-black. Within seconds, we were blind.

"Night vision," I hissed. A few clicks and everything was lit up in green and blue hues along with the yellows, oranges, and reds of my brother's body heat.

"Stay at my six," the Marine ordered. "We've found a clearing about half a kilometer up that could work as a blast site. It's wide open enough to collapse everything above it, so the entire section will crumble with God's will. Hope you've brought enough power."

I checked the weight of the backpack still hauled over my shoulder. "Just get us there," I bit out. "We know what we're doing."

Heavy breaths sawed through my lungs as we carried on our upward trajectory through the warrens of tunnels. A musty, dampness assaulted my senses, making a muscle tic inside my jaw. If death ever had a smell, that would be it. Pure and utter filth. The scent of the devil.

Within minutes, we were at the blast site.

My eyes took in the vast cavern, calculating where to detonate and cause the most carnage. I needed to think about it for a few seconds.

"How many meters above us? I asked, turning to the Marine.

He twisted his mouth as he thought. "I'd say no more than a kilometer, give or take."

"Back wall?" Benny suggested.

I closed my eyes, imagining the collapse. Feeling my way around the image until I came up with a solution. "Close," I agreed. "We'll bring it out between three and four meters. We wanna make the structure unstable but give the blast some room to blow upward, too. Two birds, one stone."

Benny's eyes hardened as he took the backpack from me. "You're a fucking machine."

I didn't argue because, at that minute, I kinda was. "Set it up. I'll connect the switch while Simmons programs it. Then we'll get the fuck outta dodge. We'll detonate as we hit the mouth of the cave and be away before everything above collapses in on itself."

He pulled the contents of the bag out. "Gimme three minutes," he said, moving to the spot I pointed out and getting started.

"Start programming," Simmons suggested. "You're faster than us. I'll go help set up." He picked up a tac torch the Marine had laid down and followed Ben.

"Three minutes," the Marine muttered, moving toward the tunnels and peering out. "That's as fast a time as I've known. It's usually around five."

"You've worked with our team before?" I asked mockingly. "Don't you use your own EOD boys for this shit? Heard your jarhead EOD loves blowing shit up. They always were noisy, gung-ho fuckers." I parked my ass to the ground and began programming the equipment on the laptop I pulled from the bag.

A grin split his face. "Our boys are as good as they come, but Command wanted a special task force on this one. It's a sticky mission, so they required something more subtle. Our EOD exists. They can all be pinpointed as we speak. You guys don't, at least not on paper. Therefore, if the higher-ups wanna deny involvement, they need ghosts."

I tapped on the keys, breathing a satisfied sigh when I picked up the switch's signal. All kinds of shit could go wrong on these missions, dud equipment being one of 'em. You could take all the precautions in the world, but explosives were unpredictable at best. Though I needn't have worried, we'd triple-checked everything before coming here, then checked again.

"Charges are in," Simmons called over. "We're wired up and ready to go. Just need the switches."

I glanced at the Marine. "How long will it take us to get out?"

He weighed the answer up in his head for a few seconds. "'Bout four to five minutes. It's quicker going down than up."

I shut the laptop down. "Ben, get everything packed away. What we leave will go boom."

He nodded and began to pack a small set of tools away while I shoved the laptop back inside the bag. "Got the switches, Simmons?"

"Yeah." He carefully held them both up. "It's time to party."

I gripped the small black detonator while reaching for my knife. "D it, and let's go."

I heard two clicks as the switches were fitted, then we all moved swiftly toward the tunnel we came in from. Cutting our moonbeams as we approached the pitch-black, we switched back to night vision. I held the detonator tightly. Whatever happened, the mission was to blow the place, so that's what would happen.

As my thoughts went there, my stomach started to churn. I nearly puked with the reminiscence of the last time that nausea hit me so hard. "Watch for trouble," I hissed. "Gotta bad feeling." It was like I'd manifested the devil himself because a red-hued figure suddenly loomed to the left of my night vision as I spoke.

Without thought, I whirled around and struck out with my knife. My heart jerked with a sense of satisfaction as the figure staggered back with a curse. "Kuss modar."

A scuffle broke out. I could only make out the outlines of two figures on the floor.

"Asshole, fucking piece of shit," I heard Benny grate out before more shuffling sounded. The thuds of rhythmic punching cut through the air.

"Fuck," the Marine muttered, clicking his tac torch on.

I switched off night vision to see what was happening, lungs almost bursting out of my chest. My guts leaped when I saw Benny on his knees beating the shit out of a big fucker in robes. Blood from the deep slash across the insurgent's face flew everywhere, including on my teammate, whose fist flashed back and forth, beating the guy like a wild animal. He was going fucking crazy. "Fucking asshole, motherfucker," Ben snapped, spittle flying out of his mouth.

"Ben," I shouted. "We gotta go."

"We can't leave him alive. If he gets inside that cavern, he could fuck everything up." The Marine grabbed my fist and held it up, looking at my knife pointedly. "Gunshots will draw the enemy."

His meaning registered, and without hesitation, I stepped forward, knife still in hand, and moved behind the insurgent, lifting his head by the hair. I felt a hot, sharp pang in my solar plexus as I slid my knife into his jugular.

The whites of his eyes filled with blood as he gargled, his life force bubbling from his mouth.

Emotionless, except for my sneer, I watched the Reaper come to collect. My stare slid to my friend, still on his knees. "Benny. Let's fucking go," I ordered, pulling him by the arm as I rose.

He nodded, face covered in blood while his dazed stare was still glued to the insurgent's voided eyes, and stood.

I grabbed his arm. "Come on. We need to beat feet." And we were on the move again but with more urgency than before. Suddenly, my collar seemed too tight, and my heart began to hammer, but I breathed through it.

After a few seconds, it calmed. My thoughts raced with the realization that we needed to get the fuck out. I tamped the dark thoughts down, making my mind go blank.

A pinprick of light shone like a beacon just as the Marine's watch beeped. "That's four minutes," he called back. "We're nearly there."

We raced toward the light. "Gonna detonate now!" I yelled. "Fucking move."

My finger went to the switch and clicked. The deafening sound of an explosion ricocheted through the air. The cave began moving around us like it had come to life. Dust particles started to fall around our heads. Just another twenty feet, and we'd be out.

Two more Marines stood at the mouth of the cave, waving us through. "Go. Go. Go."

And suddenly, we were outside in the cool night air, pulling in deep, gulping breaths as we ran to get clear of the mountain. My eyes automatically went to where the Insurgents had been bound and gagged earlier. They were gone.

"Humvees. Now!" The Marine ordered. "Our orders are to get you boys back to the airport immediately." As we approached the vehicles, he called, "Are we cleared out?"

"Yes, Sarge," someone confirmed. "All present and correct. All we've left behind are bullets in heads."

One of the Humvee doors flew open. "Go," the Marine ordered. "We gotta get outta here before it all turns fugazi."

We leaped inside the back of the vehicle. The Marine sergeant stuck his head inside the open window. "It was a pleasure doing business with you, boys." He barked out a laugh and banged twice on the vehicle roof before we sped away.

Simmons slumped back in his chair. "Jesus, fucking Christ," he said with a heaving breath.

Snow

I glanced at Benny, looking out of the window behind me. "Fuck me," he murmured.

Turning, I took in the sight of the eastern tip of the mountain caving in. It almost seemed to implode with the hammering force of the collapse. A vision swam through my mind. The view of that mountain burying everything underneath was reminiscent of two towers collapsing.

A slow smile swept across my face. Finally, an eye for an eye.

"Snow," Benny murmured. "You okay?" I followed the direction of his stare downward. My hands jerked along with the force of the tremors suddenly crashing through my chest. All the adrenaline I'd shut down suddenly came to life and whooshed through my veins.

Everything inside me seemed to burst open. I tipped my head back and bellowed a loud, "Yeehaw!" Laughter filled my throat, along with the same euphoria that seized me back at the dance club in Vegas. Within seconds, Simmons, Benny, and I were all whooping and hollering.

Simmons's eyes shone. "Did you see how that blade slid in that fucker's throat?" He shook his head. "Never seen anything like it."

"I shit myself when you detonated." Benny laughed, his expression contrasting with the blood streaked across his features. "Need to check my shorts, fucking ASAP."

"What a fucking rush," I yelled, punching the air. "Boys. Just gotta say one thing." I hooted out another loud chuckle, my eyes darting between my two buds. "I fucking love my job."

We all began to laugh again, riding the high, the excitement, and the rush. Our first task force mission was a success. We'd taken out an entire fucking T-Man cell. My body sang with a joyous sense of achievement. But, little did I know, it would all come crashing down hours later.

"Enter!" Hollister's voice ordered from inside his office.

I flung the door open so hard it banged against the back wall. Jaw locked tight, I stalked toward my LT's desk and laid my palms flat. My face twisted. "There were kids in there?"

Hollister's face blanked. "Shut the door," he ordered.

"What the fuck?" I demanded.

Slowly, Hollister stood and mirrored my pose until we were eyeball to eyeball. "I gave you a direct order, SPC Stone. Now. Shut the fucking door."

I turned, hands balling into fists. My jaw was clenched so tight my back teeth gnashed together. I closed the door, whipped around, and marched back.

"Sit!" my lieutenant ordered. "Take a fucking breath and calm down before you do something very fucking stupid."

I closed my eyes, bringing my hand up to rub my temple. "Five kids, sir," I croaked. "Nobody told us there'd be kids there."

"What makes you think I knew?" he asked.

I slumped in the chair in front of his desk, all anger seeping out of me. "Didn't you?"

Hollister did his classic pose of steepling his fingers to his chin, regarding me thoughtfully. "No. The order came down from intelligence. I knew little more than you. But let me be very clear, Snow. If I had known, I'd have still given the order."

My gut dropped. "Huh?"

He paused for a minute, his eyes still boring into me as he thought. After a minute, he finally spoke. "We're fighting a war, Snow. There are always casualties. None of us want it, and I admit it's hard to stomach, but those kids in those caves indicate two things. They were being prepped for an attack or belonged to the people there. Either way, that makes them the enemy." He leaned forward. "How do you know those kids wouldn't have gone out tomorrow, the next day, the next week, and ran at a group of U.S. soldiers while wearing a tricked-out vest?"

I scraped a hand down my face. "How do you know they would?"

"Stone. They were inside a cave system used by the Taliban to hide out, operate, and plan. Whichever way you look at it, those kids had been radicalized. If they were the offspring of the people in there, they grew up hating everything we stand for. You do the math."

Jesus, my head was splitting apart with everything that had gone down. The high from the mission still coursed through me. Then I found out I'd just blown up some kids, and the high remained but turned caustic, like acid flushing through my veins.

"It just doesn't sit right with me," I told him. "Even if they were radicalized, they still didn't deserve that."

"Maybe not," Hollister replied quietly. "But would they have deserved in five or ten years when they hijacked an aircraft and flew into our White House? The fact remains, Snow, we had orders. I'll sign the release now if you want off the task force. This won't be the last time a kid gets caught up in this shit. It's a daily occurrence, task force or not."

The image of Kitten's face flashed behind my eyes, and my stomach jerked.

Being on the task force made sense in so many ways. If I wanted it all, I didn't have a choice. Maybe Hollister was right. It wasn't what I wanted and gutted me, but this was my life. I wasn't gonna give up after one mission. "No. I wanna stay, sir." I confirmed.

Hollister nodded, giving me a wry smile. "If it's any consolation, we've had word that you took down the target. A high-up in finance. A criminal who laundered money for the enemy all over the world. I know you're fighting with yourself. Been there and done it many times, too. But it's clear to me and your superiors, you men saved a lotta people tonight."

I nodded, even though my head was still at war with my heart.

"You feeling wired?" LT asked.

I nodded. "Yes, sir. I'm struggling to settle, especially after the kid thing."

"Gym. I'll see you there in thirty."

My head snapped up. "You wanna spar with me, LT?"

Hollister shrugged. "I'll bring Espinoza down too. He's a goddamned hammer. Sarge will fuck you boys up in minutes. It'll make my week to see you bleed. Payback for those fucking rubbers you burned at my window."

I grimaced. "Dunno what you're talking about, sir."

Hollister's lips thinned. "Course you don't." He jerked his chin toward the door. "Now get the hell out. I got a report to finish up before I can take you kids out to play."

I stood, back snapping straight, a grin tugging at my mouth. "Yes, sir."

I dodged Espinoza's fist as it came flying toward my jaw.

"That's it, Snow. Make him work for it," Hollister yelled. "We'll make a fighter out of you yet."

The smartass fuck wouldn't say that if he knew I'd been sparring since I was six when Grandpa Bandit stuck me in a ring with Bowie and made us slug it out. I'd broken one of my brother's toys, a soldier of all things. After five minutes of Bo chasing me around the bar, Gramps made us sort it like men.

Snow

That was the first time I got my ass kicked, but I learned a valuable lesson that day.

Don't get caught.

Sarge hurtled toward the side of my face. I ducked again, left and right, avoiding his flurry of punches.

"Slippery little SOB," he panted.

"You're too slow." I laughed, bouncing on the balls of my feet. "Maybe you're getting too old for it."

Laughter went up from the boys standing outside the ring.

I pulled my gloves up in front of my face and aimed a jab.

He dodged, and it glanced off the side of his face.

I jabbed again and again. The last pummel hit, and he let out a quiet 'oof.' Encouraged, I did a flurry of two-one punches.

Espinoza jumped back and swung at my kidney.

It landed hard, and I let out a grunt.

Hollister cackled from below. "See, boys. Experience wins every time."

A fire lit inside my gut, and I struck out, catching the sergeant's jaw. I followed that with a blow to the other side of his head. It cracked back before he recovered and jabbed back at me.

The fire began to burn through me. I focused on Espinoza's face, going to jab again, but he was ready for me that time and moved.

My heart raced, skin feeling raw where my nerve endings heated. The gut churn started, and my eyes narrowed on my target. I struck out, a satisfied smile taking over my features when it landed.

Sarge twisted, ducked, and threw an uppercut that hit its mark.

My teeth rattled.

I stretched my jaw out and went for Espinoza's kidneys from the side. Another one, two before I landed a flurry of blows to his body.

Espinoza came at me, baring his teeth. "Now you're getting it, Snow." He punched himself on the side of the head with a glove-covered hand. "More, boy. Show Papi what you got."

Everything around me seemed to slow down. My ribs felt tight, and the burning need to hurt someone made me see red. I lashed out again, one, two, and caught Sarge again on the temple that time.

He laughed. "You punch like my mama, asshole." He beat himself once, hard on his stomach. "Is that it, boy?"

My world shrank down to one point—Espinoza's face. I pulled my arm back and threw a blow to the side of his head.

He skipped out of the way, laughing and landing another jab across my ear.

Incensed, I let out a guttural roar, planted my feet, and threw a punch. It hit home, and his head snapped back. My chest seemed to explode, and in that minute, I could've killed him. My blood pumped so hard that my ears roared with it, and I barreled toward him, throwing another punch.

On I went, releasing all the pent-up shit. We traded blows for a good minute before I felt someone grab my arm, pulling me back.

"Stand down, Snow. That's an order," Hollister said calmly in my ear. "Breathe."

I obeyed, taking huge gulps of breath, trying to get myself under control. After a minute, the rage seemed to seep out of me. The world came rushing back in, and my shoulders slumped.

Espinoza took his head guard off, laughing. "Feel better now, Snowy? Did you get shot of all that built-up young, dumb cum? See? See, Papi made it better." He blew me a kiss, still wearing his boxing gloves.

I turned to Hollister, whose lips twitched as he looked between me and Sarge. "Like the way you jab, Snow. If I'd have known you had that much spirit, I'd have brought you here before." He cocked an eyebrow. "How you feeling?"

I took stock for a few seconds and grinned. "Better," I said confusedly. "Good even."

"That's what I'm talking about. You'll sleep well tonight now you got all that out of ya." He looked down at the floor where Benny prowled. "You're up, Benedetti."

"Yes, sir." Benny climbed into the ring and helped me remove my gloves while eyeballing Sarge.

"Love it when my boys eye-fuck me." Espinoza smirked, banging his gloves together. "Let's go!"

I helped Ben with his gloves, then transferred the head guard over. It was sweaty, but Benny didn't notice; he was so fixated on the sergeant.

"Get down, dry off, and watch the show," Hollister ordered. "I'm gonna stay in the corner for this one. Seems Benedetti's got some major pent-up shit he needs to get rid of. Don't want him to get hurt."

I jumped down from the ring, pulled a mat over, and parked my ass next to Simmons.

My nausea had settled, and my chest felt lighter. Getting in the ring was an effective way to calm down after a mission. I'd been on a razor's edge since we returned to base and heard about those kids.

My mind went back to the conversation we'd had in Lieutenant's office. What he'd said made more sense now that I'd tired myself out and could think clearer. I'd never condone killing a child, but Hollister was right. Sadly, some were more innocent than others.

My thoughts turned to Kitten, and I smiled.

It seemed years since our week together. I wondered if the LT would authorize some leave soon. I'd called her a few times, but our task force training took a lot out of us, and the conversations had been short and to the point. We were on restrictions, so we couldn't travel more than two hundred miles from the base. Until Hollister lifted that my hands were tied. The old me would've sneaked out anyway and hoped I got away with it, but I was trying to turn over a new leaf since making SPC.

I checked my watch; maybe I could call my girl. It was early Friday night; she'd be at work but probably not on stage yet.

Decision made: I got to my feet and moved toward the door.

"Where you going, Snow?" Hollister called over.

I stopped and turned. "Gonna go check in with my family, sir."

His eyes bored into me. "You straight now?"

"Yes, sir."

He jutted his chin up before turning his concentration back toward the ring.

Jogging into the corridor, I weaved through the halls and took the stairs up toward the living quarters two at a time. The base was well on its way to becoming one of the largest military installations in the country. Thousands lived here, and thousands more lived in the surrounding counties, too. The fort was like its own town in many respects.

I swept into my dorm room, went to the nightstand beside my bed, and grabbed my cell. Easing onto the bed, I laid back and called Kitty. I'd programmed her number with the prefix which hid my caller ID. Couldn't have her calling here at awkward moments, like when Hollister was bellowing 'Stone' at me. I knew it was a conversation we needed to have, but like I'd told Benny, I wanted it to be face-to-face.

I found her number, tapped it, and raised a relaxed arm behind my head.

The lines connected, and her sweet voice said, "Hello? Snow? Is that you?"

My heart swelled. "Who else would be calling you this time on a Friday night? How you doing, baby?"

Snow

She giggled down the line. "I'm good, honey. I'm so happy to hear your voice."

I swear my heart did a backflip. "You at work?"

"Yeah," she replied. "I'm due to go out there in about ten minutes."

I frowned. "Early tonight? Thought you went on last?"

"Raven had another gig at Underground, so I'm dancing twice."

Something stabbed inside my lungs, and my stomach hardened. "What the fuck?" I snapped. "Can't someone else do it?"

"I guess," she said slowly. "But Marco would only give Raven the night off if I covered for her. And I thought the extra money would come in handy for Harvard."

A brittle laugh burst out of me. My fingers twitched with the urge to hurl my cell across the room. "More like you can't wait to show yourself off to that boss of yours." I sneered. "That's if he *is* just a boss."

The line went silent.

My breaths turned heavy, nostrils flaring. "Kitten. The fuck?"

"I'm here," she said, voice timid.

"Tell him you can't do it," I demanded. "Fucker can go swing."

I heard her sharp intake of breath before she whispered, "I can't do that. Marco's my employer."

Even my girl saying his name caused a flash of heat to scald my chest. A deep growl rose through my throat.

"Snow?" she said softly, tone laced with confusion. "Honey. I'm sorry if I did something to upset you."

Jesus.

The internal burning rage left me as quickly as it came on. "Fuck," I croaked, throat still heated. "Kitten. It's not you. I'm sorry. I've hardly slept for two days. It's making me an asshole."

I heard her sigh down the line. "Are they working you too hard? Why haven't you slept?"

My hand went to the back and rubbed the tension away. "We were out on maneuvers."

"Oh," she replied.

The line went awkwardly silent. Jesus, I couldn't fucking stand it. "Baby. I'm so fucking sorry for speaking to you that way."

"Apology accepted. We all get cranky when we're tired. Nothing I can't handle." She paused for a few seconds. "But you know Marco's just my employer, right? To him, I'm nothing more than a commodity."

Of course, I fucking knew that. "Kitten. You don't have to reassure me. I dunno what got into me. I'm not even jealous usually—but—" my voice trailed off.

"But what?"

I smiled. "Never been in love before, baby girl. You bring out feelings I never thought I'd experience."

She giggled again, and I breathed a relieved sigh. "Me too, Snow."

"I need to see you, baby," I mused. "Maybe I'm having withdrawal from my girl, and it's fucking with my head."

"Well, I'm definitely having withdrawal from something," she said in a sultry voice.

Immediately, my cock thickened. "Yeah?" I said before I heard a voice at her end call her name.

She sighed audibly. "I'm sorry, Snow. I have to go. I'm due on stage."

My cock deflated. "Okay. Love you, baby."

"Love you too," she said before the line went dead.

My hand dropped, and I stared unseeing at my cell, skin tight as a drum.

I'd made Kitten uncomfortable, which was the last thing I wanted. Rationally, I knew there was nothing unprofessional between her and Marco, but for a minute there, I lost my shit. I was definitely experiencing Kitten withdrawal, plus I hadn't slept because of the mission.

That had to be it.

My eyes drifted closed as I thought about her skin, her scent. All the mental snapshots I'd taken of her flickered through my mind like a movie reel, making my chest slowly loosen.

I smiled, thoughts of my girl taking over my thoughts until clean replaced dirty and good replaced evil. With my mind exhausted, I finally drifted off to sleep.

Chapter Nineteen

Snow ~ Four Weeks Later

"How's your ma doing?" Benny asked.

I shrugged, gaze still on the small row of terraced houses we'd been watching for the last five hours. "Okay. Called her yesterday. Seems like the same old."

Ben and I were in some backwater woods in a place called Tamworth in the U.K. We'd flown in, holed up in some scuzzy hotel, and awaited orders. Turned out it was a hurry-up-and-wait kinda day. My worst nightmare. I'd been pacing, fingers jittery, gut jumpy. This mission was a whole new level of bullshit. In Afghanistan, the government could explain away the shit we did; it was war after all. But here. If we got caught by the authorities, we were on our own. Hanging fire made me think, which made me restless, and restless didn't bode well when dealing with explosives.

Finally, after twelve wasted hours, our contact called.

British Counter Terrorism had pinpointed a man on their watch list. They suspected he was preparing to commit an act of terror and needed it shut down quickly and illegally. They believed the suspect, a man radicalized online, was dangerous enough to be taken out.

Our objective was to wait until he slept, go in, and eliminate him, along with any IEDs he may have built. We were to take what we could for analysis but leave enough to blow his house up without causing too much damage to the neighboring properties.

It was a little past 02:00. The last light from one of the houses a few doors from our target had gone off about an hour before. We'd waited until the street was sleeping.

I breathed through my nerves, steepled my fingers, cleared my mind, and shut my shit down. Once in robot mode, I watched Benny thread his rosary beads through his fingers and zone out.

It was time to move in.

We donned our ski masks and moved in. We were like shadows flitting down the street, taking cover against walls, and creeping through backyards until we reached our position. The house had a back entrance, which Benny immediately got to work on with a lockpicking kit. Within a minute, we'd sneaked inside a small galley kitchen leading to a dining room.

Benny signaled for us to take a quick look around.

We did so silently.

Nothing seemed out of the ordinary. A few dirty pots rested on the stove, but the place seemed clean and tidy.

We moved from the dining room to a small living room. On the right-hand wall, stairs led up to the second floor. Under the stairs was a built-in cupboard. Light shone through the crack of the door.

We'd seen the floor plans of the house, so we knew that door led to a cellar as extensive as the plot and large enough for a workroom.

Bingo.

I signaled Benny to do a weapons check while I got prepared.

My partner pulled out his MK-23 while I fisted my knife, and with a nod, he cracked the door open. Missions like this required finesse. Benny went in with the gun, me the blade. This was our fifth mission with the task force. Each one had resulted in us killing at least one person. Death was becoming a regular part of the job.

The U.K. didn't have a gun culture like we did in the States. The average person didn't own one. Weapons were highly regulated and mainly illegal to own. That meant if we left a bullet behind, it would look suspicious.

Instead, Britain had prolific knife crime, and that suited me perfectly.

The insurgent from the Tora Bora caves, whose jugular I'd knifed, was the first of many. It was becoming a regular occurrence. We found ways to stay in the shadows. Silencers weren't completely silent, so my weapon of choice became my knife. It did the trick. Plus, I found I was learning to enjoy the process of sliding my blade across a throat and watching life drain away. It almost gave me a high.

Benny stopped just inside the door and pointed down.

The dry-walled cellar's stifling heat made my collar stick to my neck. I glanced at the stairs leading down, noticing they were enclosed and carpeted. Good. Whoever was down there wouldn't know we were coming.

Low voices wafted up toward us, indicating more than one person occupied the basement. I looked at Benny, and he gave me a nod, telling me he was aware. The space appeared dim, a dull glow coming from beyond the stairs, leading us to our target like a night beacon.

Room didn't exist for fear, feeling, or emotion as we slowly began to creep down, except for a faint prickle in my chest, almost like muted excitement. We reached the bottom of the steps, and I slowly poked my head around to see into the room.

Two people, a man and a woman, sat at a table full of wires with their backs to us. They chatted softly while watching a video of an insurgent building an IED on a flat screen attached to the back wall. The man said something to the woman, and she giggled softly.

Immediately, a vision of Kitten flashed behind my eyes. I shook my head, trying to push her out. She had no place amongst this. She represented everything good in my life. A pillar of decency and the reason I was here, doing this.

I concentrated on the face of the terrorist still flashing across the TV. My lip curled, and all thoughts of my girl disappeared.

I sensed Benny creep up beside me, and together, we moved.

The couple sat about eight feet away from the stairs, but our approach seemed to take hours. We crept closer. Our most effective weapon was the element of surprise. We always used that to our advantage.

It was too fucking easy. They didn't have a clue we were there. It wasn't until we were upon them that the woman must've sensed something. She stilled for a split second and whipped her head around, craning her neck.

Terror filled her eyes, and she opened her mouth to scream, but Benny was already there, wrenching her hair, pulling her head back, and stuffing her mouth with a gag.

The guy went to jump up, but I punched the back of his head and grabbed his ears, dragging him back down. One hand slid across the front of his throat, pinning his windpipe, and I began to squeeze.

His eyes bulged, and he gargled, face and neck turning purple as he fought for life.

Holding my knife, I raised my hand, found the sweet spot, and slowly slid the blade into his throat. More gurgling rattled through the room as his throat filled with blood. His chest gave a final heave before he slumped in his seat.

My eyes slid to his partner.
Next.

Her entire body shook. Wide brown eyes filled with horror as she stared at her dead terrorist lover, who oozed blood from beside her.

Benny dragged her head back by the hair and held his MK-23 to her temple.

She immediately froze. She could've been a statue without her tiny whimpers and eyes darting fearfully around the room.

I didn't wanna drag it out. Flipping my knife, I struck out and stabbed through her heart. Dark eyes flickered before she let out a quiet cry and fell sideways from her chair.

She was dead before she hit the floor.

Benny's dark brown eyes caught mine. "Let's blow this place."

The table was a mass of wires and switches. The target hadn't got very far. He was nowhere near assembling anything that looked remotely dangerous.

"Fucking amateurs." Ben sighed exasperatedly. "Come on. Let's get to work."

And that's what we did. Within fifteen minutes, we'd made two low-power IEDs, big enough to blow the basement up and maybe the floor above, but not much else. We set up timers and placed them carefully on the table, ensuring we slumped the dead bodies upright on their seats. They'd be incinerated, but it was amazing what the CSIs could pick up. Everything had to be set up right.

"Ready?" Ben asked.

I dipped my chin, stuffing a few charges and wires in a ruck to hand to British Intelligence. We quickly changed gloves and footwear from the extra kit in our ruck—to avoid leaving bloody prints outside—before Benny clicked the timers on, and we moved toward the stairs.

"That one was tame," Benny said, sounding almost disappointed.

"In and out, brother," I replied in a low tone. "That's our job, and we did it well tonight."

We slinked upstairs and through the house, letting ourselves out the same way we entered. Keeping to the shadows, we returned to the small, wooded area quickly and efficiently. By the time we heard the explosion, we were already clear of the woods and about to get into the vehicle waiting for us on the other side of the trees. An hour later, we boarded a small, private plane that was fueled and ready to take us home.

Hollister called demanding a report. That took a while, so it was hours before I could finally come down from the high. I managed to sleep, albeit restlessly. I dreamed of dark, shadowy, faceless figures chasing me through Camp Eggers. One minute, Benny ran by my side; the next, his body began to fade. He stretched his hand toward me, begging for help, but I froze, completely paralyzed. I couldn't flex a muscle, speak, or even blink. Something made me look down. My gut roiled when I saw my body start to fade, just like Benny's had. Something was wrong. I was disappearing.

I came awake with a start, everything around me pitch-black. My throat burned hot from the horrifying dream. Sticky with sweat, I had to think about where I was for a few seconds. Was I in my CHU at Eggers? Eventually, my racing mind caught up. I felt the whir of the plane engines thrumming around me, and I heaved out a low groan. But I couldn't settle again. The dream had unnerved me.

Pushing my blanket back, I quietly got up to avoid disturbing Ben—sleeping in another chair—and went to the bathroom. Splashing water on my face, I looked in the mirror. My face stared back. All present, all correct. Still here. Still whole. Still me.

So why was my heart thumping out of my chest? Why did my fingers tremor when I went to thrust a hand through my hair? Why did my skin feel too tight for my body?

It was just a dream, Kit. Go chill out.

So, I did. I returned to my chair, pulled out my cell, and started scrolling. I went online, checked my emails, and caught up with the news.

What I didn't do was go back to sleep.

Chapter Twenty

Snow

My head hung as my hand went to my temple and rubbed. "So what's the problem, Kitten?" I asked impatiently.
I heard her sniff. "Ed's never there anymore, Snow. Neither is Paulie. They'd never leave without saying goodbye. I'm worried."

I sighed exasperatedly down the cell.

I'd called Kitten to talk about her and us, not Ed and fucking Paulie. It was all she'd babbled about for the last ten minutes. Explaining twice how she'd gone down to their alley the previous few mornings to find they weren't there. It was like I didn't fucking exist to her sometimes.

"So, what's the problem?" I demanded, a thread of irritation in my tone. "They're grown fucking men. They don't need you on their asses all the time. It's no wonder they fucked off." I winced as a sharp pain slashed behind my eyes. "Stop crowding them, woman. They probably need space."

Her voice took on a steely edge. "All they've got is fucking space, Snow. The streets *are* space. That's probably why they've taken up residence in a fucking alley. Because they're sick of having space. They're my friends, and I care about them. Why are you acting like this? I thought you liked Ed."

My jaw clenched at her tone.

She was pissing me the fuck off. The head pain had been making my mood spiral. Sometimes, it was excruciating. I knew it was probably down to stress, so I called my girl, thinking she'd calm me down, but all she did was make it worse with her fucking whining.

"Jesus. Kitten. You can't save the entire world. People have to take responsibility for themselves, too. Ed and Paulie probably wanted a change of scene or got into a shelter for a few nights. Stop reading so much into everything."

"I can't," she retorted. "I'm worried about my friends. Everything's changing. The rents for the stores where my friends work are increasing. Martha can't afford to keep the lease on, so she's closing the bakery. Mr. Kowalski had a fall a few days ago. He's in hospital. The doctors don't think he can run the store anymore, not that it's probably viable for him to with the extra money he has to find. Ed's fallen off the face of the Earth. Everything's going to shit, and I'm going out of my mind because I don't know how to help them."

A burn began to rise through my gullet. Jesus, why did she have to take everyone else's crap on? I didn't want to hear her 'save the world' bullshit. I had my own fucking problems, like this goddamned head pain. Everything coming out of her mouth was so goddamned fucking annoying. Even her voice was jarring.

My throat rasped with the outburst that flew out. "Maybe the best thing you can do is mind your fuckin' business, Kitten," I roared. "Maybe they don't want your help. Mr. Kowalski is heading for ninety. Let him enjoy the last years of his life. If Martha can't afford the goddamned rent, let her move somewhere she can. Why is everything your problem to solve? The sooner you're outta that fucking strip joint and settled at Harvard, the better. Perhaps then you'll be too busy to nag the fuck outta me about petty bullshit. Channel your energy into doing something worthwhile with your life instead of being a nosy do-gooder who flashes her tits to half of America."

Her sharp intake of breath was audible. My angry words hung between us for what seemed like forever before I heard another sniff. "Fuck you." She sobbed before the line clicked and went dead.

My throat rumbled as a growl filled it.

Bitch had hung up on me.

I pressed her number again and got her voicemail. "Kitten. You better answer your fucking phone." I ended the call and hit her number again.

Again, I got her voicemail. Something inside me snapped as the sharp stab of pain clapped through my head again. "Fuck you too," I sneered before ending the call and pocketing my cell.

Fuck her. Who needed her bullshit anyway?

It took approximately twenty-three minutes for the acid in my veins to ebb away and for my heart to stop banging against my rib cage.

It took approximately one further minute to go over the conversation in my head and realize that not only had I been a cunt, but I'd also been a cunt to her.

I didn't know what the fuck was wrong with me. The headaches were debilitating, and my mood changed the minute I felt one coming. Lack of sleep didn't help my stress levels. I was constantly wired from the adrenaline of my missions. I found it challenging to wind down, so after our debriefings, we started spending more time in the gym.

It was the only way to exhaust myself enough to catch a few hours of rest. Lately, though, even that hadn't brought me relief because I had wild dreams, bordering on nightmares, all the time.

Thoughts and visions in my subconscious always involved me, Benny, Simmons, and sometimes even Kitten being chased through Camp Eggers by shadowy, faceless figures. Every time, I'd be paralyzed with fear as my friends held their hands out, beseeching me to stop them from slowly fading away.

I fucking hated the way I'd wake up with a yell in my throat, how my fingers tremored, and my insides would surge. For a minute after waking, I'd see my CHU in Afghanistan and think my dream was a reality.

I reached for my cell and redialed Kitten's number, breathing through the temptation to cuss her out when I got her voicemail once more. I needed to keep my cool. "Baby," I murmured. "I'm sorry. I'm so fucking sorry. I'm tired, and I took it out on you. I'm stressed to hell. I'll call back later. Hopefully, you'll have listened to this, and we can talk properly. If you answer, I promise I won't be an asshole." I clicked the end call button and returned to lying on my bunk.

A tingling sensation flooded me before my heart began to throb again. I raised a hand and rubbed at the palpitations.

Jesus, *another* surge.

They were becoming more frequent.

My heart would beat irregularly, almost painfully, like it was about to race out of my chest.

I raised my hand to my face to see my fingers trembling. My jaw clenched as spots swam in my vision.

Hollister's voice filled my head. *Shut it down, Snow.*

I sat up and swung my legs over the side of the bed before steepling my fingers to my head and breathing.

In through my nose, out through my mouth.

Rinse and repeat.

After a few minutes, my heart slowed, and my shaking lessened.

Snow

Heaving a hard breath, I laid flat on my back again, hands behind my head as I continued my breathing exercises. I imagined myself on a mountain, watching the sun rise over Vegas, the smell of peaches around me. Then I pushed all the negative, toxic shit down, burying it deep.

But one feeling remained; one emotion refused to leave me. A tiny sliver of dark, thick, bitter despair.

Deep down, I knew I was fucking 'us' up.

Every time I called my girl, I felt what I what doing to her.

Our deep connection meant I felt what Kitten felt. It was gnarly.

Piece by piece, her effervescence and her zest for life were waning, only to be replaced with the toxicity that ate away at her incredible spirit.

Restless. I sat up again and scraped a hand down my face. Why was I self-sabotaging? Something dark and twisted had latched on to my soul—a demon hell-bent on eating up every spark of light in order to thrive amongst the darkest parts of me.

I needed my girl's help.

She'd exorcise it, bring me back into the light. Her goodness would fill me, make my spirit whole and complete again, but we had back-to-back missions to carry out for the task force.

As soon as I could, I'd go to her and explain. My Kitten would understand. She'd save me.

I just needed to keep it together until then.

Chapter Twenty-One

Kitten ~ Six Weeks Later

Snow hadn't contacted me in weeks.

His calls had always been sporadic at best. He seemed to go for stretches with no contact, then, out of the blue, he'd call me every day for a while before disappearing again. But still, he'd never stayed out of contact for this long.

Even though my heart lay in pieces, I understood.

Raven explained the same thing happened with her dad. When soldiers were training, on maneuvers, and on missions, they couldn't make contact, but I still missed him.

When Snow did call, I tried to stay as positive as I could, but his moods were up and down, and he often confused me with over-the-top reactions to the slightest things. Sometimes, his volatile temper made my head spin.

Long distance was hard, especially when things weren't going well. Sometimes, I wondered if I should let him go, but then I'd remember the golden boy I met, and my heart would swell with so much love that I'd feel bad for even thinking it. Snow continuously told me he was stressed. Maybe that was it. Perhaps I needed to be more understanding. He told me he dreaded getting 'Dear John'ed' by me. I could never be that girl.

I got it. Snow's job was difficult, but usually, I came off the phone not really comprehending what had happened. More often than not, he brought me to tears.

Something had changed, but I knew it wasn't Snow's feelings for me, not after the week we spent together. His elation and joy were off the charts when he was in a good mood. He told me he loved me and that I was his girl. But I couldn't help the sharp pang that speared my heart whenever I thought about the other, darker phone conversations.

I always knew it would be hard. Always knew the odds were stacked against us, but I never imagined this. Snow seemed moody, sullen, and almost rude one day, then upbeat and overly animated the next. It was hard keeping up with him and stressful for me, too.

However, giving up on him wasn't an option.

Imagining the pressure of his work and putting myself in his shoes, I understood it would affect anyone's peace of mind. I knew he'd be okay once we spent some time together again. We were young and in love. We could overcome anything, including this bump in the road.

We'd be fine. I'd make it so.

That was if he ever fucking called.

"Kitty," Raven called over. "You're nearly on."

I jerked out of my daydream, eyes widening as they darted to look at Raven.

She smiled at me through the mirror. "Penny for them," she joked.

"Sorry." I unscrewed the red lip gloss I'd been holding distractedly and swiped some on. "I'll be ready."

"You still haven't heard from him?" she asked.

I shook my head, the back of my throat burning.

Her lips twitched. "You will. I just know it. Gotta good feeling, Kitty."

Snow

I rose from my seat, checking the Velcro on my black leather bra was secure and that my matching thong was where it should be. Running a finger up the back of my black stockings, I made sure my garter belt held everything it should before I held out my arms for Raven to slip my black fitted tuxedo jacket over my shoulders. I pushed a top hat on. "See? Right on time."

She smiled and handed me a black cane. "There. You better go. Marco will have a seizure if you leave it much longer."

I turned to my friend and grabbed her hand. "Thanks, Rave."

"Anytime," she said, mouth still curved in her beautiful smile.

I squeezed her hand and dropped it before exiting the dressing room and moving through the corridor to the back of the stage, saying hellos to the stagehands and staff as I went. My mind was still half-preoccupied, so I didn't immediately feel anything. I climbed on stage, settled onto the chair that was part of my act, and struck my opening pose, waiting for the curtains to open.

My heart fluttered as my tummy gave a tug, and I knew.

Snow.

He was here.

I could feel him.

My throat hitched as the compere announced me the same way he always did.

Ladies and gentlemen. It's the moment you've all been waiting for. Please put your hands together for the last act of the night. She's known as the sexiest woman in Vegas. I give you the one and only... Kitten!

A roar went up, the curtains raised, and every spotlight shone on me as the opening bars of 'Say it Right' thumped through the room.

Keep it together, girl.

My hips jerked, my legs splayed open wide, my modesty only covered by a thin strip of leather, and the back of the chair that I gripped onto for dear life.

I stayed in the pose for a few beats, more shouts and yells sounding over the music.

Bumping and grinding my ass, almost in a twerk, I swung my legs together, rolled to the side of the seat, leaped up, and began to dance.

Nelly Furtado's sweet voice washed over me. Almost in a trance, I danced to the routine I'd perfected a few days before. It was softer than my usual routines. Some street dance mixed with hip hop and even ballet leaps and contemporary twists.

I got lost in the haunting words of a woman lamenting her struggle to communicate with her lover. Her desire for him clashing with fear. How he made her conflicted.

The song hit home in a certain way. It reflected so much of me.

I twisted, turned, and thrust, losing my costume as I went. I used the chair and the cane. My hair flew, my hips twisted, and my ass jerked in time to the hard bassline.

Not once did I look for Snow. I knew he was there. I didn't need to throw him seductive looks or come hither glances. What was the point when he already knew he owned me so completely?

So, I just danced for him.

I danced with everything I had, baring more of my soul each time I lost a piece of clothing. I wanted Snow to see the real me. Not the body, not the blonde hair, not the character. For the first time ever, when I danced, I wasn't Kitten. I was Kennedy, and I was his.

All too soon, the closing bars played.

With my back to the audience, I unclipped my bra from the front. I pulled it off before spinning around while simultaneously hanging my head as the song faded out and the stage turned black.

The curtains closed to a deafening roar and yells of 'encore,' 'more,' and chants of 'Kitten, Kitten.'

Throat thick with emotion, I shrugged my tuxedo jacket back across my shoulders, turned, and moved down the steps. Maybe I should've covered up and gone to the bar to look for him, but something told me not to. Deep down, I knew he'd find me.

I smiled at the stagehands, waving at them as I turned back down the dark corridor toward the dressing room. My stomach prickled as I saw a shadow flicker at the far end. On any other day, I wouldn't have noticed, but my senses were heightened, and my stomach tugged gently.

"Snow," I breathed. "Honey, is that you?"

He stepped into the light, his bowed head covered by a hoodie.

I froze, noticing immediately that he'd bulked up. He wore head-to-toe black and huddled into the thick sweat material of his top. I hated seeing my golden boy hiding like that when he usually stood so tall and proud.

My feet began to float closer to him like he was a magnet pulling me in. As I approached, he lifted his head and locked eyes with mine.

I nearly cried out from the ache that slashed through my chest. I bit down hard on my lip to stop the sound from escaping. God, what had happened to him? He was different. It wasn't him. I mean, it was him, but he wasn't *my* Snow.

He'd insisted on staying clean-shaven on our week together, but now he had thick stubble. His cheekbones jutted, and his jaw clenched, all his softness gone. He seemed unkempt like taking care of himself was an afterthought. He'd aged years in the space of months.

But, the most significant change of all was his eyes.

Once golden, sparkling orbs, full of life and laughter, were empty. I used to look into them and see a world full of love and light. They used to smolder at me until I could see inside his soul.

Now, a cold shiver prickled my nape at the dull, empty voids that stared back at me. This wasn't my Snow. This was someone else entirely.

My fingers lifted to cup his cheek, heart aching as I stroked my thumb gently across his jaw, the same way he always did to me. "What have they done to you, honey?" I croaked. "What happened?"

He frowned, staring at me from under his heavy brow, almost like he'd never seen me before. A hand reached out and touched my breastbone through the gap in my jacket. "You're so beautiful, Kitten," he rasped in a low voice. "So fucking sweet and pure."

My throat thickened with emotion, but I swallowed it, sliding my hands around his neck and curling my fingers tightly. "Let me help you. Let me make it better."

He stared through me. "Help me sleep, Kitten." His hand fisted the hair behind my head. "I can't fucking sleep, baby. I need to hold you so bad." He buried his head in my throat and breathed in deeply. "When I close my eyes, everything's so dark, and it's killing me. I need to hold something good."

"We'll go home," I assured him, stroking his hair. "It's okay. I'll look after you." I pulled back until he lifted his head again, and his eyes met mine. "How long have we got?"

His face shuttered. "Forty-eight hours."

"Right." I nodded to the dressing room. "Let me get my bag."

He nodded distractedly.

I pushed the door open and stepped inside, hauling my costume off as I moved toward my station. After I stripped, I shrugged into my sweats, not bothering with underwear because I was so intent on getting to Snow. Seeing him that way made every beat of my heart thud painfully despite every cell in my body tingling to be close. My forehead creased as questions raced through my mind.

Snow

Am I in over my head?
How can I help him?
What am I going to do?

Grabbing my bag, I buried the weak and worrisome thoughts deep, swiftly moved toward the door, and pushed it open.

Snow stood in the same spot, head bowed, huddled into his hoodie.

I moved into him and curled my fingers around his arm reassuringly. "Hey."

He jerked as if my touch burned before slowly relaxing again. "Fuck. I'm sorry. I'm jumpy as hell. I'm so fucking tired, Kitty."

"It's okay, honey," I whispered. "I'm gonna sort you out, okay?"

Snow's eyes slowly lifted to mine, and my heart curled in on itself when I saw the pain that ravaged his face.

That was when I knew.

Something dark had marked his soul.

He'd experienced something traumatic. I had no clue whether something had happened to him or it was something he'd done, but whatever it was had affected him deeply. Something fundamental had changed my golden boy. Altered his core, his aura.

I led Snow out the back door and around to my car. For the first time ever, I didn't throw him the keys. He wasn't in the right state of mind.

The drive home was silent and strained, the atmosphere in the car thick, dank, and heavy.

Snow stared at nothing out of the passenger window, as cold and still as a marble statue.

A swarm of butterflies fluttered inside my chest, fighting to be set free. My fingers tremored, and a heavy lump formed in my throat as one dark thought began to form.

What if I can't get him back?

I parked my car, switched off my engine, and sat for a few seconds, trying to make a plan.

From what I could see, Snow had shut down. My first objective was to get him talking and communicating, at least enough to tell me what he needed.

My head turned right. Snow still looked out of the window, lost in his own world. It was hard to know what to do for the best. Did he need time, or should I take over and usher him inside?

I leaned into the backseat for my bag, which seemed to startle Snow out of his trance.

"We're home, honey," I said, touching his arm lightly.

He looked around, confused, like he didn't know how he got there. "Right."

"You wanna go upstairs or stay here a bit longer?" I asked.

"Up."

Smiling reassuringly, I exited the car, ran to his door, opened it, and held my hand out. It was weird how the tables had turned. He wouldn't usually let me out of the car unless he was at my door, helping me.

He unfolded his bulky body, grasping my fingers as he stood.

I closed the door with a soft thud, beeped the locks, and led him to the elevator. His demeanor may have been offhand, even almost aloof, but his warm fingers seemed to hold on to mine for dear life, which gave me hope. Our hands stayed locked together all the way to my apartment. I even got my keys from my bag one-handed and unlocked the door.

"You're home now, honey," I said, pushing the door open. We walked inside together, but I went ahead of

Snow

Snow, switching lamps on as we moved toward the bedroom.

He stood at the door, silently watching as I lit the room dully from the small lamp on my nightstand.

I approached him slowly, leading him to the bed and helping him sit on what had become 'his side.'

He bent forward and held his head in his hands.

"Hey." I fell to my knees, moving between his legs. "What do you need, Snow? Tell me what will help."

Something flashed behind his eyes before he uttered a solitary word. "You."

I grabbed his fingers, looking up at him imploringly. "You've got me." I placed his hands on my thudding heart. "I'm here. See. Flesh, blood, and bones. I'm here, Snow. I'm yours. Do what you need to come back to me."

His eyes darted between mine, flashing again, but that time with a hint of fear. "I can't, Kitten."

He dropped my hand, nostrils flaring as he steepled his fingers to his head.

"No!" I said. "Don't you shut down on me." Gently, I took his hands back. "I'm here. You can be real with me, honey. You're safe."

"Baby," he croaked. "I can't. It's too much."

"Take what you need," I demanded, voice containing a thread of panic. "Take it. Take it. Snow. Take what you fucking nee—"

His hand shot out, cutting me off. He grabbed the back of my neck and hauled me up, lying back on the bed and dragging me on top of him. "I *don't know* what I need. I just need you to seep inside me again. I need goodness."

My hands came up and clutched his head. I looked deep into his eyes. I needed to show him I'd do anything if it meant he came back. "Then take it."

He pulled me closer, his face burrowing into my throat. "Fucking peaches," he murmured into my skin. "Fuck!" he muttered as he started to shake. "Fuck. Fuck.

Fuck." His tremors became stronger and more violent until his entire body jerked repeatedly.

I stroked his hair. "That's it," I whispered soothingly. "Take it all. It's yours anyway. It all belongs to you." I kept whispering words of encouragement and love.

After a few minutes, he finally began to calm down. "Jesus." He sighed. "Fuck, baby. I'm so cold."

I took his face in my hands. "Bath or shower?"

His eyes searched mine. "Bath, but I want you there too."

"Of course." I gave him a light kiss on the lips and slowly got up, walking toward the bathroom.

I counted down as I went. *Five. Four. Three. Two. One.* On the last number, I shut the bathroom door and sank down on the side of the tub. Silently, I began to cry. My heart ached so painfully that everything inside hurt, even my bones.

My Snow, my golden boy, was damaged to the core.

It didn't take a genius to realize that he was suffering mentally. I'd seen and even read about soldiers' PTSD extensively, but that didn't mean I knew what the hell I was doing. Snow seemed empty like he'd buried everything that made him who he was so deep that he couldn't tap into it again. I only had forty-eight hours to get him right. I didn't know if I could do it, and even if I did, what was he going back to? More of the same?

I thought about calling Uncle Hustle. He knew some vets in his MC who'd been through similar trauma. Maybe he could tell me what to do.

My teeth sank into my lip.

I couldn't. First, my cell was inside my purse in the bedroom. Snow would want to know why I needed it. He was skittish enough already. He'd probably bolt if he heard me talking to Hustle about him like that.

Second. If my uncle knew I had a guy here whose mind was poorly affected enough for me to call him worried and stressed, he'd be riding through with the MC at his back within fifteen minutes, ready to kill Snow.

Fuck. I'd have to go with my gut.

My back straightened. Yeah, that was it. My intuition had never let me down before; it has always served me well. I trusted my instincts enough to know I could pull Snow through whatever was ravaging him from the inside out.

I stood from the tub and ran the taps, squirting some muscle relaxant foam in the water before swishing it around. Next, I got some toothpaste ready on a spare brush and pulled out the bag of disposable razors and shaving gel Snow left on his last visit out of the built-in cupboard under the sink.

I'd clean him up, then take him to bed. All I could do was listen to my gut, take my cues from him, and go from there.

Okay. You can do this, Kennedy.

I took a determined breath before quickly swiping the tears from my cheeks. Plastering a reassuring smile across my features, I went to the door, unlocked it, and poked my head around to see Snow still in the position I'd left him.

His unseeing, dazed eyes slid to me, and he heaved himself to sit. "I'm exhausted," he croaked.

I moved toward the bed, motioning for him to lift his arms.

Slowly, he raised them, and I pulled off his hoodie, then the tee underneath. He toed off his sneakers and lifted his ass from the bed while I peeled off his jeans, shorts, and socks before tossing his wallet on the dresser.

I ran into the hall where my washer and dryer were stacked. Throwing all Snow's clothes in together, I set the wash up before returning to the bedroom.

"Come on, honey." I helped him up, walked him to the bathroom, and turned off the faucet.

He sank into the warm bathtub and watched as I stripped to nothing, climbing in with him and settling myself onto his lap. His sigh seemed to be full of relief. I imagined the toxicity being expelled along with the heaviness from his lungs as I grabbed the sponge and began to wash him.

He closed his eyes and heaved out another breath.

"That's it, honey. Let the crap out. You don't need it." I continued to sponge him down before starting to wash his head. "Your hair's grown." I tickled his chin playfully. "And you have a beard."

He scraped a hand over his jaw. "Haven't shaved for a few days. Had back-to-back missions for what seemed like forever. Hollister gave us leave as soon as we got back to base, so I got changed, grabbed my wallet, and walked straight out. Caught the first flight I could into Harry Reid."

"Hollister?"

He nodded absently. "My lieutenant."

"Right."

Not for the first time, it hit me then how little I knew of his life. I didn't know where he was from. If he had family, siblings, friends. I knew his name, and I knew him, but that was it. I guessed it worked both ways. I also hadn't talked about anything except what happened with my parents. I hadn't told him about Hustle or Sophie. All our time had been spent fucking, laughing, and watching Game of Thrones in a little world containing just us. All we'd ever done was build our connection. Nothing else seemed important.

"What you thinking about?" he asked.

I smiled, rubbing shampoo into his hair. "Just about how we connect so deeply, even though we don't really know about each other's lives."

That was when I saw it. A smile tugged at the corner of Snow's mouth, and his eyes sparked.

Warmth flowed through me, and I smiled brightly, letting out a relieved giggle. I dropped the sponge into the water, lightly grasped his jaw, and angled his face toward me. "There he is," I murmured, gazing into his eyes. "There's my Snow. My golden boy."

He barked a short laugh, and I glanced heavenward, sending a silent prayer of thanks.

A strong hand cupped my cheek lovingly. "Kitten. I'm gonna tell you everything. You're gonna know everything about me soon enough. You'll get it all. Good, bad, and everything in between. And one day, I'm gonna give you a family. A posse of men and women who'll have your back, and they'll be military, blood, and chosen family." His hand stroked across my stomach. "One day, I'll plant my babies in there, put a ring on it, and give you a traditional family too, but there's a lot I need to explain first. Right now, I'm so fucking bone tired that I know I'll fuck everything up. I dunno if I have the words, baby. Just need you to trust me a little longer. Can you do that for me?"

"You lost me at babies," I murmured with a dreamy sigh.

He threw his head back and laughed. The sound threaded through my soul like a current of joy that fused my cracked heart together. My tummy fizzed and popped with excitement and pure, bone-deep relief.

I'd done it.

Snow was back.

The way he fucked me later that night was different.

Whereas before, his touch was light and full of reverence, now it seemed rougher.

We'd started off fine. Snow had eaten me out the way he usually did, which was beautiful. At some point, though, his gentle sucks turned hard enough to mark me and his nips to stinging bites.

I couldn't say I hated it. It still turned me on, just in a more painful way. What made me uneasy was that he seemed to keep zoning out, getting so into it that my breathy murmurs of, "Take it easy, honey," and gasps of pain fell on deaf ears.

It was nothing I couldn't handle, but I was worried about the evidence he was leaving behind.

In my job, it was unseemly to be covered in hickeys, bite marks, and bruises. It reminded me of a different type of stripper, and as much as I didn't judge, that wasn't who I was. The only way I could get through taking off my clothes for a living was to keep things as classy as possible.

I groaned as Snow lay flat on his back with me straddling his face.

I'd changed position because he got rough. If I was top, at least I had more control. His fingers gripped my thighs and squeezed as he pulled me down to his mouth, almost feeding from me.

I winced as he nipped my clitoris painfully, but I didn't pull away. Instead, I white-knuckled my headboard and breathed through it, letting him take what he needed from me.

Suddenly, I felt a stinging slap across my ass, the type of sting that took my breath away, and I cried out in pain.

He seemed to like that because he groaned and slapped me again. "Give me one, Kitten," he demanded, growling the words into my pussy. "Come in my mouth."

I didn't see how I could. I was wet, but I wasn't into it. A bite of pain here and there was pleasing and enjoyable, but the harder he went in on me, the less my body seemed to respond. I grimaced as his fingers dug into my thighs, pinning me to his face.

Snow

He must've mistaken my soft yowl for one of pleasure because his fingertips pressed into my skin. Then he lifted me up slightly and slapped my pussy hard. "Give it to me, bitch," he growled.

I froze as the pain registered, then his words.

Huh?

"Snow," I said gently, but he either didn't hear me or didn't care because he went back in and began to suck my clit really hard. I tried to settle into it, tried to enjoy his touch. This was my Snow. There was no need to freak out. I knew he'd keep me safe.

But will he? A voice in the back of my mind whispered.

I knew this wasn't me. In a way, I hated myself for being so submissive and allowing it to continue. But maybe he needed to work through something? Wasn't it what I was meant to do? Be there for him? Honestly, I didn't know? My instincts told me something wasn't right, but it was a one-off. Maybe this was his way of dealing with his frustrations.

And part of me wanted to be everything he needed, even if it wasn't what I needed.

I bit my lip, trying again to settle into it, but every time he got too rough, it pulled me out of the moment. Maybe it would've been okay if I knew he was the same old Snow mentally, but witnessing his mood from before, I couldn't help the dark feelings that knotted my belly. Something was wrong.

Should I stop him?

Suddenly, he pushed me off, lifted me in the air, flipped me onto my front, got behind me, and pulled my hips up.

Okay, this was good. At least Snow couldn't bite me anymore. I sighed as he reached for a condom and slipped it on, wriggling my hips enticingly.

I jolted as he slapped my ass hard again. "Fucking whore," he muttered from behind me.

Whoa! Say what now?

Before I could utter a word, he slapped my ass again and shoved his fingers inside me.

I almost shot off the fucking bed. "Snow!" I snapped. "That hurts." But he ignored me, continuing to fuck me roughly with what felt like half his hand. "Snow!" I yelped louder that time, pulling away.

He tugged my hips back and, with an animalistic grunt, slammed his cock into me so hard that my skull almost bounced off the headboard.

He let out a loud moan and a 'fuck, yeah' as he started pounding.

I shuddered but tried to relax.

Okay, this was fine. Snow was fucking me roughly, but I could deal with that. I let out a small groan, pushing back to meet his thrusts. His hands went to the outside of my thighs, and he held me still, using me to get himself off. It was kinda hot, so I let out a whimper of encouragement and, at last, started to loosen up, letting myself get lost in the feeling of his cock moving inside me.

Snow was long and thick. He used that to his advantage, gliding in and grinding as he went deep before pulling out and repeating the movement. I felt myself get wetter as my body finally began to respond to the way he was fucking me and getting into the rhythm.

His hand slid up my back to fist my hair, bunching it in his hands, much like he did when we fucked at 'Underground.' The memory of that night hit me. Moisture flooded my pussy, and I began to whimper louder at the thought of what we did that night.

I remembered how he watched me through hooded eyes when I danced for him. How he dragged me off the dance floor into that corridor. The noise as the bar door opened and closed. The fantasy of someone seeing him fuck me like that.

Snow

"Yes," I moaned as my pussy started to heat. "Fuck me, Snow," I begged as pressure began to build in my lower stomach as the promise of my orgasm swirled.

He pounded harder, fist flexing as he tugged my hair.

I moaned louder as he took me higher.

"Come on my cock," he rasped, slipping his hands around my hips and rubbing my clit. His touch was all I needed to shoot off like a firecracker. I mewled loudly, clamping down on his cock like I never wanted him anywhere but inside me.

"Jesus, fuck!" He shouted as his cock swelled, and he started to come.

My orgasm ripped through me, making me cry out louder. My pussy contracted so hard around Snow that he cursed.

I cried out again as he pulled me up by the hair. His hand slid around my throat, and he began to squeeze. By then, I'd started to come down from my orgasm, but Snow still bucked and thrust as he cursed and groaned, filling the condom with his cum. His strong fingers squeezed harder, not cutting off all my airways but choking me enough to make me nervous.

A pang hit my chest. Something felt off. I coughed. Surely, now Snow would let me go, but instead, he turned his head and bit my neck hard.

I let out a whimper at the stinging pain he inflicted until, finally, his hand loosened, and his thrusts began to wane. He pulled out with a jerk and collapsed face down on the bed. "Jesus, Kitten. I've never come so hard."

I fell beside him. My whole body ached inside and out. My pussy, my ass, my boobs and throat, even the skin he hadn't touched hurt, and my head ached.

He cracked one eye open, looking at me with a dopey grin. His gaze flicked down my body and up again, finally resting on my throat. His eyes widened a fraction. My neck must've been a mess.

I braced, ready for him to jump up, check on me, and apologize for hurting me. He went to open his mouth but closed it again, instead reaching out to touch my neck. I closed my eyes, psyching myself up to tell him it was okay, that I was good, but silence hung in the air.

My eyes opened again and caught his.

His golden orbs gleamed as they fixated on my throat. "Look at those pretty marks," he said huskily, fingers trailing over my darkened skin. His hand rested on my windpipe, stroking it with his thumb.

A cold shiver trickled down my spine.

I jerked back, suddenly feeling really uncomfortable.

Snow's body jolted like he was being pulled out of a dream. He reached out and splayed our fingers together. "Fuck, baby. I'm sorry. I don't know my own strength. Shit's been getting real at work. I needed to let off steam, and I've taken it out on you. Usually, I'd get down the gym and box it out with the boys, but I came here as soon as my LT said I could have a couple of days."

My eyes searched his, and my shoulders relaxed, relieved that Snow was back again, present and aware. "Sleep, baby," I whispered, leaning over and kissing his mouth softly. "I'll be here when you wake up."

I watched as, within minutes, his face relaxed, and he released a soft snore as he drifted off peacefully.

For the next hour, I watched him sleep, mind going over everything that had happened since I met him months ago. It seemed so much longer than half a year since we sat at Lone Mountain and watched the sunrise together.

It seemed crazy looking back–even over that short time–how we seemed so young and idealistic. We both wanted to make our marks on the world in our own ways. Everything was easy back then. Meet, fall in love, and eventually be together, but I was starting to realize we'd both been naïve. Still, even if I could've seen into the future, I wouldn't have changed a thing.

Except tonight.

For the first time, sex with Snow wasn't beautiful. I felt used. I was pissed at myself for not stopping it; it took me by surprise, and I didn't know how I should've reacted. My inexperience was coming into play. I'd never had to deal with anything like this before and realized I was out of my depth.

My hand strayed to my throat. It ached from all the pressure off Snow's hand, skin sore from his marks. I thought about getting up to see to it, but I was too tired. Our sex session had taken a lot out of me, and I just wanted to sleep.

I turned over, back to Snow, and tried not to think of the niggling doubts that coursed through my mind. There was nothing I could do while he was sleeping; he was exhausted and needed to recuperate. Maybe after he'd rested, he'd be back to himself again.

Snow would still be here tomorrow. We could talk then.

Chapter Twenty-Two

Snow

I woke up with a massive jerk, knifing up to a sitting position.
Sunshine filled the room that I instantly recognized as Kitten's. My brain, still groggy from sleep, kicked into gear, and everything flooded back to me.

My hands lifted to massage my temples. I was disorientated but probably more cognizant than I'd been for days. We'd had a tough few weeks. Back-to-back missions, all including more destruction and deaths, most of which were at my hand.

Our last mission had been to infiltrate a convoy of T-Man out in the desert and set explosives on their transport. As soon as they started on their way, they went boom.

As I set those bombs, I fantasized about how easy it would be to sneak into their camp, carry one away, and slit their throat. That wasn't our mission, but I couldn't get it outta my head. It played on a loop over and over, exciting me. Until I caught myself and quickly shut it down. However, it bothered me, the rush I got from all the kill fantasies swirling through my mind.

My guts churned constantly. I ate for fuel, not enjoyment, and only because if I didn't, I'd keel over, seeing as we were always on the go. In our free time, we boxed the fuck out of each other to get rid of our aggression. The violence helped me keep my head straight and my emotions in check; what it didn't help me do much of was sleep.

I didn't know if Benny and Simmons were having crazy dreams like I was, but I reckoned so because when we should have been catching naps on planes, we all stared silently at our cell phones, scrolling but unseeing, like zombies. Over the weeks, Benny's and Simmons's eyes became more bloodshot, and their moods more withdrawn, just like mine. Laughter and jokes were replaced with blank looks and stretched silences.

What we didn't do was talk about it. Nobody complained. Nobody wanted to look weak or suggest we were struggling. So, we just got on with it and quietly shut down.

Finally, as we returned to Fort Campbell from our last mission the day before, Hollister took one look at us and told us we had a few days' leave and to blow some steam off. We all headed to Nashville Airport and got flights out. Benny parked his car there so we could meet and drive back to base together.

Hambleton and my family never entered my head. I just needed to get to Kitten. I needed her warmth, her spirit, and her love. Standing at the back of the club and seeing her dance with so much emotion hit me, and for the first time in weeks, I allowed myself to feel something.

And it fucking ravaged me.

I remembered sneaking backstage, but everything was fuzzy after that. How I approached her, the journey to Kitten's apartment, everything was a blur. I couldn't think straight. Images flashed through my mind, but nothing meshed together. My waking moments were hazy at best. Nightmarish at worst.

A shooting pain flashed behind my eyes, and I groaned out loud.

The headaches were debilitating. They'd be set off by the slightest noise, sometimes just by bright light. It was probably just a symptom of being so overtired all the goddamned time. I lifted my eyes, and sure enough, the room spun, so I laid back down and waited for it to pass.

My stomach whooshed and churned like a washing machine, nausea making it clench painfully. I felt so hungry, but I wasn't sure I could eat if I wanted to. Then, my body started to jerk. A heavy weight settled inside, and I struggled to get air inside my lungs.

Jesus, this was fucked up.

I began my breathing exercises, trying to calm the weird thumping of my heart. Eventually, it slowed, and the gut churn eased.

The smell of peaches assaulted me, and I smiled, relaxing as I went to my happy place. A girl, a mountain, and a beautiful sunrise. Except—something touched my hand—it fucking burned. I shot to a sitting position and grabbed an arm, lip curled, almost ready to snap. That was when I heard a soft cry of pain.

Fuck.

My eyes opened to see Kitten. Her eyes were wide and full of confused fear, her face screwed into a grimace. "You're hurting me," she whispered.

I released her immediately, my heart withering to nothing as I watched her eyes grow wary of me. The neckline of her silky robe fell open. That was the moment I saw the dark purple bruises.

I froze before knifing forward and pulling her robe apart. I sucked in a deep breath, nostrils flaring at the state of her body. Her arms and breasts had marks everywhere. Her tits had fucking bites on them. Turning her head, I stopped breathing as I saw the teeth marks and bruises on her throat.

Heat pooled in my stomach, so hot I thought I'd internally combust. It was like a volcano starting at the pit of my gut and rising through me until I fucking exploded.

"What the fuck happened?" I bellowed in her face.

Kitten shrank back slightly.

I heard the robe tear at the seams as I tugged it away to examine her beautiful, soft, painful skin. I took sawing breaths, trying to calm my shit as I stared at her, horrified. My lungs were on fire.

Her fingers curled around my nape, and she pushed her face to my throat. "It's okay, Snow," she breathed. "I bruise easily. I'm fine."

Another sucked in heaving breath. Shit, my heart raced so fast it was so painful.

"Breathe, honey," Kitten ordered gently.

I obeyed, pulling in more air, holding for a few counts, blowing it out, and then repeating the action until my heart came under control. I pulled back slightly, cupping her face and angling it so her eyes couldn't escape mine. "What happened to you?" I asked, calmer.

She frowned curiously. "Don't you remember?"

My gut panged. "Remember what?"

"Our sex. Last night," she replied simply.

I wracked my brain. Okay, so I knew we fucked the night before, but the details were a blur. I remembered a bathtub and a flash of emotion as she made me laugh about something. I recalled touches and whimpers. The problem was that I was so bone-tired and weary that everything felt like a dream, just out of reach.

She took my hand and kissed my palm. "It's okay. You were just really into it. I don't think the intent to hurt me was there. You just got carried away."

My spine prickled with a sense of awareness. "Huh?"

"I told you to take what you needed. It's fine."

That was when the meaning of her words washed over me. My jaw clenched tight at her voice. It was low and carried a tinge of apprehension like she was nervous as she tried to explain. "It was both of us. We—you—"

My heart sank into the pit of my gut, and I thrust a hand through my hair. "Are you saying I did that, Kitten?"

Her hand stroked my face, and she smiled brightly, too fucking brightly. "It's fine."

Bile rose through my throat at the ramifications of what I'd done to her. What the fuck was she talking about? Jesus Christ.

I dragged her robe off her shoulders and down her arms, pointing at the marks, and bellowed, "That's not fine. That's nowhere near fine, woman. That's a goddamned tragedy."

"Honey," she murmured so softly that I strained to hear her. "I told you to take what you needed. If this is it, then I'm good."

I pulled away from her and kneeled on the bed, inspecting her body. That was when I saw the deep teeth marks, and my throat thickened with bile. Why was she saying it was good? There was no goodness in this. It was as far from good as you could get. It was fucked-up and abusive.

I raised my hand, rubbing at the deep ache in my heart. "Stop saying that. In what screwed-up world is that shit ever okay?" My stomach jolted as the realization of what I was doing to this incredible soul hit me. I'd hurt my Kitten badly.

Jesus.

For the first time in years, tears sprang to my eyes. What made my lip curl was that I didn't even remember doing it. The night was so fucking hazy, like I was here but not. My fingers rubbed at my temples again, thoughts all over the place as I wracked my mind for clues. My brain hurt with it all.

What the fuck was I turning into? And even worse, what was I turning her into? Why was she just accepting this bullshit? This wasn't her.

Soft arms slid around my back, holding on tight, and my face was in *her* throat. I sucked her in, trying to take all the goodness I could from her. The ache in my heart spread through my chest and into my bones, veins, and blood as I memorized it all. The way she smelled, the feel of her skin. Her warmth. The way she made me whole. My heart clenched painfully because it dawned on me that it would be a long time before I saw her again, if ever.

A beautiful memory of watching her dance for me in a Vegas nightclub flickered behind my eyes. The recollection of my back against a wall, making a vow to myself, kept going over and over in my mind.

I'd keep her shining bright—I'd protect her and keep her safe. I'd always put her above me, every fucking time. No question. No doubt.

I knew I was dimming her light, and it wasn't just about the abuse I'd left on her body. Every phone call. Every conversation. Every flash of temper. Every heated accusation. It all broke her spirit a little bit more. Every snapped phrase. Every sneer. Every irritated sigh all extinguished her fire.

I was slowly hurting her, over and over, without thought or care.

And it had to stop here.

If I stayed, I'd hurt her physically and emotionally. I'd wreck her, not just from the inside out but from the outside in. She wouldn't go to Harvard, or even if she got there, she'd drop out because how could she cope with the pressure of school while I continuously did this shit to her? Maybe, if she was lucky, I'd get myself killed, and eventually, she'd become a washed-up old stripper. Suppose she was unlucky, and I lived through these murder missions? She'd be saddled with a fucking animal who'd break her soul into fractured pieces along with her skin and bones.

If I stayed, I'd ruin her.

Leaving would ruin me, but I was already damned. There was no hope for my soul—redemption wasn't mine to hold. The least I could do was allow her a decent life and protect her from all the trauma, head fucks, and violence that had latched onto me. At least I could protect her from myself.

My heart sank. Maybe we'd get it right in the next life. Perhaps a thousand and one would be our magic number.

"Let me go, Kitten," I croaked.

Her arms squeezed tighter, and she melded her body to mine, and I couldn't help holding onto her for a few seconds more, just breathing her in. She knew what I was gonna do; she could feel it.

Putting my mouth to her ear, I whispered, "Baby. You'll always be my fire—"

"–Don't say it," she begged. "Please."

"I have to," I softly kissed her neck where my teeth had broken her skin. "Look what I did to you."

She started to cry, great wracking sobs. I felt the wetness from her cheeks mingling with mine. "I-It's f-fine," she stuttered through her tears. "I-I don't care about the bruises." She ran her hands over the purple marks and lacerations. "This wasn't you. You're not well, Snow. This was a result of what *they've* done to you, not what you've done to me. You could come out of the military. We could get you help, honey."

I pulled away and cupped her cheeks, staring intensely into her eyes. "Kitten, don't you see? You should care. Nobody should treat you like I have been, and you make excuses for them. That's fucked up in itself. You're worth so much more than this. Don't you see?"

A tear tracked down her face.

I nuzzled my nose with hers. "I've taken a girl who dances on mountaintops, a girl full of life and love, and turned her into someone who doesn't even care that she's being abused."

Her eyes welled up with hurt. "It wasn't like that," she whispered.

"Did you ask me to stop, Kitten? Did you make it clear I was hurting you?"

She fell silent, and there was my answer.

My heart twisted painfully. "That's abuse, Kitten."

"It's not your fault," she cried. "It's what they've done to you. You were fine on your last visit, Snow. I can bring you back to that man. Let me try and help you. Just don't give up."

God forgive me, but I thought about it. My mind reflected on that time and everything good I felt when we were together. I remembered how I'd behaved at Hambleton. How restless and on edge I was. The monster in me had been born before then. I just didn't wanna accept it. Kitten spoke the truth. She did bring me back, right? I was so profoundly and irrevocably in fucking love with her that for one fleeting second, I contemplated doing as she asked. I contemplated staying.

But then my eyes slid to where I'd grabbed my beautiful girl's throat so roughly that I left purple smudges on her golden skin. I'd handled her so brutally, so fucking savagely, that her tiny, perfect body was battered, and I knew I couldn't stay for the same reason I yearned to.

I was so profoundly and irrevocably in fucking in love with her.

I was going to hell, but I had no intention of dragging her there too. There was only one thing I could do, and it was the best thing I could do. The most unselfish thing I would ever do.

Sitting back on the bed, I began breathing deeply. I steepled my fingers, brought them to my chin, and sucked air in and out of my lungs. Slowly, I pushed it all down. All the hurt, all the pain, and finally, all the love.

When I lifted my stare to hers, it was blank. "I'm going now," I said almost robotically.

Her eyes flicked over my face. She saw something she didn't like because she shook her head sadly. I watched her shoulders slump, all determination leaving her body. That was the moment I saw she was done, too.

"I can't fight for us alone, Snow, so yeah. Just go." She rose from the bed, secured her robe, and quietly left the room.

Even with my emotions shut down, her words filtered through. I felt the sting of them deep down inside my fucked-up black soul.

However, I got up, went to the bathroom, brushed my teeth, and washed my face before returning to the bedroom to dress. My clothes had been washed, dried, and folded on the dresser.

Didn't even notice. I put them on, slipped my wallet and cell back into my pocket, and left the room. I glanced at her sitting on the couch, staring blankly at the black screen of the TV, a broken, abused girl sipping coffee. The ether was filled with a dark cloud of devastation. I could taste its bitterness in the back of my throat.

Without pausing, I went to leave. I heard a whisper as I approached the door, "You never even knew my name."

My steps faltered.

"I have a nickname," Kitten said huskily. "My uncle calls me Kenny. He has since I was a little girl. It's the one thing of any importance I kept."

I closed my eyes. *Shut it down.*

I heard my girl stifle a sob before softly clearing her throat. "Take care of yourself, Snow."

Too late, Kitten. I thought. *I'm ruined without you.*

But I didn't say it. Didn't say a goddamned word. I walked out of that apartment without a backward glance and kept walking until I could flag a cab down. Still dazed, I went to Harry Reid and caught the next flight to Nashville.

Years later, looking back, I'd see I left so much of the man I was behind that day for her to keep safe, and I didn't even know it.

Emotionally, I left everything with Kitten. My path, at least for the next few years, depended on being without them. All they'd do was bog me down and make me feel things I couldn't handle. I was about to commit heinous acts that would further stain my soul. Emotions would just screw everything up.

My spirit? Well, I left that with Kitten, too. It was broken without her, anyway, and I'd never be at peace again, so why keep it?

In a way, I left everything Snow was behind—she owned it, after all. At least the version who fell in love with a girl on a mountaintop. The version who laughed, joked, and loved like a Stone man. Hard, fast, and forever.

During the hours I traveled from Vegas to Fort Campbell, I shed my skin like a snake. I interred everything good and decent, becoming something else entirely.

Throughout the many death missions I'd completed, Kitten's love had kept a spark of humanity glowing. The day I lost her, the last ray of light died.

I shut everything down. I became a monster. The thing inside me might have been born long ago, but I finally opened the cage. I let it out.

But, what I didn't know was that sometimes, from monsters came angels.

And I had no clue that I'd left two of those behind as well.

Chapter Twenty-Three

Snow ~ Three Months Later

01:30, and we were in the gym boxing. We'd been trading blows along to Katie Perry singing 'Wide Awake,' one of the favorite tunes many of us big, strong, burly military men loved rocking out to. Music tastes varied in camp. Night duties never went by without a blast of 'Don't Stop Believing' or Jason Deluro. The men needed more upbeat songs to get them through.

Personally, I just needed to punch something.

Ever since I left Vegas, I'd been empty.

I hadn't felt a spark of anything. I spoke only when spoken to. Conversed only about work and missions and kept myself to myself. My friends also began to distance themselves, which was okay with me. I didn't feel the devastation of losing Kitty because I didn't let myself.

I grabbed a few hours of sleep here and there, but I mostly lived on my nerves. My sins caught up with me in my dreams and carried me straight to hell. I could handle the sick images; they weren't much different from the ones I witnessed—even created—on missions. What made me sweat and ache were the emotions that I couldn't shut out of my subconscious.

The military had turned me into a killer. A man demon who thrived on violence. Many times, I put my hand to my cock, thinking about Kitten and how we were when we met, but it was the fantasy of wrapping my hands around her throat that finally made me come. Acid would burn through my veins in those weak moments. I knew it was fucked up, but at least it made me understand I'd done the right thing by leaving her. I doubted I'd ever be with another woman again unless they were sadistic bitches who got off on pain. But it would never be about love. It would be about something entirely different.

Even though I ached with missing my girl, I was never once tempted to call, write, or visit her.

Kitten didn't need a defunct wannabe serial killer who thrived on inflicting damage. For her sake, I needed to stay away. The only pure fantasy I had left was for her to live a beautiful life. I wanted that so badly for her. I wanted her to have Harvard and become a CEO of a multi-million dollar corporation. I wanted her to have it all, even if she didn't have it with me.

Once, I thought about emptying my bank account and sending her everything I had. I would've loved to help her get there and do something to try and make up for all the heartbreak, devastation, and pain I caused. But I knew she'd instruct her bank to send it straight back.

My girl was independent.

That was another weird thing. I'd clearly fucked everything up with her, but I still thought of her as my girl. Always would. After all, Stone men fell hard, fast, and forever. Being a monster didn't change that. It would never take the love or the obsession away. In moments, I'd feel a warmth entombed deep, but I kept it buried because it was what I was best at, shutting it down.

Hollister had trained me well.

I watched the LT fight with Espinoza, Benny on one side of me, and Simmons on the other.

The aggression contained in the ring with those men made me feel something. My blood pounded, and my heart thumped in time to every punch crunched into skin and bone.

They wore head and mouth guards, but that didn't lessen the brutality, which made my excitement flare as I watched. Bruises bloomed, blood spray splattered, and I felt a tingle in my lower back as the almost invisible drops fell upon me.

Sick? Yeah. Totally. But that was precisely what I'd become. Sick—inside and out.

A verified creep.

I didn't notice the buzzing sound at first. I was entranced by the hard blows and punches the LT and Sarge kept throwing at each other. Eventually, though, I was pulled out of my trance by Hollister's cell, which sat on top of his gym bag, the screen a beacon in the muted light of the gym.

I reached for the stereo remote control and turned the music down.

Hollister whipped around, saw me grab his cell, and walked to the ropes, taking off his head guard and gloves. Taking the cell from my outstretched hand, he tapped it, put it to his ear, and barked, "Hollister."

A thread of acid wound through my gut. It could be a job. Maybe I'd get my fix.

Sure enough, Hollister motioned for Espinoza to follow, and they jumped outta the ring. "Yes, sir. Now?" He listened for a minute. "Sounds like a shitshow. Are my men guaranteed safe passage?" Another pause. "How many?" Silence. "Yes, sir. Sergeant Espinoza and I will accompany them. They'll need guidance on this one."

Benny, Simmons, and I looked at each other, wide awake and alert. This was just what I needed. It had been about five days since our last mission. Too long for men who were used to being in and out on a loop.

"My office," Hollister snapped.

We grabbed our shit and followed our superiors out the door and up the stairs. Within minutes, we were all sitting in front of our lieutenant in his office, waiting expectantly.

Hollister did his usual pose of steepled fingers to his chin as he regarded us thoughtfully. "Ever heard of the Kabul to Kandahar Highway?" he asked.

Heat surged through me. "The Highway of Horrors?"

The LT nodded. "Next question. Ever heard of the 'Bloody Hump?'"

A smile spread across my face as we all leaned forward. "Yeah."

The 'Bloody Hump' was in the Province of Wardak, Central Afghanistan, a small, humped structure on the Kabul to Kandahar Highway, one of the most dangerous roads in the world. NATO and Afghan soldiers were forever getting attacked by bombs and IEDs as they passed over it. It was placed perfectly for people to hide out on, seeing as it was in a blind spot. Good for the T-Man, good for us.

Hollister eyeballed us all, one by one. "How do you feel about blowing it up?"

My heart beat a little faster as adrenaline hit me. Benny's and Simmons's eyes slid to mine, and we all grinned, suddenly elated.

"Good answer." LT's lips twitched. "Now. How do you feel about blowing it up while evading a fuck load of insurgents who'll no doubt be on the lookout for U.S. Military with a view to shooting us in the heads?"

Benny actually laughed. "Sounds like a normal day at the office, sir."

We all chuckled.

"This is a big one, boys," Hollister explained. "If we get this right, we'll take out some high-up T-Man. But they'll make it as hard as they can for us. Play on every emotion we've got. There's nothing they won't do to appeal to our base instincts."

Ben and Simmons nodded while I smirked, thinking, *Bring it. Ain't got no fucking emotions left.*

Snow

"Sergeant Espinoza and I will be joining you on this one. Intelligence thinks the targets will be passing through in about a week. We need to get there and set up discretely. If anyone shows up to do checks, we need to be ready for them, too."

My excitement grew. It sounded like my kind of job.

Hollister checked his watch. "We fly out in four hours. We'll do our checks now. Get loaded up and rest on the plane. It's gonna be a big week. Plenty to do, plus we'll need to have each other's sixes at all times. The area may be crawling with the enemy for all we know." He gave us all 'the look.' "Make sure you call your loved ones before we go."

I saw Simmons stiffen slightly out of the corner of my eye. Couldn't blame him. Whenever the LT told us to call our loved ones, it was code for, 'There's a high risk of you not coming back.' While on leave, Kyle asked his girl to marry him. She was pregnant, and the date was set.

It was shitty, really. While I was losing the love of my life, Simmons was locking his down. Talk about bittersweet. I was happy for him but gutted for me. Though, I doubted Simmons took his fucking hand to his girl, leaving her black and blue, so there was that to consider.

"You've got an hour," Hollister told us. "Get organized, and we'll meet in the tac room."

We all rose and saluted while a chorus of "Yes, sir" went up.

Hollister looked at us one by one. "Dismissed."

Twenty-four hours later, we were dropped off along with four U.S. Rangers in the desert, about three miles from the target.

The Rangers ascertained our position before we picked up our rucks and started to walk.

Our first objective was to set up a small camp about a mile away from the bridge. There, we'd work on building our explosives while the Rangers patrolled the area.

It was a tricky job.

First, we were heading into the winter months, and the nights around here dropped well into the minuses. Being from Wyoming, I was used to the cold, as was Alaskan boy Simmons. Benny was from Connecticut, also used to it. Hollister, hailing from Southern Cali, was a fucking heat freak, as was Florida native Espinoza. Had to say, I was looking forward to seeing those two fuckers suffer some.

"There's an Afghan police checkpoint about a hundred meters from the culvert," Espinoza explained as we started walking toward where we'd decided to set up camp. "We don't want them knowing we're here." His lips thinned, and I knew why.

Afghan Police were notoriously corrupt.

One of the most complex parts of ISAF being here was weeding that out. The Afghan people had lived with that corruption for years, decades even, often to their detriment. It was a big reason why a lot of Afghanis supported the Taliban. To them, they were the lesser of two evils. The police were easily bought. It was for that reason they couldn't know we were there.

It posed an awkwardness, but it didn't worry me. The fact was that the Afghan police were also notoriously lazy and inept. There was no way they'd outwit us, but even if one of them managed to, I'd slit his throat.

Two Rangers went ahead with my boys and me at their six. Hollister and Espinoza were at our six, and the other two Rangers had theirs.

Snow

We were still a couple of miles away when Hollister said, "Benny. Why don't you tell us one of those pathetic lieutenant jokes you're so fucking fond of?"

My lips twitched while Simmons and Espinoza chuckled.

Benny's eyes widened, and he grimaced.

"Come on, big shot," Hollister insisted. "Make me laugh."

Benny cleared his throat. "Did you hear the one about the sergeant and the lieutenant?"

"Nope," Hollister confirmed.

"A lieutenant and a sergeant took their unit on a mission into the desert," Benny began. "As they got ready to bed down for the night, the sergeant said, 'Sir, look up into the sky. What do you see?' The LT looked up and said, 'I see millions of stars.' The sergeant asked, 'And what does that tell you, sir?' The lieutenant looked up again. 'Astronomically, it tells me that there are millions of galaxies and potentially billions of planets. Theologically, it tells me that God's work is divine and that we are small and insignificant. Meteorologically, it tells me we will have a beautiful day tomorrow.' He paused. 'What does it tell you, Sarge?' The sergeant rolled his eyes. 'Well, sir. It tells me that somebody stole our tent.'"

Warmth spread through my chest. Me and Simmons began to chuckle.

The Rangers ahead of us looked at each other with wide grins.

Espinoza started laughing behind us, albeit quietly.

"Worst joke I ever fucking heard," Hollister grumbled. "You need to update your material, asshole. That one's older than me."

Benny's lips curved into a smile, and he shot me a knowing glance. "Yes, sir."

Over the next few days, we set up a small camp and started building our IEDs.

The Rangers were cool. They didn't mix much with us, just with each other; we were the same. I didn't mind it. At least we could cut the small talk bullshit and get on with what we were there for.

We worked in shifts, not only with bomb-making but with patrols, too. The Rangers were highly efficient, but there were only four of them, and they couldn't be everywhere.

The Afghan police didn't venture out from their checkpoint at all. A lot of the time, they weren't even at the fucking checkpoint, which I guess proved how lazy and stupid they were. It was to our advantage, though. It meant we had plenty of opportunity to sneak under the bridge, set our shit up, and get ready for detonation day, or D-Day as we unimaginatively started to call it.

We worked tirelessly until everything was set. The explosives were buried deep and strapped inside holes and small craters in the rocks that the human eye couldn't detect without looking closely. We planted some underground, too, making sure the foliage around them didn't appear like it had been disturbed.

We were all set.

It was just a case of waiting and hoping nobody could detect what we'd done.

Turned out we did our job a little too well.

"There's something not right," Hollister muttered. "I can feel it."

Snow

My gut had churned all morning, but I didn't say a word, even though I agreed.

We'd had word that the target was en route. Intelligence had kept us notified well. The T-Man convoy was a few miles out. We were waiting in position, ready to detonate.

Transport out had been informed that we were prepared to head out and were waiting. All we had to do was blow shit sky-high before completing our three-mile trek. Then, we could pop smoke.

The devastation we were about to inflict would enable us to leave unnoticed. Whoever survived wouldn't be in the mind to look for us.

Everything had gone according to plan.

We were observing from as far away as our signals would allow. If we wanted a manual detonation, we had to stay in range. We couldn't put anything on a timer because we couldn't be sure when the enemy would appear. But we had triggered the bombs to detonate like domino pieces. As we signaled for one to blow, that signal would set off the next switch, and so on. Hence why we called it the domino effect.

So, why did my stomach clench? Why were my lungs so heavy that they pressed against my ribs? Why did my blood sting like bile coursing through my veins? And why did I feel so goddamned fucking antsy?

I sat with Benny on one side and Hollister on the other. Espinoza sat next to the LT with Simmons next to him. We were all dirty from moon dust and camping out for a week. Even in our short time here, the nights had turned distinctly colder. The ground was still frozen from the night before, but I hardly noticed.

My brain hurt with thinking. *What's off about this?*

I went over everything we'd done. Where we'd hidden, where we'd placed, how we programmed the switches. It all added up right in my head.

The week had gone so calmly. It had been almost disappointingly easy. I hadn't had a kill because there'd been no opportunity for one. Why? Shouldn't those assholes have been out in force? Shouldn't the enemy have checked this notoriously dangerous stretch of road?

"Permission to speak, Lieutenant," I asked.

Hollister's eyes jerked to me, narrowing. "Go ahead, Snow."

"What would happen if we transported our POTUS over this bridge?"

He let out a quiet snort, going back to his binoculars. "It wouldn't happen."

"What if there was no choice?" I asked.

He dropped his binoculars again, eyes sliding back to me. "Spit it the hell out, Snow." He swept a hand down his dusty as fuck U.S. Army-issue uniform. "Do I look like Cedric the fucking Entertainer? This ain't Who Wants to be a goddamned Millionaire. Dunno if you've noticed, asswipe, but I'm a bit of a cunt; therefore, I ain't got a friend to phone. Get to the goddamned point."

Funny fucker.

Espinoza snorted.

Benny chuckled.

Simmons pressed his lips together.

Hollister cocked an eyebrow, waiting.

"Why haven't they sent anyone on to check the bridge?" I asked.

Espinoza let out another snort, his binoculars still glued to the bridge. "Been thinking the same thing as Snow," he admitted. "Anyone with half a brain would've been all over that motherfucker."

Hollister heaved out an audible breath. "Yeah," he muttered, eyes slashing to Espinoza, who finally glanced around and met his eyes. A wordless conversation took place between them.

"What?" I asked.

"Think I know what's goin' on," LT said thickly.

Snow

At that, Benny and Simmons looked turned toward our lieutenant, and we all waited.

"Thing is, boys. Sometimes in war, we gotta sacrifice a few to save the many," Hollister began. "The enemy relies on our sense of honor to get away with their crimes, and sometimes just to get away. Whatever happens today, remember, it's on them, not us."

"Sir," Espinoza grated out. "We got movement." As he said that, Hollister's cell buzzed.

The lieutenant checked the message and went back to his original position. "Get ready," he ordered. "They're coming. If you can't do what needs to be done, tell me now, and I'll do it."

I returned to my binoculars, eyes straining to see what was happening. I had no fucking clue what he meant, but I had a sinking feeling. God only knew what Hollister was getting at. Espinoza knew, so I guessed we would soon enough.

It took about five minutes.

The first alert was the faint sound of a child's pealing laugh.

My throat thickened at the sound. It seemed to resonate in a place I thought I'd buried deep. But still, a pang shot through my heart as the sweet, infectious noise carried over the breeze.

Two Afghan policemen came into sight, followed by a herd of people.

My body locked.

Curses went up from Benny and Espinoza.

Simmons dropped his binoculars and fell back flat on his ass. "Fuck, no. We can't."

A roaring began in my ears, and my heart began to thud hard as realization swirled through my head, making me dizzy. Jesus. They were gonna use those villagers as human fucking shields. Pain shot behind my eyes, and my fingers started to tremor.

Hollister's low, calm voice infiltrated the whooshing in my ears. "Shut it down, boys."

I heard Benny begin to argue, tone pitchy with emotion. "We can't, sir. It's women and children."

"Benedetti," Espinoza barked quietly. "You've been given an order."

I heard a scuffle and a frustrated sound escape Benny's throat. Jerking my head around, I saw Espinoza wrestling the laptop away from him while Simmons stared at them, eyes wide with shock.

"Stand the fuck down, Benedetti," Hollister grated out. "Or I'll court-martial your ass so fucking quick you won't know what hit you until you're sitting in fucking prison, rotting."

Benny's face twisted with anger. "I've done everything you asked, Lieutenant, but don't ask me to do this. I won't."

Hollister's face was an emotionless mask. "Nobody asked you to do shit, Benedetti. I told you already. If you can't do what needs to be done. I will. We've got orders, and we carry them out. That's the way it is and the way it'll always be. Following orders is what wins wars. T-Man higher-ups don't come out to play, ever. This is an opportunity we have to take because chances are we won't get another. Do you fucking get me? *We don't have a choice*. Why the fuck did you think those Rangers were really here? Protection?" He let out a brittle laugh. "They're here to make sure the mission's completed. If we don't follow it through to the bitter end, those assholes will, and then we'll all be fucked up the ass. Whatever happens, that bridge is getting blowed up today. End of fucking story." He nodded in the direction of our target. "This is on the T-Man, not us. We haven't brought those poor souls here. They have. They're cowards, every one of 'em. They're playing on our emotions, but what they don't know is they're outta luck. This isn't about emotion. It's about following through

Snow

with our objectives and carrying out orders. So shut it the fuck down. Now!"

Espinoza sat back on his ass and started tapping on the computer just as Hollister's cell buzzed again. The lieutenant glanced at it. "Get into the position or fuck off and leave it to us," he snapped. "And that's a fucking order."

Pain stabbed through my head. The sunshine, which just minutes before hadn't posed an issue, suddenly seemed too bright. My fingers still trembled, my guts jerking with sharp, shooting pains.

Fuck.

Bile rose through my gullet, and the edges of my sight blurred and darkened.

Jesus. I'm gonna pass out.

"Snow!" Hollister barked. "Shut it down. Breathe, Snow. Remember your training. Shut it down."

I fell back, ass to moon dust, bent my neck, and steepled my fingers to my forehead. I sucked air in through my nose, let it fill my burning lungs, and breathed out through my mouth. I repeated it while I cast my mind back to a mountaintop and a sunrise, allowing myself to settle.

Slowly, the shaking stopped. My mind cleared, and I pushed down every sliver of emotion that betrayed me.

Within minutes, I'd followed my lieutenant's orders and shut it down.

I looked up calmly. My voice was emotionless as I asked, "What do you want me to do?"

Espinoza was still clacking keys. "Help me with this fucking thing," he demanded. "I'm not as fast as you."

I got to my feet, staying crouched, and moved over, seating myself next to him and taking the laptop. Without a thought, I started keying in the codes. My fingers that minutes ago tremored like I'd seen a ghost, were suddenly calm. Muscle memory took over as I punched in the final sequence of numbers we needed to arm the explosives. "Ready," I confirmed. "Press enter when you wanna go." I looked at Espinoza blankly. "Want me to do it?"

"Fuck you, Snow!" Benny muttered.

The vitriol in his words didn't penetrate as I glanced at Hollister over my shoulder, who must've given a sign to the sarge because he shook his head. "Nah. I'm good now."

I got it. After Benny questioned orders and my little tweak, Lieutenant was hedging his bets. Couldn't blame him, but he had no need to stress over it. I'd have done it. Already had countless stains on my soul. Another few dozen wouldn't have made much difference.

The lieutenant's cell buzzed again. "Okay. Fall back to the edge of the signal zone."

Crouched low, we moved toward the Rangers, who were about ten meters back. They all wore smirks. Probably because they witnessed the shitshow with us minutes before. "Everything okay?" their leader asked. His face straightened out as he took in Hollister's death glare. He was saved by the buzz as our LT's cell flashed. "It's time," he said.

Turning back toward the bridge, I picked up the rumble of heavy engines. A convoy of four old—probably stolen—Humvees approached the bridge fast.

"They're coming in hot, Sergeant," Hollister said. "Get ready."

The vehicles turned the bend and picked up speed as they raced toward the bridge. I couldn't blame their method. It was what I would've done, too. Sped through ASAP.

Shit for them that it wouldn't help them whatsofuckingever. I'd set those bombs. Those fuckers were about to blow high. Screaming started to rise up from the crowd. Some blocked the insurgent's path, not that the fuckers slowed down. They just knocked them flying in the air, probably killing them outright.

Snow

Then, a miracle happened. The crowd began to run. Within seconds, they'd cleared the tiny bridge. The Afghan police ran after them, shooting warning bullets into the air.

The first Humvee hit the bridge, then the second. As the third approached, Espinoza clicked once. There must've been about a half-second delay before the sky was filled with a rumble as the detonators did their jobs. All four vehicles blew up into the fucking sky.

It was perfectly timed.

I watched, fascinated, as metal exploded a good twenty, even thirty feet up in the air as the Humvees were taken out. The noise was incredible. Different from the rumble off the mountain we brought down months earlier, but just as fucking awesome. We couldn't feel the blast or its heat from where we stood, but I could imagine the beautiful force of it.

One of the gas tanks must've caught fire when the explosion threw the vehicle up because another ear-splitting bang fractured the air with the unmistakable sound of burning hot metal being torn apart. Rubble from the bridge flying high and in all directions.

The people who weren't entirely clear of the bridge were caught in the explosion. Others were thrown clear. Most were on the ground, screaming, but at least they were alive. There would be casualties, but it could've been much worse.

For us, it couldn't have worked out better.

The fire burned hot, bright, and satisfyingly destructive, feeding the darkness within me. A shuddering breath left me, and my shoulders relaxed.

"Time to clear out," Hollister announced from behind me. "Mission completed."

I bent down and picked up my ruck, hoisting it onto my back.

All the heaviness inside disappeared. It had been blown to hell, just like the bridge and those trucks.

Warmth replaced it, the lightness suddenly making a quiet laugh rise through my throat.

I moved between Simmons and Benny, clasping their shoulders as we walked to meet our transport. "Benny," I said loudly. "Tell us a lieutenant joke for the road."

Hollister glanced back with narrowed eyes before he shook his head exasperatedly, lips twitching, and looked ahead again.

Thank fuck. Looked like our LT was giving us a pass.

Benny muttered, "Fuck you," before letting out a juddering sigh, his shoulders slumping defeatedly. "Did you hear the one about the lieutenant and the hooker?" he finally asked.

I clapped my best friend hard on the back. "No, Ben. But I'm sure you'll tell us."

Snow

Chapter Twenty-Four

Kitten ~ Three Months Later

In the six months since I lost Snow, everything had changed.
The morning he left and shattered me into tiny pieces, I called Sophie. I couldn't speak through my sobs and heartbreak. I could barely breathe.

She knew how much I needed her because she let herself into my apartment nine hours later, crawled into my bed, and held me through my heartbreak. I was so grateful for her. So fucking happy that she was in my life.

Our friendship worked because we were opposites.

I was outgoing. Sophie shy.

I was spiritual. Sophie was scientific.

I was an independent loner. Sophie missed home desperately while she studied medicine at college. Her mom and I were everything to her, and she hated being away from us.

But still, I looked at us as two sides of the same coin. We had an identical make-up, the same morals, and the same yearning for family and connection. Maybe that was why we fit so well.

Sophie always said I was the strong one, and I could handle anything life threw at me, but she was wrong. My best friend had an inner strength and a quiet determination that made her a force to be reckoned with, and that night she proved it.

Within an hour of being there, she'd bathed me and dressed my wounds.

I'd already told her about Snow. Just the surface stuff. How we met and instantly connected. How great he was to me. How utterly and completely I fell in love with him. That night, I told her everything else. The phone calls and the changes in behavior he displayed.

We discussed PTSD at length. Sophie had researched it extensively, even done a paper on it. She told me that one event could set it off, or it could develop over time through exposure to traumatic events. Some people displayed instant symptoms, while others developed over weeks, months, and years. Like any mental health illness, there was no rhyme or reason for who it affected, how, and why. Treatments even varied. What worked for one wouldn't necessarily work for another. She explained how it was tricky to deal with and how the medical community had just scratched the surface.

After all, the human mind remained an enigma.

I think Sophie being there that night saved my life and stopped the downward spiral that losing him sent me tumbling down. She made me see that our being apart was for the best because it didn't matter how ill he was; there was still no excuse for the coercive way he'd had sex with me.

I knew it anyway. I was so scared of losing Snow that I'd have done anything to keep him, but she was right; this was too much, too toxic.

She didn't judge him, though, and I was grateful for that because I knew it wasn't my Snow who left those marks. My golden boy was kind and sensitive and would rather hurt himself than hurt me. She believed me when I told her so, even said she trusted my judgment because if I fell in love with him, he must be someone incredible.

Snow

By the time she boarded her flight for Raleigh two days later, she'd turned me around. She fought for me, and I was determined to fight for her the same way if she ever needed me.

And I always would.

Sophie returned to med school, and life went on.

I wish I could say I coped well. I wished I could've pulled myself up by the bootstraps and moved on, but I couldn't. Half of me was missing. My golden boy left such a vast, dark void in my life that I couldn't see the light some days. The deep resonating ache of losing him never left me. I even ached in my sleep. Eventually, I learned to live with it, though I was never the same.

Loving Snow was the most profound thing I'd ever experienced, and so was letting him go.

I'd learn months later that I wouldn't have a choice.

All my life, I'd dreamed of going into business.

I'd tailored my studies around it, buying books on management styles, how to influence, body language, employment, and tax laws. I'd even interned in corporations.

While Snow was on deployment and at Fort Campbell, I started to help out the lawyer who worked for Uncle Hustle's MC. He wasn't exactly on retainer because they didn't get caught for the big stuff. However, he was forever bailing them out for riding at the speed they wanted to ride in places they shouldn't have been. They had difficulty following United States laws because they lived according to their own moral code.

They exasperated me, but I loved them for it, so when Hustle asked if I'd help the guy out while his usual paralegal was on maternity leave, I said yes. I thought it would be exciting and allow me to get a deeper insight into Hustle's MC. Plus, the generous check he paid would add to my ever-growing college fund.

To my surprise, I loved it.

Poring over old cases, studying opposing and defending counsel's arguments, and searching for loopholes became my new passion. When I absorbed myself so completely into my work, I forgot how much everything ached inside.

It turned out I was good at it as well.

I started to hear phrases like 'raw talent' and 'a natural.' Suddenly, the darkness fell away a little. I swapped my business management books for legal tomes, and slowly, I began to learn about another world. And it gave me a challenge.

I came to realize I could help people more by practicing law and acquiring the tools to fight for them than I ever could in business. Slowly, over the months, I began to re-think my life plan. I still wanted success and all the security that came with it, but I also wanted my spirit to fly again as it used to before him.

Then something else happened, something miraculous and wonderful and scary as hell. Something life-changing. Something beautiful.

Four months after Snow left me, I woke up and felt different, like there'd been a change in my body.

If I was honest with myself, I'd felt weird for weeks, but I didn't examine why. I'd had a lot going on. After my breakup with Snow, I'd kept busy to exhaust myself so I could sleep. Keeping busy was my go-to when I was stressed out, the same as it used to be when he was deployed.

I didn't know precisely how or why I felt different; I just did. I hadn't been sick or ill. I just felt something profound inside.

I sat bolt upright in bed after a weird as-hell dream. The clock told me it was just after six A.M.

Swinging my legs over the side of the mattress, I stood and went to the bathroom. After peeing and washing my hands, I placed my palms on the basin and studied my face, noticing it looked a little rounder. Lately, I'd been filling out. I had a little pooch, and my boobs had gotten bigger.

It was fine. I didn't believe in weighing myself just to get hung up on a number. Luckily, I was slim enough to get away with a few extra pounds, but what bothered me was I hadn't been eating. I couldn't. I'd find myself forcing down enough to fuel my body but nothing more.

I hadn't changed my lifestyle, except I was on the move more than before. I didn't rest because I didn't ache for my missing half so much while I kept myself busy.

Explanations began to ping through my mind.

Pregnancy came in at ping number three.

I froze.

No fucking way.

Heart racing, my thoughts frantically cast my mind back to the last time I'd had sex. On trembling fingers, I counted down the days, weeks, and months. My periods had always been patchy, spotty, and irregular, so I had no firm dates to count down since my last period. I calculated it had been a while, though.

Somehow, I just knew. Maybe it was my spiritual side screaming at me. Perhaps it had been calling to me for months, but in my devastation and heartbreak, I'd not taken notice. The truth was, I hadn't wanted to hear what my soul told me. It hurt too much.

But I didn't need a test.

I didn't need any confirmation, though I'd get it.

I was pregnant.

I knew it as plain as I knew my name. Kennedy 'Kitten' Carmichael.

Fuck.

The first person I told when I saw the blue line was Sophie. Then I got in my car and went to Crimson Velvet to speak to boss number one.

Marco was in the bar watching auditions when I got there.

He took one look at my face and knew I was in shock. "Sit the fuck down before you fall down, Kitty," he snapped, motioning to the bartender. "Brandy. Now!" he ordered, rolling his eyes with a look that said, 'fucking emotional females' before grating out, "It's medicinal."

That was when I began to laugh hysterically. "I–I'm too young to drink," I chortled. "How fucking bizarre is that, Marco? I'm not old enough to drink alcohol, but I am old enough to give birth and care for another human fucking being."

His eyes locked on mine.

I gave him a 'meh, what can you do' shrug before giggling again.

He scraped a hand down his face as his shoulders slumped. "Fuck!" he snapped.

I cocked an eyebrow. "You're telling me."

His eyes came to mine before he hung his head and said, "There goes my headline act."

Another laugh bubbled up my throat.

"Going by the happy announcement, I assume you're keeping it?" he snipped.

I carried on laughing.

"What ya gonna do?" he demanded. "What about Harvard?"

I shrugged. "Hope they've got a creche." I burst out laughing again.

He gave a relieved sigh. "Well, at least you're not fucking that up." His eyes softened. "The soldier?"

I nodded, laugh fading. "Yeah. The soldier."

His eyes flicked over my face sympathetically.

It wasn't like I'd gone to Marco to tell him all my man problems, but he wasn't blind and certainly not stupid. He'd seen how devastated I'd been. He'd even asked Raven to keep an eye on me. Make sure I didn't do anything silly.

My boss was a hard man, but under it, he was decent. He proved it then by reaching out, touching my arm, and saying something that made my soul bloom for the first time in months.

"We'll look after you, babe."

Hustle was next.

When I told him, his face turned purple, and he stormed out of the room.

Luckily, his ol' lady, Katie, was there, which was good. I thought he was going to have a fucking conniption.

"He's probably speaking to Prez, asking them to ride out and find your baby daddy." She laughed.

I made a face. I knew Snow used to be at Fort Campbell. Maybe he'd been moved or deployed again since. Not that Hustle would ever know that because Katie was right. We may not have lived in each other's pockets, but my uncle was protective in his own way. I wasn't going to tell him shit.

"I don't want that," I insisted. "It wasn't planned, and I'm sure he used protection on the night in question. He won't have a clue, so it wasn't like he bolted."

Katie smiled. "Are you going to tell him?"

My heart flipped over like it always did when someone mentioned Snow.

I had thought about it. I'd also thought about not. But that wasn't fair, and it wasn't me. I knew Snow didn't want me. I knew he wouldn't want to be near the baby with his anger issues, so I'd already decided to wait until the baby was born. If he turned up demanding I get an abortion, it would kill me. I'd already subjected my baby to so much heartbreak and stress. From then on, I wanted to stay calm. Plus, nothing was guaranteed, especially during pregnancy.

"Yeah," I breathed. "I'm gonna have to, Katie. But not yet. I want to enjoy this as much as I can. I don't have contact with the baby's dad at all. Not even a number or address. I'll have to track him down, which will take time."

She nodded thoughtfully. "And what about Harvard?"

"Harvard's still my plan, except I've been thinking about going into law instead."

Her eyes lit up. "Hustle would love free legal advice. Clarke costs us a fortune."

I laughed. "Hustle should behave himself then. You'd be much richer if he didn't have so many traffic violations."

She laughed with me for a few seconds before her expression turned thoughtful. "Seriously. Why don't you look for sponsors? The club would jump at it if you made a deal to give them a grace period of legal advice when you passed the bar. Maybe Clarke would sponsor you, too. He loves working with you. All the man talks about is how talented you are. He may help financially on the promise you take a job at his firm rather than one of the big, well-known ones. Having an Ivy League graduate in his company would be great for business. I'm sure of it."

Warmth spread through my blood. It was a nice feeling because I'd been cold to the bone since the day Snow left me. "I'd have to contact Harvard," I mused. "Ask if I could transfer over from business to law." I dug into my huge shoulder bag for my plastic wallet full of acceptance letters.

Snow

Suddenly, things didn't look so bleak. Maybe my dream wasn't out of reach. For the first time in months, I'd started to feel good about something, excited even.

I pulled out the file I needed and reached for my cell before laying everything out and glancing at Katie. "Only one way to find out."

It turned out that Harvard Law School was full, and it was for the subsequent four semesters.

Between them, the Three Kings MC and Clarke Law had agreed to sponsor me up to a hundred thousand dollars. I'd have to indenture myself to them for the first five years of my career, but so what? I'd secured a job and guaranteed a client.

Not exactly a hardship.

Adding that to my savings, I had enough money for law school. My only and most significant problem was that I didn't have a fucking school.

Go figure.

When I got accepted to Harvard, I also got accepted to Stanford, Duke, Brown, Princeton, Northwestern, and Cornell. So, I began to make calls. Slowly, I went down the list and made inquiries. Eventually, I got two positive responses.

Cornell and Duke.

Scotty Clarke, the guy I'd been working for, had contacts at Duke. Sophie was at Duke. Duke had a great support program for students who were also parents. It was more affordable because Sophie's roommate was moving out over the summer, so I could move in and halve the bills. Also, I'd have Soph on hand to help with the baby.

It couldn't have worked out better.

I had nearly two-hundred grand saved by then. If I added that to my sponsor money, I could leave law school without debt and not have to work while studying.

So, I applied. And I waited and waited.

All my life, I'd believed in a higher power. Everything that happened did so for a reason. If you asked the angels for help, you'd get it.

And I did. I got in.

I'd calculated the baby was due in June. I'd relocate to North Carolina to start classes later in September. I had a scan booked to check on the baby. Everything was looking positive at last.

Except my ultrasound brought up another curveball.

Two of them, in fact.

Katie held my hand as we watched the two tiny heartbeats pulsing on the screen and cried together.

"What the hell am I gonna do with twins?" I cry laughed.

Katie smiled. "You'll love them. That's all they need."

My eyes slid back to the screen filled with beauty, and my heart swelled; my babies had made it whole again. Sophie saved my life the night Snow left me, but these two beings had given me a reason to live.

My OBGYN rolled the wand over my belly. "Do you want to know their sexes?"

"Yeah," I whispered.

She pointed to the screen. "This one here, the slightly bigger one. That's your son."

My throat thickened.

"And the little one, your son has his arm around her shoulders. Can you see how he's shielding her? That's your daughter."

A tear tracked down my cheek. My strong boy was already protecting his smaller sister. It was so beautiful that a surge of warmth flowed through me. It filled me up to the brim and brought back my light.

Snow

In a downtown Vegas clinic, I swore I would be the best mom those kids could have. I would protect and nurture them with everything inside me.

They would want for nothing.

I'd make sure of it.

Chapter Twenty-Five

Snow ~ Two Months Later

The day I left my Kitten, I left everything good in me behind, too. At least, that was what I believed. Often, my mind would wander to the moment I steepled my fingers and shut everything down while she looked on, with her heart breaking.

Physically abusing her was my single worst regret, even though I couldn't remember a fucking thing about it. But emotionally destroying her hung even heavier on my blackened soul.

I'd dream about her. And in sporadic moments of slumber, all the love would flood back into my heart because, in sleep, I had no control over my emotions. Sometimes, I woke up elated, thinking she was there, but then I'd look around my room and realize she wasn't. That was when my lungs would grow heavy, and the only thing I could do to stop myself from suffocating was shut it down.

Over the months that passed and countless missions, I began to really self-destruct.

I stopped caring about anything. Often, I'd take stupid risks. Death seemed more appealing than living like I was, a tool of death and destruction with nothing of substance inside.

Everything weighed me down.

After a while, I only felt anything when I saw the life force drain from someone's eyes. I became less discriminant about who it was. Men, women, and even teens were fair game. It became an addiction. I got a rush from it. The high was something I began to crave because it was the only thing I'd allow myself to feel. I dreaded it would all come back because that was the day I reckoned I'd hold a gun to my head and go out on the ultimate high.

I'd work out my contract, pop smoke, and take it from there.

I knew I needed help, and I'd get it.

Money was accessible to me. Cash had invested my inheritance money and made me a small fortune. With that and my military earnings, I was a wealthy man. I'd spend every penny on therapy if I needed to. I'd take stock after a year and see how things were.

I'd wait until then before making any big life decisions.

I'd go after Kitten and make her mine if I could recover. If not, I'd go boom. Until then, I just had to get through by completing my time mission by mission.

Things took another downward spiral because Benny and Simmons requested to come off the task force after the bridge incident.

Hollister agreed. Couldn't blame him after Benny got tweaked. Simmons was looking to settle down with his woman. He wanted to see his contract out, leave, and use the connections he'd forged. I wished him luck.

Since the bridge, Hollister or Espinoza had been A-Teaming with us. Always one of them with us three.

After the fuck-up, and Benny and Simmon's subsequent requests to be discharged from the task force and return to our EOD team, things changed between us, too. Maybe they thought I should've requested to come out with them. Perhaps I should've, but I was too fucked up to be able to function in a standard platoon.

Snow

Benny knew me well enough to know I wasn't right in the head, and he started pulling away from me. Since I offered to blow up the civilians on the bridge, he couldn't look me in the eye. We hardly spoke anymore.

Looking back, I think he was scared of what I was becoming. Ben knew me inside out the same way I did him. He would've sensed the change inside me. Maybe he thought I'd contaminate him with the evil living inside. My friend started climbing out of the darkness but could still recognize it within me.

That was why me and Hollister were in separate Humvees. The LT and Sarge had become my go-to guys. The lieutenant probably sent Espinoza into their transport to ensure nobody got tweaked. We also had two Marines with us, one assigned to each vehicle.

Our objective was to get into Kabul and bomb a residential property where a known terrorist had been sighted. Intelligence had word that the insurgent was planning on moving in the early hours of the next day. They didn't want that to happen.

When the job came in, I was excited about it. The whole thing screamed destruction, mayhem, and death. And I was right. It was all that and more, just not in the way I'd imagined.

We flew into Bagram Air Base just after 22:00.

Security soldiers ushered us off the plane, into the two Humvees, and straight out onto the Airport Road, which would lead us to Kabul.

Everything was quiet and going to plan. Unusually, I was lulled into a light sleep by the rocking motion of the vehicle. I'd been thinking about how to talk to Benny and explain where my head was that day on the bridge. I hadn't told him what I did to Kitten because I was so ashamed. Maybe it was time to start opening up to him. I missed his friendship. Honestly, it was all I had left at that point. My military career had turned sour because I blamed it for making me hurt my girl.

By then, it was mostly just a way to allow me to kill.

Hollister had been tapping on his laptop for most of the journey. The Marine was driving the Humvee and concentrating on the road, so not much had been said between us.

The first inkling wasn't much to speak of. The rocking motion of the vehicle altered slightly, jerking me fully awake. I turned to see Hollister snap his laptop closed while speaking into the radio. "Alpha Eight, this is Alpha Niner. Update."

Espinoza's voice came through. *"Niner, this is Eight. Civilians sighted ahead."*

Hollister's eyes narrowed. "No villages in this area. Continue at speed, Alpha Eight. Niner out." He pulled his cell phone out and stabbed it. "I'm sending our coordinates for an evac. Civilians wouldn't be on this road this late."

The vehicle slowed more.

My gut gave a clench before it started to churn. Adrenaline pounded through my veins, emotions I didn't want beginning to swirl. I slowly moved my neck from side to side, waiting for the sound of the click as I locked my shit down.

The radio crackled. *"Alpha Niner, this is Eight. Weapons ready. Eight out."*

My hand went to my M4, then to my knife and pistol, and I smiled as the monster inside me stirred. A tightness began to work its way through my body. My heart bounced in anticipation of seeing the Reaper reflected in unseeing eyes.

The Humvee slowed again. "Report!" Hollister barked.

"Civilians on the road," the Marine replied.

Snow

"Drive on," Hollister ordered.

"Yes, sir."

There was a loud thud and a jolt as we ran someone over. My nostrils flared at the screams piercing the air. Another bump, more yells and shouts until, eventually, our vehicle sped up again.

I looked out the window to see what we were dealing with.

"They're using people to slow us down to set up an attack," Hollister spat. "Get your weapons ready, Snow. They know we're here and why."

I reached for my M4, allowing the monster to the surface, satisfaction coursing through my bloodstream because he'd finally get fed. I checked my ammo, got into position, and waited for my opportunity, a smile gracing my features.

You'd have thought in moments like those nerves would set in, but mine didn't. My fingers trembled but with excitement. My heart beat harder with the buzz of the kill. I couldn't have been more focused. The edges of my sight blurred until tunnel vision set in.

Aiming my M4 out of the window, I waited for a sign.

Within seconds, the sound of gunfire came from the other Humvee. A group of men in front of the other vehicle started running and yelling. Some got caught in the gunfire and dropped to the ground.

"Espinoza's clearing them away," Hollister muttered.

My gut fizzed and popped, a deep-seated need to kill rising through my sternum.

I pulled out my pistol, aimed through the window, and started taking shots at the stragglers. Cries and screams pierced the night sky. The Humvee in front commenced moving again, but quicker.

"I don't fucking like this," Hollister said under his breath. "They're gonna attack. I can feel it in my bone—"

"—Take cover!" the Marine yelled.

A split second later, a massive explosion rocked the air. Our Humvee shook with the force of it.

Automatically, I ducked, arms covering my head for protection before my eyes widened as I watched the back end of the Humvee ahead of us, carrying my team, explode. Metal shot out and up into the night sky, everything engulfed in flames.

My body locked. I screamed in horror, "Benny! No!" Just as everything around me went fucking crazy.

"Take evasive maneuvers," Hollister yelled.

Our Humvee sped up and began sliding from side to side as the gunfire cracked the air outside the vehicle. Bullets around us pinged off metal as the enemy fired on our truck. I held on tight as the Marine tried to get us outta there.

"Weapons ready, Snow," Hollister ordered. "It's an ambush."

I planted my ass, pulled my M4 up, and took an offensive position. My mind was still trying to catch up with what the hell had just happened. All I could see, hear, and think of was Benny. Still in disbelief, my brain scrambled for some kind of explanation. One minute, they were there; the next, they were just gone. How could that be? Benny. Simmons. Espinoza. All of them were wiped out in the blink of an eye.

A scene like a movie reel played in my mind on fast forward.

The day I met Benny on our first day at EOD training. The talks, pranks, fun, good times, and the bad. His face flashed through my mind. His expressions, the laughter in his eyes, the way I knew everything he felt because it was written across his face.

Heat burst through my throat, tears burning like a corrosive acid.

My friend was gone.

My jaw clenched, molars gnashing together as my lip curled with hatred for every fucking T-Man that existed. This wasn't supposed to happen. My friend was supposed to go home, start a business, and marry that girl.

My skin tightened, the need to scratch away at it unbearable.

Suddenly, I registered Hollister yelling at me. "We've got two on our tail. Help me take 'em out."

A burn from my throat sank into my gut. An all-encompassing fire spread through my chest, destroying everything in its wake. My body began to shake, not with fear but rage, as the monster inside me surfaced.

My eyes narrowed as I tried to see who the fuck fired on us as more bullets sprayed across our vehicle. The toughened metal held fast, their weapons not strong enough to penetrate.

I took aim and breathed until the world around me narrowed, my vision tunneling to a pinprick and focusing on the truck racing behind us. My breath and racing heart were loud in my ears as I fired toward the flickering lights of the enemy fire lighting up the darkness.

The truck chasing us swerved to avoid the bullets. I aimed and fired again, popping three rounds off where the driver's head should've been. Sure enough, the truck swerved and hit a rock at high speed. The van flew a few feet up in the air, letting out an almighty crash as it landed on its side.

"There's another at his six," Hollister shouted, firing at the enemy truck. "We're not outta the woods yet, Snow. We need more of that hotshot shooting."

Again, I aimed and popped off a few rounds at the driver's side. The truck's windshield smashed, exposing the driver, and two men piled into the front seats. It turned into a scene from the Wild West. All of us trying to take cover while firing shots.

I knew that something had to give, so when the thumping whoosh of helicopter propellors sounded from afar, I thought we'd be okay. We had backup coming, probably from when Hollister called through our coordinates.

The truck behind knew they were beaten. That was probably why they sprayed us with a last round of bullets. Our Humvee was well protected with its toughened steel encasing and bulletproof glass. It was perhaps those two things that had kept us alive.

The problem was our tires weren't bulletproof, and that was where they concentrated their fire before finally retreating. When the back tire blew, we must've been going eighty. I saw everything happen in slow motion. I felt a hard jolt as we hit something in the road. Felt the lightness in my body as we sailed through the air.

I knew I would die; a part of me even embraced it.

As my head slammed against something hard, I remembered the solace I felt at finally passing out, of finally getting relief from all the pain, heartache, and violence. As I sunk into blackness, I wondered if I'd be seeing my Grandpa Bandit soon. If I met anyone in hell, it'd be that old bastard.

But my last thought wasn't of Bandit, Hollister, Benny, or myself.

It was of blonde hair, soft skin, peaches, and the sun rising over a city of lights and sin. And I was finally and totally at peace.

Chapter Twenty-Six

Kitten ~ June 18th

"For as long as I live, I will never go through that shit again," I announced, laying back on the scratchy hospital sheets, wincing.

Katie laughed before placing a soft kiss on Kai's soft, downy head. "You know what they say. It's the worst pain a woman will ever experience and the easiest to forget. That's why the ladies go back for more."

"Well, I'm not," I rumbled. "It's just as well that I've given up dancing. Gotta hole in my tummy the size of Texas." I laughed, then winced again as the movement pulled on my stitches.

"Your cut's small and neat," Katie exclaimed. "One of my friends had a c-section because her baby pooped in her tummy during labor. They cut her almost from hip to hip to clean her out."

I almost gagged. "Fuck off, Katie. It's not the time to tell me horror-birthing stories. I feel like I've been turned inside out. Jesus." My eyes softened as they fell upon the beauty that was my son. "Is he okay there?"

Katie's eyes met mine. My heart lurched when I saw she had tears in them. "Yeah," she smiled, "he's perfect."

A noise came from the corridor outside my room. I twisted my head to see Sophie hurrying in. "Is she okay?" I asked.

Sophie beamed a smile so bright it was almost blinding. "Yeah. She's responding well. They're not worried about her. She was small, so they wanted to boost her in the incubator. She'll be with you by tonight. She's a little fighter, like her momma."

My throat thickened for the hundredth time that day.

I was sick of crying. Tears had flowed, first of joy, then physical pain, back to joy again, and then the same tears of heartache I'd been sobbing for months. I'd have to stop being such a sap now I had two kids to raise. I had to pull it together and get shit done.

Their dad may not have been around, but they had me, and I was determined to be everything they needed. I'd hold the fort for now, at least until Snow was well enough to come and meet them.

I'd fallen head over heels in love for the second time in my life, and it lit a fire in my belly. I had to succeed for them. They were already my everything.

Talking about love, I started looking for Snow about a month ago.

My Uncle Hustle had contacts through the MC for people who could find people. He also had military connections. I didn't know if the methods used were strictly legal, knowing Hustle, probably not, but I was getting desperate.

It was weird calling Snow Kyle.

He didn't even look like a Kyle.

He didn't feel like one, either.

What I did like was that we both had K names. That was something I wanted to continue. It would've been nice to have him to speak with about it, but it wasn't to be, for now at least, so I just picked names I loved and thought suited them, names that meant something to us both. Simmons was out of the question. There was no way my kids wouldn't carry my name, Carmichael.

Snow once told me that he loved Hawaii, especially the beach. I pored over baby books, and a name stuck out. The Hawaiian word for sea—Kai.

I fell in love with it instantly. It was strong, spiritual, and suited my son perfectly.

Another name that deeply resonated with me was Kit.

Game of Thrones had always been our thing, and the actor who played Jon Snow was called Kit. The only thing that stopped me from choosing that as his first name was that my mom had graced me with the middle name of Kitten, and the connotations seemed a bit cheesy.

So, Kai it was. He was named for his strength and his dad's love of the sea.

My daughter was small and dainty. It was like I could sense her sweetness.

Her name was more difficult to find. I looked at goddess names for her, but nothing fit until I found a word in a law textbook.

Kadence.

I loved the way it sounded and looked up its meaning. It was Latin for 'with rhythm,' and I knew it belonged to her. I loved music and dancing and wanted that for her, too. It seemed to fit her. Her middle name was always going to be Sophie. No question. I knew it took us away from our 'K's,' so I tagged Katie on, too, just to even it up a bit.

Kadence was named for my love of dance and even, in a way, my time with her dad and how we danced together on a mountaintop. How we stared into each other's eyes while our joined bodies moved together in a smoky Las Vegas club. They were profound moments for me, and I wanted to celebrate them.

So, I did it through Kady.

Kai and Kadence Carmichael—Perfect in every way.

Except, a week later, everything came crashing down.

I took the kids home to my apartment. Sophie was with me. She was on Summer break. We were packing up my apartment, loading the last few bits into my new family SUV, and going across the country on a road trip to our new home in North Carolina.

When Hustle and Katie knocked, I thought they were just visiting, maybe to lend a hand or to spend time with me and the twins before we left.

Sophie let them in, and as soon as they walked into the living room, I knew something was wrong.

Katie came straight over to me, sat me down, and clasped my hand wordlessly.

Hustle stood firm, legs planted and looked me directly in the eyes. "Found your man," he announced. My gut tugged like it was about to burst to life again, then my uncle held his hand up. "Hit a snag," he added, face solemn.

"Kenny," Katie squeezed my hand gently. "Kyle Simmons was on a mission in Kabul when the Humvee he was in was hit by an IED."

My gut sank deep, my heart clenching painfully. "He's hurt," I whispered. "I have to go to him. Where is he now? Where's he being treated?" I glanced toward my bedroom, where the twins were napping. "Jesus. How am I gonna get the babies organized?"

"Kenny. Listen to me." Katie took hold of my arm and turned me to face her. Her eyes were full of love but also sorrow. Her hand came up to grip my shoulder. "I'm so, so sorry, baby. Kyle didn't make it. He died just after the twins were born."

Something cracked deep inside my soul. A high-pitched, brittle laugh escaped me. "Don't be stupid, Katie," I snapped in a shrill voice. "That's not funny. Why are you saying that? It's not funny."

I began to shake violently. My body couldn't handle the process of everything inside me breaking. My reaction was so strong and extreme that my vision began to swim. I clutched onto Katie's hand, trying to stay grounded. I needed to be awake. I had to prove them wrong. My golden boy couldn't be dead. He wasn't. I would've felt my soul being ripped away.

My jaw clenched, teeth grinding with the heat that fired in my stomach. How dare my uncle lie to me about something like that? "I don't believe you." I eased to my feet, rounding on Hustle, getting in his face, one hand to my stitches. "Why are you doing this? Do you hate him that much that you'd do this to me?" I pointed toward my bedroom and shrieked, "To them?" I thrust a shaking hand through my hair. "Why are you doing this? Why?"

His hand shot out, and he tugged me into him, tilting my chin up with his forefinger and looking me dead in the eyes.

I froze when I saw the glitter of tears.

Hustle didn't cry. He was a big, bad biker. He never cried. The question hung in the air, but I already knew the answer. He was crying for me. "I'm sorry, Kenny girl," he murmured.

That was when it sunk in.

My Snow, my golden boy, my heart, was gone.

The sob that wracked my body started in my chest. The soul-deep, body-shaking sobs were so painful I could feel them in my bones and blood. Every muscle, artery, and cell shattered into tiny pieces like smashed glass.

The sensation of everything inside me exploding was so fucking painful that I started to get dizzy. The world swam, black spots dancing in my eyes. Darkness took me in its arms, held me close, and rocked me to sleep.

And as I fell into sweet oblivion, only one word was on my lips.

"Snow."

Two Days Later.

Somehow, Hustle got me the number for a guy called Captain Alvares. He was Snow's superior.

It took me three days to summon up the courage to call.

Deep down, there was still hope in my heart that there'd been some terrible, awful, hideous mistake. While I had a sliver of hope, I could somewhat stop myself from falling apart.

Even when Snow ended it, ended us, I always knew in my soul that one day we'd be together. I knew he loved me, knew it wasn't a lie, and I believed with everything I had that the Universe had plans for us. I mean, I'd been Snow's a thousand times before. In every life we'd ever lived.

I was his, and he was mine.

We were fated.

I felt sick because I knew all hope would be lost the instant I made that call. That was why it took me days to pluck up the courage. But I made myself do it and got everything I didn't want, but still, everything I needed to face the cold, hard, heart-destroying truth.

SPC Kyle Harvey Simmons died June 1$9^{th}$ in an IED attack about ten miles outside Kabul. He died alongside a teammate, his sergeant, and a Marine from another unit.

Simmons was an exemplary soldier. He showed promise and talent. He was a war hero who had saved countless American lives in his endeavors to free Afghanistan from the tyranny of terrorists.

He didn't suffer, and even though my soul was marked forever, I was grateful at least for that.

Funnily enough, it was only because of Kai I even made the call.

Both my babies started crying for a feed. I don't know why, but I picked Kai up first, probably because he was louder than Kadence. I sat and settled him into position, waiting for him to latch on, but he refused.

I stroked his downy dark hair, so much like his daddy's. "Come on, Son," I whispered. "Your little sister's waiting." He kept turning his face away from me, refusing to latch on. Then something beautiful happened. Kai looked up at me with big, soulful eyes, already turning golden and smoldering, and my heart stopped.

A voice in the back of my mind whispered, *he wants Kadence to go first.*

I smiled through the turmoil that roiled through my belly and the ache in my heart. "Are you sure, Son?" I asked. "Kady won't mind."

He just stared up at me.

I gazed back in wonder. *Who is this kid?*

One of a kind, my inner voice whispered.

In that incredible moment, I developed a deep, spiritual bond with my son because I knew one thing. Kai's soul was pure, but old and a little tortured. He'd been here many times before and had something to prove, just like his dad did.

He'd been sent to me for a reason. My son was my second chance to get it right, at least in this life.

I stroked his little face and whispered, "He'd be so proud of you, baby boy, for looking after her. I'm so proud of you."

I gently put him back in his bassinet and picked up his sister, who was still squawking for food. Giggling through the tears in my eyes, I held her to my breast, and she latched on immediately. My watery gaze went back to Kai. "Happy now?" I deadpanned.

He let out a little mewl, and I giggled again.

And at that moment, I knew I was strong enough to handle anything because whatever happened, I'd always have a piece of Snow with me.

He was my soulmate.

Always and forever.

Chapter Twenty-Seven

Kit ~ Three and a half Years Later

Eyes never wavering from the double doors, I rested my back against the red-bricked wall and pulled my hoodie over my face, becoming one with the shadows.

I'd been staring at those double doors for hours, waiting.

After riding into Cambridge, Massachusetts, a few days before, I'd unexpectedly begun to surge. Weirdly, I'd forgotten what it was like; it'd been so long since it last happened.

I'd kept it locked it down since leaving the military the year before.

After making Bowie meet me at Rock Springs with my bike, I'd been riding across the country and getting my head together. There was no plan. I just landed where I landed and rode until dark when I found shitty towns and even shittier motels to sleep in.

I'd stayed on the task force for two years after my buds died but mostly worked alone. Nobody else would ever live up to Benny. I didn't want to leave the military. I'd grown to hate it but was scared to be out in the world with the way my head was. Eventually, though, I knew it was time.

I had to get my life together, one way or the other. Had to learn how to live in the real world and rid myself of my demons.

I had to find her and at least make sure she was okay. Either that or go boom.

When the Humvee that me and Hollister were traveling in crashed, I'd taken a hard bang to the noggin. My brain had been scrambled, and I was put into a medically induced coma for weeks while they waited for the swelling to go down. Apart from that, I was fine. I was bruised and battered, but it had all healed by the time they woke me.

Hollister hadn't been so lucky.

His leg had been trapped under the vehicle. It was crushed so badly they'd had to amputate below the knee.

Eventually, he'd been medically discharged, of course. Given honors and a medal before being sent away and forgotten about like so many others. Broken soldiers who'd sacrificed so much had been left to rot for their trouble. Last I'd heard, he was back in Southern Cali rocking a prosthetic and living in a cabin in the woods. LT, a loner, had probably checked out and hated the world, just like me.

I was tempted to visit him once, but when I thought about it, I realized I had nothing to say. What were we gonna do? Shoot the shit about the good old days of mayhem and murder? Or maybe the decent men we'd lost? We could've always laughed about what I'd turned into, how violent I'd become, how fucking bloodthirsty. Or maybe we could reminisce about his missing leg.

Jesus. All the lieutenant jokes in the world wouldn't be enough to get me through an afternoon like that, but then I could never tell 'em like Benny did, anyway.

Nobody made me chuckle like Benny, who I didn't miss, probably because he was always there.

Every night, I sweated, moaned, and screamed as I relived his Humvee exploding.

Snow

Every night he would hold his hand out beseechingly, begging me to save him while the flames ate him alive.

I'd awaken, calling out to my friend, brother, the best man I ever knew. I'd see our CHU back at Eggers. Sometimes, I'd see the top bunk shift and hear him moan softly in his sleep before reality rushed back, leaving me disorientated. For a split second, I'd see Benny staring at me from a corner of whichever shitty motel room I was in, eyes black, void, and haunting. His voice would float through my mind.

Help her, Snow. You gotta help her.

The words played through my head on a loop.

You gotta help her, Snow. Help her. You gotta help her.

Help her.
Help her.
Help her.
Help her.
Help her.

So I went to Vegas to help her because Ben was driving me insane.

I didn't think about what I was doing. I had no clue what I would find or say when I did.

I just knew my girl needed me.

I just knew I missed her.

The space where my soul used to be now empty and void without her.

But, as much as I looked for her, she'd disappeared.

My cell had gone. Lost, broken, fucked-up on the mission, who knew? It was an old style where nothing was stored except on the device. I'd memorized her number, but it had been disconnected.

Her apartment had been leased by a drag queen from Okay, Oklahoma. When I knocked at 01.23, asking for my girl, she invited me in, but I quickly ascertained that she had no clue who Kitten or Kenny was. Some guy had lived there before the drag queen, so I reckoned my woman was long gone.

No forwarding address.

Next stop, Crimson Velvet, which had been sold and wasn't the same place anymore. I didn't recognize anyone who worked there. It was run down and sketchy as fuck. Shame really.

I even went to the strip mall. It no longer existed. A distant memory of a call filtered through my messed-up head. Kitty was stressed about rising rents and her people being forced out. The recollection of our conversation made me cringe.

Fuck, I was an asshole.

While I was jetting around the globe, killing, maiming, and living in a bubble of violence, the world kept turning. Lives went on, and things and places changed. People got on with their shit, and I was just an afterthought. A soldier passing through. A moment in time shoved into the back of people's minds because it wasn't significant enough to be at the forefront.

The story of my life.

Except with Kitten.

To her, I meant something.

Vegas was a washout, so I moved on. The next stop was Harvard, and watching the building housing their business school. I watched and waited. Stood in the shadows from 06:00 to 23:00, looking for a flash of blonde hair, golden skin, and cornflower-blue eyes, my heart tugging in all directions.

All I got was three days of nothing and an aching chest.

Finally, I'd resigned myself to the cold, hard truth. She wasn't there. My girl never made it to Harvard, and that was a tragedy. I began to wonder if it was because of me. Did I break her too severely? Did I maim her soul so deeply that she gave up?

Did I leave her for nothing?

Snow

A sudden rush of emotions flooded my bloodstream. Love, fear, guilt, and hidden ones that I couldn't even recognize anymore all came back, and it was overwhelming. Back to the wall, I sank onto my ass, steepled my fingers against my forehead, and breathed.

I went to my happy place, a mountain, a sunrise, and the sweet scent of peaches. Eventually, my guts stopped thrashing, and my racing heart slowed to a staccato beat.

Rolling the tension out of my shoulders, I willed my mind to calm before finally going over my options. How was I gonna find her? I was out of leads.

I thought my girl had a friend studying at Duke, but she'd never mentioned a name, so that was another dead-end. My eyes lifted back to the building. Maybe I could get someone on it, a professional. Pop would know someone, but that would mean calling him. The thought of that made my gut start churning again.

Now and then, I still spoke to Mom, but I got the impression things weren't going well at home. More proof that the world kept turning. Lives went on, and things and places changed. Though, I only had myself to blame for the vast canyon that stretched between my family and me, seeing as I hadn't been home for years.

I surged the last time I was there, and my PTSD hadn't even been prominent. Before I returned home, I had to get it under control, but that was easier said than done.

On my travels, I'd seen counselors, some even on the recommendation of the VA. The first time I took the plunge was when I was up north in Wisconsin. They sent me to a medical facility in Milwaukee, where I sat in a group and listened to Veteran's stories.

Joining in wasn't an option. My kill fantasies and the sexually deviant side of me were my biggest shame. I didn't want to share, so I didn't return after that. Instead, I sought private treatment. The first place I called, I told the receptionist about my PTSD and asked her to put me with a doctor who could help. I may as well not have bothered because when I turned up, the psych was female and had never even seen a war zone, let alone have experience of one.

A part of me felt like telling her everything I was feeling just to see the look of disgust fall over her face as I told her how my skin tingled at the fantasy of sliding a blade into a jugular like a hot knife through butter. How I stroked my cock to thoughts of squeezing the life from a small, delicate, soft neck. But I didn't. I walked into the room and spoke to her for five minutes before walking back out.

The whole experience put me off, and that was when I started to self-medicate.

After some experimentation, I discovered that what worked for me were beer, tequila, cocaine, and weed. Weed helped me sleep. Beer and tequila loosened me up. The cocaine gave me a rush, much like killing. It also made me wanna fight. So, I started to frequent out-of-the-way honky-tonks, biker joints, and dive bars.

More often than not, I'd find another violent asshole to take my frustrations out on. That also kept me straight, much like my time in the ring back at Fort Campbell with Hollister, Espinoza, Benny, and Simmons had.

It had been a while, though, and I was itching for a fix.

So, I glanced at the double doors before rising to my feet and rounding the corner to where my bike was parked.

Kitten wasn't here.

She was lost.

Which meant I'd stay lost, too, at least until I found her.

A Year Later

I'd hired two Private Investigators to look for Kitten, but they'd both come up empty. With not even a name to give them except Kitten or Kenny, I was fucked.

The years had wiped her existence away. My superstar stripper, who people came to see from all over the country, didn't exist anymore.

She never made it to Harvard. The first PI sent me a file of pictures taken of every woman who was enrolled in their business MBA degree course. None were her.

They investigated her apartment block. I discovered it was privately owned when my girl lived there. Since then, it had been bought and sold twice over. The original owner had died, leaving no records.

Marco couldn't be tracked down. Of course, there were records of him, but he was part of a tightly locked-down conglomerate. He hadn't been in business for a couple of years; if he was, he traded under a different name or company.

I was at a loss in every way, shape, and form. Giving up wasn't something I ever wanted to do and probably could never do entirely, but holding onto her so tight was also holding me back. I'd combed the country looking for her. Visited every state. Drank in bars in every town and city, showing her picture around. While doing that, I wasn't getting treatment for my PTSD.

So, I had a decision to make.

Get well or go boom.

Mentally, I got by as long as I had the drugs and booze. They didn't stop the nightmares entirely, but on the nights I was almost comatose from being so fucking wasted and exhausted from yet another bar fight, I found I could get sufficient sleep to function okay for a while.

I started researching VA Centers again and heard great things about one in Grand Junction, North West Colorado. So, off I went. That was the beauty of living free; I could do what I wanted when I felt like it. For those years on the road, I couldn't have lived any other way. Whenever I felt trapped or hemmed in, my skin crawled and itched so badly that I often drew blood from raking at it so hard.

After registering with the clinic, I had to wait nearly two months to be seen, so I rented a house in the middle of nowhere with the mountains almost in my backyard. I bought enough drugs and booze to keep going for a few months, got myself an old pick-up truck and a TV, and hunkered down to wait it out.

Should've known it wouldn't take long for trouble to come knocking.

Should've also known exactly who it would be.

Trouble with a capital A.

I learned something in those years of self-reflection while I traveled the country looking for the other half of my soul.

When a man had partaken in and witnessed too much violence and bloodshed, his brain became either desensitized to it, or the memories etched themselves deep inside his psyche. Hence, the slightest reminder would transport him back to that time.

In some cases like mine, both happened.

While working for the task force, I'd shut myself off. I became a monster. If I hadn't, I'd have gone insane. To keep my shit together in the real world, I'd kept it locked down, only releasing any emotions when I could take my frustrations out on someone in a bar fight.

Memories would assail me in moments of subconsciousness, which happened one morning about two weeks after my move to Colorado.

Snow

'Take cover!' A voice yelled as an explosion rocked the air, the Humvee shaking with the force of it.

'Benny! No!' I screamed. My emotions ignited and surged, love, hate, and fury rising through my body, making me tremor violently. The pain was so excruciating it made me double over.

'Take evasive maneuvers. Evasive maneuvers.'

Bullets pinged off metal. I looked outside the Humvee to see Benny standing in the moon dust, his body in flames.

'Weapons ready, Snow. It's an ambush.'

'But I gotta save, Benny,' I screamed, trying to stand, to get outside and stop him from burning, but suddenly I was paralyzed. I couldn't move a muscle.

'That's not the mission, Snow. Stand down.'

More explosions cracked through the air as Benny held his hands out to me, imploring, 'Help her, Snow. Help her.'

I watched, frozen with horror, as Benny's skin slowly charred and blackened. 'Help her, Snow,' he screamed. 'You gotta help her.'

I looked down. My breastbone protruded, pulsing in and out with every thump of my heart. I started to choke, suffocating on the smell of Benny's burning flesh.

Then Hollister's voice. 'Shut it down, Snow. The mission is all that matters. If you don't do it, I will. That's an order, Soldier.'

My eyes flew open, and I jerked to a seated position, every inch of my skin covered in sweat.

Help her, Snow. Ben's voice floated through my mind. My eyes slashed toward the corner of the room to see my friend fading away to nothingness, eyes black voids, staring, and haunted.

"Jesus," I croaked, throat parched with arid fear. My head dropped into my hands, and I sawed in a breath.

Bang. Bang. Bang.

My head jerked up again, my heart thumping wildly.

What the fuck?

My mind whirred. I was so disorientated that it took me a full minute to realize that someone was banging the fuck out of my door. I ignored it, breathing deeply, in through my nose, out through my mouth, trying to pull my shit together. Finally, when the hammering of my heart settled, and the tingling of my nerve endings eased, I hauled my legs over the side of the bed and went to see who the fuck it was.

Nothing could've fucking prepared me.

Still slightly unsteady on my feet, I moved out of the bedroom and down the hall toward the front door. I went to the peephole and froze. "What the fuck," I breathed, rubbing my eyes, praying to God that I was still in the throes of my nightmare. I didn't want this shit to be real.

I watched a big shovel hand reach out and rap on the wood again. "Lil' kitty cat!" Atlas's gruff voice boomed. "Rise and shine, motherfucker. Daddy brought you coffee."

I cracked the door open. "The fuck?" I barked.

A huge smile spread across Atlas's face as he took me in. "Long time no see, asshole. You look like shit."

He barged in, knocked me out of the way, and sauntered down the hall to the living room with two take-out coffee cups and a paper bakery bag. "Where's ya fuckin' furniture?" he bellowed. "You're a grown-ass man. You need more than a La-Z-Boy and a TV."

My jaw clenched as a booming laugh floated out into the hallway. I looked up at the heavens. "Fucking great!" I muttered. "This is all I need." I stalked after him to see he had his ass in *my* fucking La-Z-Boy, feet up, one arm behind his head, sipping his coffee, not a care in the world.

Fucker raised his eyes to mine and grinned. "Nice place, Kit. Bit far outta the way, though. It was a bitch to find."

"Yeah," I snipped. "Probably 'cause I didn't wanna be found. Shame you didn't take the hint. The fuck are you doing here, Atlas?"

He raised one shoulder in a shrug, casually sipping his java. "Come to take ya home."

I scraped a hand down my face, tamping down the telltale burn firing up my insides.

This was just fucking typical. Screw what I wanted or needed. Instead of waiting until I was ready, Pop took matters into his own hands and sent his SAA to strongarm me into doing his bidding. Well, it was wake-up time. I wasn't a kid anymore. I had my own crap to deal with. Petty club bullshit could wait.

"Ain't coming home, Atlas," I argued. "Maybe one day it'll happen, but I got an appointment with the VA coming up. I can't miss it. I've got some shit to work through from my time in the military. Dad will have to hang fire."

Atlas skewered me with a look. "Shit's happened at home. Bad shit. Dagger needs ya."

I stilled. "Huh?"

Atlas's lips thinned. "First, your ma and pa split. She's gone."

My face twisted. "What?" I demanded, tone holding a thread of disbelief.

He nodded. "Yeah. Your ma fucked off. Then Cash and Cara broke up. She caught him with his dick where it shouldn't be. Walked in on him fuckin' club gash, punched the bejesus out of his face, dumped his ass, and left town." His lips thinned again. "Fuckin' stupid prick went batshit and ended up beating the snot outta Robbie fucking Henderson of all people. Now he's looking at five years at least."

My mouth fell open.

I didn't know Cara well, seeing as I'd been in the military when Cash met her, but I'd heard great things. Mom told me she was his one, so I couldn't work out what kinda brain fart he'd had to warrant him fucking around on her.

Served him right. He always was a spoiled cunt. Pop thought the sun shone out of his asshole. Good to see that his protégé was human after all. Though there was something that didn't make sense to me.

"Why'd he fuck-up Henderson?" I asked confusedly.

Atlas shrugged again. "Got some fake pics that showed Cara getting done by him. Turned out it wasn't her, though."

"And he didn't think to ask her about it? Or did he just decide to get his dick wet to punish her? Sounds about right for the hotheaded prick." I deadpanned.

Atlas grinned again. "Your dad's goin' out of his mind."

"I'm sure he is," I retorted. "God forbid Cash has to take any responsibility for the shit he does. Who's Pop gonna groom for the gavel if his eldest is doing a five stretch?" I dug the heel of my hand into my eye. "You couldn't make this shit up."

"You're telling me," Atlas agreed. "Fuckin' club's turnin' into an episode of Maury. Shenanigans, cheating, and divorces. We need some stability back, Kit. Got a prospect intake starting next week. Want you on it. You're Prez's son. It sends a strong message."

I snorted. "Sorry, bro. No can do. Got my own shit to get straight."

Atlas sat forward, elbows to knees. "You've had years, Kit. You've been bumming around the country without a care in the world. Time to get serious. If you haven't got your shit straight yet, then whatever you're doin' ain't workin'. Maybe you need your family around. Your brothers. Maybe you should be looking closer to home for help."

My head reared back, lip curling. "How do you know I've been across the country?"

The SAA's mouth quirked up. "Had tabs on ya."

Snow

My eyebrows snapped together. "Huh?"

Atlas nodded. "Colt the whizz kid. He's been trailin' ya since Vegas. The stalky pretty boy fuckhead can locate ghosts."

My heart panged. "He can find anyone?"

Atlas kept on grinning while he nodded again. "He hasn't let us down yet. He's got mad computer skills."

Interesting.

My mind recalled a years-old conversation during my last visit home. "Wasn't he Army Intelligence?"

"Yeah. Since Colt left, all the agencies, home and abroad, tried to recruit him. Nothing's off-limits. If we wanna look into somethin', he's through the wall in a few taps and a pretty-boy smile. He's pulled the club into the twenty-first century. Add on the fact he's a crack shot and can handle himself; well, you can imagine; your pa's over the moon with him."

My forehead furrowed as I thought about that for a minute.

MI was notorious for being dogs with bones when it came to finding stuff. They wouldn't let shit go. Once I returned to the club, I could use all their resources, including Colt. I'd come to a dead-end finding Kitten. Having a hacker onside who could tap into shit that the PIs didn't have access to could be the break I'd been looking for.

My only problem was I had to get myself right, too.

Being around Dad and the club would throw up pressures I wasn't sure I was ready for. Add on the fact that I'd finally found a clinic I believed I could work with, and I saw that staying held merit, too. Finding Kitten had become almost an obsession, but being in the right head space to be good for her was just as important, especially after all the shit I'd already put her through.

"What's goin' on, Kit?" Atlas asked, voice low. "What's holding you back?"

My eyes slid to his. "Got some heavy shit to sort through, Atlas. The VA clinic here's the only one I've found in the country I think I can work with. Gotta wait a few more weeks for my appointment."

Atlas rose to his feet and approached me. "So. We're not exactly a million miles away from Hambleton. We're straight up the one-three-nine and onto the one-nine-one. It's a nice ride, just what a man would need to clear his head before and after therapy. When you need time to come here, I'll make sure you get it. It ain't fuckin' complicated, Kit."

I looked him dead in the eye. "Prospects can't just take off. What if I need a week at a time?"

A strong hand clasped my shoulder. Weirdly, I didn't come out of my skin like I usually did when someone touched me. The sensation felt oddly warm.

Atlas's eyes held mine. "Then you'll get it. You think I don't want you to be well? Jesus, Kit. You've been away too long. Your health, physical and mental, is the most important thing to me, just like every other man in the club. My job's to make sure you're good. Anythin' that'll assist you will be sorted, including trips to Grand fuckin' Junction. If we need to build our own VA center and fund it, I'll speak to Prez. You'll get what you need, brother. I'll make sure of it."

I nodded, my throat tightening with a sliver of old emotion. It was remiss of me to forget who Atlas was for a hot minute, but then he did hide it well underneath all the asshole.

It was his care and concern that I think made my mind up.

Looked like I was about to do the one thing I always swore I wouldn't.

I was going home.

Chapter Twenty-Eight

Kit ~ Six Months Later

Just like I'd feared, therapy fell by the wayside.
Prospecting for the Speed Demons was a full-time job. We cooked, cleaned, picked up dirty rubbers, hosed down, and polished bikes. In what limited time we had left over, we let off steam.

It wasn't Atlas's fault. He, Abe, and even Pop were constantly on my back to keep my appointments and attend sessions. They even found some nearer to home for me.

I attended now and again and even caught up with Renz, a guy I knew from Eggers, but it wasn't a regular thing.

The problem was I'd given up, not on Kitten, never on her, but I'd given up on myself.

All my life, I'd had a plan, and it never once included being a biker, but here we were. Over the years, I'd disappointed many people—Pop, Abe, Iris, Mom, Kitten, Benny, and even Hollister. But the disappointment that cut the deepest was how I let myself down by becoming the very thing I never wanted to be.

In the months I spent prospecting for the Speed Demons, I discovered a big life lesson. It was cliche as fuck, and I embarrassed myself even thinking the words, but they were true.

You couldn't love anyone the right way unless you loved yourself first. You couldn't be content, happy, or good for someone else unless you felt all that within.

And I hated myself.

The more I got pulled into MC life, the more resentful I felt. That resentment turned to self-loathing and anger which meant I was constantly burying my emotions so I didn't lose my shit. By then, it had been going on for years, a constant cycle of feeling stuff I didn't want to feel and not having the tools to deal with it because Hollister had trained me so goddamned well.

Shut it down, Snow.

Soldier. Shut it the fuck down.

It was all I knew how to do and as simple as breathing. It was easier to inter everything than bring it to the forefront. But it was also a toxic cycle that, at some point, I knew I had to break.

I dreaded that day. The surge would be so painful, so destructive. It would probably be the day I went boom because how the fuck was I gonna deal with years' worth of pent-up emotions?

I couldn't. I didn't know how.

In the meantime, to get by without losing my shit and shooting up the clubhouse, I continued to self-medicate.

Booze, drugs, parties, I went fucking wild. My fellow prospects were party boys, too. After work, we'd settle in the bar and have a blast. The alcohol and drugs helped me sleep, which helped me function remotely humanlike, so it worked for me. I even found camaraderie among my brethren of fellow prospects.

There wasn't anything we didn't do together. Sometimes, I even watched them fuck the club gash as I sat back with a joint, trying to get excited just so I could feel the slightest bit normal. My libido had disappeared, probably because of the self-disgust that gripped me after my dick erupted to thoughts of choking and suffocating a slim, golden throat.

I loved Kitten as much as I did on the night I whispered it into her skin, just after I'd fucked her against a wall in a corridor. I still ached for her every second of every day and always would. It was always there in my blood and bones. It was the one feeling I was never able to bury completely.

Until one night, everything changed.

I fucked up.

Every Friday night, the club threw a party. It was a biker tradition, even more so than Thanksgiving and Santa. It was the one night the club opened its doors to everyone, even the townsfolk.

We'd had a busy day cleaning the bar and bathrooms, only for them to get fucked-up again while everyone partied, but I guess Dad had a rep to protect. So, we'd done that before showering and gearing up for the night ahead.

There were four of us prospecting together. Me, Chippy, Loser, and Shoot. My prospecting name was Kit. Fuck knows how I got away with that, but small mercies, right?

Most people had gone to bed or gone to fuck.

I'd drunk enough tequila to put a horse on its back. After smoking a joint, I decided to turn in. Shot and Loser had disappeared with one of the town girls a half-hour before. Chippy was working the gate with one of the club members.

I hadn't slept for a few days and felt wired. The nightmares came when I was on edge like that, and I needed something extra to take it off.

Something like violence.

See, that craving had never gone away. I controlled it with booze and drugs, just like I did everything else, but sometimes I needed a fix, needed something more.

I'd get in the ring and fight it out with Atlas and Pop. I'd even go into the woods behind the clubhouse, punching and kicking trees like a fucking crazy person. The monster was always there, clawing under my skin to get out. He was as much a part of me as Kitten was. Sometimes, it was like I had a split personality. Kitten represented everything good that I wanted to be, but the evil inside was what gripped hold and wouldn't let go.

The corridor lights were dim. The sounds of soft music and people fucking behind closed doors filled the ether. My jaw clenched, the embers of a fire starting to burn through my belly. A slight tremor started in my fingers. I sucked in a breath as I began to breathe through it, shutting it down.

That was when I heard a woman's voice.

"Harder. Please, hurt me."

I stilled.

Laughter, then, Loser muttered, "Crazy bitch. Beat her ass harder."

The monster rose, bursting to get out. For the first time in years, the base of my spine tingled, and I felt my cock twitch.

Almost trancelike, I followed the sounds of the woman begging to be hurt, cracking the door open to Loser's room.

My chest warmed at the sight before me.

Loser lay naked, back to his bed. He was straddled by an equally naked redhead. Shoot was at her back. As she ground down onto Loser's cock, Shot whipped her ass with a belt.

The monster roared to life, flooding my bloodstream with endorphins I hadn't felt for years. I grabbed onto the door to balance myself; everything felt so off-kilter.

Snow

Shoot sensed me there because he turned around, saw me watching, and grinned. "Come in. The more, the merrier, right, sweetheart?"

The woman turned her head, and our eyes met. Hers flicked between mine, curiously at first. Suddenly, they gleamed, and she smiled triumphantly as she murmured one word, "Yeah."

On autopilot, I moved inside, shutting the door gently behind me and sinking down into the chair in the corner so I could watch.

All the while, the woman never took her eyes off me. Her retinas burned into my skin, but I didn't hate it. If anything, it added to the heat enveloping my organs. The first good kind of heat I'd not felt since—A lump formed in my throat as the comfortable feeling subsided. I reached for it again, forcing *her* from my mind.

There was no place for *her* here, not like this.

Not this way.

Slowly, the three of them started to get into it again, and the woman's eyes again fell upon mine.

My stare met hers, and something dark unfurled in my gut the second my monster recognized hers. She liked it. She loved being used that way. She enjoyed being hurt. She got off on the pain.

My cock kicked, suddenly hardening for the first time in forever.

Fascinated, I adjusted the crotch of my jeans, staring as Shoot lubed up his condom-covered cock and eased himself into her ass.

She let out a mewl of pain but didn't shy away. On the contrary, she moved so he could get deeper access. They both began to fuck her. Both slamming into her alternately.

My cock grew even harder as I watched, almost in a trance as her eyes rolled back in her head at the pleasure and pain my friends inflicted. The dark bloom in my stomach grew, meandering through my organs and seeping into my veins.

Its evil darkness fed my monster, and I felt alive inside for the first time in years. I surged, but surprisingly, I wasn't out of control. My heart beat faster but with excitement. My nerve endings tingled with pleasure instead of pain. The cold ache that sometimes made breathing difficult suddenly lifted, leaving my chest light and buoyant, almost euphoric. Much like the feeling I got when I slid a knife's blade across smooth skin.

I was so far inside my head that I didn't notice Shotgun come. As he pulled out roughly, making her whimper with pain, I jerked back into the moment.

He reached across to the nightstand, holding up a foil wrapper. "Your turn, Kit. She likes it rough, or she won't come."

My knees shook with excitement I hadn't experienced for years; I stood and flicked the button of my jeans open. Still fully clothed, I moved to the bed, pulling just enough of the denim down to allow my rigid cock to my spring free. The thought of her skin touching mine left me cold, but the notion of brutalizing her ass while wearing a condom strangely didn't.

"Hurry," the woman demanded, neck craning. Her eyes gleamed as she watched me roll the latex covering down my cock and fist it at the base. "Hard," she demanded. "Hurt me."

Those words were my undoing. I didn't even lube up. Instead, I roughly pushed forward, positioned myself, and thrust hard inside her ass.

She squealed in pain.

I heard a "dang" and a whoop from Shot as I snapped my hips back and slammed again. She almost came off the bed and probably would've if she wasn't getting impaled by Loser and me. Seating myself deep, I pulled out and thrust hard again.

She let out a pained shriek as I sneered, "You wanted to hurt, bitch. So hurt."

My balls tightened at her whimpers of pain as I found my rhythm and began to fuck her ass roughly. She was tightish, but it wasn't the sexual act that aroused me so much as her cries of pain. Every time she whimpered or cried out, satisfaction roared through my chest.

The monster was wide awake and taking control.

Every inch of skin tingled, every nerve ending, every cell. My hand snaked up her bowed back, and I hauled her up by the throat.

"Yes." Her neck swiveled, and her eyes met mine.

I could see what she wanted; I wanted it too. My hand began to squeeze as I pounded roughly inside her ass.

"Jesus," Loser cried out. "Fuck, yeah." His hips began to jerk from underneath her. "Bitch you gotta come," he gritted out, pounding from underneath so hard that I could feel the thrust of his cock through the thin layer of skin separating us.

A tingle started in my lower back, my balls drawing higher. I groaned out loud, eyes closing with forgotten pleasure. It wasn't Loser's actions or how he fucked her that excited me. What fed the monster was the feel of my hand closing around her throat. The suppleness of her skin. The way she gurgled through the pressure of my fingers pressing onto her windpipe.

Without warning, my balls drew tighter. I groaned as all the pressure of the last year burst from me. Ropes of cum filled the condom while my orgasm ripped through my insides. All my focus was on the feel of her neck in my rough grip, the knowledge that I could snap it at any time and fuck me if that thought didn't make me come even harder.

She started to squeal and buck her hips as her orgasm hit. Not that I cared if she came or not. The thought of pleasuring her never entered my head.

After a minute of shallow thrusts where I drained my dick dry, I pulled out, fell back on the bed, dick still out, and heaved in air. Bone-weary exhaustion set in, and for the first time in forever, I yearned for sleep.

I rose from the bed, removed the condom, and tied it. Didn't even look at the other two guys or the girl. I didn't care enough to. There was no thought of ensuring she was okay or tending to her. She'd done everything I needed her to do; she didn't matter after she fed the monster.

Tucking my flaccid cock back inside my jeans, I did them up, and without even a backward glance, I stumbled for the door.

Within a minute, I was in my room disposing of the condom. My head must've still been high with the drugs because I was still in a trance. I didn't give what had occurred a second thought. It was like I was on the outside looking in on the entire scene, totally disassociated from it. Plus, I was still wasted and groggy from the joints I'd smoked in the bar and bone tired from coming so goddamned hard.

My mind and body were exhausted, and my monster calmed. A new sense of lightness invaded my chest, the same way it used to after a kill.

I toed off my boots, stripped off my jeans and tee, got under the covers, and slept, satiated and relaxed.

And for the first time in years, I didn't dream.

The next day, I was a mess.

I'd had six hours of uninterrupted sleep. No nightmares, burning bodies, or messages from dead men. I should've been more settled, but was even more of a wreck than usual.

Snow

As soon as I awoke, the events of the night before came crashing back to me, making my throat burn with unshed tears. I sat up in bed, digging the heels of my hands into my eyes, breathing, and trying not to fucking jump up and trash my room.

I was losing my girl, I could feel it inside, and it was all my own fault.

When I hurt her, I was determined to leave her alone for her safety and peace of mind. I knew it would ruin me, but I never imagined this. For years I'd lived with the ache of losing her because, in my heart, I believed I'd see her again one day. But I was losing hope.

Colt hadn't come up with any new information, and I was spiraling again.

I came back to the club for nothing. And to add insult to injury, I'd screwed up in the worst way.

Fuck. Fuck. Fuck.

Logically, I knew it had been years, and she'd have probably moved on. Her light attracted people like moths to a flame, so it was stupid of me to think she was waiting for me to find her. I just fucking missed her so much. It was killing me. How long could I stay stuck in time? How long could I pine over a woman I didn't know if I'd ever see again. Logic told me to chill out. Logic told me we weren't even together, that I'd ended it.

But love wasn't logical. What we had wasn't logical. It was just us.

Always and forever.

She was my fire.

But she was also becoming my curse.

Once I broke the seal, the floodgates opened.

As much as fucking around brought on excruciating feelings of guilt and made me churn inside, it also helped keep my violent urges at bay. The redhead kept coming back to the clubhouse for me. I knew why. I sensed that I fed her monster just like she fed mine. She loved me wrapping my hand around her throat. She loved me inflicting pain on her.

The problem was the mornings after, I surged a lot more. Maybe it was the burn of guilt searing a crack into the bottomless pit where my emotions were buried and forgotten, letting them escape.

But it was okay. Shutting it down was easy, and it was what I did best.

Often, I caught my dad, Abe, and Bowie looking at me like they never knew me.

I'd always been easygoing; it was what was expected of me, what eradicated the worry in their stares, so that's what I became again. Kit, the good-time boy, everyone's friend. The other prospects and me all got patched in together. Loser became Reno. Shoot became Shotgun. Chippy became Chaps. I stayed as Kit. We were good buds. Our friendship reminded me of the one I had with Benny and Simmons, so I radiated toward it.

They were assholes at times, but so was I, and they covered for me when I was too spaced out or wasted to work. They had my back, so I had theirs.

Hiding my violent urges was a problem, though.

Chatter started going around the clubhouse about my penchant for rough sex. Dad started looking at me, more confused, and Abe's eyes held more questions.

It made me feel more disgusted with myself.

The club treated women with respect—revered them even. I'd never heard my dad raise his voice to my mom in anger, even when they were on the outs. Abe treated Iris like a precious gem. Even the burliest of brothers with an ol' lady was devoted and kind to them.

That made everything about me more shameful. I knew it as well as I knew I'd lost myself in an abyss of drugs and sadistic sex. My life had consisted of being caught in loops, and I found I was trapped in another.

Cravings for violence. Satiating those cravings with brutal, savage sex. Guilt and shame. Shutting it all down. Booze and drugs to help me sleep and function. And back to the cravings.

So on and so forth.

Rinse and repeat.

So, I began to fuck other women—nice girls who didn't want to be choked and abused—to hide who I was and disguise my real needs, and it worked. The rumors about my savagery in bed died down and became just a kink as far as the club gossip mill was concerned.

It seemed that kinks were acceptable.

Additionally, it seemed acceptable to hurt women emotionally by using them through one-night stands and whoring myself rather than choking them out. It was okay for me to charm them, leaving a trail of heartbroken women in my wake. There was no problem with bruising women on the inside rather than the outside. That shit was even celebrated, as evidenced by the road name I was finally given.

Heartbreaker.

I recognized its hypocrisy, but it suited me to play up to the manwhore image that so many were quick to pigeonhole me into, including Dad. But they understood that façade. It would naturally make them feel more comfortable around me if they thought they knew who I was.

But they didn't.

Nobody did.

Except for one person.

A person who I didn't realize since the day I returned to the MC had been quietly watching and learning everything about me. Working out what really made me tick and the needs I craved. Someone who would bring everything wrong about me to the surface and use it to her advantage.

A woman of the most dangerous kind.

One with an agenda.

Chapter Twenty-Nine

Breaker ~ Eighteen Months Later

"Saw you goin' off with Reno and April last night," Bowie muttered, nodding toward the bar. "She's trouble. I didn't like or trust her before all the bullshit with Cash and Cara went down. Can't fucking abide her now."

I craned my neck to see Shotgun with one of the club girls at the bar. My eyes squinted as I took her in. I was wasted the night before, but not enough to know I hadn't fucked anyone. However, I did recall watching Reno fuck a girl. Was that her?

I shrugged internally. *Who knows?*

Bowie's words registered through the haze of the comedown ravaging my head. If there was one thing I fucking hated, it was morning afters. They irritated me and made me combative.

"Cash was the one with a woman," I argued. "You can't blame the girl for doing what she's here to do. If we tell her to jump, she has to ask how high, or she's out."

Bowie glared at her while he took a swig of beer. "Still, I don't trust her. There's somethin' off with her."

My eyes slid to her again. Bowie was right. I could tell without much effort she was calculating, but then so were most of the bitches in this place. MCs, by their own definition, were dog-eat-dog. Survival of the fittest. That was why so many military men prospected after they popped smoke. The rules were much the same. Hierarchy. Give and take orders. Brotherhood, and fight for what the MC stood for.

"She fucks men for room, board, and pin money, Bo," I declared. "Hardly normal. You weren't so fucking discerning before you met Layla. You liked to break in the new ones. Am I right?"

Bowie glowered at me. "Never went back, though."

I laughed. "Nah. You just fucked the likes of Sydney 'hell spawn' Barrington and your stable of snooty bitches instead. I'm sure you think that made you better than the rest of us, right?"

His stare narrowed on my face. "What's your problem. Shark week?"

My fingers rubbed at the ache in my temple. "I'm just sick to the teeth of everyone giving Cash a pass. He fucked up. He cheated. He was stupid enough to beat Henderson half to death in broad daylight in the middle of town. He lost what he lost, and now he's paying the price for it."

"What if she had somethin' to do with it?" Bowie asked, gesturing toward the bar.

I lifted one shoulder in a shrug. "Then he's even more fucking idiotic than I thought. If he blamed her for what he did, it shows how entitled he is."

Bowie went quiet, drinking his beer thoughtfully.

My eyes slid back toward the bar.

To think of it, something about her pinged in my gut; it always had. I mostly stayed away from April, primarily because of the whole Cash thing—that was a shitshow I didn't want any part of—but my stomach churned slightly whenever she was around.

Bowie could've been right, but I couldn't determine why she'd go out of her way to stir. What happened with Cash put her position in the club at risk. Nobody liked or trusted her, including many of the other club girls. What would she have to gain from it?

I drained my beer and rose from my seat.

"Where you goin'?" Bowie asked.

My mouth twisted into a smirk. "Gonna go see what the fuck it is about April that would make Cash stick his dick in her and risk everything."

He muttered something about me being a disrespectful prick as I moved toward the bar, making sure I headed in Shot and the girl's direction.

As I approached, I heard her giggle at something Shot said. I tapped my empty bottle on the countertop and nodded at Sparky, who popped the top off a fresh brew and handed it to me. I turned toward them and sent her one of my smirks that made women's panties fall off. "Morning, sweetheart. You recovered from last night?"

Her eyes met mine, glittering triumphantly. "I'm a bit sore, but that's okay. I kinda like the way sore feels."

Her words resonated somewhere deep. My body locked as the monster inside me awakened.

April's eyes were full of the kind of promise that I hadn't seen since the redhead back in the day. That girl eventually left town, but not before turning up here one last time, begging to be my regular sub.

I'd laughed at her before sending her on her way. My monster wasn't about control or subservience and mastery. That was a whole other kink. My urges weren't about relationships of any kind, nor sex, and certainly not about care or love.

They were all about violence, and right then, I could see the same need for it reflected back at me in April's blue eyes.

My stare swept down her and back up again as my skin began to tingle. I cracked my neck from side to side and rolled my shoulders loosely.

She was a skinny, bleached blonde. Pretty enough if you like that type. Everything about her was fake, like she was trying to be someone she wasn't. But then, weren't we all pretending to be people we weren't in some way, shape, or form?

A small surge flooded my bloodstream as dark urges pulled inside my stomach. My monster made himself known.

I looked at Shotgun, nodding to April. "You going there?"

He grinned. "I will if you will."

My hand clasped the back of April's neck, dragging her roughly from the bar stool. "Let's go then. It's time to play."

I tipped my head back, closing my eyes and letting the effects of the white powder take over my brain. I'd gotten to the point where I could only fuck when I was high. I needed mind-altering shit to take me to a far-away place where Kitten didn't exist.

The only way I could perform was if I was in a state of darkness where it was just me and the demon inside. I needed it, though. I needed to satiate the monster to keep myself sane.

Shotgun was close to finishing.

I'd already held April by the throat while I got her off with my fingers. Shotgun had been fucking her from behind at the time. After almost an hour of my cock kicking into action and softening again, I'd pulled back and snorted a hefty line just to take the edge off. Wasted was the only way I could do this, but if I didn't, my darkness would escape.

Her whimpers and cries of pain were starting to take effect now. My demon was interested in how Shotgun slapped her ass hard while pounding into her.

My cock kicked in my jeans. At last.

Her eyes caught mine, sending a silent message. She took everything Shotgun gave with a smile, even demanding that he fuck her harder. Her stare never left my face. She was taunting me, begging me to hurt her with her calculating blue eyes, daring me to let the evil loose.

It was my catnip, everything I needed, and the bitch knew it.

Shotgun groaned loudly as he emptied himself into a condom. After taking a minute to come down from his orgasm, he gave her ass one last slap and eased out, holding the latex in place. "She's all yours, brother," he muttered, pulling the rubber off, tying it, and dropping it into the small garbage bin in the corner.

I didn't say a word as he pulled his tee and jeans back on, laced his boots, and sauntered outside toward the bar. "Lock up and bring the key out with ya," he called out as the door closed behind him.

Silence filled the room.

Still naked, April slowly knee-walked over, slid her hands up my thighs, and rested them on my crotch. "What do you want, Breaker?" she asked in a breathy whisper.

My hand reached out and fisted her hair. It felt weird, like cotton wool. Nothing remotely like the silky, smooth locks my fingers were used to touching. That helped me in a way. It made it easier to disassociate myself from what I was about to do and who with.

"I want you to shut the fuck up, bitch. Then, open your mouth wide and keep it open while I skull fuck you," I said with a growl. "The only sounds I want from you are to convey how much it hurts. Then, keep your skank mouth shut for a bit longer while I choke the life outta your little neck while I fuck your ass."

Her eyes widened slightly as a thread of shock went through them.

My monster roared as my hands went to my crotch, flicking my fly open.

Time to release the beast.

Over the months that followed, I found myself going back to April time and time again.

It wasn't the norm for me. I hardly went back to the same place twice. It certainly wasn't an exclusive thing, and I made sure she knew it by fucking other women in front of her.

I'd never have another girlfriend, and I'd never take an ol' lady or a wife. All my encounters had one sole purpose. To feed my urges and throw others off the scent of my sick fantasies. I made sure April saw me with the town girls on Friday nights, and she never got a look in. But about once a week, I found myself going back for a fix.

She seemed to know instinctively what I needed and made sure she gave it to me.

I wouldn't have given her a second thought if she didn't, and she knew it. Fucking April on the regular wasn't about sex, closeness, or connection. It wasn't even about getting off. It was merely about getting enough of a fix of violence to help me keep everything straight in the other areas of my life.

Except my life was becoming a fucking mess. As the months marched on, I was caught deeper in the cycle of drugs, booze, and rough sex with April.

My state of mind started to deteriorate even more.

By then, I think Dad had given up on me completely. He never spoke to me anymore. He averted his gaze like he couldn't bear to look at my face.

Abe tried to talk to me, but I laughed everything off and told him I was letting off steam.

Snow

Cash came home from jail. Took one look at me with April one night and clenched his jaw. All sorts of shit was going down between him and Cara, so I put the fact he was distant with me down to that. I guessed the fact I was fucking April was the final straw for him.

Not that I cared; the drugs were beginning to take over. I needed them to function, to wake up, to sleep, and to fuck.

Worse still, the dreams returned. Visions of Benny burning to death while begging me to save *her* repeatedly burned into the back of my eyes. Even more disturbingly, his ghost started to appear at random moments. I'd sit in the bar, look around, and he'd be standing in the corner, staring at me with black voids for eyes, and the same old words would float through my head.

Help her, Snow. You gotta help her.

My heart would race, and my gut would tighten as my innards felt crushed under a ton of weight. My fingers would tremble, and a vision of blonde hair and golden skin would flash behind my eyes, making me feel wanna puke from the pain of losing her that still gripped me.

I'd even find myself talking to him, begging my friend to explain, to give me a sign. *How can I help her when she's gone, Ben? I've lost her.*

My gut churn would be so acute that it would almost make me bend over double. A surge of emotion would hit me, and I'd hear Hollister's voice.

Shut it down, Snow. Shut it the fuck down.

The relief of shutting it down was immense.

Some weekends, the worry would get too much, so I'd take off to look for Kitten again.

What if Benny was right? What if she needed help? The thought of Kitten being in trouble made me wanna lose my shit, so I'd get on my bike and ride out.

I'd go all the way to Vegas. It was easy; I'd tell Atlas I was meeting some military buds for a weekend of drinking and gambling, but that was a lie. I'd go back to our old haunts, looking for her. She was never there, though. I never even saw anyone who resembled her or her friends.

It was like she's disappeared from the face of the earth.

Some nights, I'd sit in a tacky Vegas hotel room with my gun on my lap and tears in my eyes and let myself feel a fraction of the pain of missing the other half of me. I'd remember what I'd become and know I'd screwed up the only thing that ever meant something.

Even if I found her, what would I say?

Sorry, Kitten. You weren't here, so I fucked around. But it's okay, baby. I only did it to choke some sick bitches out and feed my sick, twisted soul.

A black cloud of shame circled me constantly, and I began to lose faith in everything. Kitten, my family, the MC, and, more importantly, myself. Not that I had much belief to start with.

I found with faith and hope that they were great while you had them, but there wasn't much left to live for once they'd disappeared.

The barrel hit my temple more times than I cared to admit, but I never went boom. *Her* voice always stopped me.

I love you, Snow. Always and forever.

And I'd drop the gun, my eyes flooding with tears.

Then one day, something happened that made me really hit rock bottom. Like I didn't have enough shit to contend with.

"Harder," she croaked as I stroked my cock with my other hand. "Squeeze harder."

Something loosened inside my chest as my fingers dug deeper into her skin, euphoria beginning to chase away the darkness.

When I inflicted pain, there was always a point where I hit a high. It was usually when the woman's eyes bugged out through lack of air or their throats made an involuntary gurgle as they fought for breath. That was the point where my cock would erupt, and the beast would be calmed. Except that night, it felt like I needed more.

Like any addiction, the sweet high became harder to reach and more unobtainable. So, over the months, my and April's rough sex sessions had become more extreme.

She never said anything to anyone, always took it, and never complained. If anything, she was sweet, even supportive about it. She became a fixture, ingratiating herself by becoming the person I relied on to feed my urges. It wasn't that I loved or even liked her. I saw her for who she was. What we did together wasn't clean or decent. It was always about getting what I needed and her giving it to me.

But ultimately, as much as I detested myself for it, April became someone important to me for all the wrong, twisted reasons.

I closed my eyes and let myself zone blissfully out as she whimpered and gargled. The sounds of her choking resonated with me, and my orgasm finally began to build. I stroked my cock harder with my right hand while my left squeezed her neck harder.

The beast roared, and my cock finally spurted thick ropes of cum over my stomach, my hand, and even my chest.

My groan was long and low as my mind soared, liberated by feelings of ecstasy. My mind morphed into a trance-like state, my orgasm lasting for a full minute at least. The release felt so intense that I almost blacked out.

"Fuck, yeah," I murmured, fist finally slowing. I softened my grip, releasing my cock while at the same time letting go of April's neck with my other hand.

That was when I felt her slump over.

At first, I thought she was just falling back on the bed like they all did after I'd finished. The only difference was the silence. Usually, rough pants filled the air where they gasped for breath after I'd cut off their air supply for so long. But there were no gasps, gurgles, or giggles of sweet relief as she sucked air into her lungs.

There was nothing.

My eyes snapped to her, and I froze.

Her eyes were closed, and her face grey. An outline of ghostly blue outlined her collagen-enhanced lips.

Icy fingers crept up my spine as my shocked stare took her in. I looked fixedly in disbelief for a few seconds as the blue tinge around her lips deepened in color.

I reached out and shook her shoulder. "April?"

Nothing except ghostly silence.

I shook her harder. "April. Fuck, April. Wake up." My voice, typically low and raspy, suddenly sounded pitchy with panic. I shook her even harder as my heart slammed painfully against my ribs.

Her eyes remained shut.

My trembling fingers flew to her neck, checking the angle, making sure I hadn't fucking broken it. Everything seemed intact. My hand swept over her windpipe, checking it wasn't crushed, and I cringed at the purple bruises beginning to form across her skin.

Jesus, I'd fucking zoned out and gone too far. Was she dead?

My mind scrambled for a solution, but I couldn't think straight. *Fuck. Fuck. Fuck.*

I moved next to her and felt for a pulse. My heart leaped when I thought I detected a tiny flicker of something, but I couldn't be sure. Encouraged, I tilted her head back, ensured her airways were clear, and began CPR.

Heart banging as if full of cracking thunder, I blew deeply into her mouth, watching as her chest rose, filling with air. Quickly, I moved and started compressions.

Silence.

"Come on," I muttered, returning to her mouth and giving her more of my breath. More compressions as I prayed to any god listening to please, please, please, just for once, give me a fucking break.

Nothing.

For a third time, I blew into her lungs. My heart leaped with relief as she twitched violently and gave a short, raspy cough.

Every part of my body slumped with relief as I fell back, ass to bed.

Her eyes flickered open; one was red with burst vessels, probably where I'd fucking asphyxiated her minutes before. My hands clenched into fists as heat curled inside my stomach. I didn't know whether to laugh with relief or cry over the goddamned fucking shitshow that my life had become.

Jesus fuckin Christ. Talk about a wake-up call.

"Breaker," April rasped, voice scratchy where I'd put so much fucking pressure on her voice box. "What happened?" Her hands slid up her throat, eyes widening as everything rushed back. "Oh my God," she whispered as she tried to sit up. "You almost killed me. Oh my God."

"I'm sorry," I croaked. "I dunno what happened. It was the heat of the moment."

She slumped back on the bed, her body no doubt rebelling against that small fact that seconds ago, it was dead. Her head lolled uncontrollably again, making my gut tighten.

I moved, took her hand, and hauled her gently into my arms, positioning her like a baby. It was the first time

I'd touched her outside sex, and it burned my skin. "Fuck. I'm so sorry, April." I rocked her gently. "I don't know what happened. I went into some kind of trance and forgot myself. I'm so fucking sorry, sweetheart."

She snuggled into me, looking up at my face.

She was a mess. Beads of sweat covered her brow. Her ashen grey face was enhanced by the bright red of her angry-looking, bloody eye. "I'll be fine once you get me to the hospital and they check me over," she rasped. "It's okay. I'll explain our sex games. They'll know you didn't mean it. When the police arrest you, you'll probably be okay." She stretched her neck, allowing me to see the bruises forming on her skin. "Maybe I should take the photos now so the cops get the full effect when I report what you did to me."

I stilled as a lump formed in my throat. "Cops? What the cops gotta do with it?"

April stared up at me wide-eyed. "Well," she whispered. "It's assault. Maybe even attempted manslaughter."

I shook my head disbelievingly. "No. It wasn't like that. You know it wasn't. It was just a game that went wrong."

Her hand came to mine. "We both know it's more than that, Breaker. There's something wrong about you, something disgusting and broken. It's been getting worse. What just happened proved you're out of control. Lately, whenever we make love, you always take it too far. In fact, I've been so scared of you hurting me that I took pictures of all the marks and bruises you left. I also got a couple of the other girls to corroborate that they always appear after I've been with you. I've told them how frightened I am that the beatings will get so bad one day you'll kill me. Looks like I wasn't a million miles away."

Blood rushed through my ears, my stomach hardening as I took in the smirk plastered across her face, the triumphant gleam in her eye, and the cocky tilt of her eyebrow.

Suddenly I got it. It all made perfect sense.

The bitch had hustled me.

Flashes of memories played through my mind. She seemed to know what I craved. I realized how she worked her way in over months, giving me small insights into what lay underneath. Little looks and touches. Gleaming eyes that held the promise that I could take anything I needed.

I scraped a hand down my face, smiling wryly to myself as I recalled the lowering of her lashes, her subservience, and how she'd lulled me into a false sense of security over time.

She'd played the long game, and I was fucked.

Slowly closing my eyes, I shook my head at my stupidity and heaved a breath. "What do you want, April?"

Her mouth tipped up on one side. "I want—no, I deserve to be part of the club. I'm sick of being everyone's cum bucket. I want an old man, and it has to be you, especially in light of our happy news."

Uneasiness stirred in the pit of my gut. My lip curled as I snarled, "What?"

She smiled brightly. "I'm pregnant, Kit. And it's yours."

Heat began to build inside until acid burned my throat. "Bullshit."

She shrugged. "Remember a couple of months ago when the condom split?"

Huh?

I cast my mind back, going over everything that had happened in the last few months. A memory pinged. It was so faint it could've been a dream. Jesus, I'd been so fucking wasted. I'd gotten back from Vegas hours before and drank enough tequila to put an elephant on its ass.

Add on the shit I'd put up my nose, and there was no wonder I'd blocked it out.

"Wait. You told me you were covered," I accused, voice rising to a bellow. "You said there was no chance of pregnancy, seeing as you were taking birth control pills. You told me there was no fucking chance in hell."

The cocky smile spread across her face, and she murmured, "Oops."

I clenched and unclenched my hands, trying to tamp down the new desire to punch her fucking bitch face. "You cunt," I snarled.

The bitch laughed. "Maybe I am a cunt. But I'm a cunt claimed by the great Kit Stone. One of the heirs to the empire. The last brother standing who all the girls want to lock down."

My face twisted as I lowered it to hers, snapping, "I'll make your life a living hell."

"Funny that," she retorted in a low tone. "I was thinking much the same thing." She rolled away from me, clambering stiffly off the bed and moving toward the door. "I'm gonna go get my stuff and move it in here. I need to record these injuries for insurance, and then I need my ol' man to take care of me, seeing as my neck's fucked up. May as well make myself comfortable in here. I should stay out of sight for a few days while the bruising heals." She gave me a finger wave. "I won't be long, *ol' man* of mine."

My eyes stayed on the door long after she closed it softly behind her, throat burning with five years- worth of pent-up tears.

I was well and truly fucked. April had played me like a goddamned fiddle, and I'd been too high and too screwed up to even notice. She'd well and truly trapped me with a baby, of all things. Poor little bastard would come into the world with a drug-addicted, twisted son of a bitch for a father and a conniving cunt for a mother.

Snow

A sudden rush of emotions flooded my bloodstream as old, forgotten feelings began to batter me from deep inside. My hands shook violently as a memory came to mind, fragments of a conversation. My heart squeezed as an image of Kitten sponging my body in a warm bathtub, caring for me the way she always did–with everything good in her heart. Cornflower blues gazed at me, full of love and concern, as the memory of a whispered promise hit me like a Mack truck.

One day, I'm gonna give you a family. A posse of men and women who'll have your back, and they'll be military, blood, and chosen family. One day, I'll plant my babies in there, put a ring on it, and give you a traditional family, too.

I closed my eyes and allowed myself to be transported back to a time, allowing myself to feel the love and connection once more before I shut it down again, forever.

It seemed like a dream. Maybe it was. I couldn't be sure. But if it was a dream, it was the most beautiful one I'd ever had. If I could've relived that every night instead of my best friend burning to death, I might have been a better man for her. Maybe I could've been stronger and not given up on us like the worthless piece of shit that I was.

Maybe I could've been enough.

My black, broken soul panged when I thought about our years apart and everything that had happened. It was crazy, after so long, how I still loved her like it was only yesterday when we watched the sun rise over Vegas, and I had her in my arms. In my heart, she was mine, and she always would be. I still burned for my Kitten. She was my fire. My always and forever.

Nine long years had passed since we met, and I still remembered everything about her. The way she looked, her scent. How she moved as she danced for me in a smoky nightclub. The way she smiled and laughed.

How she made me feel so alive.

Without her, I was just a vessel. A bag of bones and blood. My humanity went up in flames alongside Benny on a road outside Kabul. But the instant I wrapped my hands around my Kitten's throat and betrayed her in the worst way I could, my soul burned.

Maybe having my one, but not being with her, was my punishment for all the evil things I'd done. April was my penance, everything I deserved, and there was only one way I could cope.

My heart twisted as I reached into my jeans pocket, still slung low on my hips, and dug out my cell phone. I clicked on my recent call list and waited a few seconds for my dealer to answer. Everything may have gone to hell in a handbasket, but there was always one thing I could use to numb the residue pain that I'd never been able to fully inter.

I'd give myself a year and see where I was. In the meantime, if the drugs didn't kill me first, I could always go boom.

Honestly, it would've been a relief.

Chapter Thirty

Breaker ~ Four Weeks Later

I groaned painfully as freezing-cold liquid splashed across my face and head. Jerking awake, I sat up in bed, looking around through sleep-filled eyes. "What the goddamn?" I yelled. "I'll fucking kill you, bitch."

"Now, now, now," Mom's pissed-off voice snapped. "That's no way to speak to your loving mother. And believe me when I say this, Kit. I'll kick your ass from one end of the clubhouse to the other if you dare talk back to me like that again."

My eyes jerked up to see my mom holding a water jug over my bed. "What are you doin', Ma?" I yelled. "Jesus, woman. You're fucking crazy."

I yelped as a sharp sting went through the back of my skull, the clapping sound of a hard slap cutting through the air.

I glowered at my mom. "What the fuck are you hitting me for? Jesus. I just woke up. How the hell have I made you pissed already?"

Another sting made me groan as Ma slapped me again. My head already banged painfully. The woman was a bigger sadist than me.

"Ya goddamned idiot. You're up shit creek without a paddle. Your dad's forehead's been popping veins like whack-a-mole lives in his brain. Abe and Iris are worried sick. You've upset your brother and Cara. Bowie's given up on you. Freya thinks you're suffering from a fucking aneurysm. Atlas has been down the Cell all night, getting nowhere fast. And all for that two-faced, traitorous bitch." She slammed the jug onto my nightstand and punched her hands to her hips. "You're not leaving this room until you explain yourself, Kit Stone. Enough is enough."

Bringing my knees up under the comforter, I rested my elbows on them and held my head in my hands. "Jesus, Ma. Stop nagging. I can't fucking take any more. She's pregnant. I'm stuck with her, and that's it."

The bed mattress moved as Mom sat on the bed, took my hands in hers, and murmured, "Look at me, my beautiful boy."

My eyes slowly lifted to hers.

"Do you even know it's yours?" she asked simply. "I'm sorry, but every instinct tells me something's way off with the whole ridiculous affair."

I continued to stare at Mom as my thoughts scrambled.

Nobody knew the shit April held over me. I'd told everyone I was with her because of the baby. Their confusion and disbelief were evident. They weren't far off with their suspicions that something wasn't right, but how could I explain what happened? I wasn't sure the baby was mine. I knew the condom split, though, so there was a good chance. Also, it still deserved a chance, even if it wasn't mine. Once she'd had it, I could at least ensure it was cared for, even with her as its mom.

My biggest regret was the children I'd killed while I worked for the task force. It burned like lava in my veins. Maybe I could keep this one safe. Perhaps that would bring my fucked up soul a slight sense of peace.

"Ma," I muttered. "You have to let it go. I'm stuck with her, and that's the end of it."

Snow

Her face took on a confused look. "Well, the only person with her now is Atlas, and I highly doubt she'll be having a good time with him."

My eyebrows snapped together as I looked around the room, her words not sinking in. "What the fuck am I doin' here anyway? The last thing I remember, I was at my apartment." I scraped a hand down my face. "What the fuck's goin' on?"

Mom's eyebrow raised. "You don't remember?"

I wracked my brain, trying to figure out what I'd done. As soon as Dad shut the auto shop down for the holidays, I'd holed up with a stash of drugs, beer, and tequila. "I don't even know what fuckin' day it is, Ma."

"It's the day after Christmas, Kit," Mom whispered. "Don't you remember anything about last night?"

"Jesus." I rubbed the ache in my temples, wincing. "I've lost the last four days."

She looked to the heavens, murmuring what a little shit I was under her breath. "Jesus, Kit. You're thirty years old. When are you gonna grow up? It's that bitch isn't it?" She sniffed. "Bet she's been drugging you to keep you putty in her hands so you didn't work out her twisted game."

My gut dropped at the thought of April opening her trap. What the hell did Mom mean by games? "Huh?"

Mom looked me dead in the eye. "It came out last night. Seraphina saw her at the Sinner's compound. Turns out she's Bear's ol' lady. We think he sent her here to stir shit up and spy."

I held up a hand to silence Mom as my brain whirred to keep up. "Wait. Who's Seraphina? And she's Bear's ol' lady?"

"Kit," Mom said quietly. "April. *She's* Bear's ol' lady. She's a traitor to the Demons, has been for years."

All time seemed to stop. Mom kept speaking. I could see her lips moving, but the blood started rushing so fast in my ears that I couldn't hear a word.

April was a fucking spy? A traitor?

Jesus.

Heat flickered through my body, rising up and surging to the surface. The room distorted, spinning slowly as the edges of my vision darkened. I held a trembling hand up in front of my face. "Fuck," I muttered. "Jesus, Christ."

"Kit?" Mum asked urgently. "Baby, what's wrong?" Her voice sounded a hundred miles away.

I laughed as my heart slammed against my ribs so hard that I wanted to cry out in pain. Fuck, maybe this was it. Was I dying? My lungs seemed to harden to steel, and I struggled to catch my breath.

"Kit!" Mom said urgently. "Baby!"

I laughed again. The Reaper was playing with me, making me suffer before he spirited me away. I laughed again, gasping for air as I heard Mom speak in hushed tones.

"Iris. Kit's room, now. Don't tell anyone. I think he's having a panic attack. Bring water and something to help him breathe. Hurry, Iris."

I looked at my mom's stricken face. "I—It's okay, Ma," I rasped through short puffs of air. "I don't care." Relief flooded me as I closed my eyes and tried to succumb to the darkness clouding my vision. Before I knew it, I was being gently rocked.

"It's okay, my boy. You'll be okay," Mom murmured.

Suddenly, it was easier to breathe. My gut panged because I didn't wanna take air anymore. I just wanted it all to stop. I was so tired of being broken and incomplete. The world wasn't good for me; I was a stain on the Earth.

Still being rocked gently, I heard my door open and close gently.

"How's he doing?" Iris asked in hushed tones.

"Kit. Have some water," Mom demanded softly. "You'll feel better."

Snow

I lifted my head from my mom's shoulder and took the glass from Iris. "Thanks," I muttered, taking a swig. It was cool and refreshing on my hot, cracked throat. After a couple more sips, the room stopped spinning, and everything came back into focus.

After a few minutes of getting my head together, I glanced between Mom and Iris's pale, worried faces. "I'm okay now, Ma. You shocked the fuck out of me, is all. Tell me what happened."

"Mum positioned me against the headboard and snuggled into my side. "Last night, you turned up here with April. You were so drunk that you couldn't even stand up. A few weeks ago, Cash and Atlas rescued a couple of kids from the Sinners. Your dad thinks they were about to sell the girl, Seraphina. She and the boy, Mason, have been down in the Cell, out of sight for their own safety."

I laid my head back and closed my eyes, trying to understand. "So what's that got to do with April?"

Iris took my hand. "When you walked in with her last night, Sera recognized her immediately. She told us April was Bear's ol' lady, and she'd seen them together at the Sinner's clubhouse."

Iris snorted. "As you imagine, Son. Shit's hit the fan. Atlas and Dagger had her locked down in the Cell within minutes. They've questioned her all night. She won't talk. Just keeps asking for you."

"That's why I woke you up the way I did," Mom explained. "Dad wants you down there, stat, to see what you can get out of her. I didn't know you were sick, though, Son. You don't have to go anywhere if you don't want to. I'll clear it with Dagger."

I dropped my head back against the wall, trying to think straight.

If April was down the cell for being a traitor to the club, I couldn't save her. Her crime carried the death penalty. The only reason she was still here was because

353

she was pregnant. If I knew Dad, they'd keep her alive, but only until she'd had the kid.

I could feel what little control I had over the situation slipping.

It would all come out about what I was and the things I did. Maybe I should just come clean to Dad, go pack, and get the fuck out. I could always hole up somewhere and take care of business. The fact was, I knew I wasn't gonna last much longer. Living was getting to be unbearable.

Help her, Snow. You gotta help her.
Help her.

My head shot up to see Benny's ghostly figure standing in the corner of the room.

Help who, Ben? I thought, staring at him. *Give me something. Do you mean April?*

His black void eyes stared in my direction, but he didn't say or do anything. Jesus. What did he want from me?

A plan started to form. Maybe I could talk to April and see if she'd turn rat. It would help her case with the club. If she gave me something, I could help her strike a deal. She couldn't stay, but maybe she'd leave the kid with us and disappear forever.

"Ma. I'm going down the Cell. Maybe she'll talk to me. It'll help the Demons if we know exactly what she's been doing and why. Dad's probably tweakin', and Atlas will be ready to stomp on her. Plus, I need to know the truth about the baby and what's gonna happen next."

Mom's lips pursed. "Just know you've got options. If the baby's yours, I'll move back, help raise it."

Iris let out a huff. "Like you'd need to, Del. Me and Abe would take the babe. Kit could still be its dad, but we'd take it in until Kit could. There's a lot of us who'd help. He wouldn't be alone."

My cold heart jerked, and my lips twitched into a smile. "You'd do that?"

"Of course." Iris laughed. "You're the closest thing I've got to a son."

A flash of warmth spread through my gut.

It was crazy how an MC-born-and-bred military Stone man had always felt closer to the women in his life than the men. Growing up, I spent most of my time with Mom and Iris in the kitchen. I was definitely a momma's and Iris's boy. Mom always said I was more sensitive than my brothers and Dad. I fought against it because Grandpa Bandit said it was sissy, but still, the women made me feel more at home, accepted even, where the men never did.

Maybe Mom and Iris saw the same thing in me as Kitten did back when I was clean.

I swung my legs over the bed, reached for my jeans, and pulled them on. "Gimme five minutes. Need to brush my teeth." I glowered over at Mom. "Already had a wash, eh, Ma?"

Mom and Iris chuckled as they headed for the door. "I'll let Dagger know, Kit," Mom called back. "I'm glad you're feeling better."

I went to my drawers for a clean tee. "Tell Dad I'll be there in five. I'll find out what she's been up to if it kills me."

"Kit," Dad barked through the cell. "Get April out here. Her ol' man's here for her."

"But Pop," I began, "she's fuckin' pregnan—"

"Kit. Do it. Now!" he barked before hanging up.

My eyes lifted to stare at April. "I'm sorry. Bear's here. You're outta time."

Her face dropped as her body began to shake. "You can't just hand me over, Breaker. Please," she implored. "If he's got no use for me, he'll kill me."

I tried to summon up the will to care but came up empty. "Is the baby mine? Tell me the truth. I may be able to appeal to Dad if it is."

"Yeah," she whispered, lowering her eyes.

Lie, my inner voice breathed.

My eyes flicked to the corner where Benny stood, arms outstretched. *Help her, Snow. You gotta help her.*

My hand lifted to grab my hair. "Jesus, fuck! I'll sort it, but we have to go." I took my knife and cut through her restraints before hauling her up from the chair. "I don't gotta choice. We'll go out and speak to Prez."

"Please don't," she begged as I dragged her across the room of the Cell. "Prez doesn't care."

I rounded on her, getting in her face as the beast roared to life. "What the fuck do you expect, April," I bellowed. "You betrayed the goddamned club! You fucked with all of us."

"I'm sorry," she wailed. "I didn't have a choice. Bear would've killed me if I didn't."

I threw the door open, dragging her into the hall. "Everyone has a choice. You could've left. You could've gone to Dad. He would've helped you disappear." I cuffed her elbow, pulling her up the stairs. "It's not even a one-off. You've been fucking us over for years. Jesus, woman. Are you even pregnant?"

"Yes," she screamed. "I am. I am."

The bar was full of club members and women looking out the windows at the stand-off. Bear had stormed the gates to our compound and somehow gotten hold of Cara. I'd been in the Cell, questioning April with Atlas, when it shit hit the fan.

I caught Mom's eye, and she shook her head worriedly. Iris held a crying Freya while Sunny wailed in Layla's arms. Men stood at the windows yelling at the women to get into the kitchen in case more shots were fired.

The place was fucking bedlam.

Snow

April started to wail as I threw the main doors open and dragged her outside to the parking lot. "I'll talk to him," I snapped. "Don't say a fuckin' word."

I pulled her toward Pop, my face a snarl. "She's not going with him," I bellowed over to him. "How could you do this, Pop? You know she's carryin' my kid. I'll shoot every one'a ya if you think you're gonna let him take my kin."

Ice filled my veins as the sound of laughter filled the air. My eyes lifted to see Bear holding a gun to Cara's head.

My gut churned painfully, my heart panging at the devastation on her face.

"How fuckin' gullible are you?" Bear shouted. "Is that what she told you? That the kid's yours?" The fucker winked at April. "Nice job, doll. I'll reward you well for that one."

Bile rose through my throat as Benny appeared next to me.

Snow, you gotta help her.

My throat tightened as Bear's words registered. I looked between him and April disbelievingly. *Bear's fucking kid?* She tried to pass *Bear's* kid off as mine? Just minutes ago, I begged her to tell me the truth. I promised I'd try to help her. Now it was completely fucked. What kind of woman did that? What kind of woman would lie about that shit? I should've fucking known. I *did* know. Didn't make it any easier to believe, though.

I mean—Bear?

"You're lying," I accused the asshole holding Cara before turning to April. "He's lying. Isn't he?"

The bitch wrung her hands. "Kit. I had no choice."

My voice rose to a bellow. Anger, hurt, and shock erupted from my body. "Why the fuck did I ever believe you?" I yelled in her face. "I must be fuckin' touched in the head."

April's eyes widened as she took a step back from me. "Believe me? What do you mean, believe me? Tell me, Kit. How long would it have taken you to get a paternity test and then kick me out?"

Was she fucking crazy? She'd sat in the Cell and swore the baby was mine, and she'd been lying all along. Why would anyone trust anything she said?

"Are you shittin' me?" I shouted. "Jesus. Have you heard yourself? Do you believe your own lies? You're fuckin' crazy!"

She sniffed her tears back, looking down at the ground.

I shook my head at her. All emotion drained of me until there was nothing left. Deep down, I knew she was lying, that I was just a mark, but I saw the kid as a chance to do something right. She'd even taken that away from me. But, bright side, at least I was free of the cunt.

I grabbed her arm and dragged her bitch ass toward the gate. "Take her," I spat. "Pushing her toward Cash, lip curling with disgust. "She deserves him."

Turning on my heel, I stalked toward the clubhouse, checking that my gun was secure inside my cut. I planned to wait at the doors. If there was another shootout, I'd aim straight for Bear's head, then April's. The kid would be better off dead than having those two sick fucks as parents.

Help her, Snow, Benny said from beside me. *Help her.*

I stared into my friend's black void eyes and realized I no longer cared about anything. My last tiny thread of hope had died. Ben could haunt me all he wanted. I couldn't help him. Couldn't even help myself. The sooner he fucked off and left me alone to my self-destruction, the better. He could drive me insane for all I cared. The fact I was even seeing my dead friend proved I was halfway there anyway.

I took a heaving breath, filling my lungs to take away their tightness as I watched Cara stumble back through the gates, Cash with her, before mumbling the only thing I had left to say.

"Fuck off, Ben. *Just fuck off and leave me alone.*"

Six Months Later

Out of all the Speed Demon brothers, I couldn't believe it was Atlas's wedding day. We'd all landed in Vegas to see him and Sophie—his woman— get hitched.

The asshole had met his 'one.' She was the perfect blend of sweet and tough, hard and soft, hot and cool. She was also a fucking doctor who was smart, too smart sometimes.

And he loved her to distraction.

I came out a few days before the others. I'd been trying to get out here every couple of months, still looking for my Kitten.

Being without her still hurt as much as the day I left her, but my brain wasn't addled with drugs and booze anymore, so at least I'd broken away from the self-destructive loop I'd been caught up in.

A lot had changed since Bear took April.

Without her hanging shit over my head, I'd become more involved with the club. Atlas pulled me into his little SAA circle, and admittedly, I felt useful again. It hadn't given me a new lease of life exactly, but it had given me something. It gave me enough to do to keep me ticking over. I'd even gotten some murder and mayhem under my belt over the last few months, so I'd kept the monster at bay. I spent a lot of time in the ring and the woods, though it was preferable to self-medicating.

Another significant change was that I hadn't fucked a woman since the night I'd almost killed April.

The whole sorry experience taught me a big lesson.

I'd never have a woman again unless it was *my* woman. I sickened myself with what I'd done. Looking back, I realized just how fucked up it all was. I recognized it as a form of self-harm in a way. A way to punish myself and push Kitten even further away.

It hadn't worked, though. After nine years of loving the same woman, I knew my heart would always belong to her. The only difference now was I'd accepted it. It felt good in a way. There was no pressure, no façade, no acts or masks, no hiding, no judgment.

It was just me.

Another change was my time spent at the VA in Grand Junction. I went there for three days every month for treatment. I hadn't worked my way up to telling my counselor everything. I mostly talked about my time at Eggers. He'd pinpointed the event when they thought my PTSD had been triggered. Back when I found a little girl's severed body in the aftermath of a VBIED.

I tried to talk to him about Benny, but each time I attempted to bring him up, my emotions surged, and I wasn't ready to feel that pain. I still heard Hollister ordering me to shut it down, and I was grateful for it in a weird way.

The heartache from being without the other half of me was torture enough.

One day, I'd be ready, but not that day.

That day was for Atlas and Sophie. For them, I'd keep my shit together.

All morning, my stomach had done backflips. My churn was back, but not in a painful way; that morning, it felt different. I should've known it was a sign. My instincts had never let me down before.

It happened in the car on the way to the wedding.

I didn't feel the sign. I saw it.

Snow

Literally.

A fucking billboard.

It was surreal. The car slid down the I-15 at the back of the strip, taking us from the diner we'd just had breakfast to the 'Little Chapel of Love.'

I sat up, back slowly straightening.

Something made me look, take notice, a feeling. My breath caught inside my throat when the image of a woman suspended in mid-air appeared directly above.

A massive billboard was ahead, twenty feet high in the air.

Clarke and Carmichael Law.

Women—Know your rights.

On the billboard was the most beautiful girl I'd ever seen. Her blonde hair curled down to her waist. Cornflower-blue eyes stared out at me. Her sexy little smirk hit me in the chest.

As Axl screamed, 'Welcome to the jungle,' from the in-car stereo system, taking me back to almost ten years before.

My body jerked as something punched me in the chest.

Heart hammering and pulse thrumming, I leaned forward, resting my arms on my knees, hands dangling down, eyes glued to the woman I hadn't stopped loving for the last ten years.

I couldn't look away.

She was incredible. Long blonde hair flowed down to her tiny waist. The swell of her hips, long, shapely legs. Her perfect tits were encased in a designer suit, silk shirt molded across her perfect tits.

Palms suddenly clammy, I rubbed them absentmindedly against my jeans. I thought about glancing at my boys, just to see if they were as mesmerized as I was, but for the life of me, I couldn't look away from that goddamned billboard. I rubbed at the goosebumps trailing down my arms, still unable to wrench my stare from the sex kitten. With trembling fingers, I pulled my cell from my pocket and, just in time, snapped a picture and quickly sent it to Colt.

Within seconds, my cell phone beeped with a message.

Colt: *Jesus, fuck! She's fucking gorgeous.*

My gut twisted.

An urge to pull his eyes out of their sockets hit me. I wanted to stop him from looking at her. My fingers twitched with the compulsion to message him back and cuss him the fuck out.

She was mine.

Emotion hit my throat, and for the first time in years, I allowed myself to feel the love residing in my heart. Tears hit the back of my eyes. It was so fucking joyous that I had to let out a laugh.

I've found her. I've found my fire.

Atlas's eyes shot to mine, and he quirked an eyebrow. "Are you fuckin' high, Breaker? This is my goddamned weddin' day. I told you when I asked you to stand up with me, nothin's gonna fuck this up. Any shenanigans, and I'll flip my lid. Do you fuckin' feel me, brother?"

Holding my cell up with shaking fingers, I stared at her picture again. A huge grin spread across my face. She hadn't changed a bit. She was still my dream woman, my heart, the other half of my soul.

Every piece of skin tingled. My mind whirred.

She's flipped a switch and brought me back to life.

My always and forever.

Epilogue

Breaker

"They're here," Cash said, grin wide and cocky as he sat on the chairs behind us.

His words fell on deaf ears. My mind was still on the billboard I'd seen on the way here.

Had she been in Vegas all along? It seemed that way. I assumed she was a partner in the law firm she advertised. Either that or they used her for her beauty to sell their services.

My jaw clenched; the thought of people taking advantage of my girl suddenly made my back stiffen. That shit would stop immediately.

I looked toward the heavens, trying to keep my tremoring fingers and tweaking under control. I couldn't believe I wasn't out there getting my girl. Atlas would have a conniption if I walked out. Everyone already thought I was a fuck-up. Letting my brother down today, of all days, would just take the cake. I'd get this done, then I'd get gone.

My knees shook with excitement. The cell in my pocket had been buzzing like it was alive for the last ten minutes. Colt had no doubt tracked her down already, but every time I reached to check, Atlas gave me a fuckin' death glare.

A song began to play.

Tender is the night...

My eyes rolled so far back in my head they hurt. That fucking bullshit English band Atlas and Sophie were into drove me insane. Raleigh Ritchie was where it was at. I smiled. Hadn't listened to him for years. It made me feel too much. Maybe now I'd found Kitten, I could–.

My thoughts were interrupted by the banging of the door behind us.

I glanced at Atlas, who remained looking ahead, chest puffed out, a massive smile across his ugly ass face.

My eyes shot behind, resting on Sophie. "She looks amazin', brother. Wait until you see her. She's sexy as fu...." My voice trailed off because right then, something happened, something beautiful and magical. Something I'd forgotten in the mists of time.

Warmth tugged inside my gut.

My mind went blank for a few seconds before a fire flickered to life inside me as stunning cornflower blues met mine.

My heart swelled so big that it started slamming against my ribs because standing next to Sophie, staring at me like she'd seen a ghost, was the most beautiful girl in the world.

My girl.

Her soft, silky blonde hair looked the same, wild and tousled down to her waist. Her face was still beautiful but slightly more angled than before. Weirdly, I could see she'd aged barely but somehow still didn't look any different.

My eyes swept down her body, taking in her fire-engine-red silky dress, not unlike the dark pink one she'd worn for me almost ten years before.

Immediately my cock thickened. *Jesus.* My eyes widened. It was the first time that had happened in ten years without needing evil fantasies to flicker through my mind.

Snow

It felt good, clean, and normal.

My stare slid back to Kitten's. My heart sank when I noticed her blue orbs glistening with tears. But the word she spoke next made it shatter into pieces.

"Kyle?"

Fuck!

I felt all color drain from my face as she stared at me in shock. My mind spasmed as the same chant went through it. Kyle was dead. He died years before. Kyle was dead.

Fuck. Fuck. Fuck.

I closed my eyes as the room began to spin. Jesus. I was about to pass the fuck out. She never knew my name. What if she'd been looking for me all this time but never knew my name? What if she tracked Kyle down? What if she...?

My stomach gave a jolt and began to churn. I had to press a hand to it to stop myself from puking. What if she thought—.

Fuuuuuuuuck!

Dad must've moved toward them because suddenly, he appeared on the edges of my vision. "Jesus Christ," he rasped, glancing at me. "He looks exactly like you when you were a kid. What the fuck's goin' on?"

My gaze moved right until I was met with golden eyes.

My heart jerked because they were *my* golden eyes. Stare traveling lower, I took in his sneer, identical to mine. The way his arms folded across his chest, just like Dad did.

I couldn't take my eyes off him.

He was so fucking beautiful.

And so fucking mine.

Something flickered from deep inside me, a light, a warmth I'd forgotten. The soul I thought had burned to nothing stirred back to life, and it ached.

That was when all hell broke loose.

"You're dead," Kitten whispered, eyes still glued to mine. "I looked for you. I gave them your name; they told me you were dead."

My throat thickened with emotions I hadn't felt for years. They burned my insides to dust as the consequences of my actions ten years ago hit me like a freight train.

God forgive me. What the fuck have I done?

"Whoa. Whoa. Whoa." Abe's wide eyes darted between Kit and the blonde. "Who the fuck's Kyle?"

Sophie's mouth dropped open, and her eyes gleamed as realization dawned. Her shocked gaze slashed straight toward me. "Shit. Breaker's Kyle?"

A thread of panic seized my chest, reaching into my throat and strangling me. I had to make my girl understand. I had to explain.

I moved toward her, arms outstretched, the need to touch her overwhelming. "I didn't die, Kenny—Kitten—I can explain. There was a fuck-up. I'm not Kyle Simmons."

Atlas turned to me, lip curled, eyes promising death. "Well. You've fucked up this time and at my wedding, too. I'm gonna kill you, motherfucker."

Bowie hovered in the background, his eyes darting between me, Kitten, and the boy. "Oh shit."

My heart curled in on itself as I saw pure, raw pain slash across my Kitten's face.

"What kind of mix-up are you speaking of, *Kyle?*" she snipped. "There wasn't a mix-up when you told me your name was Kyle Simmons. There wasn't a mix-up when we met years ago, back when you were on leave from the army. There wasn't a mix-up when you kept returning to Vegas to see me. There wasn't a mix-up when you left the last time, and also left me knocked up." Her voice turned steely. "And there certainly wasn't a mix-up when I pulled strings and tried to find you through Military records. Your commanding officer told me you died in an explosion just after the twins were born. So tell me, *Kyle,* exactly what kind of mix-up are you speaking of?"

The boy next to her shifted. "Asshole," he muttered, glowering at me. His arm reached out, and he tugged someone protectively against him, trying to shield her.

I caught a flash of silky blonde hair, and the most beautiful creature I'd ever seen appeared in my vision.

A small girl with white-blonde hair, rosebud pink lips, and huge cornflower blues gazed at me like she could see inside my soul. "Mom?" she cried.

The room spun again. My heartbeats stuttered as my soul reached out again, blistering everything in its wake.

Mine. Mine. Mine. It whispered as the heavens seemed to open from above, shining a light down upon them. My Kitten, my boy, and my girl.

Pure fucking goodness.

Dad's shoulders stiffened. Slowly, he turned to me, and I could see the fury rising through his barrel chest. "You fuckin' idiot!" he bellowed.

My heart did a backflip. *I know, Dad.*

"Jesus, Bro," Bowie murmured, his disappointment palpable.

His words struck home alongside his disappointment. Its darkness mingled with the utter shame that made my organs clench.

Kitten's eyes swept away from mine, and I shivered with the coldness they had left behind.

She turned to Dad. "Hey," she greeted him with a wry smile. "My name's Kennedy Carmichael. These are my kids, Kai and Kadence."

Kennedy. Kai. Kadence.
Perfect.

"I'm gettin' that, darlin'," Pop muttered, his voice getting louder as he glanced at me, eyes spitting hatred as he bellowed, "Seems we have a mutual acquaintance.

And it just so happens to be my complete fuck-up of a son!"

My gut roiled as I looked at my kids. I thought back, mind frantically working out what was going on. Two? How...? My lungs burned when I realized they must've been twins.

Jesus Christ. I've got twins.

My attention was caught up by my Kitten again as I watched her pop a sexy as fuck hip. "I can't believe this shit. I've come to my best friend's wedding only to discover that one of the groomsmen is my dead fucking baby daddy. And hallelujah. Praise the lord," she threw her arms up, "he's gone and risen from the dead."

There she is, my inner voice whispered. *There's her edge. That's my girl, giving me sass.*

The sharpness in her voice made my face fall into a wince. "I'm not dead, Kenny—Kitten," I corrected.

She sashayed her beautiful ass over to me, got in my face, and shrieked, "Well, duh!"

The smell of peaches assaulted my senses. My eyes closed as a memory from long ago floated through my mind.

"You watch The Walking Dead?"

She cocked her head to one side, looking at me like I belonged in the asylum. "Well, duh."

I made a grab for her, laughing. "Who the fuck are you 'well duh'ing'?"

With a giggle, she scurried across the bed out of my reach before I grabbed her around the waist and hauled her back into my lap, arms holding her close.

I smiled at the sweet memory. *My fire. Always and forever.*

"Kit?" Dad grated out.

My eyes snapped open to see Dad glowering at me like his head was about to explode. "You're on my shit list, boy."

Snow

My eyes were drawn like magnets to my little girl. She was so fucking beautiful, I couldn't take my eyes off her. That was when it hit me in the chest.

Everything I'd missed.

Nausea rolled through me, and my skin turned clammy.

My stare went to my son, Kai. He glared at me with a face so familiar it was like looking in a mirror. "Asshole," he snapped straight at me.

I closed my eyes again.

Fuck.

Everybody started to talk, chuckle, and whisper. I heard Cash the asshole laugh and Atlas muttering to Sophie, "Why the fuck does shit have to hit the fan on our weddin' day, baby?"

She heaved out a long sigh, lips pouting as one shoulder lifted.

Atlas pointed to the door. "Everybody out," he ordered. "Sort your 'Days of Our Biker Lives,' Maury Povich goddamned 'he *is* the father' shit out somewhere else. Me and my woman are gettin' hitched, and shock fuckin' horror, *your* fucked-up shit is screwin' with *my* fucked-up shit. How would you like it if I did a 'who's the daddy' routine at one'a your weddings, huh?" He looked up, spitting out a curse.

Through it all, my gaze fell back upon Kitten.

Our eyes locked, and for a split second, I heard it, her soul calling to mine. Her eyes conveyed all the love and goodness in her heart. She was still there. My fire.

Dad shook his head, muttering obscenities under his breath. His angry stare fell upon my little girl, then toward my mini-biker boy.

Then something crazy and wonderful happened. I watched, open-mouthed, as realization slid across Dad's features. He was a Grandpa again, and there were three more additions to the Stone family. A huge grin spread across his face, and he proudly puffed out his chest.

"Kids. I'm your grandpop, John. Welcome to the fuckin' family."

I glared at him, hands clenching to fists.

Fucker needed to watch his goddamned language. My baby girl didn't need to hear that shit. I didn't want him corrupting her innocent sweetness.

Atlas almost choked as he stifled a laugh, clapping my shoulder so hard that he made me wince. Then he said something that made my blood run cold.

"Yo, motherfucker." He nodded toward my mini-me son, who still glared at my face with his arms folded across his chest. "I think you've got some explainin' to do."

THE END

**Breaker, Kennedy, and the twin's story will continue in Breaker: Speed Demons MC Book Four.
This time I promise ;)**

Snow's Playlist is Available on Spotify

https://open.spotify.com/playlist/3KQ49S91ECxBiqiZnMaJ3z

Author's Note

Good Lord, this book was a joy to write and the hardest thing I've ever done.

As I started researching Breaker's original book, I began to worry. I knew there was more to Kit and Kennedy's love story than everyone thought—that he met and slept with her, then ghosted her.

I always knew Kit was more profound, and his 'one' was a life-changing love who he lost. How else could he be so damaged? There were reasons for his actions. I knew he'd been in the military. I also knew he suffered from PTSD. I knew it wrecked everything around him, including his relationship. What I didn't realize until I started to write was to what extent.

I would like to thank Katie, herself ex-military, who held my hand so beautifully as she helped me navigate the waters of Kit, his unit, and Camp Eggers. Every song mentioned at Eggers was listened to by Katie and her fellow military personnel during the timescales mentioned in this book (roughly 2009-2014). Thank you for your service, and thank you for your generosity and your guidance.

In the next book, the dark will turn to light. Not immediately, because Kit has to go through the healing process, but he'll get there, fingers crossed. I'm so looking forward to returning to some of the old humor and shenanigans we're used to seeing with the Speed Demons.

Thank you to my people, my support system, and my tribe.

Elizabeth N Harris— Gawd, we've been through the wringer already this year, book wife babs, but better times are ahead. I feel it in my bones. Here's to you, your grace and humor, and for always being there for a natter.

Em's. It's been a joy to get to know you. Thanks for your loyalty and for being so good to my Annie. Also, thanks to Sam for putting up with my mad ideas and working hard to make them a reality.

Jayne, oh, Jayne. Thank you for working so hard in the background. You're my rock, and I appreciate you more than you know.

Nicola. You've been a godsend. Already, I'd be lost without you. I see your artist's soul. I love our vibe and our 'playlist song finding.' You're my witchy soul sister.

My Tribe ladies. You bring me joy. I love you all. You're my safe place. Thank you.

Mylene, Victoria, Elizabeth, Nicola, and Jayne. My alpha readers extraordinaire. The books wouldn't be what they are without your guidance.

My ARC ladies. Thank you for the fun times and enthusiasm. I adore what you all bring to the group and how you treat each other—and me—with so much love and respect.

And thank you, readers. Your messages of love and encouragement mean the world to me. I appreciate you all.

Love and light.

Julia XOXO

Stalk Jules

Jules loves chatting with readers
Email her
julesfordauthor@gmail.com

Join her Facebook Group
Jules Ford's Tribe | Facebook

Instagram
Jules Ford (@julesfordauthor) • Instagram photos and videos

Printed by Amazon Italia Logistica S.r.l.
Torrazza Piemonte (TO), Italy